THE BABEL APOCALYPSE

SONGS OF THE SAGE, BOOK 1

BY

VYVYAN EVANS

NEPHILIM PUBLISHING

The future of science fiction writing

NEPHILIM
PUBLISHING

The future of science fiction writing

NEPHILIM PUBLISHING
Suite 82428
PO Box 6945
London, W1A 6US
United Kingdom

For all enquiries relating to this book, please visit the book series website:
www.songs-of-the-sage.com or email: info@songs-of-the-sage.com

A CIP catalogue record for this book is available from the British Library
Library of Congress Control Number: 2022911277
ISBN: 978-1-7399962-2-2 in paperback (print) format
ISBN: 978-1-7399962-3-9 in e-book (ePub) format

First published: May 2023
Typeset in England: Design by SMR

DISCLAIMER
While this is a work of speculative fiction, it is inspired by events, businesses, incidents, technologies, and theoretical concepts that have some basis in reality. Certain long-standing institutions, agencies, and public offices are mentioned, but the characters involved are wholly imaginary, as is this novel's story.

ⱭB⅂Ǝ⅃Ɛ ⱭⱢꞮ ⅂ƆƎ⅃

"They who control language control everything."

From the *Babel Apocalypse Manifesto*
by Professor Ebba Black

PROLOGUE

It wasn't her cold beauty that marked out Ebba Black as unique—her *chilling looks*, as she called them—although her looks invariably made an impression on all who met her. Rather, it was the fact that she was the last nate in the automated world. That made her famous. Undoubtedly she was celebrated for other things too—Ebba Black the Babelist, the heiress, the conspiracy theorist, the charismatic professor. Maybe even the oddity. After all, Ebba was the last speaker of languages that would die with her. With Elias's passing five years prior, she had no one left to speak them with. And Ebba Black would not marry. Commitment of that sort wasn't her thing, and she would certainly never have children. You could say she wasn't the maternal type.

Ebba knew she was unique in other, ineffable ways, too. For one, she listed things to herself, silently, in her head. *Reasons to know me. Reasons not to know me. Reasons to hate me, to admire me.* But not *reasons to love me.* Never that. That was forbidden. Ebba never allowed anyone to get that close.

Sometimes Ebba even indulged in one of her trademark waspish grins. To no one in particular, while she mentally scrolled through one list: *reasons to kill.* The list with the names. Her *list of lists.* The grin was the only outward sign she was

5

performing a mental stock-take. It wasn't good to be on that particular list. Ebba Black was neither the forgiving nor the tolerant type.

Ebba was all too aware that she was viewed as an anomaly by pretty much everyone; she was neither feral nor out-soc. So, some of her students—especially those from outside the Republic, such as the Grand Union, and other places too— thought she must be breaking the law. It was a common misconception. She had even once been reported to the authorities by one of those types. For being an unchipped *ghost*, as they called her. That made her laugh; a dark laugh at the irony of it. The *mutes*, she called them. Those who had been fitted with Universal Grammar tech.

But while she officially resided in the Nordic Republic, and as long as she remained there, Ebba wasn't doing anything illegal. The Republic was something of a curiosity even among Tier One states, never having passed a lang-law. Yet this singular absence was offset by the special requirements of Nordic birth licenses. To have one granted, prospective parents had to consent to their newborn being fitted with Universal Grammar tech. So everyone got a language chip at birth anyway, together with an ear implant transceiver. Which meant that voice command tech was, for all intents and purposes, *de rigueur* even without a lang-law. But that was the Scandinavian way. In the Nordic Republic, they organized freedom.

For her part, Ebba knew it wasn't her. It was everyone else who had the problem. "That's what you *would* think," her braver, typically male students told her. "You're Ebba Black." *Ha! Whatever that means. How do they know what Ebba Black would think anyway?*

And despite all the false idols—intelligence, wealth, beauty—

that others admired and envied in her, they didn't know the things that had made her the woman she was. No one knew that her will of steel was, in fact, forged from sorrow. But Ebba knew. And she knew that her losses were more than any ordinary person could bear. *Shapes her into who she is.*

What sustained the blackness of her sorrow was vengeance. Vengeance past and vengeance yet to be dealt. Ebba nurtured it in the dark palace of her mind—the innermost, most private mental shrine where she kept the one list, the list that was actualized and ritualized. The list of lists. There remained three names. They were the toughest ones. Especially his, at the very summit.

But something preternatural happened that Ebba knew would change everything. She was witness to an apparition, unheralded early one morning. And it brought with it a warning, a prophecy, and a gift. *Makes you want to read.*

* * *

On the morning of October 5th, Ebba had risen before dawn, as she did each day. She never slept much; she felt guilty wasting time on sleep. She had been for her customary five-kilometer run through the early morning Kattegat fog that often enveloped her vast estate at that time of day, at that time of year. She always finished at the cliff top, high above the Kattegat Sound, overlooking the straits and the distant landmass of Zeeland far out in the sea. On that particular day, Zeeland was occluded by sea mists. She then began her daily Wing Chun routine.

Ebba always started with relaxation techniques before moving through the gears, visualizing each gesture in her mind's eye a fraction before execution. And all the while, she kept her petite, lissome body in perfect balance as she followed her corporeal center line, which guided every attack. She performed her armory of rapid strikes while moving forward, aiming at an unseen assailant on the cliff top.

Afterward, Ebba would normally have completed her morning workout in her live-action pistol range—a concrete bunker adjacent to the orangery, behind the herb garden to the rear of her neo-Baroque manor. Her favorite weapon was her original Beretta 92. She loved its accuracy, and the single-action trigger from the second shot. But most of all, she loved its shape—the esthetics of a step-slide design that hadn't been manufactured for nearly a hundred and fifty years. Ebba had no time for modern coil weaponry. No finesse, no skill required, she was wont to sneer. *You have to make them feel it.*

But that particular October morning, as Ebba completed her final Wing Chun move, punching through the thick fog, a misty doorway opened. Out of nowhere in midair. And what emerged was a shimmering, winged creature, burning in orange-red flame.

Ebba watched what she believed to be a fiery angel descend from the sky through wreaths of mist. A six-winged seraph, to be precise. Ebba knew her mythology—tradition placed seraphim in the highest rank of angelology. Ebba was as well-read as she was lethal with a pistol. She also knew it was nuts. Completely. She would be classed as certifiable—yet, she was witnessing it. And Ebba was not the emotional type. She had learned, out of necessity, to regulate her emotions a long time ago, to hide what she truly was—a high-functioning sociopath with psychopathic tendencies. And Ebba was okay with that.

Yet, on account of knowing she wasn't imagining what she was seeing (because Ebba seldom, if ever, doubted herself), and also on account of knowing (or at the very least, believing) that such creatures didn't in fact exist, Ebba froze in disbelief. And it took one hell of a lot to make Ebba Black freeze.

Crazier still, as the apparition touched the rocky ground two meters in front of her, the seraph transformed into a woman. A beautiful woman in black attire, with red-orange flaming hair and piercing emerald-green eyes—nuclear green, maybe. The type of eyes that locked your gaze and arrested your heart. Eyes that burned into Ebba's own coal-black eyes.

And then Ebba had a further shock. The woman was someone she recognized. After all, Ebba was a hacker extraordinaire. She had back-door access to live sec-cam footage of all the most important law enforcement agencies in the world, including Interpol. But the woman before her looked much younger than her live feed, by around two decades, Ebba guessed. Which placed her in her early twenties. That couldn't be right. *What the beep?*—Ebba thought, censoring her would-be expletive. Ebba Black never swore, even in her head. She remained too refined a lady for that.

As Ebba took an involuntary step back, belatedly wondering whether she was imagining the whole thing, the flame-haired woman began speaking. She was using King's English. Not just the quaint accent, but the whole assorted verbiage of the Old Standard's grammar and vocabulary too. And as it so happened, this was a variety no longer supported by Unilanguage. Tier Two states like the Old Kingdom were no longer permitted independent state official varieties. The decree had already taken effect, at the start of the year. *Is this one a nate too?* Ebba thought. She knew all too well that she was all that remained of the old ways throughout the Tier One and Two states—the automated world.

"Don't be afraid," the flame-haired woman said softly. Ebba shook her head. She wasn't afraid. She never was. But here and now she felt something she had never experienced before, although she wasn't entirely sure what it was. "I don't have much time," the woman continued.

"This is ..." Ebba began. *Impossible*, she thought, shaking her head at herself. She didn't like the word—no agency in it. Ebba was all about agency. She was always in control.

The woman continued smiling. "This will sound crazy, but I'm from your future." Ebba nodded in agreement. It sounded crazy all right. "In five years, you will save me from a subterranean prison beneath a salt flat—Groom Lake, Nevada. Which means I can help you here." Ebba felt her mouth opening before she remembered to close it.

"You're from the future?"

The woman's smile became rueful. "Marc Barron must be stopped. But you haven't managed it."

Now Ebba's mind was racing. How did this woman know about that? Her list? The Appleton gang of three: Hadean Burr-Alston, Darya Zao, and, top of the infamous list, Marc Barron himself.

"It's not so easy to ..." Ebba stammered.

"To get to him? To end him? You've tried, I know. You told me." Ebba was now completely perplexed. The woman laughed, watching Ebba's expression intently. It was a warm laugh, spontaneous, open, her voice soft, gentle. Not at all prickly, as Ebba had imagined, given her reputation for being ornery and ruffling feathers, while solving the world's most vexing cybercrime cases. Ebba liked that. She somehow felt a connection with this one. "What I mean is, you *will* tell me," the woman added, correcting herself, staring at Ebba with her green eyes. "But you can't get to him without help. You can't do it alone."

"He's protected somehow," Ebba murmured.

The woman nodded. "One month from now, there will be a global language outage. Something you've predicted, right?" Ebba stared in further amazement. "You must prepare."

"Prepare how?" Ebba asked.

"There is a man, a Europol commander: Emyr Morgan. You must find him, recruit him. Help him with your Language Unplugged protocol." Now Ebba was even further taken aback. *How does this woman know about the protocol? And why would she need to seek out this man?*

"Emyr Morgan?" Ebba whispered.

The woman nodded. "You need his help to accomplish your goal. He will save your life. And you'll also need this." With that, she reached inside her black leather jacket. As she pulled out her hand, holding her palm out toward Ebba, the nothingness she seemed at first to hold materialized into a semitranslucent orb the size of her palm. The orb was spinning on itself or within itself. She proffered it to Ebba. Ebba saw that within the object something was shifting, transforming between misty spiraling shapes that looked like some sort of eternal knot of translucent motion. As she peered into the swirling orb, Ebba saw that the shapes were in fact one single shape—a strange, winged creature that morphed incessantly into some new, languid version of itself, from serpent to bird and back again. As the cycle of transformation peaked, the winged-serpent-cum-bird creature pulsated red before dissipating back into translucence. *Some weird Gestalt-like perceptual trick.* Ebba scrunched up her eyes and shook her head. She felt she was being hypnotized.

"Take it," the woman said finally.

Ebba did as she was bidden. The orb dropped into her palm. But she felt nothing; no weight, no texture. Just nothingness. And as she closed her hand around it, the orb disappeared. Ebba gasped in amazement and shook her hand open to make the vanished orb reappear. But no matter how hard she gestured, there was still nothing. Just thin air.

"It's gone," Ebba whispered.

The woman shook her head. "It's still there. But now bound to you. It will reappear when you need it."

"What is it?" Ebba asked. "A weapon?"

"This is far better than a weapon. It's called a void prism. Marc Barron is protected by something powerful—a gaseous being, a Watcher. That's why you haven't been able to kill him. This will make many things possible, even changing the very shape of time."

"But how can I kill him?"

"Inside the prism is a Chol, which will summon me again. When the kairos moment arrives. I will draw out the Watcher, then he will be unprotected. You will have your shot."

"A Chol?"

"A consciousness, an ancient soul, connected to my own master Chol, located at a distant place in spacetime—the alpha and omega point of time. Remember everything I have said. But most of all, this. When we meet again, in five years, it will be the first time for me. I won't recall this meeting. Remember the chronemics. I will need the time and place markers to find you here." And with that, the woman began fading from view. *Chronemics? Place markers?* Ebba thought. *This is all surreal.*

"Wait," she stammered. "You're Lilith King, aren't you? Director of Interpol's Global Cybercrime Center. In Singapore?"

Lilith smiled wistfully at Ebba as her form continued to fade.

"Lilith," she murmured. "That's one name I've been called—an old name, given by my father long ago to strike fear into the Sage."

"You have other names?" Ebba asked, amazed by the strangeness of this woman and her response.

"Echoes in time. On this planet, my second coming has been foretold. Abaddon, Apollyon, Exterminans." And with that she was gone. The apparition vanished into the thick Kattegat fog that swirled around Ebba anew.

CHAPTER 1

a little confusing

talking to Emyr.

My mother's dying wish was to be buried in Wanstead earth. The place of her birth. Near the end of her existence, her skin became veiny and translucent and her memory as frail as her body. By then she had begun to address me by my late father's name. I felt repulsion. *I'm Emyr*, I had wanted to scream, *I'm not him.* I was nothing like him. I was tall, dark, and had a strong moral compass. He was slight, with a ruddy complexion, and lacked scruples. But at least I no longer harbored anger for my mother's betrayal, ~~for my boyhood trauma; that had gone.~~ The solace of time. But I hadn't forgiven her either. And as I hurried away from the cemetery once it was done, I felt only ambivalence.

By the time I reached Manor Park, twilight had become darkness. I walked along the pedestrian corridor, heading back to where I had parked my Skyraider. The cold air swirled around me, so I pulled up the collar of my Napa coat against the chilly November evening. Soft grain leather. Italian design. I loved that fur-lined coat. I hated this foreign city. I wanted to get back to my life, and my job across the water; to get home.

The networked system of LED streetlights slowly dimmed behind me before slipping into darkness, while those ahead flickered on, transmitting my location to one another and

London's communication nerve center, hosted on an aging server in space. The electric glow dappled the walls of the buildings, making the windows appear to pucker in the shadowy light.

I heard a group of drunken revelers behind me. "He always has a line for the ladies," said one slurred voice. The boozy pitch contour wobbled toward me, bouncing along the polycarbonate surface. Then came an eruption of cackling.

As I was about to glance back at the voices, a light flickered in my peripheral vision, drawing my gaze upward to the night sky. A soft white glow, high up in the dark. At first it was indistinguishable from the airway lights. But it persisted, the size of a small disk at first, before shifting to red-orange, getting larger. At that point I realized it definitely couldn't be a hover car. This was farther up, probably low Earth orbit, which explained the initial white. But the shift in coloration—that meant a detonation, producing nitrogen dioxide, which turned deep orange when mixed with air. *A gaseous cloud has reached the atmosphere*, I thought. I was witnessing a chemical explosion in space large enough to be visible to the naked eye. But what was exploding?

As I continued looking up, the orange grew in intensity until it flared across the skyline, illuminating the entire landscape around me with an eerie red-orange. It was only then that I became aware of the newly hushed silence of the drunken revelers nearby. And the silhouettes of other people too, who had also stopped and peppered the pedestrian corridor. We were all now strange red creatures, watching transfixed in rapt silence as the night sky was on fire. And just as suddenly as it had appeared, it was gone; the orange light faded back into a deep well of pitch black.

I was pulled out of my reverie by the sight of a hover car descending onto the vertipad ahead of me. A three-wheeler autonomous hackney cab; mass-produced model. I watched in idle distraction as the glass frontage descended level with my eyeline, not twenty meters from me. Inside, I saw a woman, illuminated by the interior safety lighting—late twenties, perhaps, with a small child, a boy of about three or four. The red glow of the vertipad's perimeter security lights bounced sharply off the polymer composite shell, which advertised the taxi company in holographic lettering. The vehicle came to a standstill on the vertipad.

But something about the hover taxi held my gaze. I realized it was the autogyro system. Something was wrong. Instead of self-stowing, it remained deployed. And the vehicle stayed in place where it had landed, in the middle of the vertipad. *Strange*, I thought. It should have taxied away onto the transit corridor by now. Maybe the explosion had affected the landing telemetry circuit. Stranger still, given the passengers were now stuck inside, why hadn't they voice-activated the exit? The gull-wing doors remained closed.

I climbed over the thermoformed pedestrian barrier, ignoring the warning sensors as they flickered on, blinking at me, and walked up the vertipad incline toward the hover cab. The woman peeked out, panic etched on her face. As she glimpsed me through the glass, she suddenly began banging as if in desperate supplication. I mouthed that she should issue her door deactivation voice command into the piloting VirDa. She didn't seem to understand me, so I spelled out Virtual Digital Assistant with my forefinger on the window—*VirDa*; a crude attempt to make her react.

She stared out at me with wild eyes through the gull-wing window; a look of incomprehension. I realized that her apparent lack of understanding could only mean one thing: ~~she was feral. Her language streaming service was out.~~ She had no idea what I was saying, nor could she communicate with her VirDa. And then she screamed.

Helpless, I watched the terror contained within the soundproofed confines of the plastic hull. The little boy's upturned face shifted to fear and then distress as he witnessed his mother's frenzied panic; the child began to cry. I watched through the glass, witness to the sobs I couldn't hear.

Just then, I heard the roar of VTOL thrust engines. I glanced up. Another hover car was descending, way too fast, dropping directly onto the vertipad, destined for the hackney cab that lay stationary beneath.

I was trained to process details happening in real time with the precision afforded by the slow dilation of protracted duration. With focus, I could unpick the frenzy of multiple rapid events within a temporal landscape perceived with an ethereal slow-motion calm. I observed that the descending hover car was a private vehicle—it had four wheels with expensive alloys that glinted in the marker lights of the VTOL corridor. And as it dropped, I saw that it had air capture ducts underneath and a CO_2 cooling condenser, allowing supersonic flight in international sky lanes. This was a beast of car with a truly global range, an expensive piece of engineering.

There was a man seated at the piloting console. I glimpsed him in the shimmering red of the security lights. To my shock, I realized the descending car was in manual flight mode, which was not permitted in class R airspace, above the city. What was the guy thinking? A collision was now inevitable.

Just before the two vehicles came together, I saw the woman

following my gaze. She glimpsed what was about to befall her, the edge of the other hover car tumbling fast toward her. She made a sudden, startled move for the child. An instinctive shielding gesture, perhaps.

To protect myself, I ran back several meters from the vertipad as the falling vehicle smashed into the roof of the stationary cab. Then came a deafening bang. The impact severed the autogyro blades of the vehicle beneath, which snapped off the roof bearing and spun across the adjacent taxi lane, making a sickening scything sound on the hard plastic surface. I squinted through the darkness as smoke rose from the wreckage. A hissing sound was coming from the tangled mess of the upper vehicle. The hackney cab underneath had somehow resisted the impact. Its reinforced plastic structure appeared largely intact.

I returned to the crash site and climbed onto the protruding front hull, from where I was able to peer into the stricken car on top. The lighting on the piloting console was dimmed, but I could make out splashes of blood on the inside of the cracked windscreen. Some of the ceiling safety lights were still lit; they dimly illuminated the twisted, seemingly lifeless body of the pilot, lying across the front passenger seats where he had been tossed by the collision.

I jumped back down onto the vertipad, searching for the woman and child in the car underneath. My training dictated aiding the most vulnerable first. I turned to a group of onlookers, and called for assistance with getting the injured out.

It was then that I became aware that they were strangely silent, especially given what they had just witnessed—the first hover car crash in years. Each individual was eyeing the others, attempting to mouth something. Only one man seemed still able to speak. He began talking excitedly. But, to my surprise, he was speaking in a non-Union official language. I recognized it as Mandarin. Others nearby stared at him in startled bafflement. And as he heard the strange sounds coming from his mouth, his words slowly lapsed into silence as a look of darting fear flashed across his face.

I resumed my rescue attempts on the vertipad, picking up a broken piece of carbon-reinforced sidebar lying next to the wreckage. I used it to try and prize open one of the gull-wing doors of the hackney cab, but the weight of the upper vehicle prevented the door from deploying. I ran around to the other side. This time I managed to apply enough pressure to gain leverage. The door hissed as the hydraulic mechanism deployed and the gull-wing slowly opened up and out. The woman and child lay crumpled and still on the floor of the vehicle beneath the concave splintered roof.

As my first aid training kicked in, I checked they were both breathing. Then I lifted the child out, supporting his head, followed by the woman using a shoulder pull. I quickly carried the boy down the vertipad incline, away from the vehicle, then carefully pulled the woman along until they were both a safe distance from the wreckage. The woman's nose looked broken and blood oozed from her nostrils. She had been thrown forward against the glass passenger cabin frontage. I suspected there may be internal injuries, too.

Just as I finished placing them both in the recovery position, a flicker of flame began nibbling gently from somewhere beneath the plastic front of their cab. I smelled the distinct odor of rotten eggs—the toxic combination of sulfur at high temperature that had leaked from the ion-sulfur battery and reacted with hydrocarbons in the taxi shell to create hydrogen sulfide. The flames began spreading rapidly. Before I could act, they had engulfed the second vehicle. The man, even if still alive, was now beyond my help.

I felt the vibrations of an incoming alert in my ear implant—I tapped my left wrist to activate my holotab. The chip in my wrist glowed briefly green before projecting a holographic screen. There it was—a Europol alert banner scrolling across the small translucent screen floating above my wrist. A red alert status had been triggered.

"Global language outage. Report to HQ." The hairs on the back of my neck stood up. *A language outage. What does that even mean?*

I knew I had to get help for the hackney cab passengers before responding to the alert. That was the protocol: ensure no immediate danger to life before answering another request.

I scrolled through the menu on my holotab using the eye-tracking sensor tech, selecting the London emergency services app with a blink command. Then I issued an in-app voice command, placing a facecall.

The connection should have been instantaneous. But instead, I heard the distinctive shrill pitch of an unrecognized call attempt. I frowned and tried again. This time I was patched through to a human dispatcher. An actual human! But then again, the Old Kingdom was just a Tier Two state. Soc-ed classification and the United Nations' job automation agenda didn't fully apply.

The dispatcher was a young woman with her headset slightly skewed. She appeared surprised to see me through her screen.

She began speaking: *"Toate serviciile de urgenţă sunt indisponibile."* I regarded her in surprise. As my auditory nerve activated, my language chip began to auto-parse. I recognized her words as the state official language of Romania. *What the hell ...*

"All emergency services are down?" I asked. She looked at me, both confused and alarmed. It was clear she had no clue what I had just said. I blink activated the language app on my holotab before issuing my voice command.

"Switch to Romanian as default," I said. The single vibration in my ear implant indicated that my language setting had been changed. I addressed the woman again. *"Toate serviciile de urgenţă sunt indisponibile?"* I repeated, this time in Union Standard Romanian.

"Da." She nodded.

"Eşti româncă?" I asked. She shook her head. *If she's not a Romanian national, then why does she have her language set to Romanian?* I thought. Especially working in the London emergency services center, where the VirDas operated solely on the local state official standard. Last time I'd checked, there was only one state official language in the Old Kingdom. And since Unilanguage's decision to stop supporting King's English at the beginning of the year, all official VirDas in London now only ran on the North American Standard variety.

"Nu mai pot vorbi engleza, nu înţeleg ce s-a întâmplat," she replied with a small shrug, tears welling in her eyes. And abruptly, she pulled off her headset and ended the call. She seemed equally shocked at her inability to speak English anymore.

"Dezactivează limba română. Setează limba engleză ca implicită," I said, issuing my voice command into my holotab to deactivate Romanian and return to English. "Facecall Europol SOS."

I was patched through to the Europol virtual emergency response center. The standard, flaccid face of the dispatcher VirDa appeared on the holographic screen, which projected from my wrist like an ethereal membrane in the dark of the autumnal evening.

"Commander Emyr Morgan," the VirDa said, addressing me in the Europol default, North American Standard English.

"I've received a code red alert. And I have civilians down. The London emergency center is no longer operational."

"Yes, a catastrophic language outage has been reported," the VirDa confirmed. "What do you need, Commander?"

"An air ambulance, a paramedic, and direct access to a local ER."

After a slight pause, the VirDa responded. "I have placed an emergency request. A Union crew is assigned, traveling across the Old Kingdom channel via the South Holland airway."

"Copy, thanks. End call," I said. *Catastrophic language outage? What the hell's going on?*

CHAPTER 2

Still Emyr?

I glanced down at the unconscious woman and child. They lay on the cold modular surface at the foot of the vertipad where I had placed them. I took off my Napa coat, draped it over them, and slipped off my black mourner's jacket and placed it under their heads. As I finished, I became aware of the unnatural behavior of the people in the High Street pedestrian corridors that gave off from the vertipad.

It was the near silence that was most striking. The evening chatter had evaporated. Bystanders were now dispersing from the scene of the crash, some in silent panic, while others cast furtive glances at their companions. Further down the pedestrian corridor, people were moving around in a hushed trance, seemingly unsure what to do. I watched one man sit quietly against a polycarbonate barrier. He began sobbing.

I heard one voice finally: a man. He was speaking in an unusual language, addressing a woman; a wife or girlfriend, maybe. The couple were moving away from the crash site as my language chip began auto-parsing the words. It was Hindustani, one of the two state official languages of the Indian Republic. The woman studied him fearfully, shaking her head. She began speaking something else in response. It was a variety of Lusitanian! I recognized it as the state official language of

Brazil. Each of their pitch contours became increasingly plaintive until they lapsed into silence, shoulders hunched in mutual incomprehension, glancing at one another in visible distress.

I heard another voice about a hundred meters away, along Manor Park High Street in the direction of East Ham. It was a woman. Her voice was muffled at this distance, although at least it sounded something like English. She had activated her holotab and was speaking to someone. Her silhouette appeared ghostly under the pale streetlights. I had the impression she was trying to summon help. I hoped she'd have better luck than me if she was calling the local emergency services.

As I took in the strangeness of the scene, a new commotion caught my attention. Two menacing figures were accosting passers-by farther down Manor Park High Street. And they were brandishing bladed weapons. They moved deliberately, threatening, targeting individuals—searching for someone, maybe. People scattered from their path as they approached like a pair of wrecking balls.

Then they zeroed in on the small figure of the woman, still on the facecall on her holotab. The larger of the two figures grabbed her by the throat from behind. She screamed as she turned. Her voice was high-pitched, the unexpected attack prompting a shrill cry of panic.

They began half dragging, half pulling her along the pedestrian corridor toward a grocery store entrance, while other people nearby were dispersing in silent fear. At the store entrance there was a further commotion. The two armed figures—definitely male, I now saw—were gesturing at her to do something, threatening her. I heard her muffled replies, the words indistinct at this distance. Then I saw the large fist of one of the men as it came into full view under the streetlight. It smashed hard against the side of her face. As the woman hit the ground, the sound of the impact echoed in the new stillness of the night.

There was another man nearby. He stepped forward, coming to the fallen woman's aid, braver than the others. He also seemed still able to talk. As he reached the woman, his muffled words carried to me. But the tall, skinny silhouette slashed him with his blade, and the man stumbled. The armed men then picked him up, abandoning the fallen woman, dragging the injured man to the entrance of the store as he cried out in pain. Within a few seconds they were inside, still dragging the man.

I flinched. This was distress I couldn't ignore. It drew me in; I knew I needed to do something while awaiting the air ambulance. I began jogging toward the stricken woman. She was now sitting on the ground, her hands clasped around her ankles. She began jabbering as I neared. It was English, but a variety I didn't have access to.

"Rah! Wagwan? Dem man dun grunt. Man knew it was sus. Two roadmen from upsuh. Dem man had rambos. Da tall one, my man pointed da skeng. Man squealed."

I didn't have a clue what she was saying. But I could see that despite her animated demeanor, she was badly shaken. The smoldering flames from the hover cars behind me illuminated her face as she spoke. She was young, maybe twenty, and pretty.

"Why dem man dun dat for?" she asked. "It hurt innit. Man felt da ching, a sharp one. Da shorter roadman, my man was blacked up. Dem man dun be red spicers. My man was mean crazy. Big man ting! Da look in dem eyes. My man was clapped. Dem man wanted in Grocerido. Tried to make man operate da

Welcome VirDa. Man dun scream, dun hav no account." As she finished, I followed her gaze toward the self-service store entrance nearby.

"I'm sorry, I don't understand. Something about Grocerido?" I asked. She stared through me. But then she was off again.

"Man was shook. Real bad shook. And man a baller. Man was gonna leg it, ain't gassin. But den, man saw you. A bossman? Peng, big one. Wagwan piff ting."

"New Blinglish?" I asked, guessing that's what she was streaming. Part of a high-end package, a non-standard variety used by posh moots. But for that class of rich kid, non-conformity, not being readily understood—that was kind of the point.

"Yuh dun know," the woman replied, nodding.

"Can you switch to North American Standard?" She shrugged. I sighed. "Look, I have access to two hundred and fifty varieties. But only the state officials."

She frowned and then pressed on her wrist chip, reactivating her holotab. She issued a blink command to select her language app before speaking an in-app voice command. "Variety: English, North American Standard."

The woman stood gingerly. Her eyes wandered along my white starched shirt and the line of my black kydex shoulder holster, reaching an abrupt terminus at my coil pistol.

"It's all right. I'm with Europol," I said, trying to sound reassuring as I placed my hand on the weapon. "I'm Emyr Morgan. What's your name?"

"Arlo Sallow. They're feral," she declared, eyes wide as she gazed toward the store. She was still shaking.

"It's shock. You'll be safe now."

"They wanted me to voice register so they could loot the place. But I couldn't …"

I got it. She was still in her Blinglish default. Not the state official variety. New Blinglish wouldn't work on any public VirDas in the Old Kingdom. "They grabbed the other guy, to get them in. He was streaming official English. They cut him bad. With their knives. And they were both manic, on something." Arlo was standing unsteadily now, rubbing a tear from her eye.

"Looked like zombie blades," I said. The top of her head barely reached my chest. I watched her lips tremble in the flickering neon of the Grocerido holographic adverts. The store frontage scrolled through various waveguide displays. The garish advertising promoted the deals of the day, ranging from toothpaste to chocolate. The prices bounced across the frontage in yellow and red splashes. "Appleton subscriber? I assume, with a lexical package like that." She nodded. "Gun activate."

Arlo watched, slightly alarmed, as the bright green glow of the capacitor slowly crept on as the gun's electromagnetic coils began far-field charging. She probably hadn't seen a coil pistol up close before.

"I'll take it from here," I muttered as I approached the Welcome VirDa, moving away from her. I wanted to get in, to see what I could do for the guy the two ferals had snatched.

At the entrance I heard banging from inside, behind the opaque glass of the storefront. Someone was trying to get out.

The virtual face of the VirDa faded in, wearing a simulated peaked Grocerido cap. The store name was written on it in mustard-yellow lettering, with ostentatious flourishes running beneath the letter "r."

"Welcome to Grocerrrrido," the pasty-looking male face said with a fake broad grin, rolling his r's in lavish welcome. The sec-cam in one corner of the display blinked at me, while the language streaming orb of the registration terminal above the screen began to vibrate, scanning the live rebounds from my language chip. "No account, *no* problem," the talking head continued. "Register your voice print and come on in. We are Grocerrrrrido!"

I spoke into the mic protruding from the beveled side of the VirDa screen. "Emyr Morgan. Europol business. I request immediate access."

The dumb AI ignored me and just repeated its standard greeting. "No account, *no* problem. Register your voice print and come on in. We are Grocerrrrrido!" I sighed. Europol had no jurisdiction in this neck of the woods.

"I give permission for registration of my voice print and DigID credentials," I said quietly, issuing my voice command. As I spoke, the sec-code encoded in the metadata of my acoustic signal was registered by the VirDa. *I now have a retail account with Grocerido,* I thought with a grimace. *A cheap chain based somewhere in the Old Kingdom—up north, no less.*

"Welcome, Emyr," the pasty face boomed with a fake-friendly flourish. "Registration complete. Your voice commands are now recognized. You're good to go." My voice print could be matched with the unique LS rebounds from my language chip, now stored in the Grocerido database.

As the glass door opened, a middle-aged woman ran out, scarcely taking me in as she brushed past, panic etched across her face. I glanced after her in surprise as she disappeared into the night.

I was standing on the threshold of a brightly lit store with rows of neatly stocked shelves. Music was playing softly from the ceiling speakers, and navigational VirDa displays blinked at me from the end of each aisle. I could hear groans coming from somewhere.

The VirDa's pasty face materialized in front of the first aisle on the navigational screen. "Hello, Emyr. This is the canned food aisle. The first heavyweight on our best canned foods list is the mighty salmon. We also have canned pinto beans, soups, tomatoes, kidney beans, white beans, even canned clams. You say it, I'll find it. Let me be your guide."

"Shush!" I hissed in irritation. I was attempting to locate the groaning while also listening for the ferals. The pasty-faced VirDa suddenly looked crestfallen.

"No need to be rude, Emyr. I'm just doing my job. Do let me know if you need me." The VirDa's face faded out and was replaced by more scrolling mustard-colored marketing.

As I turned into the third aisle, I saw the injured man. He was lying against a stack of breakfast cereals, where he had been abandoned. He was badly injured, his white shirt almost completely bloodied. His eyes flickered closed as I approached. He was slipping into unconsciousness. I crouched next to him and undid his shirt, revealing a long but superficial gash running across his stomach. I did a quick take. It was a nasty wound but survivable. It wasn't immediately clear why there was so much blood on the floor.

Then I saw it. The knife stroke had extended across his entire body, cutting through part of his wrist, clipping his radial artery. Blood was gushing out. It had been several minutes already. I scanned for an aisle that contained toweling, then dashed to retrieve what I could. I returned after a moment to bandage the man's wrist, but he was now completely still.

I felt for a pulse, but I knew I'd lost him. This was senseless butchery of an innocent bystander whose only mistake had been to try to help Arlo outside. Just then, I heard it again—the annoying sound of the VirDa's booming voice from a few aisles away.

"Sir, we don't have you registered yet. I can help. Welcome to Grocerrrrrido." There was no response. ~~I knew that could mean only one thing: the two ferals~~.

I jumped up and moved toward the sound. As I rounded the corner, I clapped eyes on the taller feral who I had seen slash the now-dead man. He had matted, straw-colored hair and dirty-looking pants, and was helping himself to liquor bottles, tossing them into a shopping cart, ransacking shelves as he moved steadily down the aisle.

"Hey," I called loudly. The feral froze and slowly turned around. He grinned as he clocked me, pulling something out of his jacket. I was right. It was a zombie knife. It had a nasty-looking twisted, serrated blade with a blue-threaded handle.

"Put it down," I grunted menacingly as I pulled my coil pistol out of its shoulder holster. The feral paused, the grin slowly disappearing from his face.

I suddenly heard a noise behind me. Hoarse breathing. And as I turned, I saw the other feral, who had appeared seemingly from nowhere. This one was shorter; a youth in his late teens with bad teeth, blotches of red pustules on his face, and dilated eyes. *Arlo was right,* I thought. They were Red Spice users. Or at least this one was. And judging from his crazy eyes and sweaty demeanor, his Deep Brain Stimulation implant was offline, just like his language chip. He was beginning to struggle with cold turkey.

The short feral charged, aiming to shoulder-barge me. I braced myself as we collided. The impact knocked him backward. He fell, coming to rest against some shelving while beholding me above him in surprise, standing unmoved. But he had succeeded in knocking the pistol out of my hand. It clattered onto the floor, the green activation coil slowly fading into inertness as it stopped spinning across the tiled surface. The fallen youth jumped up and scrambled toward it in sudden glee. He picked it up clumsily, squealing as he turned and pointed the gun at me. And then he attempted to fire.

Nothing. His glee was short-lived. The feral looked bewildered, staring back up at me wildly, almost accusingly. He couldn't have known that Union weapons were fingerprint locked.

The feral began shaping to throw the gun at me, hard. I watched his arm as it bent, focusing on its trajectory. These two were dangerous; they needed taking out before anyone else got hurt. Myself included.

The stillness I felt inside my mind in the maelstrom of erupting violence was the result of dedication and training. But I also knew that, in some measure at least, I could trace it back to the physical abuse I had experienced from an early age. Growing up with a violent father, I had learned to compartmentalize; I didn't feel pain in a conventional way. And the skills I'd learned as a Heddlu cadet, and later in advanced combat training courses and in Muay Thai competitions, had further taught me that when someone brought violence, be it a perp or an opponent, even this could be leveraged to take out the other guy.

In that moment, just before the feral could throw the gun at me, with his arm raised, he had exposed himself. He was vulnerable. He didn't see it that way, of course. But that was the moment for me to unleash a sudden decisive move to neutralize him. I took one stride toward him and delivered a forearm smash to the side of his neck near the carotid artery. A brachial stun.

The feral collapsed to the floor. He would be out for between five and thirty seconds—forever, in a fight. This was not an ordinary knockout. The feral's entire nervous system was completely messed up. It would take him several more minutes to manage effective motor control after regaining consciousness. That would at least provide me with some breathing space to deal with the other one.

I stepped over the limp body on the floor. "That's mine," I hissed at the unconscious form, picking up the gun. I holstered it, then turned to the taller feral. He was still there, having taken in the entire scene. But as I faced him, he took an involuntary step back before spinning around to flee. This was the one who had already killed. I wasn't going to let him get away.

I began marching after him with long, fast strides. He disappeared around the end of the aisle, heading toward the exit. I knew I would catch up. The store's automated checkout system had no way of charging him for the goods he'd removed from the shelves. He was stuck in here.

I heard him before I rounded the corner of the final aisle. He watched as I approached, his eyes fixed on my looming figure. I studied the long knife, which he had raised, threatening me as I approached.

"Gun activate. Stun rounds." I only wanted to incapacitate him. Lethal force was always a last resort. I heard a click. Now only polymer bullets had been loaded, with a low muzzle velocity setting. I aimed low and fired. The feral toppled over and lay motionless underneath the exit VirDa screen, just in front of a self-checkout scanner. A bottle of liquor he had been clutching in his other hand rolled out of his grasp and grazed the supermarket floor with a rhythmic clinking. Its holographic sensor fusion label sprayed refracted beams of reds at random into the air.

"You have a security breach in your store," I said, speaking into the beveled mic on the exit VirDa screen. The pasty face appeared on the display. *What else should I say?* I wondered. *Someone is dead? Killed by feral drug addicts, now incapacitated?*

"Thank you, Emyr," the face said cheerfully. "I will notify local law enforcement."

I sighed. *Everything in London is down.* Outside, I saw that Arlo had already disappeared. I didn't blame her. I headed back to the mother and child.

CHAPTER 3

As I walked back to the vertipad, a call-back alert vibrated in my ear implant. I activated my holotab. It was a request to facecall my boss. I blinked to activate the facecall app before issuing my voice command: "Facecall Lina de Bolle." *Boss*

Lina's stern, bird-like face immediately appeared on my screen. Her gray hair was pulled back into her customary tight bun. She eyeballed me with an intense expression through her horn-rimmed glasses. She was old-fashioned; no laser correction for her. She was the least vain person I had ever met.

"Emyr," she began, before pausing, as if not knowing what to say next. Not like her at all. "We have quite a situation."

I frowned. "There's some kind of language outage, right?"

"The official line is an accident. To avoid panic. High Representative Lopez has just released a statement to that effect via the Imperium press service." *The foreign affairs and defense supremo, and the highest-ranking official in the Grand Union after the joint presidents, issuing a statement himself? This has to be really serious, then*, I thought.

"What's the unofficial line?" I asked.

"Sabotage. A series of cyberattacks hijacking state cyber apparatus in Tier Two federations to create some sort of massive botnet attack. The target seems to have been the language

34

streaming satellite systems. Just commercial, though. None of the Tier One state military systems were targeted."

"How bad is it?" I asked.

"Unprecedented. At least two LS systems in low Earth orbit are down," she began. "The Samkee and Tele3 satellite systems are definitely affected ... we're waiting to hear from other providers." Lina paused, her piercing amber eyes holding my gaze.

"So that means—what? The outage has to be global?"

Lina's eyes narrowed slightly. "We think so. The Union is in bad shape. All the other Tier One states are affected too. The Chinese Republics are currently completely incommunicado. We haven't been able to reach anyone there. And communication is patchy with the Japanese." *Then the attack must have been huge,* I thought.

"Weren't fail-safes supposed to kick in?" I asked.

Lina sighed. "This is what we know so far. There was a series of malware attacks that embedded rootkits in at least two African Federation servers. There's also evidence that governmental servers from the Confederation of South American Republics and the Arab League of Nations were weaponized. All those servers were then remotely coordinated to launch a focused tsunami of distributed denial-of-service attacks. The Tele3 and Samkee Command and Control servers were overwhelmed." Lina appeared to twitch. "I've just spoken to von Böhm. He says the relevant team at CyberForce is trying to get a ping on the origination point of the attacks as we speak."

I knew what that meant. My counterpart in CyberForce, that idiot Marchaud, would have been assigned by General von Böhm.

"What's the prognosis for getting systems back online?

There's all sorts of crazy going on here. Never seen anything like it."

Lina grimaced. "The Skylight system is offline. Samkee engineers are working on it now." She adjusted her glasses as she spoke. "The situation is worse with Tele3. The attack caused thermal damage to the battery system on several Bluesky satellites. Catastrophic failure of propellant storage units and a chain reaction explosion. It looks like the entire Tele3 system is gone."

"Gone? That must have been it," I muttered.

"What?" Lina asked.

"The explosion. Lit up the sky here. It was quite something."

Lina stared at me grimly for a moment before continuing. "Everyone saw it. Across the entire northern hemisphere. All Tele3 subscribers are offline ... feral. We're still trying to get data from Samkee, to assess the impact on their users." She paused, running out of words for a moment, staring directly at me out of the screen. "Sorry for your loss, Emyr, by the way. But ..."

"You need me back?"

Her forehead creased. "I have to cancel your leave."

"I understand," I replied. It was due to end the following day anyway; and I was always ready to serve.

She studied me for a moment. "What's your status?"

I smirked. "You mean how quickly I can get back?" Lina smiled faintly. "I'm waiting for a medivac for two ferals. At a hover car crash site in East London."

"A crash? There hasn't been one in the Old Kingdom for, what ...?" Lina asked. I could tell she was genuinely taken aback.

"One this bad, well over a decade at least. I'll be back as

soon as possible. But definitely tonight." Lina stared out at me thoughtfully. "And my assignment?" I asked.

"I want to know who's behind this. Their motives and if there is more to come. I'm assigning you and your division to that. We need answers, and fast."

I nodded solemnly. I was relieved not to have been assigned to crisis management. Not my forte.

"What does the Proelium think?" I asked. I assumed that von Böhm's lot at the Union's military command in Brussels would have picked up advance chatter, especially on something this big—something global.

"You know CyberForce. The usual. Pointing fingers at the Russian Federation. But the director's keeping an open mind ... for now. He wants to know whether this could be the work of Ebba Black. He's asked for a briefing. You and me. In the morning."

"I'll get Pieter to call in the confidential informant, see what she knows. Whether the Babelists really have the capacity for something like this. The kind of DDoS attacks they've carried out before ... well, they were never on this scale."

Lina's brow was knitted with furrows. "Speak to your informant first thing tomorrow. We meet the director at eleven a.m. He's then meeting the High Representative at twelve noon."

* * *

When I reached the vertipad and the stacked wreckage of the two vehicles, the feral woman was conscious. She was sitting up, clutching the child, who was also awake. Both watched me suspiciously.

"An ambulance is coming," I said. They looked at me blankly. I pointed up the VTOL corridor and the woman followed my gesture. We watched in silence as the liquid CO_2 condensers underneath the medivac descended, dropping slowly within the LED marker lights. In the flickering flames from the vertipad, the distinctive blue and yellow Europol livery of the medivac unit had morphed into a surreal crimson. The vertipad itself was unusable, still littered with the flaming remains of the two damaged hover cars. The medivac had to land a bit farther away.

The door slid open and a disembarkation ramp deployed. Two paramedics emerged in their green uniforms, moving down the ramp to the foot of the vertipad where I was crouching next to the mother and child. The first was a service gynoid, as expected. She was a standard maquette model, gray outer casing without integumentary finishing. It was cheaper that way, without a synthetic skin overlay. No hair or nails. In her line of work, being pleasing to the eye was not part of the job description. Still, she was dressed in a medical overall a size too large. Deliberate, probably. She was also wearing a cap. Probably to hide her lack of hair. *Poor thing. They have feelings, after all.*

But upon seeing the second, I did a double take. This paramedic was an actual human, a man.

"Commander?" the man asked, smirking as he saw my surprise. He was heavyset, around sixty, and moved slowly. "You weren't expecting me," he said cheerfully. "Not many do. Paramedics aren't on the obs-jobs list. Not yet. I'm one of the last, though. But at least this gynoid has a sense of humor. Not bad for biomechatronics and synthetic consciousness." He gestured at his companion. She threw him a withering look.

"She'll be taking my supervisor spot—I'm retiring next month."

"You'll need patient transports," I called back as I stood. I watched as he activated his holotab before issuing a blink command. Two self-loading patient transporters emerged from the ambulance, drawn by wheeled daemons. The daemons rolled sleeky down the ramp. Their head-mounted consoles flickered, spraying the darkness with threads of light. As they reached the ferals, the daemons deployed the medical contraptions— body-length hinged metal plinths, which slowly extended beneath the injured woman and the small child. The plinths delicately lifted both patients in an upward arc, creating angled seats above the trolley base. When both woman and child were seated in the transporters, safety straps deployed across their chests and legs, the daemons recoupled to the transports before reversing back up the ramp into the ambulance. I watched as they docked the transporters in secure berths within before locking their own wheels into strong magnetic clamps.

The gynoid followed the daemons into the ambulance. I glimpsed her lithe silhouette against the backdrop of the interior lights as she stood next to the docked patients and issued voice commands quietly into a portable ER VirDa. I could see the ER unit auto-attaching ECG sensors to both patients, beginning diagnostics for triaging purposes.

The gynoid looked like one of the newer Einstein-chipped models. Taller than the other gynoids I worked with at Europol. *More real than ever.* That was the logo of Appleton's droid tech division. The Appleton CEO's grinning face was all over the MyPlace ad flashes these days. Somehow I despised the way he came across, the way his hologram leered out of the blink-through advertising. There was something off about Marc Barron. He gave me a bad vibe.

The male paramedic clearly wanted to chat. He loitered at the foot of the ramp.

"I'm curious, Commander. Your first name: Emyr. That's a bit of an unusual one, isn't it?"

I sighed. I got that a lot. "I'm from Cymru. It means 'king' in Cymraeg."

He chuckled. "Talking of a king, the Old Kingdom's just announced martial law. Requested Union support."

"Oh," I replied absently. I was still preoccupied with the crash. Highly unusual, even in a Tier Two state. *Why would someone be flying a hover car in manual mode in restricted airspace?* The paramedic ignored my lack of enthusiasm. He shook his head grimly. "The old king made the request himself, by all accounts. Just heard it on the way across over the comms."

"The king?" I muttered, just catching up with the conversation. "He asked for Union intervention?"

"And the prime minister's gone feral. Probably a Tele3 subscriber. Not the smartest. Never could stand him," the paramedic said before tutting. "We saw it from up there. The one that blew up. Lit up the South Holland skyway."

"Gone feral?" I asked.

"And the government's a shambles. Old Kingdom's gone to shite. Military command offline too. They reckon over seventy-five percent of their armed forces is now feral. No separate military satellite system, you see. But you know that, right, Commander?" I muttered under my breath. "The lower ranks only have commercial language streaming subs. Tele3, apparently. Which explains things. So the Union has to step in, as always."

"Samkee's offline, too," I whispered, more to myself, still processing what Lina had told me. I was still stunned by the enormity of the looming catastrophe.

"The Appleton servers are working, though," the paramedic added. "Military-grade cybersecurity systems. You get what you pay for, I always say."

"Anyway ..." I began.

"The king's gotta be with Appleton," he surmised, ignoring my signal to end the conversation. "It's all right for him, I guess. At least he has some sense. And can pretend his title means something. As for the rest of them here ... serves them right. Always thought too highly of themselves. Must've been a shock, it all went downhill fast. Losing the Celtic partnership nations to the Union, downgraded to Tier Two," the paramedic hissed. There was venom in his voice. The Old Kingdom didn't have many friends left.

"Where will you take them?" I asked, glancing toward the ambulance. I wanted to find out whatever I could about what had caused the mother and child to become feral. And who their provider was. That would be a start, at least.

The paramedic touched his wrist chip, activating his holotab, and glanced down at the screen. "We've been green-lit for Guy's. Neurology department," he replied.

I frowned. I had expected Saint Thomas's. It had an ER department, while I knew that Guy's Hospital didn't.

"Neurology, not ER? You're sure?" I asked.

But he just nodded. "Onboard AI has completed prelim diagnostics. No internal biological injuries. A neuroprosthetic problem detected. Already triaged for a UG tech failure." He put his holotab into hibernation mode before looking back at me. "That's why it has to be Guy's. We just deliver them where we're told," he muttered.

"I'll follow in my vehicle," I said.

The paramedic shrugged. "Be seeing you, Commander."

He moved back up the ramp and disappeared inside the vehicle. The ramp auto-stowed, sliding back into the undercarriage, before the door slid shut. I watched as the medivac climbed jerkily up into the night sky before abruptly swaying back into the VTOL corridor.

I turned and began walking toward the public elevator stack, to get back to my vehicle beneath the terrestrial level. Again, I felt a vibration in my ear implant. I pressed on my wrist chip to activate my holotab. This time an alert banner was scrolling across the screen: a memo to all Europol staff. A state of emergency had just been declared across all the Union's thirty-four nation states. A curfew had been announced by the joint presidents in the Magisterium, effective 10 p.m. Central Union Time, later that evening. All civilians were to remain at home between 10 p.m. and 6 a.m. Family members and acquaintances were requested to facilitate homestays of all ferals. Union Emergency Command would escort isolated ferals to safe holding tanks.

I drew in a sharp intake of breath. *This is all completely messed up.*

CHAPTER 4

The elevator shuddered to a gentle stop. The door opened and the underground hover park safety lights booted on. As I approached my Skyraider, I ran a hand across the hood tenderly, my fingertips brushing the polished claret finish, as I always did while walking around the side. It still gave me a thrill. The bronze rota grid alloys, the tall spoiler fin on the rear of the shell, a top speed in the supersonic range, a climb speed of 4,000 meters per minute. Not to mention the state-of-the-art security linked to my sec-code alone. The lights flickered twice as the security protocols deactivated. I loved that car.

Before getting in, I folded my long Napa leather coat and black mourner's jacket and placed them carefully on the spare seat. I activated my VirDa, Siena, absently watching the console lights boot up. Her virtual face bobbed onto the display screen: blue eyes, a perfect aquiline nose. She was only AI, but still, I loved her nose.

"Where to, Emyr?" Siena cooed with Tuscan accent differentiators. All this—the Italian accent and the female persona for my VirDa—didn't come cheap. But then again, I did have expensive tastes. I gave a tap on my wrist chip. The eighteen-centimeter holographic screen projected in front of me. The Europol MyPlace channel was live streaming

43

in background mode in one screen quadrant. I moved my wrist to see better, and the screen moved too, floating translucent silver in the darkness inside the cabin.

The feed was direct from the Magisterium, the epicenter of the Union's administrative heart in downtown Brussels, the capital city. A joint presser with the Grand Union's two highest-ranking officials, the Commission president and the president of the Council of Leaders. I ran my gaze along the audio-slider bar, increasing the volume. The Commission president had a somber air, her forehead creased with worry. There were reports of looting in several Union cities. Local police had been overwhelmed in Berlin, Bratislava, Paris, and Sofia. Warrior-class droid units had been deployed by Proelium military HQ. To the Old Kingdom, too. Ferals were running riot, the Commission president announced. *Quite literally*, I thought, having witnessed it with my own eyes. Hence the Union had deployed a rapid reaction force, ten battalions of biomechanical soldiers heading across the Old Kingdom Channel. An act of solidarity for a neighbor, the president intoned. *More like self-interest to prop up a failing state before it becomes the Union's mess*, I thought. I gave a blink command to mute the feed and another to activate my facecall app.

"Call Lotte van der Meer," I said, issuing my in-app voice command. I needed to speak to her anyway, now that we were formally assigned to the case. But in truth, I just wanted to hear her voice and see a face that cared.

With a flicker, her freckled face, long auburn hair, and familiar coy smile occupied my screen. I took in Lotte's trademark pale red eyeshadow on her lids and lower lashline.

"There he is," Lotte announced, looking directly out at me.

"And there she is," I replied, "one radiant, psybient beauty."

"This is a Europol line, Emyr," Lotte said in prickly reproach, pinning me with her look. I knew I shouldn't be commenting on how she looked, alluding to *us* on this line. "You're in your Skyraider, then," she stated, shaking her head. My console lights were blinking next to me. "Your one true love!"

"No, Lotte, that's—" I stopped myself before I said *you*, as I saw her arched eyebrow, her glanced warning. She threw me a quick shake of her head before a faint smile reappeared.

"I'm just your hard-working chief analyst," she said quietly. She knew what I had been about to say. Then she narrowed her eyes as she became somber. "How did it go?"

I sighed. "It's done. She's buried," I replied, solemn too.

"Wanstead soil, as promised?"

"One and the same. As she requested." Then I paused. "Before the Bastard took her away to Cymru," I muttered, trying to pull a wry face. But now I was only able to summon sadness, which somehow reflected back at me from Lotte's hazel eyes through the screen. I'd known she would ask about my mother. But somehow, unexpectedly, traces of sorrow needled me.

"You look tired," Lotte whispered. "Poor Emyr."

"You're at Eiserhowerlaan?" I asked, changing the subject, knowing she was speaking to me from Europol HQ. I could tell from her expression that she saw the topic was now closed. And Lotte knew I didn't do feelings. They were buried too.

"Sleeping quarters being set up."

"Not going home, then?" I asked. Lotte shook her head. "Jaap won't be happy." She gave me a fake grimace in response as she brushed a wayward strand of hair from her eyes.

"You've spoken to Lina?"

I grinned. "My compassionate leave has been canceled. We've been assigned to the case. She wants to know whether

Babel is behind the outage. The director wants a full report tomorrow."

"Is that what you think? *Your* mystery woman caused it?" Lotte asked. I frowned, ignoring her snide remark.

"For now, I don't think anything. Let's gather the evidence ..."

"So, what do you want me to do?"

"Two things. Can you get a trace on the origination of the DDoS attacks? A geographical origin. It would be a start at least, to help figure out who's behind this. Lina says Tier Two state servers were taken over to launch the cyberattack in low Earth orbit."

"Isn't that CyberForce's job? Marchaud's team in the Proelium will already be on it."

I rolled my eyes. "That genius?"

Lotte smirked and wagged her finger at me. "Same old Emyr. Fine. I'll get a team of droid analysts on it. And the second thing?"

"See whether there's any chatter in cyberspace between Babel cells. See what comms you can intercept."

"So you *do* think it's Babel, then?" Lotte asked.

"Ebba Black's up to something. We've known that for some time." Lotte let out a long sigh in response. "What?" I snapped, now slightly accusingly. Lotte claimed I was obsessed with the woman. It was true she was a conundrum—and it wasn't just that she was a ghost and a nate. Still, Lotte's insinuations had started to grate.

"Babel's encryption is always difficult to crack. You know that, right?" Lotte muttered absently.

"Right. But you'll try anyway," I said, smiling. "I'll call Pieter later. As soon as I'm back at my apartment. I want to pull in Karen Hoekstra first thing. See whether she knows anything. Shake the tree a bit."

"I'll get the team all over the comms. We'll do our best," Lotte replied.

"That's all I ask. One more thing, though."

"You said *two* things." Lotte stared out at me with insouciance.

I frowned at her. "Okay, third thing," I began with slight irritation, "there was a crash here. A hover car dropped down a VTOL corridor onto a vertipad at the following location." I issued a blink command to my holotab, sending the location pin of the crash site via a memoclip to Lotte's Europol portal ID.

"A hover car crash!" Lotte exclaimed. "Isn't that supposed to be impossible these days, with LiDAR autonomous hover car tech?"

"I know. It doesn't make sense. Can you try and retrieve the diagnostics—get a fix on what caused the crash? The vehicle looked to be running on manual mode."

"Self-driving in R city airspace?" Lotte exclaimed. "One sec." She glanced down, issuing blink and gaze commands at her console VirDa screen. "I have something. The driver is listed as male, one Dhruv Gasper, CEO of … Drones Kineto, a drone-tech surveillance company in the Republic of California. The company also manufactures robotic medical equipment, apparently." Lotte then began muttering, "Very high speed in an unrestricted intercity skyway." Then more loudly, "Apparently on a transatlantic flight path. You're right, the vehicle was on manual. No VirDa engaged."

"So he *was* piloting himself," I exclaimed.

"Apparently. It was all legit. He was operating on manual mode in unrestricted airspace. Nowhere near London city R space. The outage hit as he reached the Paris-to-London skyway intersection. He took a descent VTOL corridor for the transatlantic skyway. His LS rebound records cease at exactly that point."

"Hmm, something happened to his language chip ..." My words trailed off.

"Looks like it," Lotte replied. "My guess: the outage hit, his language chip went. Maybe his telemetry system got shorted. And then he couldn't use voice commands to have his VirDa take over, switch to auto mode."

What a way to go, I thought. To become feral, unable to switch to the vehicle's autopiloting system. The guy would have just kept traveling down the intersection corridor at high speed, dropping into London's R airspace, until he hit the ground.

"Can you see which provider he subscribed to?" I asked. "Something's off. Surely a rich guy like that would be with Appleton? Especially as he was based in the Republic."

Lotte played with a strand of her hair absently. "Good point. Appleton's not affected by the outage. I'll look into it. You're heading back now?" she asked.

"Later. I want to check something out first. Two ferals I sent to a local hospital. They've been diagnosed with some kind of UG tech failure—I want to see what's causing the loss of language streaming."

"Isn't that obvious? The explosion," Lotte said. I studied her thoughtfully. The explosion would only have affected Tele3 subscribers—the system that blew up.

"Weird things are going on. Some people here are feral. But others seem to have some kind of linguistic scrambling— Romanian, even Hindustani."

"Hindustani?" Lotte sounded surprised.

"I have a feeling I might start getting some answers at the hospital," I muttered.

"Following your famous itch?"

I grinned. "Lina calls it *interfering*."

"And when you're back ..." Lotte's voice cracked unexpectedly.

"What is it?" I asked with concern. Lotte shook her head. Now she seemed off; something was up. Tears welled up in her eyes. She brushed them away and attempted a smile.

"I have something to tell you. See you soon." With that, she called off. *That sounds ominous,* I thought.

* * *

My hover car approached Guy's Hospital tower from the north, crossing over the river. I taxied down a small incline away from the vertipad before coming to a stop on a parking platform.

I approached the security console to register my DigID credentials underneath the language streaming orb, facing the VirDa display screen. The orb auto-activated, glowing green as it moved back and forth above me, scanning the sec-code rebounds from my language chip. A simulated female face bobbed onto the VirDa screen.

"Emyr Morgan, Commander Europol, Cybercrime Division head. State your purpose."

"Request access to the neurology department. I referred two patients." With that, I activated my holotab, issuing a series of blink commands at the image gallery app, sending facial stillgrams of the two ferals to the VirDa's sensor.

"Proximity alert received. Patient data matched. Thank you, Commander. Access granted to floor 144. Follow the PosNav instructions."

The glass security doors slid open. Once inside the entrance vestibule, I saw my name being broadcast via a stillgram blinkable on the display panel next to the relevant door on the elevator bank. I blinked to activate the stillgram and waited just a few seconds before the elevator arrived.

Inside, I was alone. The ceiling speaker emitted faint splashing water sounds, creating an eerie echo, before my elevator slowed to a gentle stop. The doors opened onto a busy atrium: daemons, mobile medical units transporting patients, nursing auxiliary gynoids, and even human medics. A squat janitor droid was moving in concentric circles around the floor.

I heard the ceiling-mounted personalized Positional Navigation system activate: "Commander Morgan, take the corridor on the far right."

I followed the intermittent overhead prompts as it picked up my LS rebounds, directing me. Access entry VirDa screens signaled what lay behind a series of large sliding doors that lined the corridor: Amyotrophic Lateral Sclerosis Unit, Autonomic Neurology, Brain Tumor Program, Cerebrovascular Diseases and Critical Care, Child and Adolescent Neurology, Clinical Neurophysiology. I gazed in bemused incomprehension at the names. Activating my holotab, I issued a blink command to select the Union-DEF language app. Once active, I issued an in-app voice command: "Download medical lexical package, default language." I felt a slight vibration in my ear implant as the command was confirmed. And with that I now knew that the Amyotrophic Lateral Sclerosis Unit treated patients with motor neurone disease.

After a few minutes, I reached my destination: the Universal Grammar Tech Neuromedical Care Unit.

"Welcome, Commander Morgan. Access granted." The glass door slid open, revealing a large vestibule lined with smart LED walls and ceiling panels. As I crossed the threshold, the distinctive antiseptic odor of ammonium hit me, combined with hypochlorite and phenolics. The aroma was a little bitter.

Dead ahead was a large reception console. Behind it stood a gynoid. This one was dressed in blue medical-style scrubs. She was a consumer-facing model, finished with a mid-brown skin tone modifier and short brown hair. The gynoid was in hibernation mode, but as I approached, her eyes flickered open. Also brown. I knew she would be scanning me, confirming my sec-code credentials for the umpteenth time since I'd arrived.

"Commander Morgan, you are here about your referrals ..." she began. *A statement, not a question?* I wondered, before a glitch kicked in. "Yrrrr ... yes?" A question, then. This one was clearly an older model, not a newer Einstein-chipped synthetic.

"Yes," I replied. The gynoid paused. Just for a moment, but long enough for me to know she was communicating with another VirDa via neural linking.

"You may wait over there," she announced, gesturing to a small recess with some seating. "Mr. Singh, the duty consultant, will be with you shortly." With that, the gynoid slipped back into hibernation mode. *Mr. Singh. That means a real person.*

As I waited, my thoughts drifted back to my mother. She had once been a nurse herself, here at Guy's Hospital. Back in the day, before soc-ed classifications, before human jobs were replaced with AI. Before nursing was declared obsolete and put on the obs-jobs list.

My mind wandered back to the afternoon, to the service led by the chaplain. Chaplains remained human. At least that was one job that hadn't been proscribed. A sentimental thing. You had to be human to preside over death. *The irony.*

CHAPTER 5

"Commander?" asked a pitchy voice behind me. I turned around to see a small harried-looking man. About my age but wrinkled, with male pattern baldness already taking hold. His shoulders were hunched, which diminished his stature further. He had an air of defeat, or fatalism, or maybe both. Or perhaps it was just extreme fatigue after too many long shifts. He rubbed an eye absently. As he craned his neck to look up at me, I saw surprise in his eyes. I probably looked like a giant next to him. To most people, standing at 198 centimeters, even without my luxury Ferrogami shoes. ~~"I'm Mr. Singh. Neurosurgery consultant,"~~ he muttered.

"Do you have a few minutes? I have a couple of questions."

"Of course. This way, Commander." His accent was clipped in the effete way provided by some of Appleton's high-end packages. The accent Singh was streaming was meant to sound plum and impressive. I just found it pompous. But that was me.

I followed Singh's diminutive figure past the reception console. As we walked, I glanced through the glass wall on the left of the vestibule. It was an intensive care ward with some serious state-of-the-art internet of medical tech—a series of gleaming white patient booths, open-sided polycarbonate canopies with virtual sensors, protruding lights and diagnostic devices, containing smart beds. The beds were electronically segmentable, mounted on plastic polyformed platforms fitted with an array of monitors and robotic inspection units hanging over them. I was surprised to see that the facility was almost full of patients.

As we passed, I watched with idle curiosity the focused activity of a daemon rolling between patients situated in their polycarbonate units. The daemon was clearly a top-end multifunctional robotic unit. With advanced synthetic consciousness and computing power, it would be interpreting multiple streams of data from the array of smart diagnostic units attached to each patient, providing a continuous data feed.

Nearby, there was a glass medical monitoring hub with several banks of VirDa monitors mounted on consoles. The displays pulsated with colored bar charts, and graphs faded in and out, livestreamed from the smart ward. A medical gynoid, this one in green overalls, was focusing on the data. I vaguely wondered about the significance of the different-colored uniforms.

As we turned into a corridor leading off the reception vestibule, I saw another glass cubicle containing a stationary daemon in powered-down mode. It was equipped with a portable oxygen unit and suction apparatus, a crash cart, and a resuscitation kit, as well as what I recognized as a pulse oximeter and glucometer.

Singh led me into an office a little farther along. As he half turned, gesturing for me to follow him inside, I noticed how his oversized white tunic appeared to envelop his thin body like a shroud. He sat down in a synthetic leather chair next to a VirDa console and pointed to another.

"I referred two patients," I began as I sat, "a woman and—"

"Yes, yes," Singh said impatiently, cutting me off. "We've examined them." He fixed me with a piercing gaze. "They both have scarred language chips. It's conclusive."

"What does that mean, exactly? Scarred?"

"The Wi-Fi transceiver component, the ear implants, they're working. But there's no streaming signal getting through to the core Universal Grammar component." I was taken aback. I'd never heard of scarred language chips before. Singh nodded solemnly. "We've run a series of LS rebound tests. No neurological damage. The patients' brains remain intact—healthy."

"But what you're saying is—what? It really is the language chips?"

Singh's brow furrowed. "Non-functioning. Completely dead…" His voice trailed off absentmindedly before continuing as if rediscovering his line of thought. "It turns out it's the electrode pillars." He saw my look of confusion. "In the microbattery that powers their language chips."

"The battery? Hold on, there hasn't been a battery failure in decades. It's supposed to be impossible." I knew there were all kinds of safeguards to protect the tiny unit that powered the language chip.

"The electrodes consist of a series of tiny thin films, multiple stacks, barely a few hundred micrometers thick. Now completely fried. Probably from the same pulse that triggered the satellite overload."

"The explosion, you mean."

Singh nodded absently. "Didn't see it myself. Heard it was impressive. I was overseeing surgery. Did you?" he asked, watching me with sudden curiosity.

"So these two are Tele3 subscribers, then?" I asked, ignoring his question. His eyes narrowed as he watched me with something bordering on suspicion.

"How did you know that?" he asked sharply.

"That's the satellite system that blew up," I explained. "The other internet-from-space ecosystems appear undamaged. Physically, at least. Although there are reports of streaming problems. Samkee, definitely. Maybe others."

"That explains one thing," Singh said quietly, as if to himself, before addressing me. "We're seeing the same pattern with other ferals admitted. Tele3 subscribers all have scarred chips, non-functional. A WHO medical alert broadcast a few minutes ago confirmed the same thing. Thousands of similar cases already in the Union, United Federation of America, and other Tier One states, including the Korean and Indian Republics. All Tele3. No data currently available from the Chinese."

"So all Tele3 and Samkee subscribers have scarred language chips?" I asked. Singh shook his head brusquely.

"That's not what I said." There was irritation in his voice.

"Sorry, Dr. Singh, I don't follow."

He glanced at me with a piercing look. "*Mr.* Singh," he said. I looked at him quizzically, now thoroughly confused. "I'm a consultant, a specialist, more than a mere doctor. That's only for those generalists ..." He shook his head slightly dismissively. "Address me as Mr., not Dr."

They're always so stiff-assed in the Old Kingdom, I thought to myself. It took all my meditation techniques to stop this one getting right up my nose. He was especially prickly.

"Mr. Singh it is," I said quietly.

Singh nodded and carried on. "All the Tele3 subscribers we've admitted have scarred chips. But the Samkee users coming in ... their language chips are functional. No battery damage. It's just a signal scrambling problem. Probably some streaming glitch. Language registration protocols, I'd guess. Nothing amiss with the neuroprosthetic tech itself."

"That explains it," I muttered.

"What?" asked Singh, watching me.

"Someone suddenly talking in Mandarin in Manor Park High Street immediately after the outage hit. And a dispatcher from the London emergency center speaking Romanian. Then someone speaking Hindustani, of all things."

Singh scowled. "Hindustani is a perfectly respectable language. I have family in northern India."

"I just meant—" I began, shaking my head.

He held up one hand to silence me. "I know exactly what you meant," he said huffily. "But you probably witnessed the effects of the outage on Samkee subscribers. Scrambled linguistic status. Presenting as locked out of their default language settings. Highly disruptive. Language streaming randomly reset to a single state official variety from a different country. Which means all affected Samkee subscribers won't be able to communicate with holotabs or security VirDas here."

"So it's serious, then?"

Singh glanced at me and gave a slight grimace. "If you think being locked out of your home, checking and retail account is serious, then of course it's serious. But in theory, nothing permanent. Assuming Samkee can get their streaming protocols reset."

"First Samkee has to get its satellite system back online," I muttered. *But more pressing, what about the Tele3 subscribers?*

There's a lot of them. My mind was whirring. Tele3, with its HQ in Brussels, was the closest thing the Union had to a state-sponsored language streaming provider. After all, it was the Union's designated partner for streaming services to the entire Unskill population. Like all UN-designated Tier One states, Unskills qualified for gratis state-provided official language streaming. In the Union, that meant around fifty percent of the adult population, with Tele3 receiving the entire federal annual budgetary allocation. It was a big deal, and a hell of a lot of money. So if Tele3 had been taken out, it wasn't just the lower soc-ed classes that were screwed. The economy would tank, too.

I studied Singh for a moment. "So how do we fix a scarred language chip?"

He began shaking his head. I knew that wasn't a good sign. "That's just the thing. This has never happened before with second-gen chips. And before that—well, the last time a first-gen language chip failed was before the first lang-law referendum. These new ones, the micro-electronics run on a Lazarus loop. They are pretty much indestructible."

"Except that turns out not to be the case," I muttered. "But you can replace them, right? Fit a new chip? Change the UG tech or something?"

"It's not that simple," Singh said. I threw him a confused look. He took a gulp of something from a cupstock. "Cold!" he exclaimed with irritation. "You want something?" he added absently, gesturing toward his cup.

Not something like that, I thought. "I'm good, thanks."

He moved his head in a strange sideways motion. Then he began monologing. "You, me, and everyone else in Tier One and Tier Two states are subject to lang-laws, right?" I wondered where he was going with this. Hopefully not a history lesson on the Californian mandatory language chipping experiment that had gone global within five years. "Did you know that the language chip is in fact an array of ultra-thin flexible polymer threads?" Singh carried on. "Each chip contains several hundred threads, each a fraction of the width of a human hair, with thousands of electrodes distributed across each thread."

He watched me, waiting for my reaction. He wanted me to say something. After all, UG tech was his bread and butter. I got it; he found it all impressive.

"Cool, I guess."

He rubbed his hands together in glee, warming to his theme. "And did you also know a robotic surgeon can sew threads into the living tissue of a newborn's brain at the rate of ten threads per minute? With absolute precision! The language chip itself connects to the two significant language areas of the brain." Things had changed since my day. I was chipped at eighteen. Today kids got chipped at birth—that was the law.

"The brain has language areas?" I asked, vaguely surprised at this new revelation.

"It certainly does. Wernicke's area and Broca's area. Wernicke's is where we process language. Language understanding, the ability to comprehend words and phrases. Broca's does the production part."

"What, like speech?" I asked.

"Right. The language chip is basically a bridge between these areas and a remote language streaming server. When we stream, we're in fact calling up words and patterns of grammar on demand. And data from the language streaming signal activates the two language areas but without the nuisance of having to learn vocabulary and grammar. The bit of the brain that used to store all that, well ..." Singh looked at me knowingly. I got it. Humans didn't do that anymore. At least, not in the automated world. Tier Three populations still had to do things the old-fashioned way.

Back in high school, when UG tech was still shiny and new and the Union wanted to maximize uptake by the transitional generation, it was drilled into us teenagers what an astounding feat of technology it was all supposed to be. Anyone with a multilingual LS subscription package could move across any state language boundary line and use any of the world's official languages. What the teachers hadn't said was that it only applied if you could afford it. Marc Barron, Appleton, and all the other new tech gods of language—well, let's just say they weren't doing any of it for charity. *Cognition offloaded.* That was the slogan of the day. *Take the load off,* our teachers had said back then, trying to be funny.

"Who do you subscribe to, Commander, if you don't mind?" I wondered where Singh was heading now, asking this question.

"Union-DEF."

He raised his eyebrows, impressed. "A non-commercial provider, then."

"A perk of the job."

"I imagine more of a necessity in your line of work," he added. "So your language server gives you words to label things you want to talk about. And a grammar system to link them up, so you can verbalize your thoughts. And because of your provider, well, you can do that in pretty much any language." He took another sip of the cold liquid and grimaced again. He had forgotten. "Cold!" he repeated with a new shudder of irritation before continuing. "These days, the second-gen chips that newborns get, they have developmental protocols built in. Basically, as the child starts building a head full of concepts, it can use language streaming to begin articulating what it feels, what it wishes to express, without the hassle of having to actually learn a language anymore."

"But I still don't see why you can't just replace the damaged language chips."

"The two patients you sent my way …" Singh made a swirling gesture with his left hand, vaguely indicating somewhere outside the office, "… the little boy can be rehabilitated. He's young enough. Enough brain plasticity, no danger of damage to the brain's vasculature. If his family can afford it, we can fit a new second-gen language chip in around thirty minutes. It would take just a few hours for his new voice print and other DigID credentials to propagate. He'd be up and running, back to normal, the same day."

"And the adult?" I asked.

"That's where the problem is. She also has a second-gen UG chip—she was chipped at birth. As things currently stand, she'll never be able to stream language again."

I gasped. "Never?" I asked, completely astounded.

"Not without a miracle." Singh held his palms out as if about to examine them. But I realized it was just his distracted state.

"But why not? Can't you just fit a new second-gen chip? Like with the child?"

Mr. Singh sighed. "Therein lies the problem. The second-gen UG chip isn't like the original chip used for the transitional generation, like us. It's designed for the brain of a newborn. The outer casing of the second-gen chip is in fact a liquid membrane, a biological component to allow it to adapt to a growing brain."

"But what about a first-gen chip? Couldn't you replace the woman's damaged chip with one of those?"

"That's why we would need a miracle. They're not manufactured anymore." I guess my face showed amazement. Singh smiled at me faintly. "When were you chipped?"

"2103," I replied.

Singh moved his head sideways again. "That would make you ... what? Forty, right?" I nodded. "And by the end of 2115, all the world's transitional generations had undergone the neuroprosthetic implant procedure. First-gen chips were obsolete. After all, they were designed for an adult brain."

"But surely there must be some somewhere."

Singh shrugged. "Appleton's patent expired after twenty years. Marc Barron and Hadean Burr-Alston, they were clever and wanted to protect their invention. So they renewed the patent in case Tier Three states ever decided to make the move. They wanted to future-proof Appleton. But today, only second-gen chips are being manufactured. No one makes first-gen chips anymore, not even Appleton, to my knowledge. You can't get them. No market. There aren't any nates left outside Tier Three."

"Except Ebba Black," I murmured.

"Ah, Professor Black—a famous unchipped outlier. Anyway, you see the problem? I literally have no solution for adult patients like the boy's mother. We simply don't have any stocks of first-gen chips here at Guy's."

The woman will now be out-soc. That means all adult Tele3 subscribers will be out-soc. This is crazy. I racked my brain trying to come up with a solution.

"What about this?" I began. "A first-gen chip user, like me, learned language the old-fashioned way, right? I started out as a nate."

Singh shrugged. "So?"

"Doesn't that mean that in adults like me, if their language chip failed, their original knowledge would kick in—the language they acquired as a nate? Couldn't their original language knowledge reboot or something?" I asked.

"If the brain were a computer. But the brain doesn't work like that. Basically, with language, it's a case of use it or lose it. Let's take you, Commander. Your age is forty. Which means your own personal store of linguistic knowledge, what we call the mental lexicon, is now a pale shadow of its former self. Hypothetically, even if we could restore your brain to its eighteen-year-old linguistic state, it would still be the brain of a forty-year-old man who hasn't used his linguistic neural networks for, what, twenty-two years? There wouldn't be much language left. You'd be essentially a feral. And the female adult patient, she doesn't have any linguistic memories of her own to draw on. She never learned language to begin with."

"I guess you and I are the lucky ones, then," I said.

"How so?"

"Not subscribing to Tele3. Or Samkee, for that matter."

"I subscribe to Appleton ... I need it for the medical lexical package. It's the only provider that offers the specialist terms I need to do my job."

"You've been helpful, thank you," I said. Singh gave me a faint smile that merged with fatigue, or maybe it was irritation. I wasn't sure.

"What do you think caused this?" he asked.

"The outage?"

"The news bulletins are claiming an accident. Although it makes no sense ...." His voice trailed off. I looked at his small frame as he kept shaking his head to himself. I knew what he was thinking: *what are the chances of both the Tele3 and Samkee systems failing at precisely the same time?* I also knew that the better question was not *what* had caused the outage, but *who*. The world seemed suddenly to have changed.

CHAPTER 6

I was in my Skyraider, finally heading back to the Union. I felt relief as I left Old Kingdom airspace. The London–South Holland airway was completely deserted. My passage home had been auto-cleared.

I idly scrolled through my holotab updates. Europol MyPlace news broadcasts were full of chatter about emergencies and curfews across the Union's thirty-four-country bloc. Bulletin refreshes brought live ticker updates of the millions of out-soc directly affected by the Tele3 outage; there were millions more Samkee subscribers with scrambled linguistic status, now all feral. I instructed Siena to shut it all down. I craved calm, silence, at least for now.

My mind wandered back to my own temporary experience of being feral at twelve. That in itself was ironic, because back then I wasn't actually feral. Not technically. I was still a nate when Cymru transposed Union lang-law into national legislation. The term *transitional generation* was even laid down in the Union lang-law directive.

The lang-law public conversion fund, subsidized by Appleton, ensured that at my age of majority I was fitted with UG tech, whether I wanted it or not. There was also a national subsidy to have a wrist chip fitted if you complied within the first six months of your eighteenth. ~~It was quite an incentive~~. And I ~~longed to have the cool-looking tech~~. And the biopersonal computing system, the holotab, was essential to manage a language streaming subscription effectively.

At twelve, still a ~~monolingual speaker of Cymraeg,~~ I went on a school trip to the Old Kingdom. The memory of that trip always stayed with me. Maybe because of the awe I felt passing the row of sleek Union border droid units at Cardiff hover port. But certainly because after we arrived at the zoo, on the other side of the River Severn, ~~I couldn't communicate with any of the public VirDas around me. It was a surre~~al ~~feeling of helplessness~~. I knew that didn't make much sense— helplessness—given the violence of my domestic life, but there I knew what to expect. ~~And at twelve, I was already nearly as big as my father.~~ The dynamic was changing. But across the border, I was quite literally out of my depth.

King's English was still supported by Unilanguage back then, the state official language—the so-called Old Standard. That was the only variety run by the public VirDas in the Old Kingdom. By then, only adults had already undergone chipping. ~~The state official language in Cymru was Cymraeg. Among us~~ ~~transitional kids, that was what we spoke too. Not one of us~~ ~~spoke English.~~ We had been assigned a multilingual Welcome Unit that accompanied us, translating the virtual signage and granting voice command access to our pre-paid exhibits, the zoo restaurant, and snack bars.

Back then, I didn't like being chaperoned, being told what to do. So another kid and I snuck away. It was fun at first. Until we became trapped in an exhibit; we couldn't get the door-lock VirDa to work. Someone—a large man, I remember— wanted to help. But he didn't stream Cymraeg, of course. He spoke loudly and was agitated. When I got spooked and tried to run, he grabbed my arm, hurting me. In my panic, I saw the Bastard's raised fist in every stranger's movement, in every shadow, making me jumpy. After that, the fear of being feral, not being able to issue voice commands, being locked out by VirDas I couldn't communicate with—that never went away.

* * *

The Skyraider taxied away from the vertipad toward the cavernous underground parking zone beneath my building. Siena powered down the piloting system and I picked up my jacket and coat, climbing out. I activated my holotab and switched my language setting, as I always did when I arrived home. The Netherlands operated just one state official language for all public VirDas: Union Standard Hollandic.

I took the elevator, moving silently up toward the top floor. I stepped out into the hallway in front of my apartment door. The security VirDa screen blinked at me.

"*Ontgrendel de deur*," I said, issuing my voice command to unlock. The VirDa parsed my voice print, blinked again, and the door opened.

Inside my apartment, lights booted on. I issued a blink command on an eye-tech fusion sensor to activate the auto-stow closet, which opened from behind a wall panel. I placed my coat and jacket on hangers inside. I then eased off my kydex holster and pistol, stowing them inside the weapons safe before the closet retracted, disappearing behind the paneling.

"Florence," I called out. The digital contour of my VirDa faded into view on the large wall screen as I entered the lounge.

"Welcome home, Emyr." Her Tuscan accent rolled over my

name, just the way I liked it. Inside the apartment I could do as I pleased with my own software. Union lang-law didn't apply inside private residences. My VirDas ran on North American Standard English with Italian accent differentiators.

I gazed around the expanse of my apartment, taking it in as I always did after being away. I loved this place! Over five years before, with my promotion to Head of the Cybercrime Directorate at Europol HQ in The Hague, I had swapped my bachelor pad in Bridgend, Cymru, for the glamor of a penthouse apartment overlooking Scheveningen beach.

I went straight to the spiral staircase, manufactured from brilliant white carbon-fiber panels that supported glass steps with brushed chrome rails, to get to the second floor. I desperately needed a drink. Once upstairs, I went through my open-plan relaxation area, past the bedroom suite, to get to the bar and seating area. The bar featured my own bespoke design, a 3D holographic waveform display of iridescent redshift flames. I placed a tumbler into the drink-maker.

"Rusty Nail," I said into the service unit's local VirDa. A glass tumbler quietly dropped from the machine's supply chute, followed by three ice cubes, a double measure of Irish whiskey, and a slice of brûléed orange. I tried to limit myself to two drinks per evening. It wasn't always possible.

With drink in hand, I sat down on a high bar stool across from my beautiful TechSportif billiard table with stunning red cloth, imported from Québec City in the United Federation of America. I gazed up at the pièce de résistance on the upper level: the pitched glass roof. It dropped from the center of the high ceiling toward glass doors that gave out to the upper-level roof terrace. I glanced around in quiet satisfaction.

I turned toward the large VirDa screen on the adjacent wall, taking a gulp of my drink. Then I issued my voice command: "Florence, facecall Chief Inspector Pieter de Bruijn."

There was a momentary pause before Pieter's round face appeared on the large screen in front of me. As he glanced up from his console to look out at me, for just an instant his short-cropped hair filled the screen with brown blur. His connection identifiers showed he was still at the office on Eiserhowerlaan. He had an air of fatigue about him, and his cheeks were even more flushed than usual.

"I need one of those, boss," Pieter said with a rueful grin as he eyed the glass I was still holding. For the very first time since he had transferred to Europol, I noticed that his eyes were brown. I realized I hadn't paid much attention to him. He was reliable, and that was good enough. His grin rippled across the contours of his face. I gave the slightest of nods—I didn't do chit-chat with anyone at work. Except Lotte, of course.

"Our brief is to find out who's behind the outage," I began.

Pieter's grin disappeared, replaced by a look of weary earnestness. "I heard we'd been selected. All other divisions have been assigned to crisis management, under direct command of the Imperium and the Magisterium. Now even Europol's taking orders from the bureaucrats in Brussels," he muttered.

I cleared my throat. I wasn't interested in his opinion. "I need you to put together a list of possible suspects—commercial, private, state actors, terrorists ..." I began as I took a final sip, finishing my whiskey before placing it on the bar.

"But we start with Babel, right? Lotte already mentioned you want to bring in the informant."

I nodded. "Let's see whether Karen has heard anything—any chatter. The director wants a briefing in the morning."

"I've already made arrangements, spoken to her," Pieter began. I nodded approval. "We're picking up Professor Hoekstra first thing. But in terms of chatter, something interesting. My team intercepted a call thirty minutes ago. We passed it to Lotte for analysis. She said you'd asked her to do a trawl of all Babel comms."

"And?" I asked, keen to hear what Pieter had.

"Her team managed to decrypt about ten seconds. It's between two Babel cells. The handles have the IDs *Datashizzle* and *The Tower*. But we've only got audio for one. It's a bit mumbo-jumbo. Something about a *Language Unplugged protocol* ..." Pieter's words trailed off as he watched my expression change; he'd piqued my interest.

"Language Unplugged! A reference to the DDoS attacks earlier, maybe ...?" I mused after a moment.

"I know. That was my first thought too. But Babel always claims responsibility immediately after a DDoS attack. This time, nothing. Nada. And Babel hasn't ever done anything on this scale."

I mulled over Pieter's words. Could this really be the work of Ebba Black's cyberterrorist outfit? After all, Babel wasn't anti-people, just anti-big-tech. And this was clearly having a global impact on Tier One and Tier Two populations. Still, this had been no accident. Someone was responsible. Despite what we were briefing to the news outlets.

"Send me the recording and transcription. Any luck identifying the cells' locations?"

Pieter squinted back at me. "That's the funny thing. You know, these guys are impossible to hack. Usually. But one of the handles wasn't properly cloaked: Datashizzle. We already have coordinates. A location on the south coast of the Old Kingdom."

"And identity?" I asked.

"Still working on that. Will send you full details as soon as we have DigID credentials. One more thing—I've just come off a call with my contact in Marchaud's division in the Proelium. CyberForce are saying it's the Russians. Get this—BeeDirect is the only other major commercial provider unaffected." Pieter nodded as he saw my mouth open wide. "That was my reaction too," he added.

Now I really was taken aback. BeeDirect didn't operate outside the Russian Republics, being the Federation's state-sponsored provider. And given its security protocols were woefully below par compared to the world's other major commercial LS providers, it was vanishingly unlikely that it could have withstood a cyberattack that had impacted the likes of Tele3 and Samkee. *Which can only mean it hasn't been targeted*, I thought.

"Why would BeeDirect be spared?" I mused aloud. "If this really were Babel, then all LS providers are legitimate targets, right?"

"Unless it really was the Russians after all," Pieter said. "Of course, Bulchovi is denying any involvement. But he would, wouldn't he? The High Representative, the whole of the Proelium and Imperium security apparatus, they seem to be working themselves into a frenzy about the Federation as usual."

"The Russian Federation wouldn't be that dumb. Bulchovi doesn't want economic sanctions imposed by the Union, by other federations," I replied.

"Or maybe something worse ..." Pieter muttered, making me glance up at him on the screen.

Just then I heard a gentle vibration in my ear implant, a high-priority alert. I activated my holotab and saw that Pieter had sent through the audio file and transcript for the intercepted Babel call to my Europol secure portal.

"Let's pick this up first thing." I gave Pieter a terse nod as I deactivated the call.

I made myself another drink before going back downstairs. I needed some air. On the lower floor, I went past my study— which also housed my isolation booth—the kitchen, and my mini gym, before reaching the expansive lounge with its eye-sensor-operated luxury retractable furniture. The lounge featured large glass windows on three sides, giving out to my private glass-enclosed balcony which allowed me to walk around the exterior of the building.

"Open," I whispered softly. As the glass panels slid apart, a cold breeze encircled me, rippling my shirt. I felt its icy pull against my tired face. I stepped out onto the balcony, which overlooked the black beach and the foaming sea in the cold November night.

I loved the long, sandy dunes; smooth, tranquil, and yellow in the heat of summer, churlish and gray in the unseasonable winter months. A stream of lights to my far left drew me back to this strange new reality. From my vantage point, I made out Union transports descending the VTOL corridor near the Beach Stadium, about a kilometer and a half away. The venue was aglow, the retractable roof closed against the night. It had been turned into a holding tank for ferals. South Holland was one of the most densely populated regions in the world, with nearly two thousand people per square kilometer. And with so many ferals without guardians or family support, the local Union command would have a busy night. I returned inside.

Before turning in for the night, I spent a few minutes

catching up on briefing updates on my Europol virtual portal in my isolation booth. The news made for grim reading.

It was now confirmed that an electromagnetic pulse, triggered when the Tele3 satellite system had exploded, had permanently damaged the micro-electronic circuitry of the language chips of all Tele3 subscribers. Millions were now out-soc in the Union alone. If the medic back in London was right, a large percentage would remain permanently so, unless production of replacement first-gen chips could be restarted.

While I already knew that subscribers to the other main service provider in the Union, Samkee, were now feral and so temporarily offline with scrambled monolinguistic status, commercial providers in many other markets had been impacted in the same way. These included Avalon, based in Toronto; the Japanese-based provider, Dokomo; and the Mumbai-based provider IndiaCom, as well as the South American conglomerate Brilhante. The outage was truly global.

The default languages of subscribers to these providers, like Samkee, had all been randomly reset by the DDoS attacks and all ID credentials deleted. Across the world, users were unable to reset to their country's official language. Their voice commands no longer worked in their home states. Most people could no longer operate public VirDas.

Across the Union, around eighty percent of the population were either Tele3 or Samkee users. Many of those affected were trapped inside buildings and vehicles, or locked out of them. I watched live security telecast feeds on my holotab. The scenes were surreal.

But one thing was becoming abundantly clear: if you were an Appleton subscriber, you were one of the lucky ones. Appleton had better security protocols than the national defense systems of some smaller Tier One states. It even supplied the United Federation of America's Space Command with core ballistic infrastructure. Marc Barron had contracts with UFA governmental agencies running to trillions of e-Continentals. And, of course, Appleton had invested in countering Babel's cyberattacks for the last five years.

I finished my final drink of the night. I could already tell that tomorrow was going to be quite a day.

CHAPTER 7

It was day two of the language outage. I rose from my bed at first light, finally giving up on my restless attempts at sleep. I spent twenty minutes on a short calisthenics routine in my personal gym. Once finished, as I was warming down, I listened to the decoded ten-second excerpt from the Babel communication that Pieter had sent through. I was curious to hear what one of Babel's tech ninjas actually sounded like.

"Florence, play audio file 2125-11-05-Babel on loop."

It repeated through the ceiling speaker directly above me. Some acoustic quality had been lost during the decryption. It also hadn't been possible to decrypt the transmission channel for the first voice, The Tower. There was only static. The second voice, Datashizzle, was male. The words were clear enough. He was repeating part of what he had just been told.

"The protocol?" Then a short pause. "Is it time to reveal the Language Unplugged protocol?" Finally, after another longer gap of static, Datashizzle's final words—three words: "Operation False Flag." And that was it.

Operation False Flag, I mused. *What's that?* I knew what a false flag operation was, of course. But Babelists were no pirates on the high seas—maybe pirates of the automated world. I chuckled to myself. And whether they hoisted the colors of an innocent party or not, innocent they most certainly were not. *So what did False Flag mean in this context?* I wondered.

In the brief excerpt, Datashizzle spoke with an oddly guttural accent, harsh, with pronounced "r" sounds. The accent sounded regional. An expensive subscription, probably. Maybe Appleton? Still, it wasn't an accent from a lexical package I recognized.

As I showered and dressed, I continued to ponder Operation False Flag. As I turned it over in my mind, I was reminded of what an instructor had taught me many years before, during my training at the Heddlu Seiberdroseddu detective academy in Cymru: solving a cybercrime case was like trying to solve a jigsaw puzzle when pieces belonging to several similar-looking puzzles had been mixed together. Neither straightforward nor easy. After all, any black hat worth their salt could cover their tracks by throwing a dozen extra pieces into the mix to sow chaos and confusion.

Solving a case always entailed an act of creation, a mental feat of integrating the improbable to connect the possible, to find the likely. It wasn't just about the laborious collection and cataloging of evidence. In cybercrime, an obvious solution was a *non sequitur*. Which was why more than fifty percent of all cybercrimes remained unsolved. And also why many of my colleagues from my cadet days were languishing in junior ranks while I was heading to the top. I could do it all, examine the puzzle in a different way, from a different angle. And now I had the *itch* again. Something bugging me. *Hmm, I'll check out Ebba Black's old Babel Apocalypse Manifesto when I get to the office,* I told myself.

As I was about to walk out the apartment door, I received

a new Europol vibration alert in my ear implant. It was from Pieter. I paused to activate my holotab. A person-of-interest file on Datashizzle. We now had DigID credentials, including biometric and facial records, full bio details, and even a current location. *Good job, Pieter!*

I scanned the key details. Datashizzle's real name was Erebus McDenizen, a twenty-eight-year-old national of Alba, one of the Celtic partnership countries together with Cymru and Éire, all Union member states. But he held an Old Kingdom residence permit where he was now based, which figured. It was easier to operate under the radar outside the Union, in a Tier Two state, where surveillance protocols were lax.

A black hat hacker and convicted felon with an extensive rap sheet, McDenizen had the dubious claim to fame of having a first arrest at the age of just fifteen on a misdemeanor charge. At seventeen he was convicted of several cybercrime felonies, including unauthorized computer access, conspiracy to carry out a distributed denial-of-service attack, data theft, and wire fraud. He was sentenced as a minor and served just twenty-four months in an Old Kingdom young offender institution with early release for good behavior. He was rearrested twice for parole violations and spent a further twenty-four months in medium-security penitentiaries before a final spell in an open prison. Later, after a court-enforced rehabilitation program, McDenizen was permitted to work as a security researcher, a white hat, disclosing bugs to corporations as part of bounty programs. This he did responsibly—at least initially, according to parole service records. But McDenizen's LS rebound records halted abruptly around three years ago, at which point he dropped off the grid. Until now.

Pieter's team had used triangulation to identify McDenizen's street address near Southampton, on the south coast of the Old Kingdom. And local drone surveillance had now confirmed McDenizen was physically present at the property. ~~We need to bring him in, I thought~~. I needed more intel on whatever the Language Unplugged protocol was. And Operation False Flag. These were our best leads so far. Our only leads.

* * *

I lived a short walk from Europol HQ. Once outside my apartment building and onto the esplanade, I was instantly enveloped by the fine sea salt aerosol that laced the cold, moist air, customary for this time of year. But as I turned a corner, a novel sight greeted me: a hover car abandoned near a vertipad on one side of a beach transit corridor. Its passenger-side cab screen was smashed, apparently from within. More unusual still, on the main Scheveningen transit corridor, streams of Union transport vehicles were heading to and from the Beach Stadium, arriving with ferals, leaving empty.

I turned into the Scheveningen Badplaats, walking past some recently smashed house fronts. A Union sentry post had been set up across the transport corridor—a squad of Challenger-class infantry droids stood in the pedestrian corridor. The droids were over two meters tall, the hydraulic casings in their neck and arm joints pulsing as their head-mounted orb scanners swiveled in a 360-degree surveillance pattern. I strode past.

As I reached Old Scheveningen, there was a commotion adjacent to a small row house. A military hover vehicle was parked nearby on uneven cobblestones, in the monumental area of the old quarter. The high-tech vehicle looked strangely out of place amid the stonework and vestiges of early morning sea mist.

Two Challenger-class droids and a small group of distressed human onlookers surrounded a figure on the ground. As I moved closer, I saw a frail-looking elderly woman lying supine on an open porch in front of a house door. The adjacent security VirDa blinked red: secure settings engaged, door locked. The woman's face was puffy, her eyes closed. On her exposed arms there were large blue spots. She lay perfectly still, as if asleep. Her gray hair was arranged in rigid wispy strands, semi-frozen from the night before. One of the droids was checking for a pulse, while the woman's neighbors were talking quietly among themselves. As I approached, the head-mounted LS orb on one of the droids auto-scanned my sec-code rebounds.

"I'm with Europol. What happened here?" I asked quietly, using North American Standard, the official variety for internal comms across all Union agencies, including military droids.

"She was offline, feral. Locked out of her house," the droid replied.

A middle-aged woman in the group was wringing her hands. She had red eyes and was still in a nightrobe, outdoor boots hastily put on. She glanced at me and away again. Then she spoke.

"*Ze woonde alleen. Ik wist niet dat ze buitengesloten was.*" As soon as my auditory nerve activated, my language chip began auto-parsing the words. Union Standard Hollandic, with no accent differentiators, I switched to Hollandic. The old woman had lived alone, apparently, and could no longer issue voice commands. Her neighbor hadn't realized she was shut out outside. No one had come to her aid.

The droid now kneeling by the old woman was communicating with its paired droid via neural link—I could see the status lights on the side of its visor. I kneeled too. *Hypothermia*, I thought. That looked to be the cause of death. The kneeling droid then communicated with the hover-vehicle VirDa; a medical transport emerged from the vehicle, supporting a black body bag. I heard someone gasp in the small group of onlookers as they realized what that meant.

"Gecondoleerd," I muttered in Hollandic in the direction of the distressed neighbors, before turning my back and walking away. I heard the distraught sounds of subdued sobs behind me. The sobs felt accusing as I moved down the brick-paved street.

Once on Eiserhowerlaan, I saw the familiar imposing Europol building. The five towers, interconnected by linking glass bridges, housed each of the major divisions, sub-divided into departments and units. The exterior glass corridors, which had garnered architectural awards, snaked around the structures. And beneath, there was a majestic entrance hall running along the base of the towers. From this angle, I could even identify my office window high up in Tower 3 on floor 33. It had a great view of the Scheveningen woods opposite.

Somehow, entering the marble-floored lobby of Europol always gave me a sense of purpose. I walked past the circular green-cushioned seating in the center. As I reached the employee auto-security console, I paused briefly for the language-streaming orb to clear my sec-code and DigID credentials.

I stepped out of the elevator at my floor. A bleary-eyed human detective walked by. Once inside my office, the motion-activated closet adjacent to the door opened. A long, thin shelf and hanging bar slid out. Once I'd hung up my coat and jacket, it auto-stowed, disappearing back inside the wall. Glass paneling on one side of my office gave me a partial vista across the large open-plan office suite of my management team—only human assets on this level. Several heads glanced up as they saw me arrive. They averted their eyes as they met mine staring straight back out at them through the glass.

I wanted to check out the Babel file before Pieter came to collect me for our interview with Karen Hoekstra. I sat at the chair behind my work console, with large windows behind me overlooking the woods opposite. I then activated my holotab before using my Europol portal to sync with my office VirDa. The mic aperture opened next to the inlaid fusion sensor bar in the center of the console. A stalked mic rose from inside.

"CC-33-001 VirDa, activate mirror display." As I issued my voice command, the holotab projecting from my wrist vanished. In its place, a large translucent screen was projected from the sensor bar in the center of the console, with my DigID credentials displayed in the bottom notification panel. I glanced around distractedly at the inert gray LED wall panels opposite me. I had a slight headache from lack of sleep. Or maybe too many late-night whiskies. "Set environment to Rest at Work mode." The smart walls directly opposite, around my door, and on the left transformed into a restful natural hessian shade. "Display the Ebba Black dossier visuo-map."

The index field of Europol's Ebba Black data pool appeared on the large holographic screen projecting from the console. It consisted of an array of nested stillgram and hologram blinkables. With a single blink command I could call up an entire data stream, and with further in-app voice commands, cross-reference what was being displayed with any other data stream.

The itch! I wanted to check out the *Babel Apocalypse Manifesto* that Ebba Black had published ten years ago. Links to various dossiers and documents appeared on the display, together with the few available images of Ebba Black. Not much. The woman was an unchipped nate; we couldn't monitor her movements. And zero social media presence, so there was little intel to draw upon.

But before I could activate the manifesto file, something caught my eye, blinking at me. There was a new hologram on file, just uploaded to the Europol server by our security algorithm. A reflowable image I hadn't seen before. I suddenly felt a flutter of butterflies in my stomach as I activated the blinkable. It was her!

I gazed at her face—the famous linguistics professor who remained a ghost. The same woman whom Europol had labeled a cyberterrorist. A graduation event for the hologram was listed, dated a few months before, recently uploaded to the public MyPlace channel of Gothenburg University.

I knew the lines of her face by heart. I had studied the few images we held of her many times. The woman was an enigma, and while I barely acknowledged it to myself, she fascinated me. In this new image, her hair was raven black, as usual. But this time, as the holographic camera app had caught her stylized pose, the iridescent blackness of her hair glinted deep obsidian green. Her hair appeared to shimmer on the screen in front of me as her holographic image moved. Her face was stern, striking, with an upturned, aristocratic nose. There was a haughty aloofness about the way she held herself. It was clear she had both poise and self-confidence. And I detected a hint of cruelty pulling at the corners of her faintly smiling lipsticked mouth. She was wearing a red sleeveless cocktail dress with a halter neck and holding a matching clutch in her right hand. I didn't know what I was hoping for as I stared at the hologram. Some kind of epiphany, maybe? Was she really capable of all this—the mayhem now being unleashed on the world?

Through the glass paneling to my right, I saw Lotte approaching. Her tall, shapely figure was unmistakable as she stood up from her console station; her long dress bounced as she moved. I watched as she acknowledged a seated colleague, his console facing me in the outer office. As he looked up at her, his eyes clocked me staring out of my office. He quickly lowered his gaze. Lotte stiffened ever so slightly before slowly turning her head, her eyes meeting mine across the room and through the glass of my office wall. She threw me a faint smile of acknowledgment.

As she opened the door to my office, I instinctively blinked to close the 3D photo and deactivate the Ebba Black dossier before she could see it. I could tell something was definitely up. Today she was no longer her usual insouciant, coy self. I could sense an awkward stiffness toward me and her palpable tension. Without the trademark psybient-style red rings around her eyes, she also looked different somehow—oddly pale. All freckles and thin nose. It changed her appearance in a way that suddenly took me aback. I realized I had never before seen her without her alternative, fashionable persona; the pale hazel of her eyes stood out. Even her hair was now strangely overrun with unbrushed disregard. More tousled than usual.

"CC-33-001 VirDa, hibernate," I said. The last thing I needed was my own tech spying on me should I accidentally trigger its security algorithm with one wrong word.

"Shutting down, Commander," it confirmed from a ceiling speaker above.

"Hello, beautiful," I said, smiling once the door was secure. Lotte watched me, a nervous smile flickering briefly across her face. But her eyes were sad.

I began to move toward her, around my console, which was now back in inert mode. Normally I could smell the delicate indolic aroma of her jasmine and rose fragrance. But today there was nothing. She involuntarily stepped back from my approach in slight alarm.

I stopped. "What is it?"

"You mean the thing about Europol's strict policy on workplace relationships?" she responded, frowning at me. I knew that wasn't it. That had never been a problem for her. This was something else. She was clearly on edge.

I looked her up and down. Lotte was tall, even for a Dutch woman. Her deep crimson suit jacket, black ribbon choker, and the lacy ruffles down the front of her dress, now slightly crumpled, gave her a retro steampunk look. And those high-laced boots with heels lent her an unconventional air.

"Something's up, isn't it?" I asked, quietly, disconcerted by Lotte's newly guarded behavior. I studied her face as she averted her gaze; she bit her lower lip before tentatively glancing back at me.

"Emyr, I did something dumb ..." Tears suddenly welled up in her eyes as she paused. Just then, there was a tap on the glass paneling. Pieter was looking in, pointing to his wrist.

"Damn," I muttered as I gave a half-tap on my wrist chip. My bioclock appeared in iridescent green beneath my skin. I realized I had to go: Pieter and I needed to align before Karen Hoekstra arrived. Lotte examined my face before sighing.

"Go. It can wait. It's nothing," she said quietly.

"Nothing?"

She paused before replying. "Of course," she whispered back, attempting a reassuring smile. I knew she was lying.

CHAPTER 8

The interview suite was large and windowless, at basement level. Pieter synced with the VirDa and began setting up the room. We still had a few minutes before Karen was due to arrive. I helped myself to a cupstock of coffee from the service unit in one corner. Meanwhile, Pieter issued voice commands.

"IS13 VirDa, activate mirror display. Chief Inspector Pieter de Bruijn, Commander Emyr Morgan present. Voluntary interview. Subject Karen Hoekstra, Professor of Cybernetics and Director of the Research Institute on Hacktivism, Cyberterrorism, and Public Policy at the University of Amsterdam."

I turned around, holding the hot coffee, watching him as he sat at the console. He was a big man but out of condition. His thin black tie was loosened, his top shirt button undone. Today he was also unshaven. I knew he'd pulled an all-nighter.

Once he was done, he looked at me, his eyebrows raised. There was something on his mind. "I always did wonder how you'd managed to get the world's leading academic authority on cyberterrorism as a confidential informant."

I smirked before replying. "I can't actually take the credit for that. She came to me out of the blue, five years ago." Pieter threw me a look of slight surprise. Of course, he didn't know the full story. He had only transferred in from the Belgian National Police Agency two years prior.

"She and Ebba Black have history, right? Was that the reason?"

I frowned. "It's not entirely clear. Karen was involved romantically with Elias Black, or at least that was my impression. And after his suicide, she blamed Ebba somehow."

"Found on a beach in the San Francisco Bay Area after blowing his brains out with a coil pistol," Pieter muttered. I glanced at him in mild surprise. "Elias, Ebba's brother. Last night I went back through some parts of the file, including the Californian autopsy report from five years ago." I gave Pieter a faint smile. He was conscientious. I respected that.

I shrugged. "When Karen reached out to me, Babel had changed tack. That's when the DDoS attacks started. She said Ebba was on a path she couldn't follow."

"The Brain Deep attack?" Pieter asked.

"You have been doing your homework," I said as I sniffed the cupstock. The coffee was cool enough to drink.

"Brain Deep Tech, incorporated in the Bay Area. It developed and licensed Deep Brain Stimulation implants, sold under medical license or commercially for those who subscribed to nicotine supply apps," Pieter announced.

"Yep. And also the unlucky recipient of Babel's first ever cyberattack after five years of relatively harmless ethical hacktivism. That was actually why Karen reached out. She said she wanted to do the right thing." I paused. Pieter's eyes narrowed. I could see he was curious. "Karen claimed Babel had intel showing Appleton was bankrolling Brain Deep, and that it was a front for the illegal trade in the Red Spice app. That the profits were being siphoned off to fund a secret Doomsday cult. The Brethren of the Sacred Vessels of the Grigori, she claimed."

Pieter shrugged. "Cool name. Never heard of it."

I grinned wryly. Pieter clearly hadn't been through the entire file. "Also known as the Dark Court, apparently, if you want an even cooler name. According to Karen, anyway. But we couldn't find any trace of it—either name. Passed on the intel to the relevant security agencies in California. Came back a dead end there, too."

"And you didn't manage to stop the attack ..."

With that, my grin evaporated. I sighed. "Babel beat us to the punch on that one. Put Brain Deep out of business. Permanently. But at least I got a former insider as an informant. Given Babel's command structure and autonomous, non-identifiable cells, using standard infiltration methods was a non-starter. I was happy with all the reliable intel I could get, to be honest."

I moved next to Pieter and sat down. It was nearly time. I saw he had the Ebba Black dossier open on the large holographic screen projecting from the console.

"She's a strange one," Pieter muttered as he blinked through the visuo-map index field. I glanced at him. "Did you know that Ebba Black is on the UNESCO Intangible Cultural Heritage listing? The only human with that distinction."

"The world's last natural speaker of multiple dead or proscribed languages," I replied. Pieter shook his head; in wonder, maybe.

"I didn't know," he muttered. I smiled wryly again.

"Ebba Black is quite the polyglot. She's a nate in the one Nordic state official, Riksmål. And some others. But what's interesting is that she also speaks a number of unsupported languages, including King's English, Old Swedish, and Meänkieli."

Pieter glanced at me, nonplussed. "Never heard of that last one." Then he laughed. *"History belongs in the past."* It was the well-known slogan of Unilanguage's Technical Committee. Unilanguage only stored proscribed languages for five years after removal from streaming platforms, then they were permanently deleted.

"Something like that," I replied. "Meänkieli was a minority Finnish language by all accounts. Once spoken in the Torne Valley of northern Sweden, before unification of the Scandinavian states. That's where Ebba's mother and family are from. At least originally."

"Ah ..." Pieter muttered. "That explains why the Johansson-Black biodegradable packaging conglomerate is headquartered up there."

"Even though the main factory is based in Stockholm. Where they make these," I said, pointing at my cupstock.

"And King's English, too ..." Pieter whispered, clearly impressed with Ebba Black's nateness in proscribed languages.

"Because of her father, of course. William Riggs, originally from Oxford, a respected professor of philology before his LangFree activism days. Ebba's parents were what you might call eccentric. Never got themselves or their kids chipped. And brought Ebba and her brother up off the grid, despite all the inherited Johansson-Black wealth."

Pieter blinked on an old stillgram of William Riggs and Alvinia Black. They were beaming, arms aloft in jubilation, surrounded by other LangFree activists and their lawyers on the steps of the California Supreme Court in Sacramento. The image was from an old news bulletin, dated 2105, reporting on their fatal hover car cash. But the stillgram of the smiling couple was from the day before their death. *Ironic, that, an image of joy from immediately after their famous legal victory*, I thought. They had been granted leave to appeal Californian lang-law on human rights grounds.

"You know what's funny?" I said. Pieter raised an eyebrow quizzically. "What if William Riggs and Alvinia Black had lived? Would the world's first lang-law have been repealed? Then maybe even here in the Union."

"And you and I would be nates too, right, boss?" Pieter said, now laughing.

"Well, let's just say Ebba Black wouldn't be on a UNESCO listing," I replied. *She certainly doesn't look like a monument*, I thought, having now seen a hologram of her in a red cocktail dress.

"Still, must have been tough for her ..." Pieter muttered, looking back at the stillgram blinkable. "Losing her parents like that. She's thirty-eight, so she would have been young— what ... eighteen?"

"Tough for her brother, too. He was only sixteen, hardly more than a kid really. And Karen. She was William Riggs's star PhD student," I replied.

Just then Pieter stiffened, involuntarily touching the back of his ear.

"She's here."

* * *

The door to the interrogation suite slid open, revealing Karen Hoekstra accompanied by a Welcome Unit. I stood and smiled at the slim woman standing on the threshold.

"Professor Hoekstra, thanks for coming in at short notice," I said. As she walked forward, she brought the smell of cold morning into the room. "Can we offer you something to drink?"

"Some water?" she muttered.

"Pieter," I prompted. He shifted suddenly before lumbering out of his seat. He returned, pushing the cupstock toward where she now sat, across the console from us. Its hard, plant-coated base made a slight scraping sound on the gray polymer surface. I observed Karen's micro-expression as she winced.

She was an attractive woman, well endowed, with long strawberry-blond hair and a lightly freckled face. She adjusted her glasses. *Glasses suit her*, I thought. Karen took a sip from her cupstock.

"We wanted to get a sense of whether you'd heard anything through the grapevine ... who might be behind the outage?"

Karen looked directly across at me before glancing at Pieter. "The chief inspector explained last night when we spoke. The organization always admits responsibility. And I understand in this case that hasn't happened."

"So does that mean it definitely isn't Babel?" I asked.

Karen coughed, adjusting herself in her seat. "I just need to remind you that Ebba doesn't recognize the term *Babel*. That's your name for what she does—for the organization."

"Sure, but we have to call it something. And now it seems apt, given she predicted exactly this—a global language catastrophe—in her *Babel Apocalypse Manifesto*, published ten years ago."

Karen's eyes widened slightly in surprise, maybe because I actually seemed to have read it. She watched me thoughtfully before replying.

"But Ebba wasn't actually making a prediction. Not about the future, anyway. The whole point of her manifesto was that an apocalypse had already taken place. The apocalypse was in the past. People rendered mute by big tech and lang-laws. The manifesto wasn't arguing for this … a global outage. It was arguing for a reset. She was more pragmatic back then …"

Pieter cleared his throat. He had pulled up the *Babel Apocalypse Manifesto* on the large translucent screen projecting from the console's fusion bar. Sitting on the other side of the console, Karen couldn't see it. She wore a look of confusion as he began reading.

"Today, language is a commodity, controlled by corporations, policed by Unilanguage, manipulated by big tech and even governments for their own ends."

"He's reading from the manifesto," I explained, smiling at her surprised face.

Now Karen smiled too. "Right. Ebba's point was that it's one thing to stream our entertainment—music, books, movies—to lease it and play it via our holotabs and VirDas. We pay writers, musicians, filmmakers for what they produce using their talent. But what about language? Language isn't a special talent. We are all born with the ability to acquire and produce it. Language isn't something that should be taken away, implanted in tech, and then leased back to us for monthly subs."

"So we regain control of language by de-commoditizing it, right?" I asked.

Karen took another sip of water before continuing. "Well, it's definitely a fact that lang-laws, together with the policies of Unilanguage, have led to the mass extinction of most of the world's languages. Today whether a language lives or dies turns on whether it represents a sound financial investment."

"And for Ebba, that's a bad thing?" I asked. Karen threw me a look of surprise. "I'm just playing devil's advocate."

Karen smirked. "Well, let's just say it wasn't sold like that

by big tech, by Appleton, with their pronouncements from
their plush campus HQ in the Republic in the late 2080s and
'90s. The glossy PR campaigns were packed with some great
slogans: *Imagine being able to speak any language you want, working
anywhere in the world, falling in love with anyone.*" Pieter giggled
as Karen mimicked the syrupy drawl of the infomercials in a
husky femme fatale voice.

"So you're saying that the reality and what was sold don't
add up?" I surmised.

"For Ebba, it *really* was all a lie, all of it! That's what she
thought when she wrote the manifesto. And I'm pretty sure
she believes it even more now," Karen said. I looked at her
blankly. She sighed. "Look, regional accents are now for the
rich. They were once for the regions, for the hard-working
locals, identifiers of place and class, of geographical origin.
Now they are status symbols. The locals have been priced out
of their own accents." She paused, her cheeks flushed slightly
red. I suddenly realized that she believed it all too, Ebba Black's
manifesto that went viral a decade ago.

"Okay. That's the history lesson ..." I began.

"But that's not why I'm here," Karen said, smiling wryly at
us both. "You want to know if Ebba has the capability for a
DDoS attack of this magnitude. And if so, would she do it?"

"And whether you've heard something—anything, you
know, through your contacts. Full disclosure: we've intercepted
some chatter about something called the 'Language Unplugged
protocol.' But we don't know what to make of it," I said.

At that, Karen glanced at me sharply before nodding slowly.
"Language Unplugged. Yes, I've heard of it. Two days ago."
Pieter and I glanced at each other. "I'd put out feelers in an
encrypted chatroom for intel on something for my research.

This black hat reached out using the handle Datashizzle. One of Ebba's. Datashizzle has been with her for at least three years. I'd heard of the handle, but this was my first successful contact."

"Go on," I whispered, barely daring to breathe.

"Datashizzle claimed the organization had developed a back-door hack to servers in low space orbit. From somewhere called Freetown. They're calling it the Language Unplugged protocol."

"What sort of hack?" I asked with nervous excitement.

"That was it. All I got. It was a cold drop. A mini info-dump. Then, well, radio silence. I tried to get Datashizzle back. But nothing."

"So that's really all you have?" I exclaimed in disappointment.

Karen nodded. "These guys are tech guerrillas. Unless they want to be found, you can't."

Pieter glanced at me knowingly. I knew what he was thinking. We'd succeeded where Karen had apparently failed.

"One more thing. Did this Datashizzle mention something called Operation False Flag?" I asked.

Karen shook her head. "Not to me."

Now Pieter interrupted. "What did you make of it, Professor?" Karen looked at him quizzically. "Language Unplugged. Any thoughts on what they might be up to with this?"

Karen shrugged. "I didn't think much at first. Typical Ebba name, all mystery, grace, and danger. But then the outage happened. And you got in touch. So now, if I were to hazard a guess, I'd say Freetown is where Ebba has a command base. And this Language Unplugged protocol, well, it sounds ominous."

"Ominous in the sense of a cyberattack to take out global language streaming capabilities?" I asked.

Karen frowned. "The Ebba of ten years ago, of the Babel Apocalypse, would never have done anything like this. But she's changed. That's why I had to move on. Ebba became obsessed with Appleton, with Marc Barron. She has always been intense. Never really an idealist—that was Elias. She did her own thing. Didn't really get involved before she published her manifesto. And then, five years later, with Brain Deep Tech, there was this new, sudden violent vibe to her activism." Karen glanced at me. Her eyes appeared to be imploring me to understand something, though I was unsure what.

"Do you know why she became obsessed with Appleton?" I pressed.

Karen straightened her back. She picked up the cupstock and took a long sip, averting her gaze. When she spoke again, there was a stickiness to her words. Tension; dry mouth, maybe. She looked suddenly upset, trying to retain her composure.

"Elias. I think his death broke something in both of us. He should never have done it ..." Karen's words petered off.

"Killed himself? We never really know—" I began, but Karen shook her head.

"I don't mean that. I mean, after everything he stood for—his parents, me, even Ebba. He goes and gets chipped, just like that, at the age of thirty-one, when he was a nate—the last one apart from Ebba. And then, worse, he goes off to work for Appleton at their campus in northern California. It was a real jaw-dropper. Turning his back on everything he'd believed in. We argued. He refused to explain. Said he couldn't. I knew Ebba was in on it. She wouldn't talk either. He made me a promise: he would tell me everything when he came back. But ..." Karen shook her head ever so slightly, a tear in her eye. *He never came back,* I thought.

"People can be unpredictable," Pieter suggested quietly, trying to offer some sympathy.

"That was it for me, after that. And Ebba started with the Brain Deep attack."

"So this outage could be caused by whatever the Language Unplugged protocol is?" I asked.

"It could be, except …"

"Except what?" I probed.

"Why wasn't Appleton targeted? Ebba hates Appleton. You've never seen anything like it, hate like that."

"Their security protocols are—" Pieter began. I knew what he was going to say. I held my hand up to silence him. Karen wasn't done talking. I wanted to know what she still had to say.

Karen shook her head again. "From what I hear, Appleton really wasn't targeted. Their security defense systems were never even tripped."

CHAPTER 9

As I waited for Pieter to complete the security logout from the interrogation suite VirDa, I received a vibration alert in my ear implant. I activated my holotab. It was a memoclip from Lotte with a status update. *Good! Just in time for my briefing with the director.*

Pieter glanced at me expectantly. "It's Lotte. She's discovered something important about the origination point of the cyberattacks. She'll join us as soon as we're back up."

"Sounds good, boss."

Back in my office, I stared out the window at Scheveningse Bosjes, the wooded park below. Pieter was issuing voice commands into the service unit in one corner behind me while we waited for Lotte; I needed more caffeine. I finally turned and sat down on the sofa adjacent to the glass paneling. Pieter sat in a chair opposite and handed me a cupstock of coffee. I could see Lotte approaching through the glass. I couldn't help but wonder where she would choose to sit.

Pieter watched me intently. I knew what he was thinking.

"We need to interview the hacker, Datashizzle. I want to bring him in for questioning," I muttered.

"From the Old Kingdom? Do you think the director will go for it? The Union doesn't have jurisdiction."

I turned to Pieter thoughtfully. "The Old Kingdom's now under martial law, propped up by Union Warrior-class droid battalions. Their National Crime Agency isn't functioning. We're way past following protocol."

"The director might go for that."

"And I think it's high time we also interviewed Ebba Black."

Pieter frowned. "She's a Nordic national. Not part of the Union. A bit trickier."

Just then, Lotte entered. Pieter nodded at her. She glanced at me nervously as she sat in a chair next to Pieter, away from me. I would have to confront whatever it was she needed to get off her chest. As soon as I was done with my meeting with Lina and the director.

Lotte began speaking. "We've managed to unmask the originating IP address of the DDoS attacks—"

But Pieter interrupted her mid-sentence, activating his holotab. "Sorry, just gotten a high-priority alert."

"What is it?" I asked, as I watched him parsing something on the screen projecting from his wrist chip.

"CyberForce is certain it's the Russian Federation. A memoclip just in from Marchaud. The High Representative has apparently asked von Böhm to provide military options. A full briefing is scheduled for tomorrow in the Imperium."

I groaned. *The bumbling Marchaud again. That's his level. Sending memoclips to rile us up.*

"Marchaud couldn't command his way out of a paper bag, let alone a cyberattack," I muttered in irritation. Pieter looked at me in slight surprise. I knew I needed to keep my thoughts to myself. *But dammit, Marchaud sure knows how to play politics, I'll give him that. And the last thing the world needs is war on top of a global language outage.* That last thought made me angry. "Typical, jumping the gun like that. Last time I checked, this is still a civil inquiry and not a military matter. Until we are told otherwise, we have the lead," I said more forcefully than I had meant to.

Pieter was staring at me, eyes wide. "The Russian Federation doesn't have the AI capabilities for cyberattacks on this scale." I nodded. Even Pieter, unimaginative as he was, knew that the Russians, for all their dirty tricks, were unlikely to be behind something this big. "And in any case, General von Böhm's probably not the most clear-eyed when it comes to the Federation," he added, shaking his head.

"What makes you say that? You mean—" Before I could finish, Pieter completed the sentence for me.

"The home heating intelligence scandal. My old commander in the National Agency said it was nigh on criminal the way CyberForce missed that one. All the intelligence they had, all the signs. And *boom*, Union-wide cyberattacks on home thermostatic heating systems during that winter."

"That was a bad one. I remember thousands died. Worst cold snap for a decade."

Pieter's eyes narrowed. "The public inquiry cost Marchaud's predecessor his command. A convenient scapegoat, saving von Böhm his own position. I mean, Russian state-sponsored actors behind the whole thing after all." *But on the bright side, for Marchaud at least, it gave him his lucky break,* I thought to myself sarcastically. After all, there was nothing bright about Jacques Marchaud. *Promoted to Head of Military Cyberintelligence, to his level of incompetence.*

"The scandal was a major embarrassment for CyberForce all right," Lotte added. "But it's more than just that. For von Böhm it's personal. His wife gunned down in broad daylight on the banks of the Moskva River—and in front of their children. Imagine his guilt, living with that. Knowing he was the intended target."

"I remember reading about it," Pieter said. "Talk about justice not served. The show trial of the young punk the Moscow City police beat a confession from. Something like that could only have been sanctioned at the very highest level of the Russian state apparatus."

"So maybe now von Böhm sees an opportunity—" I began, but caught myself before saying more than I should.

Lotte coughed, breaking the awkwardness. "Anyway, we've figured out why CyberForce is so certain the Russian Federation is behind the outage."

I raised an eyebrow. "And why's that?"

"As I was saying, my team has been triangulating IP data. All the DDoS attacks used VPN tunneling protocols to mask the originating IP address."

"And ...?"

"Multiple secure entry and exit points were used to bounce the attack signals across different territories, including IP addresses in low Earth orbit. But the origin point appears to be an IP address in ..." Lotte studied us, waiting for our reaction as she prepared to drop her bombshell, "... Siberia."

"Of course. The Russian Federation!" Pieter exclaimed.

"Are you sure, Lotte?" I asked.

"The data is solid. We've checked and re-checked. We're certain."

I was glad I had this intel before I went up to see the director.

"There's something odd, though," Lotte added.

"What?" I snapped. *This still doesn't make sense*, I thought.

"The degree coordinates show that the IP address is located at Lake Baikal."

"A lake?" Pieter asked.

Lotte pursed her lips in response. "It's a massive rift lake in southern Siberia, just north of the Mongolian border."

"But what's odd?" I pressed.

"Well ... the IP address is located right in the middle of the lake."

"Hmmm," Pieter muttered. "Perhaps the attack originated from a boat." There was silence for a moment.

"Just because the cyberattacks may have originated from Russian territory, doesn't mean that Russia is behind it," I announced finally. Lotte and Pieter stared at me. "Look, the Russians don't want a war with the Union or any other Tier One state. Their economy is fragile."

"And their cybersecurity systems would be knocked over in a day. The Union's drone army could take Moscow within a week," Pieter added.

"Exactly. Bulchovi might be a despot, but he's not dumb," I asserted. "What about Operation False Flag? The chatter between the two Babelists you intercepted, Pieter?"

Lotte began smiling. "You think the IP address in Siberia is deception? That's Operation False Flag?"

"I think that whoever is behind this wants CyberForce to think it's the Russians. That's why BeeDirect wasn't targeted."

"So who *is* behind it? Your lady suspect number one?" Lotte whispered, gazing at me slightly accusingly. Pieter smirked as she spoke, before glancing away as I threw them both dirty looks.

"I don't know. Yet. But we need to know what this Language Unplugged protocol is. And Karen Hoekstra has just told us that Babel has a base somewhere: Freetown. We need to locate it."

"One more thing, Emyr," Lotte said. "You asked me to check

out the LS subscription package of Dhruv Gasper ... the CEO of the Californian drone manufacturer."

"Who?" asked Pieter, pricking up his ears.

"The guy involved in a hover car collision yesterday evening in London," I replied.

"It turns out that he *was* an Appleton subscriber," Lotte stated. "Which is weird."

"So he could have prevented the crash by using voice commands," I said.

"Which means that perhaps his issue wasn't the language outage?" Lotte suggested.

"Exactly. We need an autopsy—cause of death. And to get access to Mr. Gasper's virtual locker and the vehicle."

"We'll have to trace next of kin—permission for the autopsy," Pieter murmured. "And we'll need probable cause to get a warrant to impound the vehicle." I raised an eyebrow at Pieter until his words trailed off. "I'll deal with it, then."

"Good! I want the autopsy done today," I said. "And a full background check. I want to know everything about this Mr. Gasper."

* * *

I arrived at the Directorate on the executive command level of Europol Tower 1. Lina was already in with the director. I seldom had cause to visit the executive level; I was spared by Lina in her capacity as his deputy.

As I sat waiting, something Karen Hoekstra had said stayed with me. She'd reminded me of the PR campaign, the slick advertising selling the idea of UG tech and voice command technology in the early days. It took me back to my squalid room as a kid in our damp house in the Swansea Valley, watching the MyPlace news broadcasts. The distant wonder of the Californian lang-law referendum. The excitement, the buzz. UG tech was sold as a form of leveling up. Removing barriers to aspiration. The vote passed with a massive majority. The lower soc-ed classes were most in favor. Once the legislation cleared the Capitol in Sacramento, all adults were legally bound to be chipped. It was dubbed the Great Experiment by some: a six-month window in which an entire population voluntarily gave up language and had neuroprosthetic technology implanted. And at midnight on January 1, 2092, at a stroke, voice command technology became the only available means of adult communication with public VirDas anywhere in the Republic.

And then the miracle. California became a new utopia. Everyone could be identified, anywhere, anytime. All forms of crime dropped by over fifty percent across all categories by the end of the year. And making voice command technology the legally required system of public security systems simplified and even improved the lives of ordinary people. The LangFree movement began, led by William Riggs and Alvinia Black, claiming a massive erosion of civil liberties. But from the perspective of nearly everyone else, there were no downsides to language streaming. Everyone won.

Other nations looked on absorbed, watching the experiment, as skepticism quickly turned to increasing awe and eventual envy. Lawmakers and the public in other Tier One and Tier Two states soon clamored for their own lang-law referenda. But as a kid, in Cymru, it was unimaginable then that this strange, distant, foreign tech ideal would touch me. That it would become the norm. Back then, no one thought of the dangers—a language outage. People losing LS signals, going feral. People's language chips becoming permanently damaged, going out-soc.

A vibration in my ear implant took me out of my reverie. I was being summoned. I cleared my throat and stood. *Here we go.*

CHAPTER 10

The director's suite was a large room with off-white LED smart walls and eggshell marble flooring. A long table with high backed chairs dominated one half of the room. Lina glanced at me as I entered. She was seated on the opposite side of the table. She gave the slightest of nods. Her skin appeared even paler than usual. The smart wall behind her featured the Europol insignia, the hologram flickering briefly and transforming into the Union flag.

The director was standing at the far end of the room with his back to us, beyond a small meeting space with lounge chairs around a metallic coffee table. He was staring out of the tall window facing the distant sea.

"Rodrigo?" Lina said quietly, drawing the director's attention to my presence. I knew from Lina that she and Rodrigo de Eusebio Dominguez went back a long way. He'd handpicked her as his deputy when he'd taken the top job at Europol. She made the revelation to me over drinks and canapés at her chic Belgisch Park apartment, during the most recent annual social she'd hosted for her management team at the start of the winter holidays. The director trusted Lina's judgment, sometimes more than his own. I'd seen it with my own eyes. There was something about her. It was hard to explain, but she gave off a good vibe.

The director turned to face us.

"Commander." He smiled at me faintly, gesturing to a seat opposite Lina. He had a round, boyish face that always appeared to glisten with a hint of perspiration. Today he was wearing a blue Garbo shirt from Barcelona. The man-about-town brand, functional and affordable. *Not something I'd be seen dead in*, I thought. *And he isn't wearing it well. Unbuttoned at the top, loosely tucked in; the shirt looks at least one size too small. He hasn't updated his wardrobe for a while.*

"Director," I replied in acknowledgment as I sat.

"We have an unprecedented situation," he said, sighing distractedly as if about to carry on. But his initial pause lapsed into sustained silence. He moved forward and sat to the left of Lina, directly opposite me, watching me thoughtfully. I could sense the tension, the pressure he was under. He was almost reeking of it.

Lina adjusted her small body slightly, placing her wrinkled hands on the table as she began speaking. "We're facing a high-impact, low-probability event, for which we are completely unprepared. Most major cities are either already in or about to go into lockdown. Children separated from parents, people locked out of homes, mass looting by packs of ferals."

"Crisis management ..." the director muttered, frowning before looking across at me sharply. "But that's not your assignment." He drummed his fingers on the table.

That was my cue. "We now know the origination point of the cyberattack. Russian Federation territory—Siberia, to be precise," I said.

The director nodded. "I just got off a facecall with von Böhm. He seems pretty convinced the Russians did it. What do you think, Commander?"

I shifted in my seat and stretched out my long legs under the table. "I think that's a bit too fast. We've intercepted chatter between Babelists mentioning a false flag operation." The director looked at me quizzically. "It's possible that someone wants us to think it's the Federation."

"So you suspect the Russians are being set up?" Lina asked sternly. "By who? Babel?"

"It's one explanation. Babel has developed something called a Language Unplugged protocol. And they have a secret base called Freetown. We're not yet sure what Language Unplugged is, but our intel suggests it has something to do with hacking language streaming servers."

"And this place, Freetown. What do you have on that?" the director asked.

"We only just learned of it an hour ago from an informant. We don't yet have a fix on the location, nor a clear understanding of its purpose."

The director scowled. "How is it that your command can know so little about this cyberterrorism outfit? About this Ebba Black?" Irritation rippled through his voice as he leaned forward. Lina touched his arm lightly. His posture shifted and he eased himself back into his chair.

Lina leaned across the table toward me. "What the director means is that we need confirmation of your hypothesis. As the powers-that-be, military command in the Proelium and the Ministry for War in the Imperium are both increasingly convinced it's the Russians. We only have a small window to come up with evidence."

"Before the High Representative asks the joint presidents in the Magisterium to sanction military strikes," the director added with a growl.

Lina paused before fixing me with her hooded gaze. "So how do we go about getting confirmation of your hunch, Emyr?" *Same old Lina,* I thought. *Always cutting through the thickets of emotion that bogged down clear decision-making.*

I smiled faintly. "I have two requests. We've identified a Babel operative currently residing in the Old Kingdom. He's an Alba national, so a Union citizen. We believe he has knowledge of the Language Unplugged protocol. I'd like to bring him in for questioning."

"The Old Kingdom. What do you think, Rodrigo?" Lina asked as she glanced sideways.

The director made a slight whistling sound as he sucked his teeth pensively. "It had to be the Old Kingdom, right?" he asked, glaring at me. "Beyond our jurisdiction. An extradition request will take months with the mess they're in …" he muttered.

Lina glanced at him and craned her head slightly. "The Old Kingdom's under martial law. And with the state of emergency here, we probably need to expedite this one if Emyr's right. Surely there's a workaround?"

"What do you have in mind?" the director asked her.

"A rendition. It would certainly avoid any … complications." Lina glanced at me, throwing me a furtive nod.

"That would definitely speed things up," I added, addressing the director.

The director glanced at us both. "I'll need to talk to von Böhm again. He has a special forces unit embedded with CyberForce, human assets, CounterRevolutionary Warfare capability. I'll have to ask for a favor." The director paused before continuing. "But he'll want something in return. I know him."

Lina nodded. "Oversight," she muttered. The director sighed.

"But this remains a civil inquiry, right? I need to have the lead."

The director squinted at me thoughtfully. "Okay, so this is how we'll play it. We'll ask for an immediate rendition. Questioning can take place in the Proelium, which also gives you access to a NocioPerception rack. You might need to use duress. Time is of the essence, Commander." I didn't like the sound of any of that. And compromising on where we'd interview McDenizen, not bringing him to Europol HQ … it was starting to get messy.

"Will that be enough, Rodrigo?" Lina asked. "Suggesting the Proelium for questioning? If von Böhm thinks we're running a different line of inquiry from the Russian angle, well, he might not be willing to cooperate. He's a wily old fox." I watched her in admiration. She was always good at anticipating the politics.

The director nodded. "You're right." He turned to me. "How would you feel about having your opposite number at CyberForce participate in the interrogation? What's the guy called again?"

I groaned inwardly. "Lieutenant Colonel Jacques Marchaud." Lina smiled as she saw my expression. She knew.

"Don't know him," the director muttered.

"The one with the dress uniform and very thin mustache. Presented at the interagency cyberconference in September. Talked about cryptography and cyberintelligence. Remember?"

"Oh yes, the one who kept his kepi on all the time." The director smirked as he seemed to remember. "Put in a formal request for rendition when you can, Commander. I'll need today's date stamp. But I'll speak to von Böhm as soon as we're done. Can you give me the target's details, DigID credentials, location … now?"

With that, I activated my holotab. Using blink commands, I quickly sent Erebus McDenizen's details to the director's Europol portal. He nodded as soon as he'd gotten a data receipt alert in his ear implant.

"You said you had a second request," Lina said, watching me intently.

"I'd like to interview Ebba Black."

There was a moment of stunned silence before it was broken by the director.

"It's one thing arranging an extraction from a failing Tier Two state under martial law and Union administration. But the Nordic Republic, Tier One, an old ally—that's an altogether different matter. And as you know, they have a strict non-extradition policy for their citizens."

I shook my head. "Just an interview. Nothing more. In the Nordic Republic. I'd travel there."

"Oh, I see. What do you think, Lina?" the director asked, glancing at her.

Lina adjusted her glasses. "It's all a bit sensitive at the moment. The Nordic authorities are quite twitchy about Professor Black. We've just heard that the United Federation's Justice Department has unsealed an arrest warrant for her. Charges were authorized by a Federal Grand Jury a while back, it seems. Long-standing pressure from Appleton's lawyers. I guess they haven't appreciated her special attention. The UFA's attorney general had to be seen to be doing something. Anyway, timing isn't good, especially with the outage, should the Republic start thinking we suspect one of its leading citizens."

"You're saying that the Republic won't agree to let us interview Ebba Black?"

"I'm saying that the Nordic authorities are in full stonewalling mode. The professor is their wealthiest private citizen. But if Professor Black were to personally agree to such a request, then that would be a different matter." Lina was still staring at me. "What's your feeling, Emyr? Would she agree to meet you?"

"It's definitely worth a try."

"Then I can have my assistant put out feelers," Lina said.

The director looked at me. "Commander, wait outside. I'll talk to von Böhm. The deputy director will let you know what we manage," he said, glancing at Lina.

"Very good, sir." I stood and took my leave.

* * *

Back outside, I processed the rendition request using the in-app voice commands in my Europol portal on my holotab. Once I was done, I waited to see what the director and von Böhm managed to figure out.

I didn't have to wait long. I became aware of Lina's birdlike presence in front of me. She fixed me with a gimlet eye. I stood up smartly, now towering over her.

She adjusted her gaze and smiled ruefully at the discrepancy in our heights. "You'll be pleased to know it's been agreed. A CyberForce Alpha team has already been dispatched. You're to report to Proelium military command in Brussels at one p.m. today. Use of a NocioPerception rack has been authorized. You retain full authority as civil law enforcement lead, but Colonel Marchaud will be present." I nodded. "As will the Alpha team commander in charge of the rendition, who will be assisting. At von Böhm's insistence." I groaned inwardly at the prospect of further interference.

"And who's the special forces commander?" I asked.

Lina studied my face. "You won't like it."

This time I groaned out loud. "Don't tell me it's Aapo Törni?"

For the first time today, Lina produced a broad smile. "I said you wouldn't like it. Attempts are also being made to arrange an interview with Ebba Black later today," she disclosed. "I'll let you know more later, if we can reach agreement with the authorities north of the border—and, of course, with Professor Black herself. You'll also be accompanied by someone from CyberForce. Between you and me, von Böhm is very suspicious of our line of inquiry."

I nodded absently. I was still absorbing the news that I would need to work with Törni. Lina paused for a moment while she studied my face.

"You'll remain professional, as always. Right?"

I glanced down at her, feigning surprise. "What are you insinuating, Lina?"

Lina raised her eyebrows before allowing herself a wry smile. "I know you and Captain Törni have some history. But we do need to get this all figured out. Before CyberForce does something rash." I sometimes suspected Lina thought of herself as my surrogate mother. But she *was* right about one thing: I didn't like it one bit that he would be there, in my face again. Törni was a real bastard.

"I'll be professional. But will he?" I shot back darkly.

CHAPTER 11

When I returned from the director's suite, Lotte was hovering near my office. She glanced at me sheepishly.

"How did it go?" she asked before I could say anything.

"I have to be at the Proelium in less than two hours. CyberForce is bringing in our hacker for interrogation," I replied as I activated my door.

"Why not here? Why there, in Brussels?" Lotte asked, following me inside and sitting on the sofa by the glass panel.

"That was the deal with von Böhm. So that he can keep an eye on what we're up to. And you'll never guess who will be assisting me."

"Marchaud?"

"And Aapo Törni," I whispered. Lotte's eyes widened.

"Oh no, not him. After what he did at the Games in Cantina. What will you do?"

"I'll try not to punch his lights out," I whispered venomously.

Lotte smiled. "You need to do better than *try*. Probably another brawl is not what either CyberForce or Europol would like to see—ideally. Especially not between their leading shooting champions."

"Ideally?" I smirked, raising an eyebrow. "You're right ... I do have a few minutes, by the way. If you want to ... "

"I was hoping we could, you know ... talk," Lotte mumbled. But all of a sudden, she was no longer managing to hold it together. Her eyes welled up. I frowned. *This isn't good.* As I studied her, the tears, I realized how ironic it was that just as I sensed the end was coming, I started to think about the beginning.

Our affair had been initiated by Lotte soon after she had transferred to the Cybercrime division. She would linger after management meetings. She eyed me coyly, catching my gaze, gently brushing her hair away from her eyes when she spoke to me. And all the time, she drove me crazy with her perfume and the psybient-style red-ringed make-up around her eyes.

It began one weekday afternoon. We were alone in my office, conducting secure analysis in the isolation room. Lotte kept brushing against me as we sat alongside each other in front of the work console. Finally, she blurted it out. She couldn't stop thinking about me! I grabbed her impulsively and kissed her hard. Really hard. I came to know that was the way she liked it.

I was usually disciplined with coworkers. I had to be. My thoughts were my own, but I tried not to look. And never touch. But her fragrance had so infected me I could no longer resist her. At least, that's what I told myself. She told me she loved her husband and said she wanted us to be discreet. We had to be. I was in breach of my employment contract by fraternizing with a coworker for whom I had line management responsibility. It was a summary dismissal offense.

But it turned out that Lotte was exactly my type. Married! I worked with her, I had sex with her, but I didn't have to live with her—I went home to my own space and my own bed. That was the perfect level of commitment for me. After all, I was married to the job, as Lotte liked to tell me.

"Shall we?" I asked as I moved to the far wall of my office and the sliding-panel access to the isolation room that lay beyond. "VirDa, unlock isolation room." Lotte stood, following me. "One of the perks of being a division commander," Lotte muttered. I glanced back at her, confused. "You get an actual isolation room all to yourself. The rest of us mere mortals have to share a poky isolation booth just like the ones at home," she added jokingly, as she always did, making light of a tense situation.

I smiled. "You're no mere mortal," I whispered as I led her into the isolation room behind the LED paneling.

The access panel slid shut behind us and the low-level lighting booted up. Inside the conductive polymer-lined interior, our communication was now perfectly secure. We could no longer be observed, surveilled, traced, or identified. The only downside was that Wi-Fi reception of language streaming signals was no longer possible. A hard-wired connection was required.

Usually, Lotte and I didn't need to plug our ear implants into the VirDa console. We used my isolation room for an altogether different purpose. I knew others would have judged me if they'd known; I judged myself sometimes, being quite the cliché. *The boss having an affair with an employee—a much younger employee— with trysts hidden from prying eyes and sec-cams,* I thought.

I slotted the long, thin translucent cable into the small jack behind my ear, and Lotte followed suit. I turned, waiting for her to begin. She looked crestfallen.

"I did something a little bit stupid," she began, continuing from where she'd started earlier that morning, before swallowing. "You know I keep a video journal ..."

I shook my head. "I didn't, actually."

"Yeah, I do. I record a few times a week in our isolation booth at home. I like it to be private, even from Jaap."

"What sort of things?" I asked, genuinely intrigued. I'd never kept a journal; I saw such things as overly self-indulgent. I didn't go in for feelings that much. Or at all.

Lotte shrugged. "Oh, different kinds of stuff. How I feel about things, situations, dilemmas, people ..." She paused. "And about you."

I raised my eyebrows. "Really?" I was flabbergasted. I hadn't considered Lotte might dwell on me—on us—out of hours, so to speak.

"Yeah ..." She paused. "It helps me process things, as I have no one else I can confide in. I can't talk to the occupational psychologist about us at work, as they'd immediately report us to Lina de Bolle. And if I spoke to a private shrink, I'd be breaching the Official Secrets Act. I confide a lot in my journal."

"Oh," I said, suddenly unsure in which direction this was going.

She nodded. "The thing is, Emyr ..." Lotte gulped. "The thing is ..." She turned to face me. "I realized I love you." Now it was my turn to gulp. I could feel the blood drain from my face. She let out a sharp laugh. "Don't look so scared, tough guy."

"So what was stupid?" I asked, keen to change the subject.

Lotte sighed. "Probably a bit more than stupid. I didn't secure my video journal log in my virtual locker. I got distracted by an alarm in the kitchen and popped out. It was odd, though. When I got there, the alarm stopped."

"So?" I prodded.

"For a couple of minutes, the video log was open and live on the VirDa console." She watched me, letting the implications of her words sink in.

"And Jaap saw it?" I asked as I realized what Lotte had meant by something stupid.

She glanced away before looking back at me, giving a small affirmative nod. "He was loitering. He'd become suspicious—he kept telling me he sensed I was distracted. I guess we hadn't been intimate for a while. It's the little things." She sighed again. "He seemed to know I'd leave the isolation booth. Somehow. He waited until I'd stepped out, then he went in while I was in the kitchen. When we first got together, he found it endearing that I still kept a journal ... I record in Hollandic, because that's my default at home. Jaap only has a standard, single language package. So, of course, he understood exactly what I was confiding in my journal." Lotte eyed me carefully.

"Go on," I pressed gently.

"There's one thing I don't understand, though. The journal normally locks after a few seconds of inactivity. I still don't get it."

"Get what?"

"It should've auto-locked. He should never have seen it—anything. It was almost as if Jaap knew he would find my journal open, unlocked, at that particular moment."

"What did he see?"

"He had full access to my entry. He played back the last few seconds. It was enough."

"Enough? What did you say, Lotte, in the video?" I pressed, becoming anxious. Lotte instinctively placed her hands over her face for an instant.

"I was thinking aloud about you, about us. I said that you made me feel like no one ever has. I think I may have said that I was falling in love with you."

"That's not good," I said, grasping the scale of the calamity unfolding. Lotte suddenly threw me a dark look.

"That I think that?" she asked, with a hint of bitterness.

I shook my head. "I meant that you recorded yourself saying it. That Jaap watched you say it. How did he react?"

"How do you think?" Lotte asked. I looked at her in pained silence before she continued. "At first, he was angry, madder than I've ever seen him. And he wanted to know details—when, where, how often. I told him about our meetings at Café de Renbaan—you know, our secret lunches there—and about ..."

"About in here?" I asked, mortified.

Lotte gulped as she glanced at me. "He wanted to know why—why I had betrayed him. He always felt insecure around you."

"Insecure around me?" I asked, confused. Lotte suddenly burst into laughter.

"Look at you. Tall, handsome, athletic, super smart. A real man's man. Most men feel like that around you. Haven't you noticed here in the office ...?" Her words petered out. "And then he became hurt, sad, and ..." tears began rolling down her cheeks, "... suicidal."

"Oh!" I replied limply. Lotte brushed away her tears.

"Yeah. We were up most of the night, talking. Me trying to reassure him. He's a good man. He may not be you, but I married him, I made a commitment to him. And I do still love him. I know it's crazy, being in love with two men, but—"

"And what did you decide? The two of you ..."

"Oh, Emyr, always getting straight to the point." She smiled faintly. Her face was now streaked from her tears, which somehow only added to her quirky charm. "I offered Jaap a divorce, but he refused. He said I have to give you up. I told him I didn't know if I could do that, but then ..."

"Then what?" I asked impatiently.

"You have to understand, Emyr, he's not a bad person."

"Then what?" I insisted.

"He told me that unless I give you up, he would expose the affair." Lotte stopped and watched me expectantly. I blinked.

"And destroy my career," I said in a matter-of-fact manner.

"You have to appreciate he was hurt, upset ..."

"But he would do it," I said. She remained silent. "Answer me. Wouldn't he?"

"I believed him," Lotte replied finally. She pursed her lips, thinking for a moment, before speaking again. "You remember I told you this wouldn't be forever." I didn't need to reply. I remembered. "That's because I knew you would never love me. You are married to the job, as I keep telling you. But I have a husband and he is in a dark place."

"I understand."

She shook her head. "I'm not sure you do. But it doesn't matter. If I don't give you up ... I don't want you to be harmed. Jaap has agreed we will erase the video journal. There will be no record. You'll be safe."

"So you're ending this ... us ... because your husband is, what, blackmailing you?"

Lotte shook her head again. "No, Emyr ... I'm giving you up because I love you. And this is the right thing for you. I choose to protect you."

"But what kind of person would I be if I allowed you to stay in an unhappy marriage only to protect me?"

"It's fine. I'm not unhappy. I love Jaap in my own way. And he *is* a good man. I'm happy enough."

"Okay then, I guess."

"There's one more thing," Lotte revealed. "I have to request a transfer away from here, from The Hague, from HQ."

"What!" I exclaimed. "We need you. I need you here."

"That's the deal. Don't you see? I can't continue working with you ... I don't trust myself. And in any case, Jaap wouldn't agree. I promised him."

I fixed her with a piercing gaze. "That's fine, but you do need to stay for the time being, until we've figured out who's behind the language outage. Then I will support your transfer."

"Okay, I'll talk to Jaap. Hopefully he'll be fine with a delay. And of course, I'll do everything I can to support you and the team while we all get through this ..." Her words trailed off.

I smiled. She leaned toward me and gave me a long hug, the hug of an old friend. We had moved, apparently seamlessly, into the state of being ex-lovers.

"Thank you, Emyr. For everything. You have meant the world to me." I half turned away to avoid fully confronting the end of things. Lotte stood up and unplugged the jack from her ear implant. She straightened her dress. She gave me a faint nod and smiled weakly. I could tell she was attempting to remain brave.

As I watched her leave I felt, strangely, relief that it was over. On my own again. The way I liked it.

CHAPTER 12

Approaching Brussels city airspace in my Skyraider, I saw the gaudy government buildings in the distance, peppering the skyline of the Union's capital city. The Proelium building, home to the Union's military command, was a flamboyant Cyber Age eyesore. Some genius in the city's planning department had labeled it an architectural masterpiece. It now had listed monument status. *Go figure*, I thought.

After descending the VTOL corridor, my Skyraider taxied down the ramp to the designated Proelium visitor zone beneath Schuman Square, in the heart of the European quarter. I knew something was up when I saw the rotund figure of Marchaud himself, rather than a Welcome Unit, awaiting me at the greeting point adjacent to the disembarkation zone.

"Jacques?" I asked in surprise.

"Emyr. Welcome back to the Proelium," Marchaud said, his hooked nose wrinkling. As he smiled, his pencil-thin mustache implant curled under his upper lip, almost disappearing as the whites of his teeth showed. The black mustache seemed strikingly out of place against his natural gray. "So, we're really going to do this?" I looked at him in temporary confusion. "It's my first time," he divulged, whispering confidentially before releasing his high-pitched laugh, which was always somehow unsettling. "An interrogation using the NocioPerception rack!" He gestured for me to follow as he began leading me toward the elevator stack. He glanced up at me. "Your team gave us good intel. But I was a bit surprised ..." he paused, "... that you were able to pinpoint his location so quickly. Datashizzle."

Marchaud had the disconcerting habit of squinting as he spoke. As expected, he was attired in his CyberForce dress uniform—a light-beige jacket with red sashes and fringed epaulettes, and blue dress trousers with red lampasses down the sides. And, as always, he was wearing his kepi. No matter the occasion or location, Marchaud always had it on his head.

"I have a good team," I said, sounding slightly more defensive than I had intended.

Marchaud waved his hands absently. "I agree. Your team." He wrinkled his nose again. "But this one is cunning, this Datashizzle. He's one of Babel's top anons."

Inside the elevator, irritating music started up. Or maybe it was just me. *Easily irritated!*

"You know that Captain Törni is joining us," Marchaud began, turning to me with a conspiratorial air. "I heard something, you know, rumors ..." He made a swirling, dismissive gesture with one hand, as if he didn't bother much with tittle-tattle. I smirked to myself. "That he attacked you at the last World Military Games. In Cantina." I laughed, mainly for my own benefit. *So that's it. He's fishing for gossip. That's why he came in person to do the meet and greet.* "Your rivalry in the sharp-shooting categories, of course, that's well known. And your gold medal in the combined triple crown event at the last games, that was well deserved," he added, making a lavishly expansive gesture with both hands and arms.

I glanced at the guy. Marchaud thought he was working me, playing me. But I knew what he was—a flatterer-in-chief. And a mine of idle gossip, which no doubt appealed to the vanity of some of the Proelium senior military staff. Yet despite his bumbling manner and reputation for incompetence, Marchaud hid his dangerous side in plain sight. He used gossip for his own ends. Which was how he'd managed to obtain a promotion beyond his ability. I knew I had to be judicious in what I revealed. "Now, about Cantina ...?" He eyed me innocently as we stepped out of the elevator.

Marchaud wanted juicy details. A blow-by-blow account. I wouldn't give him that.

"Törni was still serving under the Finnish flag when I first met him. Before the integration of national militaries under Union command. He was the Finnish armed forces sharp-shooting champion, a gold medalist at two World Military Games in a row. I guess he got riled up when civilian agencies were permitted participation rights. But I can understand that."

"You being allowed to compete—that upset the apple cart, I agree," Marchaud said before whispering, "From what I hear, he has a short fuse, especially after a drink. They say he likes vodka."

I shrugged. "I don't have a problem with a man liking a drink."

"But in that bar, after he lost to you. The military police got involved. What happened?"

I smiled, glancing down at Marchaud. We were nearing the NocioPerception suite's waiting chamber in the underground interrogation center. That was where we'd be collected by the technician. "Honestly, it was all a fuss over nothing. A misunderstanding."

"But he hit you, no?"

I studied Marchaud. *What is this really all about*, I wondered, *this new-found curiosity?* At the entrance to the waiting chamber, the looming figure of Törni was visible through the opaque sliding glass. I certainly wasn't going to tell Marchaud that I had taken a sucker punch. That the Finnish giant had caught me unawares with an uppercut. And I especially wasn't going to reveal that I probably hadn't been at my most mature, although it was true that the details of who insulted whom were blurred by the alcohol fumes. Moreover, any clarity as to who was guilty of starting the altercation had since been lost in the mists of each divergent retelling.

But one thing I did know: I harbored a grudge that the punch had gone unanswered. *Because that's who I am*, I thought. Even back then, before he became the Union's armed forces super heavyweight boxing champion, Törni had a reputation for being handy with his fists. In the Italian bar on the final night of the Games, it was his hand speed that beat me, knocking me sideways. And the blow had power behind it that for a second or two had left me dazed. Once I had picked myself up, I was only prevented from retaliating using my Thai martial art skills by the fact that his unit ushered him away; the bar manager had called the military police. My only lasting injury was wounded pride.

* * *

As I entered the waiting chamber, Törni was standing in glacial stillness next to a table and chairs in the center of the room. He was dressed in military fatigues, a black beret in his shoulder strap, his blond hair in a crew cut. His face remained impassive as he watched me enter, yet his eyes narrowed as he tracked my movements.

Once I had crossed the threshold, he edged forward until his face was scarcely more than ten centimeters from mine; we were the same height. He offered me his hand. We were now working together, after all. Yet the hint of a scowl pulled at one corner of his mouth.

I glared into his cold, gray eyes, flecked with gold. They stared straight back at me, unblinking. Nothing fazed the guy. Not even me as I matched his strong handshake with a firm clasp of my own. I was vaguely aware of Marchaud scurrying in behind me, glancing up at us both.

Our moment of studied intensity was broken by Marchaud, who coughed nervously as he sat. To my surprise, he had removed his beige kepi and began fiddling nervously with the brim as it lay on the table. I went around the table and lowered myself onto a seat. Törni sat opposite me.

Törni placed his large hands on the table in front of him and spoke without modulation.

"The male target was acquired from the location in Lyndhurst, southern Old Kingdom. Target was sedated and rendered to the Proelium around thirty minutes ago." Törni's delivery matched his expressionless face.

Just at that moment I received a high-priority alert in my ear implant. As I activated my holotab, I was conscious of Törni's and Marchaud's eyes on me. It was from Lina de Bolle, with an update on Ebba Black. I raised my eyebrows. Yes! She had agreed. An interview was scheduled for later that afternoon. The Nordic authorities had also signed off on the request. We were to report to her Baroque manor at 3 p.m. I suddenly felt the involuntary flutter of butterflies in my stomach again.

As I was about to blink on the hibernation slider, the last line of Lina's memoclip took me aback. It wasn't Marchaud who would accompany me—it would be Törni, at von Böhm's express request. It made no sense. We were after intel on Ebba Black. Törni had no training in that. He was a blunt instrument with all the tact of a sledgehammer. *What's von Böhm's game?*

As I was still processing the update, Marchaud and Törni both received alerts of their own. Törni peeled his eyes away from his holotab and looked at me once he'd read his update. He treated me to a knowing smirk. I gave him the slightest nod of acknowledgment.

Then I received a second alert with a different vibration sequence. This was a proximity alert identifying the NocioPerception technician who was approaching. My holotab was still open, revealing her DigID credentials—Alodie Descoteaux—and job title: Interrogation Technician.

With that, an interior door opened in the waiting chamber. It led in from the NocioPerception suite itself. Descoteaux was a tall, slight, nerdy type—mid-thirties, I guessed. She was wearing loose-fitting white overalls with a white cap. She brought with her the faint smell of chlorhexidine gluconate antiseptic solution as the door behind her slid closed. I smirked as I saw Marchaud rubbernecking through the sliding door, attempting to get a glimpse of the rack on the other side.

"Gentlemen," she said, as she stopped in front of us. "The subject is prepped. I'll be overseeing the logistics of your interrogation. As you'll be aware, my primary function is to ensure health protocols are observed." Then, as an aside, "That's why it's me here, not a droid. A legal requirement. This is one job that'll never go on the obs-job list. Not when we're dealing with right-to-life law."

I grimaced to myself. The ostensible assertion of right to life struck me, ironically, as the ultimate dehumanization of a person, despite my own personal history of violence. Erebus McDenizen had the right to life under Union law while we tortured him. Of course, we weren't supposed to refer to it as *torture*. Torture was illegal. But in the end, that was just semantics—a linguistic artifice.

Marchaud cleared his throat. He was clearly nervous. "I have never ..." he stuttered. "I was wondering about the procedure ..."

The technician nodded and began rattling through what sounded like a well-rehearsed explanation. "Throughout our bodies we have nerve endings—nocioceptors. They detect different types of physical experiences that are potentially harmful. When a particular stimulus—for instance, the experience of heat—reaches a certain threshold—let's say above forty-two degrees Celsius in the case of heat on the skin—the skin nocioceptor kicks in. It sends a signal to the brain, which generates the subjective experience of pain. But in the case of the NocioPerception rack, there is no actual heat source. We simply trick the nocioceptors by simulating the experience of heat using electrodes."

"I know about the body's nocioceptors," Marchaud replied. "But I mean, how do you actually simulate the pain?"

"He's been strapped to the rack, one hundred and fifty electrodes inserted into various parts of his body, including soft tissue, joints, and organs. And all the standard medical sensors to monitor health parameters. We don't want to overload the brain's pain centers. He's already fitted with an intravenous drip, which provides an *added benefit*, in the not-so-technical parlance," she added, slightly apologetically.

"Not sure I understand what you mean," Marchaud muttered, perplexed.

"The IV solution contains a neuromuscular blocking drug in addition to the usual stuff. You know—standard saline solution, vitamins, electrolytes. The blocker incapacitates him. But his sensory experience of pain is enhanced. Hence ..."

"Ah, an added benefit," Marchaud repeated in hushed wonder. "So, what kinds of pain can be simulated?"

"Good question," the technician replied. "We can simulate a broad range of visceral and somatic pain. In fact, we have an entire menu. Anything from fingernail removal to drowning, from a heart attack to the sensation of bugs under the skin. We usually recommend starting low on the Duress menu to give the subject a chance to provide data points without simulating unnecessary pain." I watched with mild fascination as Marchaud visibly squirmed.

"Starting low?" he asked.

"Things like a persistent itch, sunburn, tinnitus ... and from there you can go anywhere you want. We can simulate all the standard physical forms of duress, from boiling, enema, flaying, kneecapping, sawing, or genital mutilation to scalping. We can also simulate sensory-psychological forms of torture; for instance, the simulation of starvation or stress positioning— even extreme sound or so-called white torture."

"What are the most extreme forms of torture on your menu?" Törni asked. I glanced across at him. That was exactly the sort of question I would have expected him to ask. The technician glanced at him, nodding matter-of-factly.

"Just a heads up, we don't actually use the word *torture* here. But as to your question, honestly, we can simulate any form of duress. Here we are only limited by our imaginations."

"What about the Blood Eagle?" Törni asked.

"I'm not familiar with that," the technician replied.

"The Viking form of execution. The subject's back is slashed open to give access to the ribs. The ribs are then broken by pulling them up to resemble the wings of an eagle. Salt is then poured into the wound. Finally, the subject's lungs are pulled out of the chest cavity and draped over the ribs."

The technician had a confused air. "Oh, I didn't know you had Viking heritage, I thought you were ..."

"I'm half Sámi," Törni growled.

I smirked to myself at her reaction: *Why would a Finn mention a Viking form of torture?* But I knew this wasn't a cultural reference. The guy was just a sadist.

The technician smiled faintly at him. "That's quite something, Captain. Shall we go through?" she asked quickly.

CHAPTER 13

We followed the technician through the sliding door. And just as I remembered, it was the lighting that hit you first, even before the bleak sterility of the place. The smart walls emitted such a crisp, stark white that there was a hint of blue. The interrogation suite was separated by a thick pane of transparent armored glass into two hermetically sealed compartments. I saw Marchaud's look of shock as he gawked through the glass at the subject, strapped to the NocioPerception rack on the other side.

"He's naked," Marchaud muttered, seemingly unable to peel his eyes away from the disconcerting scene. The rack was still in inert horizontal mode. McDenizen was lying on it, secured with medical straps. The rack itself was the shape of a human figure, arms outstretched to the sides, legs parted, and it was made of translucent plastic. It had hundreds of small holes drilled through it, from which protruded thin metallic electrodes attached to metal probes, which had been inserted all over McDenizen's body. Attached to the head of the frame was an intravenous unit and a further array of vital sign sensors, all strapped to McDenizen. His head had been shaved to allow the pain receptor detection cap to be fitted.

"You can get set up, Commander," the technician said. "And don't forget to begin with EEG baseline." I sat at the console to sync my DigID credentials with the interrogation VirDa. Törni and Marchaud took seats on either side of me.

"Prepare console for interrogation," I said once I had synced with the VirDa. The translucent display projected from the inlaid fusion bar in the center of the desk console and the small adjacent aperture opened for the stalked mic to rise out. The interrogation menu faded onto the screen, with a full array of blinkables corresponding to duress levels. Now I had full eye and voice command control.

Meanwhile, the technician walked toward a door at one end of the glass partition. She spoke her voice command into the security VirDa. Once inside, the door sealed shut behind her. I looked on as she settled into her own console seat on the other side of the glass, next to the subject. Once she had checked her VirDa screen for health parameters and established the subject's baseline pain threshold, I heard her green-light the interrogation system.

The hydraulic system of the NocioPerception rack began to deploy. Slowly, the subject strapped to the translucent frame began to rise into a vertical position. McDenizen came to a stop in midair, facing us through the glass pane. His eyes were wild with terror.

I used gaze commands to scroll through the Duress menu on the display in front of me—it was divided into different pain thresholds, with listings for various techniques nested under each. A single blink command provided descriptions, case studies, and pain ratings.

"Are we ready?" I asked, glancing at Marchaud and then Törni. They both nodded. "Activate two-way glass," I said into the mic. Erebus McDenizen could now see us. He barely blinked. I had the power to cause immense pain with a single voice command. I adjusted the stalk of the interrogation microphone and leaned forward slightly. "VirDa, activate two-way communication." Marchaud jumped slightly as the reverberation from my voice echoed back at us from beyond the partition. "Mr. McDenizen, we will begin the interrogation." McDenizen was staring at me, completely powerless as he heard my voice. I felt a jolt of pity for him. "You are subject to a Union rendition protocol. I am Commander Morgan, leading this interrogation as the ranking Europol officer. I am being assisted by Lieutenant Colonel Marchaud and Captain Törni, both of CyberForce." I gestured to the two men beside me. McDenizen remained silent.

"First, I ask you to confirm your full name." McDenizen snorted in an odd manner, like an untamed horse. I could see hate in his eyes.

"But we know that," I heard Marchaud mutter. I rolled my eyes before issuing a blink command to mute the two-way microphone system. I turned to Marchaud. *What does he know? He just works a VirDa console and happens to wear a uniform. He never gets his hands dirty.*

"We have to first establish the baseline for truthful answers. Questions we can verify. The VirDa operates an algorithm through EEG sensors, measuring the subject's brain wave responses," I said as calmly as I could.

"The P300," Törni growled across me at Marchaud. "Shows up there," the Finn added, stabbing a finger into the large translucent screen projecting from the fusion bar in front of us.

"A polygraph test?" Marchaud asked, still looking at me.

I shook my head. "Physiological measures spike under duress and can give a false positive. Brain wave patterns don't lie." I glanced at Marchaud expectantly. He showed me a thumbs-up gesture. I sighed before reactivating the two-way mic.

"Your full name?" I asked McDenizen again. His eyes were still wild as the silence persisted.

Törni tapped my arm. He pointed to somewhere in the medium pain intensity range on the VirDa screen. I shook my head. *The guy lacks finesse.* In one corner of the screen was a blinkable icon for my personal Europol portal. I activated the intel file on McDenizen. We were going to start low. It appeared he had a history of breathing disorders. I pointed. Asthma. I could sense Marchaud nodding next to me in my peripheral vision.

"VirDa, severe asthma attack," I said into the stalked mic. On the other side of the glass, the subject took a sudden gulp, convulsed, and began choking. His skin became blanched and pallid. "VirDa, pause," I said on the thirty-second mark. "Now, please confirm your name," I repeated for a second time. McDenizen was still struggling to breathe.

"Erebus Caelan McDenizen," he muttered. Toward the top of the screen, the customary EEG graph appeared, with its scrolling peaks and troughs.

"And your day and month of birth?"

"23rd of February," came the reply, again with the guttural accent differentiators on the "r" that I recognized from the audio excerpt Pieter had provided. The VirDa pinged. I glanced at the EEG display for confirmation. We now had our baseline.

"Strange accent," Marchaud whispered. "It's Alba, right? Appleton?"

I knew from McDenizen's file that he was born in Glasgow. I also knew that Appleton had recently stopped offering Alba accent differentiators—there was little demand anymore. I shrugged at Marchaud before continuing the interrogation.

"Is there anything you want to tell us at the outset? Please believe me, I don't want this to be any more uncomfortable than it needs to be." I felt the telltale knot of apprehension in the pit of my stomach at what I was about to do—cause extreme pain in someone who couldn't fight back; someone immobilized, drugged, restrained.

McDenizen flinched. "What do you want?"

"Information. On Ebba Black. On Babel. I want to know Babel's role in the language outage." The subject gulped. "You can begin by telling us what Operation False Flag is."

"False Flag?" McDenizen asked. "I don't know what that is," he muttered. I watched the EEG readout as its waveform scrolled across the display. He was lying.

"There are consequences when you're not truthful, Mr. McDenizen." I blinked through to his file again. He suffered from entomophobia. *We can simulate that. Still in the low pain intensity range.* "VirDa, crawling bugs on the skin." McDenizen continued to stare at us through the glass, but his breathing began to sound shallow. "False Flag?" I probed again. Still he remained silent. "VirDa, crawling bugs now *under* the skin."

"Stop!" McDenizen implored after a few seconds. "I'll tell you."

"VirDa, pause."

It was a few seconds before he was able to speak coherently. "My role was intercepting Unilanguage communications, decoding them," he began.

"Unilanguage?"

He attempted to nod, but his head was restrained. "Chaired by Appleton—you know, Marc Barron." McDenizen gave a faint sneer before muttering, "Capitalist pig."

"Go on."

"I hacked into Unilanguage's Technical Committee meetings. And facecall records from executive management meetings."

"And?"

"Appleton has developed new tech ... a type of neural implant, a new chip." I watched the sharp rises and falls of the lines on the EEG display. McDenizen was telling the truth.

"What kind of chip?"

"It's third-gen UG tech. They're calling it a *ghost chip*. Barron gave a virtual presentation recently to the executive management. Highly encrypted. That's when we first heard about it. None of the usual Committees, including the Technical one, seemed to know anything about it—it never came up before."

"And you found out something?"

"It's a high-end add-on—upscales the second-gen language chip. It works on a proximity sync with the language chip, cloaks the location of the subject—there are no detectable LS rebounds. It somehow suppresses them." I felt my eyes widening. "At the beginning of the briefing, before the executive came online, there was an informal exchange, just a few seconds, between a senior officer at Appleton HQ and Barron himself ..." McDenizen suddenly seemed to be struggling to breathe. He took some calming gulps of air. "They were calling in to the Unilanguage campus in Palo Alto. The Unilanguage folks hadn't joined the call. Barron and the woman were in the call-waiting lobby. Their comms settings pre-activated."

"And who was the woman?"

"She didn't come into view, just her voice off facecomms. I guessed his fixer, the Belarussian."

"Darya Zao?" I prompted.

"It sounded like her. She was talking of an outage, Operation False Flag, someone or something from the Inland Empire, and the *fall guy*."

I felt my body tense as McDenizen spoke. Not only could I see from the screen that he was telling the truth, but we were really getting somewhere. "Do you remember what she said?" I asked. McDenizen paused.

"Something about Operation False Flag being engaged. That the Inland Empire third party has deployed the drone. And that the fall guy would take the blame for the outage as planned."

"Those were her exact words?"

"Along those lines," McDenizen replied.

"And you still have the facecall record?"

"I forwarded it to command."

"To Ebba Black?" I asked. McDenizen remained silent. I could see Törni smirking next to me in my peripheral vision.

"How did Barron respond?" I asked.

"Nothing much. He just said, 'Good.' Maybe. Then his meeting partners connected. From Unilanguage. The Belarussian didn't engage further."

"What did you make of it?" I asked. "This exchange?"

"Not much at first. But then ... the language outage, yer know, that happened."

"Are you implying a connection?" I asked.

"Appleton is involved."

"In the outage?" I asked, bewildered, as Marchaud burst out laughing. I glanced at him and smiled.

"That's ridiculous," exclaimed Marchaud.

"You see how that sounds," I said, staring directly at McDenizen. Yet his EEG levels were still within the baseline parameters. He clearly believed what he was saying. I frowned.

"Okay, tell us about the Language Unplugged protocol."
McDenizen's eyes narrowed. I had expected a spike in his
physiological measures, an indication of surprise. But his pulse
and breathing rates were within interrogation norms. *It's almost
as if he were expecting the question*, I thought. Yet he remained
silent. I sighed. I felt Törni's gaze burning into me.

"VirDa, activate one-way microphone." I turned to Törni.
"Let's be proportionate—something like ..."

"Wire brushing," Törni replied, pointing to the medium-
intensity pain selection on the Duress menu. "And then move
up quickly." I looked at the Finn. His pale gray eyes were staring
right back at me intently, waiting to see what I would do.

"VirDa, activate two-way microphone. Mr. McDenizen, you
will now experience wire brushing."

"You have it all wrong," he began, squealing. I watched in
grim fascination as McDenizen's pupils began dilating as the
probes embedded in his skin, liver, kidneys, heart began to
enact this new horror. The scene was surreal. A suspended
figure, naked, wretched, shorn of dignity, experiencing the
inner turmoil caused by the sensation of gnawing, burning pain
from simulated rigid metal spines brushing continually across
his skin, conjuring the feel of red striations of wounded flesh.
And then McDenizen wet himself, yellow urine trickling down
his leg, dripping off the rack onto the pristine floor.

Törni smirked. "What a pussy," he said dismissively into my
ear. I threw him a withering look.

"Please stop," McDenizen croaked. "Untethering ..."

"What?" I responded.

"Stop!" he yelled. "It's untethering."

"VirDa, deactivate wire brushing." I paused. "Tell us about
untethering." McDenizen was now producing strange hoarse

grunts. His eyes glazed over before slowly refocusing.

"Babel's technology to untether language chips. A surgical procedure."

"And what does this procedure entail?"

"Don't know much. Honestly. I'm just a hacker, I'm not a medic."

"Babel has neuroprosthetic specialists?" Marchaud blurted out, surprise rippling across his features.

"And what's the purpose of untethering?" I demanded. McDenizen had caught his breath again.

"All I know is that it disconnects a language chip from language streaming services without impacting language."

"That doesn't make any sense," I said.

"Please ..." whispered McDenizen. "I really don't know." Just then it hit me. If Marchaud was right and Babel did have neuroprosthetic specialists, then untethering *was* some kind of surgical procedure. And for that there had to be a medical facility somewhere. A place.

"Freetown," I said suddenly. "That's where the facility is ... for untethering. Right?"

I could see that McDenizen was still recovering from the simulated wire brushing.

"Freetown?" he whispered.

I nodded. "We know about Freetown. Where is it?"

"I don't know ..." McDenizen mouthed. Saliva was dribbling from both corners of his mouth in a pitiful continuous stream.

"I don't believe him," Törni hissed at me. I glanced at the cold, square face next to me and pointed to the EEG display. McDenizen was telling the truth. I turned and looked back through the glass at McDenizen. It was clear from his eyes that he didn't know. No EEG waveguide was required for that. By this point, I knew he would have told us almost anything. I decided to change the direction of the interrogation.

"What was Babel's role in the language outage?" McDenizen didn't reply. "Is this untethering process connected to the outage?" I pressed.

He attempted to shake his head. "We're trying to free people from big tech."

"But hasn't the outage done exactly that?"

"Not from Appleton. That's still standing," he replied with a bitterness that took me aback, given his physical state.

"So let me get this straight. You claim Babel is blameless?" McDenizen frowned. "Your organization?"

"Yes," he replied. His EEG readout showed him still to be telling the truth.

"Tell us about Ebba Black." McDenizen remained silent. "Is she *The Tower*?" I insisted.

"No," he replied at last. This time I knew he was lying even before the EEG display confirmed it.

Törni jumped to point at foot roasting, in the extreme pain range on the Duress menu. I blinked on the stillgram and saw from the description that it was a form of torture first recorded in Ancient Rome. It was later perfected during the Spanish Inquisition for extracting confessions. Törni gestured toward McDenizen's file. I guessed he had learned something from me already about proper interrogation techniques. McDenizen had watched his pet dog burn alive in the family home as a child. *That would seriously fuck you up*, I thought.

I muted the two-way comms. "No, we're not doing that. He's just a computer geek, not a trained field operative," I said definitively. "That would exceed brain pain center thresholds. We're not sadists." *Or at least, I'm not, as confirmed by my annual psych evals.* But sometimes inflicting pain was the job. And I always did the job.

I resumed the interrogation. "Mr. McDenizen. Just answer the question. I take no pleasure in inflicting more pain on you. You need to help yourself. This is almost over."

"Yes, Ebba is The Tower," he whimpered. "What will happen to me?"

"He's confessed to corporate espionage," Marchaud muttered at me. I nodded.

"Thank you. You will now receive medical attention. VirDa, terminate interrogation," I said, speaking my final voice command. For now, I had everything I needed for my meeting with Ebba Black.

CHAPTER 14

It was a fifteen-minute journey on an international skyway from Brussels airspace in the Union capital to the Nordic Republic. And a few minutes after that, my Skyraider was approaching Gothenburg, which sat at the mouth of the River Goth as it flowed out into the Kattegat Strait. I had been surprised when Törni proposed that we travel in the same vehicle. Von Böhm had definitely put him up to something.

Ebba Black had agreed to be interviewed at her estate on Styrsö, an island forming part of the Gothenburg Archipelago. As we began our descent, I glanced down at islands with quiet beaches, pine woods, pink granite cliffs, and picturesque sea views. Once we were close to the Black estate, perimeter security sensors activated and Siena was given auto-authorization to land. The Skyraider swayed before dropping down the estate's VTOL corridor. I gazed out through the windows with curiosity at the neo-Baroque manor below. The drone surveillance footage I had access to hadn't done it justice.

We landed on a vertipad adjacent to a beautifully verdant round lawn encircled by gravel in front of the large mansion. As we waited for the beetle-wing doors to open, moving upward like a pair of scissors, I glimpsed the coat of arms of the Johansson-Black family, which adorned the protruding span in the center of the building's façade. There was small lettering beneath: *Kattegat slott*. As my optic nerve scanned the writing, my language chip began auto-parsing. *Slott* meant manor house in Riksmål, the Nordic state official language. Törni got out of the hover car first and started walking with purpose. As I caught up with him, I followed his gaze as he abruptly slowed. He had been drawn by movement coming toward us along the gravel driveway. A tall woman. Törni glanced at me questioningly.

"Horchata Chiu, Ebba Black's assistant," I muttered.

"She's an albino," he whispered, apparently mesmerized by the pale, striking, and highly unusual woman approaching us. I marveled at the oncoming figure too. It wasn't her eerie snow-queen whiteness that was so arresting. Nor was it her unusual height. It wasn't even her attire. She was dressed in a short silver skirt, silver stockings, silver glittery ankle boots with high heels, and a plunging white blouse and black velvet jacket, all at odds with the thermal requirements of the chilly November air. Rather, and most specifically, it was her gait.

Horchata Chiu moved her long, thin body in undulating synchronicity that delivered a visual overload of sultry sensuality with aplomb. Her head was up, her shoulders back. She swung her arms loosely, gracefully, with measured ease. And her hips swiveled from side to side, her weight more in her heels than anywhere else. This was the killer shoulders-hips-heels walk of the hyper-seductress. The femme fatale walk, if ever I had seen one.

"She thinks she's on a catwalk," Törni muttered dismissively next to me.

"In fact, she used to be a model," I replied. He eyeballed me in surprise. "She retired three years ago and began working for

Ebba Black. Soon afterward her LS rebound records ceased."
Törni glanced back at me with tight lips and narrowed eyes,
before turning his gaze back toward the woman. "Interesting,
right?" He didn't respond.

As Horchata Chiu reached us, she held out a long, pale arm
with fingers extended. *More to be kissed than shaken,* I thought. I
shook her hand gingerly.

"We're here to meet with Dr. Black," I said. As she nodded
in acknowledgment, I couldn't help but notice that even her
eyebrows were white.

"We've been expecting you, Commander. This way, please,"
she replied. Törni and I followed the woman toward the house.

I knew from our file that the imposing mansion before us
had been built in the late 2050s, in the style of the late Baroque
period. It was commissioned by Ebba's maternal grandparents,
Melker Johansson and Klara Black, who made their fortune in
the emerging plant-based green manufacturing technologies of
the 2040s.

The front façade of the building featured an elaborate two-
way external staircase—two sets of wide marble steps that led
on both sides to the entrance vestibule, located on the first
floor. The two wings were painted a striking shade of ocher. The
central span was of gleaming white brick. Its top jutted up above
the pitch of the roof, with a large clock in its peak. The mansard
roof was adorned with navy-blue glazed tiles. They glinted in
the crisp mid-afternoon sunlight. It was a large building—at
least four floors, I guessed—surrounded by a private wood. And
I knew from our flight over the island that behind the wood, the
estate let out onto a cliff overlooking the sea.

We followed Horchata Chiu up the steps. I vainly attempted
to avert my gaze from the sway of her derriere in front of me.

At the top of the steps, she half turned, beckoning us through imposing light-yellow paneled doors.

Inside was a large hallway with a magnificent chandelier plunging down from the high ceiling. An ornate central staircase rose to a half-landing leading to split staircases—parallel flights on either side. At the top was a large landing with a marble balustrade that overlooked us. I followed the line of the luxury red carpet runners up the staircases, noting the matching gold fittings.

Horchata Chiu led us from the hallway through a door on the left. It appeared to be an antechamber, with chairs placed around the room. The walls were adorned with sumptuous oil portraits—I assumed of family members.

"Please sit," Chiu said, gesturing to a couple of chairs. "I'll let the professor know you're here."

She approached an interior door, knocked softly, opened it, and disappeared inside. After a moment, she re-emerged.

"Professor Black will see you now," she announced.

* * *

Törni and I stepped through into the adjacent room. As we entered, I heard the strange, unfamiliar click of a door closing behind us. Horchata Chiu had remained outside. And then it struck me. There were no VirDas here, no voice commands to unlock doors. The doors had handles for human hands. *How novel!*

We had entered a dimly lit room that carried the faint odor of lavender. The floor was carpeted with several large, antique-style Persian rugs. Swirls of embroidered motifs in a range of reds played across them—scarlet, crimson, maroon, carmine, claret, burgundy, and cardinal red. The windows to my left looked out onto the circular front lawn. It was a large room, oak-paneled, lit only by a small, green-shaded lamp on a desk across from where we'd entered. Pale autumnal daylight filtered through the windows.

As my eyes adjusted to the dimness, my gaze was drawn to a mezzanine level that jutted out around three walls. The narrow mezzanine comprised wall-to-wall shelves filled with books. *Actual books! The sight startled me.* Physical artifacts made of paper with covers. The last time I had seen a book was in my childhood—just one book, once, a relic from a previous age; a ragged, dirty, musty thing with curled-up corners. I realized to my amazement that this place was, in fact, a personal library. An oak spiral staircase to my right, at the far end of the room, led up to the mezzanine.

I glanced back at the large oak desk. And then I realized there was a figure sitting behind it. Ebba Black! She was a small thing. I could already tell she was even more beautiful in the flesh. I felt an unexpected tingle run down my spine as we made our way toward her seated figure.

Ebba stood up and stepped out from behind the desk, approaching us. I caught myself feeling slightly disappointed she wasn't wearing the same red cocktail dress as in the hologram image I had downloaded that morning.

"Gentlemen," she called across to us, "I assume we're using English?" Her accent was native King's English. Now I was seriously impressed.

As she spoke, it dawned on me how husky her voice was—deeper than most women's. She directed us with an accompanying hand flourish to a seating area, a brown Chesterfield sofa in the center of the room. It looked stylish but uncomfortable. In front of the sofa was a long mahogany coffee table. Törni and I sat awkwardly next to each other. Ebba moved toward us and stood on the other side of the low table, hovering like a small dark raven.

"You are Captain Aapo Törni," she announced, fixing the Finn with a pointed look. I watched the way her lips curled as she spoke, revealing glimpses of perfect white teeth. The red of her lipstick somehow made her black hair seem even more striking. "You have the unusual distinction of having served under the colors of three flags—Sápmi, Finland, and the Union." I glanced at Törni; he was squinting at Ebba, perplexed. "You have a Finnish mother and a Sámi father, but you always felt greater affinity with your father. You took up his cause after his death and were instrumental in the Sámi insurgency of 2105, before later serving in the Utti Jaeger regiment—the special forces unit of the Finnish army. *Excelsior.* Isn't that the motto?" Ebba asked, watching Törni in wry amusement. "Shall I continue?" she asked as if issuing a challenge. His lips parted slightly, which was the only motion he made. I could sense his hostility. Ebba lapsed into silence.

"Impressive," I muttered, seeking to break the tension.

Now Ebba turned to me. "And you," she began. "Commander Emyr Morgan of Europol."

"So far, so good," I said, grinning through gritted teeth as I felt panic welling up in me.

"You've recently lost your mother. My condolences. You had a troubled childhood, first running away from home at thirteen, followed by a spell in foster care and another under social services care at fourteen when you violently attacked your father, causing him to have a detached retina." I suddenly felt flushed. "You received a Superior soc-ed classification at

seventeen, the only one that year in Cymru. My congratulations.
And later enrolled in the Cymru Heddlu Seiberdroseddu
academy, fast-tracked through the detective program. You rose
rapidly through the ranks before being tasked with setting up
and leading the Celtic partnership nations' first cybercrime
bureau. It wasn't long before Europol took notice, was it?" she
asked. There was silence for a few seconds.

"You seem to know quite a bit about us," I said.

"Given you know so much about me, isn't that fair?" Ebba
asked.

I felt unnerved as this small woman stood over us on the
other side of the table. She was eyeing us with coal-black eyes.

"There's actually not much on file ... about you. You're a
ghost." At that, Ebba tilted her head back and let out a laugh—a
tinkling laugh that echoed around the room. I watched her
in amazement as her long hair shimmered in the light from
the desk lamp behind her. Nearly everything about her was
black, from her hair to her clothes. She was dressed in a scarlet
blouse, a black jacket, a black velvet pencil skirt that fell to
just below her knees, black stockings, and high stiletto-heeled
shoes.

Ebba folded her arms, seemingly studying us as she pursed
her lips. There was something paradoxically intimidating about
her petite, perfectly poised figure.

"Can I offer either of you something to drink?" she asked,
still standing.

"No, thank you," I said quietly. Törni stared assiduously
through her without replying. I glanced at him. He looked
almost comically out of place, his oversized physique in his
military fatigues perched precariously on the leather sofa in
the large library. Ebba finally sat down opposite us and crossed

THE BABEL APOCALYPSE   147

her slim legs in an elegant posture. She was sitting upright, perfectly still, straight-backed, watching us.

"You're here to talk about the outage," she announced finally. I nodded. "You, Commander, are still minded to think I did it, despite what you have now learned from torturing poor Erebus McDenizen." I spluttered in surprise. "While you, Captain, couldn't care less, despite knowing that your superiors in CyberForce are certain I did not. Your orders are to scope out my home. Ready for what? Am I to be rendered too? Or worse?"

I glanced at Törni in surprise at this revelation. Silence fell over us for a moment. Ebba appeared to examine my expression as I glanced back at her. *What am I to make of this woman?*

CHAPTER 15

Just then, there was a sound from one corner of the room. I peered over Ebba's shoulder into the shadow beneath the mezzanine level. Törni had heard it too. As I focused my eyes, the sound attached itself to a dark figure standing almost perfectly still. Ebba turned slightly, following my gaze before glancing back at me in apparent amusement.

"Ursula," Ebba called over her shoulder. The figure slowly hove into view. She was a sturdy-looking woman, mid-thirties and at least 185 centimeters tall, dressed in leather pants, a loose black top, and black sneakers. Her mousey blond hair was cropped short. She had a rectangular face and a crooked nose that had been broken at some point. She wore a leather shoulder holster with a large handgun stowed in it. I sucked in my breath. This was an old-fashioned weapon. It looked like a Glock 19, the perfect conventional handgun for home defense. It made quite a noise and had serious recoil, unlike my high-tech coil pistol. It was chambered with 9mm Luger and, used correctly, could stop a giant.

"Why don't you take a break?" Ebba said, glancing up at the woman. "I don't think our guests will cause a disturbance."

"Yes, Ebba," Ursula replied with what I recognized as rural Wessex accent differentiators, from the Old Kingdom. *That would be an expensive lexical package*, I thought. *She's probably streaming Appleton.*

As Ursula left the room, Ebba watched me, apparently even more amused, judging from her expression. She placed a small finger across her lips as if to suppress a laugh.

"You didn't know about her, did you?" she asked. "About my bodyguard."

"Not that one," I muttered.

Ebba nodded before clearing her throat. "So, as I have you here, let me tell you a story from Genesis." She paused, smiling as she saw Törni's confusion. "You've heard of the Bible?" He nodded. "Then here's an origin myth for you: how language began. The Tower of Babel."

"I'm not sure how that's relevant," I said. "As you yourself already mentioned, we're here to ask you about the outage." She raised her hand to silence me.

"Humor me, okay?"

I shrugged, smiling to myself. Now she was about to perform. I sat back. She was quite the piece of work.

"In the generations following the Great Flood, so the story goes, there was a primal unity of humankind with a single language, spoken by all. The people decided to build a city, and at its center, a tower that would reach up to the heavens. God observed the overweening pride of his progeny and bristled with indignation at *their* hubris. And as punishment, God scattered the people over the Earth, creating different tribes and different languages so they could no longer understand one another. The city received the name *Babel*, from the Hebrew verb *bālal*, meaning to jumble or to confuse." Ebba sat back and watched us. "Today I am branded a Babelist because I want language to be free. The agencies you gentlemen represent say I want the world to return to a state of chaos. Babel is your name for us, not ours," she said with disdain. "Big tech fears loss of control when that is precisely what it provides, just to service shareholders and maximize profits." She sighed again. "Talk about hubris!" Silence followed. I didn't know how to respond to that. Törni sat impassively.

As I watched her eyes, which darted with passion as she spoke, I wondered whether Karen Hoekstra might have been wrong when she claimed that Ebba Black was not an idealist. This woman was clearly driven. But I still hadn't fully figured out what was driving her.

Törni snorted finally. He didn't like her, not one bit. I could have predicted it. "Is there something you'd like to say, Captain?" Ebba asked, now with a hint of malice in her voice.

"You and Babel are cyberterrorists. Criminals. You don't get to lecture us," he began. These were his first words to her since we'd arrived. And they were not well judged. I groaned inwardly. I knew it would have been more constructive if Marchaud had come instead.

"Let me give you some free advice, Captain. Measure your words before you utter them. Bad manners will not go unpunished here."

"Is that a threat?" Törni asked through gritted teeth. Ebba responded by throwing me a faint smile, before glancing back at him while weighing her words.

"Let me ask you this, Captain—a hypothetical. How do you win at Chicken?"

"What?" Törni replied, as perplexed as I was by this curveball of a question.

"Oh, you know," Ebba said, gesturing vaguely with her

small, well-manicured hands. "The classic car crash game. Two drivers on course for collision, driving headlong at one another. Whoever swerves first loses. Whoever doesn't blink and stays the course wins."

"Okay, I know Chicken," he replied.

"So how do you win?"

"By not blinking, by carrying on driving?" Törni responded.

"But what if the other person doesn't blink either? You'll crash and die," Ebba said. "Do you want to die?"

Törni thought for a moment before responding. "Well, you make the other person think you won't blink, so they blink first." I smiled to myself. *She's succeeded in drawing him in; he's way too easy.*

"Precisely," Ebba said coolly. "And how do you do that, Captain?"

"By driving ..."

"And if you keep driving, you might crash and die, because the other driver thought you'd blink first ..."

"Hmmm ..." Törni appeared to be genuinely struggling with the conundrum.

"Let me see if I can help you," Ebba offered. "You win in three steps. And it all happens before you even get in the car. First, you create a reputation for making credible threats. Next, you reinforce your notoriety for carrying them through. If you are rash or obstinate, that doubtless helps. And finally, you make good on your threats ... time after time."

"So how does that relate to Chicken?" Törni asked in confusion.

Ebba flicked her black hair. "Fair question. If you follow these steps, your opponent will know that your threat to smash your car straight down their throat is credible—that you will do it. *They* will swerve first. Assuming they even want to play Chicken with you in the first place." Törni smiled to himself as if he'd achieved some sort of epiphany. "And to answer your earlier question," Ebba stated, "the answer is yes."

"I don't understand," Törni said, genuinely confused.

"It *was* a threat!" Ebba said. I felt Törni's whole body convulse next to me. I glanced at him. A vein in his neck was visibly pulsating, and I could feel the tension as his body seemed to strain. I was astounded by the look of hate in his eyes. Törni clearly wanted to stand, to smash his large hand down on top of her skull. I tapped him lightly on the thigh. He glanced at me. I shook my head. He let out a quick breath as if trying to regain control and consciously released himself, sinking back into the sofa. When he spoke, finally, it was the slow, almost slurred speech of depraved anger that can no longer be concealed.

"Dr. Black, you need to get real and stop playing silly games. You're meddling in matters way above your head. You're born into privilege. You should stick to your university ivory tower. What do you know about life?"

Ebba looked at Törni, her eyes suddenly wide in surprise before she broke out into laughter. It was almost a venomous sound, perfected to drive a man like Törni, with his strengths and weaknesses, to despair. And her mouth was cruelly twisted, pulling a waspish, evil-joker grin. He suddenly rose. I rose too, because he did. And only then did Ebba seem to see the danger. The dawning realization occurred to her that Törni was, for a split second, beyond anyone's help. And in that micro-second, I realized, as I watched her, that Ebba was still not afraid. She was utterly fearless.

"Aapo, let's get on with the interview," I said firmly, quietly, and ushered the giant at my side back down. He glanced at me, and the moment of uncontrollable rage was over. The danger had passed.

Törni had underestimated this woman. In truth, we both had. He went by appearances; that was his modus operandi. I tried not to. But Törni was fundamentally a military man: he liked order, structure, and rules. He viewed the world in somewhat simplistic ways. Despite our personal history, our mutual grudge, I respected his commendations, his steel in the heat of battle, his unflinching calm under fire. But I suspected that there was much more to Ebba Black than met the eye—I sensed she had her own ghosts.

"On the list he goes," Ebba muttered almost inaudibly, as if to herself.

"Sorry?" I asked, bemused. Ebba shook her head.

"Just mental bookkeeping," she said louder, still staring at Törni. There was silence before she spoke again. "You asked to see me about the outage. My organization has no role in that. I could tell you this was the work of big tech—a land grab, so to speak, for more business real estate—but you wouldn't believe me." Ebba leaned back in her chair, folding her arms again and arching her right eyebrow. I'd never seen a woman with such dark, lacy, thin eyebrows. "You'll need to get the evidence for yourself, to see it with your own eyes, in order to believe. So instead, what I will do is tell you more about Language Unplugged."

Now I raised an eyebrow. "We understand Babel—" Ebba fixed me with a dark stare. "I mean, your organization has developed some kind of untethering technology."

"Correct. But if your respective agencies want evidence—blueprints, for instance, and proof of concept—you will have to give me and my operation amnesty, including Erebus McDenizen's immediate release. We can help, given the crisis, but I need at the very least a guarantee for my people." I was slightly taken aback by Ebba's candor. "You had no right to torture him," she muttered with quiet indignation.

I ignored her last remark. "Could you elaborate on what you mean?" I asked. "In terms of help you can provide. Untethering. To mitigate the effects of the outage. Before we get into details of any potential arrangement ... so that we're all on the same page." I was attempting to regain control. This was supposed to be our interview, after all.

Ebba lifted her hands before placing them back neatly on her lap, palms facing upwards. "We have developed an untethering technology—a surgical procedure that allows the connection between the language chip and the external language streaming source to be severed while retaining default language status and a voice print. The patient can select a single language to retain post-op without the need for streaming and subscription to an LS package."

My mind was racing. This all felt so far-fetched. Given the security protocols in place, it beggared belief that anyone could be untethered from language streaming while retaining their sec-code and hence their voice print; that they could still function in the voice command security landscape. Ebba was watching me intently. She no doubt guessed I was skeptical.

"We've developed a technique to administer a sonic shock to the ear implant without affecting the integrity of the language chip. However, the procedure does require the insertion of a memory plug, placed below the scalp, which downloads the entire lexical database, what you might think of as vocabulary and grammar, of the subject's pre-selected default language prior to untethering. This gets connected to the untethered language chip, creating a closed loop. Basically, the individual has standalone linguistic ability in their chosen language without ever needing to stream again."

I gulped, suddenly realizing the full magnitude of what she had just revealed. Language streaming was an industry that generated quadrillions of e-Continentals each year. An entire ecosystem was built on it. And Ebba Black threatened to tear it up, to make it obsolete with her new technology. Törni intervened at this point. Of course he would.

"That's illegal. Union lang-law prohibits any form of tampering with UG tech. And it's corporate theft." Ebba gave him a withering look of pity before glancing at me. She didn't need to say anything. I could tell what she was thinking. We were beyond lang-laws. People were dying in the streets; they were stacked up in sports stadiums with meager food rations while the authorities tried to figure out what to do.

Ebba's expression flickered with dark rage before she gathered herself, regaining her composure. "Full disclosure, Captain. I really don't like you. Just to have that out of the way. But I'm going to give you a fool's pardon. For the time being." I glanced sideways at Törni. His gawping expression was just priceless.

"You talked about a lexical plug—an implant that downloads a lexical database. Any provider in particular?" I asked. Ebba smiled faintly.

"I like you, Emyr. You are perceptive," she said. "You ask the right questions. May I call you that, Emyr?" she asked, staring directly into my eyes.

"Appleton," I blurted out.

"You see—smart too," Ebba replied.

"But that *is* corporate theft," said Törni, seemingly unable to control his anger, "from the world's most prestigious commercial LS provider."

"Theft," Ebba began, "is the act of rendering around sixty-five percent of the world's population mute. We're talking about seven point two billion people. Theft is the act of storing their language in space and selling it back to them for exorbitant monthly fees and then inventing voice command security protocols so that they simply cannot function in their new techno-environment unless they continue to pay." She slowly crossed her arms again. "That, Captain dearest, is the parade example of theft," she said decisively with a sarcastic flourish. She leaned forward slowly before continuing, her black eyes smoking. "Worse, governments are in the pockets of big tech. They are complicit, having enshrined this unspeakable evil in lang-laws." There was silence for a few seconds. "And in any case, Appleton doesn't own language. Language is not the proprietary technology of a single corporation. It belongs to all of us. We, the people."

"If we are to believe you, Dr. Black ..." I began.

She shook her head. "Please, call me Ebba."

"Ebba. You claim to be the ultimate altruist. Babel—I mean, your organization—has nothing to do with the outage."

"Correct. As for altruism, I'm not to everyone's taste," she said. "Some even seem to think I have a polarizing personality." She flashed Törni her evil-joker grin once more for good measure. "But you want evidence? That we have the procedure to untether chips?"

Silence reigned. Ebba stood with careful precision and walked back to her desk. She picked up a small handheld device, clicked on a button, and began talking into it. "Ursula, would you mind stepping back in? Over." There was a brief crackle of static.

"Yes, Ebba," Ursula's voice replied. Ebba turned back to us. She smirked at our expressions.

"It's called a walkie-talkie," she said, dropping the device casually onto her desk. "We don't do internet here. Well, at least not in here," she added, gesturing around the room. There was a light knock on the door and the burly female bodyguard stepped back in.

"Ursula," Ebba said, "would you mind showing these gentlemen your lexical chip implant?"

The woman walked over to us and placed her large hands on her hair. She parted it in the middle, bending slightly so that Törni and I could see. There was a small visible scar, completely healed, right in the center of her crown.

"Gentlemen, I don't suppose you have a portable LS orb to hand?" Ebba asked. Törni nodded. "Scan her, please." Ursula waited impassively as the Finn stood and pulled out an LS scanning orb from his utility belt. He issued a voice command, activating a small thin handle that slowly auto-extended from the center of the orb, and held the spherical scanner above Ursula's head. The small device began humming as he moved back and forth above her crown.

Törni withdrew the orb and inspected a readout on a small screen on one side of it. "She has no LS rebounds," he said, astounded.

"Please put your little tool away," Ebba replied snidely. "And yet she can process language. Ursula understands us and can reply."

"And she has accent differentiators," I added.

"That's the beauty of the high-end lexical packages offered by Appleton," replied Ebba. "Ursula chose hers, which we downloaded to her memory implant. So she now has the dulcet tones of a Wessex accent, as once spoken by her grandparents in Exeter, Old Kingdom. And she is free of streaming forever."

"Enough of these parlor tricks," Törni almost spat at her. "How are you really doing this?"

Ebba glanced at him scathingly before addressing her bodyguard. "Ursula, would you go and ask Horcha to step in?" The bodyguard left quietly. Horchata Chiu entered the room.

"Scan Horcha," Ebba commanded. Törni again performed the operation.

"No rebounds," Ebba said before Törni could confirm the finding. "And you have LS rebound records for her, don't you?" she asked me.

"Her rebound records stopped three years ago," I replied.

"That's when she was untethered. Thanks, Horcha. I think the gentlemen have seen enough parlor tricks for one day." Ebba nodded sarcastically at Törni, who sat back down. "I can prove that Language Unplugged is a non-violent protocol. We have a lab and we are willing to share the technology. We can help."

I frowned. "But your untethering tech, that requires a functioning language chip. Which won't help with Tele3 users. They have scarred chips. Permanently feral, hence out-soc."

Ebba shook her head. "Appleton has secret stockpiles of first-gen chips. Ready to go. Enough for everyone." Now my jaw dropped. "You didn't know! Of course not," she added. "Marc Barron's carefully guarded secret. Create a catastrophe. Hold the world to ransom. Then take control of the market under cover of a global language outage."

"You're making this up," Törni spat at her.

"Am I?" Ebba asked archly. "Emergency board meetings of all the other big providers affected by the cyberattacks around the globe, including Avalon, Dokomo, Samkee, and Zhengfei, indicate that new servers will need to be deployed to resolve the current scrambling issues. Preparation and launching of new systems into low space orbit will take months. The current internal prognosis of these companies ranges from nine months to a year to have their respective streaming issues resolved." With her words, I felt my face draining of color. My expression must have given my shock away. "You didn't know?"

"That's a long time," I whispered hoarsely.

"I know. But our technology can be scaled within a few weeks for mass production if we have access to the Union's UG tech plants and neuromedical centers. We can provide full biomedical specs and techno-surgical support. I have a team of advisors who can assist. We can solve this for everyone, once and for all, and give language back to the people."

What Ebba was proposing would require emergency legislation and political courage to set aside Appleton's legal claim, their patent. And if she were right, Appleton's stockpile of first-gen chips would need to be requisitioned.

"And where are your medical experts? In Freetown?" I asked. A thoughtful look came over Ebba's face.

"Freetown's location remains my secret for now."

"We're obviously going to have to consult," I said. "We're talking about an overhaul of legislation, governmental and corporate approvals ..."

"I think we're done here," Törni hissed abruptly, rising to his feet and his full height. "In the meantime, don't go anywhere."

Ebba glanced up at him from her seat with a hint of malevolence.

"In that case, *enchanté*, Captain. I suspect we will have the pleasure again soon."

CHAPTER 16

Back outside, the afternoon sun was already beginning to set. A damp chill was settling into the evening. And Törni was fuming. He wasn't the talkative type at the best of times. But now his studied silence carried menace, while his taut expression conveyed pent-up violence. I knew the signs.

I followed him, only stopping when we reached the parked Skyraider. But Törni walked past it, beyond the vertipad. I climbed in, watching him through the cabin window.

Once he was safely out of earshot, he began dictating a voice memo into his holotab. No doubt reporting in. To von Böhm, probably. *I'd better do the same*, I thought, *prepare a memo for Lina and the director*. I activated my holotab and selected the voice memo app before dictating.

"Interview with EB complete. Subject claims Babel is not implicated in the language outage or preceding cyberattacks. Re. Language Unplugged protocol: subject also claims that Babel has developed a neuroprosthetic implant that stores a lexical database. It syncs with the native language chip, creating a closed loop. The individual retains linguistic and voice command autonomy without the need for language streaming. EB offers the tech in return for amnesty. However, the lexical database derives from Appleton, she claims. Significant risk of legal and political fallout from this. Subject claims to have insider knowledge that the world's biggest providers, including Union providers such as Samkee, may be subject to a delay of up to a year before their normal streaming capabilities are restored. Subject also claims Appleton has an existing stockpile of first-gen chips available. Any confirmation on whether that's the case? Please advise on next steps."

I sent my message and waited for Törni. I glanced out of the Skyraider. He was now pacing the gravel driveway, apparently on a facecall. Just then, I received an alert in my ear implant. I still had my holotab activated; it was from Lotte.

When I called back, she answered and began talking immediately. She was both flustered and excited. "You need to hear this, Emyr. You really do!"

I furrowed my brow. "Hello yourself," I muttered. She nodded at me.

"Sorry. Manners. But this is important."

"Okay. Hear what?" I asked with slight irritation. It was only then that I realized I actually felt lingering resentment that she had ended it—our affair. Somehow it now stung, despite my initial relief. *Get over yourself, Emyr,* I thought, willing myself to feel less curmudgeonly as I saw her face again.

"Someone just sent through an audio file, literally right now. Deposited on the Europol secure server."

"Who?" I snapped.

"That's just it, I don't know. I received an anonymous alert. God knows how they even managed to get access to the server."

"The alert was addressed to you?" I asked.

"Only my credentials were pinged. Weird, isn't it? I don't know what to make of it. But get this ..."

"What?" I asked, becoming intrigued.

"The audio file is entitled *Catch and Kill*."

"Catch and kill," I muttered. "What does that mean?"

Lotte shrugged. "I have no clue." She was back to her rouged, made-up best. *Now that we are history*, I found myself thinking, not without a hint of bitterness. "There's reference to it in the recording. The file was clearly securely encrypted. The decryption process has degraded the audio quality. It's still not great, but you can more or less make it out. A woman's voice."

"What do we know about the source of the file?"

"That's the interesting thing. I've just finished an acoustic scan, and managed to recover a digital watermark. It's been hacked from a secure Appleton server."

"Appleton?" I exclaimed, now hooked.

"Exactly. I'll stream the audio. It's not very long." Then there was a slight crackle, a hiss, followed by a woman's voice.

"We've received the uploaded footage. He was rigged using a frog tie?" Something inaudible from a second voice, perhaps male, then, "So she used webbing to restrain him. He was dressed in a lace babydoll—nice touch. He wanted a golden shower. Very submissive and slow edging, with whip control. Just what we wanted." There was the crackle of the second, almost inaudible voice, then the woman again: "He wouldn't have invited her there unless she had the ghost chip fitted." The second voice could now be heard again. The first part was inaudible, then the voice finished by saying "... kill." This was followed by the female voice again. "Yes, we have our catch and kill. The Magisterium won't expect it. He will ensure they comply. You'll arrange for Lady Raven to be wired the e-Continentals from your secure account as we requested?" The audio stopped there. Lotte's wide eyes stared at me.

"What do you make of it, Lotte?" I asked. "Lady Raven to be

wired Continental credits. Who the hell is Lady Raven?"

Lotte shook her head. "The Magisterium?" she asked.

"Did it actually say that?" I asked with incredulity. "The joint presidents in Brussels?" I mused. "Hmmm ... catch and kill. But what could that be?"

She shrugged. "You're the smart detective."

"Powerful interests covering up the truth?" I mused, thinking aloud, starting to feel the nagging itch again, something hidden, missing parts of the puzzle.

"But what's being covered up?" Lotte asked.

"Ghost chip!" I exclaimed, as the phrase from the audio file suddenly made sense.

"What?"

"Our Babel hacker, Erebus McDenizen. When I interrogated him earlier, he was talking about ghost chips."

"And what did you find out?"

"Babel hacked into a secure Appleton server and recovered a file. He said Marc Barron was discussing these so-called ghost chips."

"What are they?" Lotte asked.

"Some new type of UG tech, he claimed. They apparently don't give off an LS rebound."

"Wow," Lotte said. She paused for a moment, stunned. "If that's true, then Appleton will have done it again! Folks will pay a lot of money to get hold of those for their newborns' privacy."

"It sounded like it was some kind of add-on—an implant that could enhance an existing language chip, cloak the LS rebounds somehow."

"In an adult?" Lotte asked, even more incredulous.

"Maybe. McDenizen didn't seem to know that much."

"Then Appleton really will have cornered the market. Isolation booths will become obsolete—no more hardwiring to a VirDa."

"In the United Federation, maybe. Their lang-law is different. No chance here," I said decisively. After all, Union lang-law required a person's location to be verifiable at all times. Something that disguised LS rebounds, well, that stood no chance of passing muster this side of the Atlantic.

"Unless the law was changed?" Lotte gave me a knowing nod.

"The Magisterium would never approve something like that," I said.

"The Magisterium ..." Lotte whispered as if in warning. "Didn't we just hear that mentioned in the audio file?" She raised one eyebrow. "How did it go?" she asked, changing the subject. "The interview with your mystery woman?"

"Ebba?" I asked.

Lotte blinked quickly. "Oh, I see. It's Ebba, is it? First names now?" It almost sounded as if there was hurt in her voice.

I frowned. "It's not like that. Anyway, she doesn't seem to be behind any of this. The outage. She wants to help. The Language Unplugged protocol—she claims it's some kind of new technology that allows a user to retain language chip functionality without the need for streaming."

"Well, that does sound impressive."

"Except that her solution would torpedo the entire language streaming industry."

"Then the wolves will be after her."

"Yes. And she's a small woman with just the one bodyguard."

Lotte smiled at me knowingly. "You like her. Be careful, Emyr, please."

And with that, she called off. I glanced out the window. Törni was also done with his facecall and was heading back to the Skyraider. I knew I had to drop him off at the Proelium, in Brussels, before I could head back to The Hague. As he climbed in, he looked pleased with himself. He sat in the seat next to me in the passenger cabin. "All set?" I asked.

He nodded. "A meeting is being set up with High Representative Lopez. This evening in the Imperium. Decisions to be made. The General wants me there to provide a briefing." I raised an eyebrow. I knew what that meant. Now that Ebba Black had confirmed that Babel wasn't behind the outage, CyberForce and von Böhm had carte blanche to lobby the Magisterium for military action against the Russians.

As I was contemplating what Törni's self-satisfaction augured, I received an alert in my ear. I activated my holotab. A message from Lina. I smiled as I read it, then glanced at Törni; his smug satisfaction would be short-lived.

Lina was conveying a message. The director would also be attending the meeting with the High Representative, albeit virtually. But he wanted me there too, in person. According to Lina, the director was concerned that a pretext to declare war would be manufactured. He wanted a cool head in the room and an evidence-based appraisal. An invitation would follow.

I turned to Törni. "It seems I'll be joining you for the meeting with the High Representative." I allowed myself a broad grin. Törni's look of dismay literally made my day.

CHAPTER 17

Once back in Brussels, we taxied to the disembarkation zone underneath the Proelium. As soon as the Skyraider was stationary and the exit doors activated, Törni jumped out and was gone. He couldn't have left the vehicle any faster if he'd tried. He knew he would see me in the High Representative's cabinet chamber in the Imperium in fifteen minutes.

I'd received a memoclip en route: Marchaud would be awaiting me again. He was also due to attend the meeting with High Representative Lopez. As I reached the meeting point adjacent to the disembarkation zone, Marchaud wrinkled his nose at me. After patting me lightly on the arm, he led me to the Link.

"All the important decisions are taken in the Imperium," Marchaud announced with faux solemnity as we moved along the Link travelator, through the underground transit canal connecting the Proelium and the Imperium buildings. "The spooks and bureaucrats in the Imperium tell the Magisterium what to do. So the reality is, the Imperium rules the Union, while we in the Proelium wait to receive our marching orders. All the really important functions sit in the Imperium: the External Action Service, the Ministry for War, the Union Intelligence Service, the High Representative himself ... You understand me?" He wrinkled his nose again. "Have you ever met *Señor Control?*" he asked abruptly.

"Excuse me? Met who?"

"Monsieur Lopez. That's what the civil service pool call him," Marchaud whispered conspiratorially. "Brash, they say. And quick to resort to foul-mouthed tirades. But above all, he likes to be in control. He demands obedience from his assistants, the heads of his agencies. Fierce eyes. Very intense … if you understand me." Marchaud nudged me while gazing deep into my eyes so that I would understand the profound significance of this information. I sighed in exasperation.

"No, I'm afraid I've never had the pleasure."

Then Marchaud wittered on about Lopez's designer suits with pastel-colored shirts from Madrid's most exclusive tailors. Tutting, he implied it all went on his executive clothing allowance. The Union was footing the bill, he claimed with a dismissive shake of his head. Marchaud frowned. He certainly appeared to enjoy engaging in his own personal psychodrama in finding the banal suspicious.

"So Lopez has taste," I remarked absently.

"Not my taste," Marchaud muttered, before taking off his kepi to wipe his glowing brow with a neatly folded khaki handkerchief branded with CyberForce insignia. I threw him a dismissive sideways glance and smirked to myself. I doubted he would know what fashion was if it jumped up and down on him.

I ignored him, half tapping my wrist chip and glancing at my bioclock. Still ten minutes before the meeting. Apparently just enough time for Marchaud to segue into the formidable Alojzija Žagar. She had been summoned to join Lopez and von Böhm after our meeting with Lopez.

"What will CyberForce's Head of Cyberwarfare be there for?" I asked, now intrigued.

"What do you think?" Marchaud replied, answering my question rhetorically before proceeding to answer it anyway. "War is coming. The High Representative has decided."

"I think that's a decision for the joint presidents. For the Union Commission and Council of Leaders in the Magisterium," I muttered dismissively. Marchaud flashed me a faint smile—pity, maybe. *What does he know, that I don't?* I wondered.

"She likes them young," Marchaud whispered as he leaned toward me, still talking about Alojzija Žagar. "Never married," he confided. *Not my type, then,* I thought wryly. "Did you know her first name means *war* in Slovenian? Fierce those slavs." Marchaud was warming to his subject. He then began describing what he called *the great scandal* of Saint-Cyr—something about how the fearsome Brigadier General Žagar had become involved with a young male cadet at the storied military school. I didn't know how Marchaud managed to find out such things. Just listening to him was exhausting. I stopped paying attention, absently watching the military staff coming in the opposite direction on the travelator, heading back to military command in the Proelium.

* * *

Törni was already waiting in the anteroom to the cabinet chamber when Marchaud and I arrived. Alojzija Žagar, a tall, buxom woman dressed in combat uniform, was waiting too. She contrived to brush against my arm as Marchaud and I walked in. She glanced at me coyly through slightly narrowed eyes.

As soon as the welcome gynoid had scanned us, it ushered Törni, Marchaud, and me into the cabinet chamber. I could feel Žagar eying me up as she remained outside, awaiting her turn with Lopez.

Inside, High Representative Lopez and General Eduard von Böhm were already present, as was my director, Rodrigo Dominguez. Lopez and von Böhm were seated, while the director was present by video conference call, his round, perspiring face bearing out via a large holographic screen on a robotic mobile telepresence unit. He gave me a faint smile as he saw me appear through the sliding door.

I glanced around the chamber, the inner sanctum of the Imperium, where the decisions taken affected the lives of millions of people across the Union and beyond. The chamber was dominated by two features. One was the cabinet table, at the head of which the High Representative was seated in a bizarre power pose, both arms stretched out and down, palms splayed downward, pressing hard on the table in front of him. My first thought was that this was a guy who took himself way too seriously.

Von Böhm was a slender figure in military fatigues with thinning gray hair, and a dramatically arched nose which lent him the mien of a hawk. He sat to Lopez's right, on the side of the long table across from us. The director was staring fixedly out from the telepresence unit that was positioned further along, to von Böhm's right.

The long, clear table was manufactured from micromagnetic piston smart glass. It featured flowing holographic waveguide displays, fading from pale white to a hint of rose and back again in a slow cascading swirl of soothing color.

High Representative Lopez was framed by the second,

even more striking feature—two tall, elongated stained-glass windows in the high wall directly behind him. They gave out onto a sealed light shaft that rose several hundred meters into the sky, allowing an artery of natural light to run down through the Imperium building. The design had won architectural plaudits. The blues and reds of the opaque refracted light cast a sinister luminescence around Lopez.

Marchaud and I sat opposite von Böhm, to Lopez's left. But Törni had to be special. He walked around the table and took the nearest available seat to von Böhm.

Lopez began tapping on the table with his fingers. He stopped abruptly as he opened the meeting. "The presidents of the Commission and Council of Leaders have asked for an appropriate response to the cyberattacks. I will make a recommendation. But, of course, your input is crucial. Which is why senior officers from CyberForce and Europol are here." Lopez glanced at von Böhm. "General, why don't you brief us?" Lopez was a large man with a full black beard. And he was portly, with hints of black chest hair peeking over his unbuttoned shirt neck.

Von Böhm cleared his throat before speaking quietly but with conviction. "We now know for certain that the cyberattack originated from Russian Federation territory. And other than Appleton, the only commercial provider unaffected is BeeDirect. Europol suggests this is just circumstantial evidence, but—"

Before von Böhm could continue, Lopez intervened. "I understand that Europol has now fully explored their theory that the cyberattack is the work of Babel, correct?" he asked, glancing at the director, who looked at me. I gave a curt affirmative nod. Törni was watching me intently. There was the merest suggestion of a smirk pulling at the corners of his thick lips. It was in moments like this that it nettled me that I had never had the chance to retaliate for his sucker punch back in that bar in Cantina.

"Sir, we have interrogated a Babel asset in the Proelium and interviewed Dr. Black in the Nordic Republic. Both deny any Babel involvement," Törni said, addressing Lopez. *He can't help himself, apparently*, I thought.

The director jumped in at that point, addressing von Böhm. "I see where you're going, Eduard. But we need to be careful not to rush to judgment. As you've rightly pointed out, the evidence against the Russians is circumstantial."

Von Böhm narrowed his gaze, shaking his head. "Not anymore. We have new intel." The director's face on the telepresence screen flashed a look of surprise. "Colonel, why don't you explain?" Von Böhm was staring at Marchaud. Now it was my turn to be surprised as I turned to examine Marchaud's face, seated next to me. He had not shared any new intel with me.

Marchaud wrinkled his nose and glanced around nervously before addressing High Representative Lopez.

"We intercepted a facecall recording a short time ago. Between the Russian Federation president, Bulchovi junior, and an aide. It appears to be off the record. Bulchovi is claiming Federation responsibility for the outage. Our cryptography department concluded that the facecall record is genuine. It was obtained from Russian Federation servers. It provides conclusive evidence of Russian involvement."

At this bombshell, I bristled in my seat while the director jumped in. "Commander, do you know about this?" he snapped at me. He could see from my shocked expression that I didn't. "Why hasn't this been shared with Europol? We also need to verify its authenticity," he demanded, clearly irate at being blindsided.

I turned to Marchaud. "Can we see the facecall recording?"

Before Marchaud could respond, Lopez intervened. "There's no need. I have seen the evidence with my own eyes. A final decision will be made by the presidents following consultation with the Council of Leaders. But it should be clear what my recommendation will be. There has to be a reckoning. That's why I'll be speaking with Brigadier General Žagar in a little while, to better understand CyberForce's tactical strike capabilities."

The director was staring out at me from the screen. I needed to buy some time. Whatever this new facecall evidence was that Marchaud had, I knew it wasn't the Russians. It couldn't be.

I cleared my throat. "High Representative," I began, "I know we need to be seen to act. But this, blaming the Federation, it's too obvious. Just give us a bit more time."

Lopez glanced across at me. I saw his dismissive look. "Commander Morgan, isn't it?" I nodded. "The evidence speaks for itself. Europol can now fully focus on crisis management. We have a humanitarian catastrophe on our hands." With that, Lopez turned toward the director. "Rodrigo, see to it that your man stands down." I watched the director's face as he stared back at Lopez, unblinking. We both knew that the joint presidents would follow the recommendation of the High Representative. The Magisterium always did. And no one liked the Bulchovis. Father and son, keeping it in the family, autocratic rule, leading a declining Tier Two regional power. *CyberForce will provide Lopez with military options that he will sell to the presidents as a clean kill. And that will be too tempting*, I thought.

But there was no such thing as a clean kill. The Bulchovi family wouldn't take this lying down. And Bulchovi junior fancied himself as the new Peter the Great. The Russians would fight back. We were heading for an even greater disaster. I decided I needed to change tack, to try and reason with Lopez. I began again. "If we're focusing on crisis management, then we could actually use Babel. Ebba Black may have developed untethering technology. It might provide a short-term fix while we reset following the outage. These are unprecedented times."

"I've heard what she's offering," Lopez said, now devoid of emotion. "The General has already briefed me." I glanced across the table at von Böhm. Törni's eyes were now full on me—a knowing smirk. "Do you know what I have had to deal with? This afternoon?" Lopez asked in a withering tone. "A one-hour facecall with the UFA Secretary of State and with Marc Barron. And just now, a further hour with Appleton's not-so-subtle legal team. If Marc Barron tells the Secretary of State to jump, she'll ask how high." Lopez eyed the room malevolently. His eyes came back to me. "Marc Barron has more financial power and more political clout than some states combined." He sighed and sank back into his high-backed chair. The unruly black hair on his arms and neck glinted in the refracted light cast into the room by the stained-glass windows behind him. There was an uncomfortable pause.

"High Representative?" von Böhm probed quietly. Lopez came back to us, his momentary distraction giving way to renewed fiery lucidity.

"The Secretary of State expects immediate action against this Ebba Black."

"High Representative, we need to tread carefully. Ebba Black is a Nordic national. She's not a citizen of either the Grand

Union or the United Federation of America," the director said quietly.

"I'm not talking about extradition if that's what you mean, Rodrigo," Lopez snapped before sighing. "With this cyberterrorist outfit on our doorstep, we're talking copyright infringements, theft of virtual proprietary assets, fraud—the list goes on. We can't be seen to be doing nothing. The Federation is our closest ally. There are political ramifications of all this. We've been asked to ... assist."

I glanced at Lopez. *Assist? What the hell does that mean?*

"Sir," I began, "we're talking about millions of people feral, and out-soc in the case of Tele3. We could negotiate with Marc Barron. Ebba Black claims to have a hack for the Appleton lexical database. We might be able to syndicate rights on a fixed-term basis to Appleton's proprietary data. Given the state of emergency, Appleton could be asked to play its part."

Lopez shook his head. "Appleton won't agree, ever!" he hissed at me. "Don't you get it?" I was momentarily stunned by his air of defeatism. "Barron has made an offer. For any ferals with scrambled status that wish to switch providers, a free extended trial period for the top Appleton lexical package on both sides of the Atlantic."

I could see the director was aghast. I was flabbergasted too. "Surely this catastrophe shouldn't be allowed to become a marketing opportunity," I retorted after a moment. "And in any case, the Appleton proposal would only help ferals. What about the out-socs—Tele3 subscribers with scarred chips?"

"High Representative," said the director from his large screen, finally intervening. "The commander is right. We have nothing to lose by exploring the Ebba Black option."

Lopez shook his head in a resigned fashion. "I wanted to go

into politics to help ..." He smiled weakly, looking around the faces arranged before him. "I ..." He seemed to be searching for words. He rubbed a finger in a corner of one eye.

"High Representative?" von Böhm asked with slight alarm. Lopez brushed away his concern by partially raising his hand, collecting himself.

"Marc Barron has graciously offered to also help with the out-soc. There's been one positive development, at least. It turns out there's a significant reserve of first-gen chips held by Appleton. We've been offered a subsidy on implant replacement procedures for all former Tele3 subscribers." I heard the director's gasp from the screen before I heard my own. "Both the external and domestic commissioners for crisis management, here and in the Magisterium, are scaling the logistics as we speak. We'll have everyone's chips replaced within a few months. They'll be offered Appleton's subscription package on discounted terms. It'll resolve the crisis. An end to the outage."

As I processed what Lopez had just announced, I knew what this meant. Tele3, the Union's homegrown provider, would be gone. Appleton would clean up and effectively take over its entire market segment. *And if that could happen here, in the Grand Union, then what about other less powerful federations and states?*

"Sir," I said, "wouldn't it be easier and much cheaper just to repeal lang-law? There are alternatives to voice command tech. Biometric-based recognition technologies are equally secure— retinal scanning, for instance."

"That's enough!" Lopez snarled, banging down a fist on the glass table as its holographic waveguide display eased past underneath his clenched hand. He was red-faced and positively fuming. "Don't forget where *you* are, *your* rank, and *who* you're addressing." The entire chamber fell deathly silent.

I was stunned by the angry response I had managed to induce. Something didn't add up. I knew that Lopez was tightly coiled, but his overreaction was extreme, even for him. Across from me, Törni was grinning. He was enjoying this. Inside, I was seething.

Lopez scanned our faces in silence for a moment before speaking once more. "Director Dominguez, I think we can now excuse you. And Commander Morgan, you are free to return to Europol HQ."

"But ... what about Ebba Black?" I asked.

Lopez glanced at me sharply. "Yes, we have to make a decision on that. Eduard, please stay on. You too, Captain Törni."

As I walked out of the chamber, I could feel Törni's gaze burning into the small of my back. I knew this wasn't going to end well.

CHAPTER 18

The next morning, in my office at Europol HQ, I had a headache that I couldn't shake. I was sitting at my office console, holding a cupstock of hot coffee. *Day three of the language outage,* I thought grimly as I synced with my office VirDa. The meeting with High Representative Lopez the evening before had left me unsettled. Too many whiskies in my apartment once back from Brussels. I never took anything for a nagging hangover; I suffered stoically. *It's good for me,* I told myself.

It was still early, and not all my management team was in yet. I absently watched tendrils of steam drift out of the cup. I knew the order would come soon, down the chain of command. Lina would deliver the news. My division would be assigned to crisis management like the rest of Europol. The politicians in the Imperium had already *determined* who had caused the cyberattacks, buying into the explanation coming out of Proelium's CyberForce command. So, I would officially be taken off the language outage case.

A vibration in my ear implant pulled me out of my funk. It was a virtual knock at my door. I'd forgotten I hadn't updated my office status to *available.*

"VirDa, open door."

Pieter and Lotte marched in together, clearly agitated about something. "How did it go with the High Representative?" Pieter asked. They stood in front of me on the other side of my console.

"A bit odd," I muttered. "Marchaud claims to have a video file in which Bulchovi takes responsibility for the outage."

"We've not heard of any such file," said Lotte, frowning. "I would need to verify its authenticity."

I nodded. "That's the first thing that's odd. CyberForce aren't releasing it to us."

"And the second?" Pieter asked.

"The High Representative was a bit too quick to side with von Böhm ... to decide on war. Especially given what that means—what's at stake."

Just then I received a reminder alert in my ear implant. My expression must have shown it. "The autopsy report?" Pieter asked. I looked at him quizzically. "It was finalized last night as you requested."

"Have you seen it yet?" Lotte asked. I glanced back at their expectant faces. *That explains their excitement.*

"The file read status shows he hasn't even opened it," Pieter muttered at Lotte before staring at me slightly accusingly. I sighed, holding my hand up for silence, and gestured that they sit. I blinked on the *new reports* icon on the screen projecting from the fusion bar of my console. And there I had it—the autopsy on our mystery CEO, Dhruv Gasper from California. It had indeed come in late the previous evening.

As soon as I began reading, I knew something was definitely up. Cause of death was brain irradiation, of all things. Gasper's language chip had exploded, which supposed to be impossible. The autopsy also showed evidence of another unexplained implant—a cortical plug inserted under the surface of the skull, with evidence of recent surgery. This new implant was connected to his auditory and optic nerves. The report was inconclusive as to whether the new implant was related to the cause of death, as the damage to the brain's vasculature was so severe, any further determination was impossible. Death had been instantaneous, coinciding precisely with the language outage.

I glanced over the top of my translucent screen. Both Pieter and Lotte were watching me intently. Only Pieter had taken a seat. "It doesn't make any sense," I mumbled.

Lotte moved slightly closer, in front of the console. "It doesn't, does it?" she asked rhetorically. "Language chips don't just explode. And we've no idea what the new implant is."

"Foul play? Meant to look like an accident?" I suggested.

"Under cover of a global language outage," Lotte said.

"Which means that whoever took out Mr. Gasper knew there was going to be a cyberattack," I added, looking knowingly at them both. "And I just happened to be there, in the wrong place at the wrong time, to witness his demise."

"Inconvenient for someone," Lotte said.

"Which is why we both did some late-night digging," added Pieter, his red face rubbering over my screen from where he was seated.

"And what did your digging reveal?" I asked.

Lotte smiled. "You first, Pieter. Then he can get the juicy details. And see her hologram, too."

I glanced at Lotte, puzzled; Pieter smirked at her before addressing me.

"My data science team has been picking through the vehicle's flight data. Gasper departed from Brussels and traveled on an intercity skyway to Paris before heading out of Union airspace, ready to cross the Atlantic to get back to the Republic—to get home."

"He departed from Brussels?" I asked.

"A vertipad on one corner of Rue d'Aerschot, north of the Gare de Bruxelles-Nord," Pieter replied smugly.

"Any idea what he was doing there?"

"I've uncovered quite a bit," said Pieter, suddenly breathless. I could sense his excitement. "Rue d'Aerschot is the heart of the red-light district. North of the main train station there's a labyrinth of brothels, clubs, cybersex parlors. An entire underground scene."

"And that's where he departed from?" I asked.

Pieter nodded. "Exactly there. I'll send you the details." He activated his holotab and issued a blink command for a proximity share. I blinked at my console to accept, and details of Gasper's itinerary popped up. I could feel Pieter's eyes on me as I scanned them.

It turned out that on November 5th, Gasper had traveled to Europe from California for one scheduled appointment. But that was in Paris at 5 p.m. Gasper had apparently first traveled to Brussels—despite having no official business there—where he had spent around two hours.

"So what was he doing in that part of Brussels? Sex tourism?"

"Probably not. Lotte will get to that. But first, you'll want some background on Gasper. It makes for interesting reading," Pieter said.

I nodded as I activated a second blinkable that appeared on my screen. It opened a mind-mapping report, prepared by Pieter, entitled 'Subject Background.' I began scanning the key details.

Gasper was forty-eight and a former employee of Appleton. *Curious*, I thought. *Everything keeps somehow circling back to Marc Barron*. Gasper had set up Drones Kineto seven years ago as both CEO and CFO. Around three years ago, he had hired a new Chief Financial Officer, one Dwayne Kline, now thirty-five, who had been promoted to company chairperson eighteen months ago. The report concluded that this Kline had bought a stake in the company, and in addition to being Gasper's business partner, he had also become his lover. But they remained discreet, not marrying or entering into a civil partnership. *So Dwayne Kline wasn't his next of kin*, I thought.

I glanced at Pieter, now curious. "Who provided authorization for the autopsy?"

"Mr. Gasper's elderly mother. Lives in Ottawa."

I turned back to the screen. Gasper had moved to California at nineteen to study advanced robotic technology at Berkeley. He had stayed on to do a PhD in Unmanned Aerial Vehicle tech. *Ha—drones, of course*, I thought. He was then hired by Appleton, eventually heading their R&D drone division. Seven years ago, he and his entourage, an Appleton engineering team, had moved to just outside LA and set up Drones Kineto.

"Did Gasper poach staff from Appleton?" I asked Pieter.

"It's not as straightforward as that. The whole thing seems to have been underwritten by Marc Barron," Pieter said, pointing. I scrolled down further.

I saw that Drones Kineto was wholly owned by a shell company, with no employees and no assets. But what I saw next made me take a sharp intake of breath. The address of the shell company was listed as Appleton HQ, in Silicon Valley.

"That's not all," said Pieter as he saw my reaction. "The shell company has two directors listed … we had to work hard to trace it all back, but …"

"Marc Barron is one, I bet," I said.

"Right. But you'll never guess the other."

"His Chief Science Officer, Hadean Burr-Alston?" Pieter shook his head. "Then tell me," I said, frowning.

"Jürgen Fleischman," he replied, watching my face carefully.

"The Head of Interpol?" I asked, incredulous.

"The world's top-ranking police officer, no less," Pieter replied somberly. *What the hell's going on?* I wondered. This made no sense.

Just then, Lotte jumped in. She placed both arms on the surface and leaned in, looking at me through the translucent screen.

"It turns out that Fleischman and Marc Barron go back a long way," she began. "They studied together in Paris in their twenties." My face must have been a picture, because Lotte started laughing.

"Paris?" I asked.

"Tell him, Pieter."

Pieter nodded. "Lotte's right. In 2087, the year after human trials for UG tech had been approved in the Republic, even before the United Federation came into being."

"Why would Marc Barron go study in Paris?" I asked, at a loss.

"Apparently to research a business model to exploit UG tech," Pieter said. "He attended the INSEAD business school. When he returned to California, that's when he and Burr-Alston made language chip technology commercially available before moving into voice command tech. Based on our mind-mapping, his time in Paris was instrumental in developing the business case for the voice command ecosystem."

And so the plot thickened. I took several sips of my coffee as I processed this new intel. The world's top law enforcement officer, Director Fleischman of Interpol, had been in the same business school cohort as Marc Barron at a time when Barron, apparently, was developing the strategy to make UG tech the unstoppable force that now ruled our lives. And Fleischman was, it seemed, more than a mere acquaintance. He was also a business partner. I wasn't sure if that was ethical, given the potential for conflict of interest, let alone legal. And how on earth did all this relate to the unfortunate Dhruv Gasper, now lying in a Europol mortuary with the inside of his head blown up?

I carried on perusing the background report on my screen. Gasper was politically active, very hard alt-right. He was an outspoken critic of the Chinese, their technology and industrial practices, which he viewed as a serious threat to the Californian tech industry even after the formation of the United Federation of America. He had been especially critical of Unilanguage. He had publicly denounced its decision to allow Zhengfei permanent member status of the management executive around eight years ago. It got quite nasty, the fallout playing a role in his decision to relocate from Silicon Valley to the Inland Empire, where he set up Drones Kineto. With that, I came to the end of the mind-mapping report.

"What else do we know about Gasper's relationship with this Dwayne Kline?" I asked.

"Aside from the age gap?" murmured Lotte.

"Not much so far," Pieter replied. "Mr. Kline's background is in corporate finance. A high-flyer. Stable long-term relationships with men of the same age until he met Mr. Gasper."

I sat back in my chair, rubbing my chin absently, thinking. If only my head weren't quite so bad. Something was bugging me. "But why Brussels? On November 5th, without any scheduled business?" I asked, staring at Pieter and Lotte. *What was he doing there, then?*

CHAPTER 19

I blinked to reactivate the file of Gasper's itinerary. "Is anyone going to fill me in on the juicy details that Lotte threatened me with?" Pieter and Lotte glanced at each other, then looked at me.

"Boss," Pieter began impatiently, "the audio file that Lotte received … yesterday."

"Catch and Kill? What about it?"

"There are two voices, a woman and a man," Pieter said.

"The second voice wasn't very clear," I muttered.

"The second was definitely male," Pieter replied. *He seems sure of himself,* I thought. "Lotte will explain. Anyway, the first voice—the female—mentions the identifier Lady Raven."

"I remember," I said.

"I reached out to an old contact in Vice, from my Brussels City police days. Lady Raven is a denizen of Rue d'Aerschot. Which is where Gasper departed Brussels." I raised my eyebrows. "A high-end dominatrix. She apparently has an isolation dungeon in an underground unit that she owns in the heart of the red-light district. She doesn't advertise—she doesn't need to. My contact tells me she has a long waiting list of VIPs. She sees clients in person and also offers virtual BDSM services using a bespoke Lady Raven app. She's very expensive and has a reputation for complete confidentiality. Her clients even enter into non-disclosure agreements drawn up by her personal lawyer."

"And you think our Dhruv Gasper was visiting her?" I asked.

"It's in the itinerary report," Pieter replied. I glanced back at the screen to resume perusing the itinerary Pieter had sent through. Based on LS and sec-cam records, Pieter had reconstructed Gasper's movements.

The afternoon immediately prior to the cyberattacks, Gasper had reached Brussels restricted airspace at 2.56 p.m. He'd then spent under two hours with Lady Raven in her isolation dungeon—there were no language streaming rebound records for him during that period. Then, at 4.46 p.m., his sec-code showed up again, with a sec-cam record a short time later near the confirmed address Pieter had for the dominatrix. There were then continuous sec-cam and LS records showing his pedestrian route to his hover vehicle. He left Brussels city airspace at 4.51 p.m. Gasper touched down at a vertipad location in Paris at 4.58 p.m. From there, he spent around one hour at a small robotic arm manufacturing plant, a French-registered subsidiary of Drones Kineto. That was the official business. Then, at 6.04 p.m., Gasper left the plant. He reached his hover vehicle at 6.09. He switched into manual flight mode once he'd left Union airspace at 6.20 p.m. His LS records ceased at 6.27 p.m., around two hours after sunset. By the time he crash-landed in Manor Park in London, on top of another hover vehicle, he was already dead.

I looked back up over my screen at Pieter and Lotte. "What do we know about this Lady Raven?" I asked.

"Not much," Lotte said. "There's limited information on her virtual MyPlace profile. We just have one image and an E-box address. Can I mirror to your console?" I nodded.

Lotte and Pieter both moved around. I glanced at them in surprise. Pieter even pulled up a seat next to me. Lotte stood behind, syncing her holotab to project to my console.

"Are you ready?" she asked over my shoulder. I nodded. And with that, a holographic image of Lady Raven appeared on the large screen in front of us.

I gasped. "Wow," I mouthed softly, before stopping myself, as I understood what the anticipation had been about.

"Doesn't get old," muttered Pieter.

I was vaguely aware that Lotte was sniggering. I turned my head, glancing behind me in surprise, only to realize that she was in fact sniggering at Pieter and me. We must have been a sight. I had my mouth wide open. And Pieter, sitting beside me, gave the impression that his eyes were popping out of his head.

"That's one sphinx," said Lotte, moving forward so that she was standing beside me as all three of us stared at the screen.

The 3D hologram was of a woman in her early thirties. She had vivid purple hair, styled in a long bob, with matching eyes the color of deep purple sapphires. She wore a silver layered chain necktie studded with diamonds that plunged between her breasts. And what breasts—large, firm, adorned with black latex nipple tassels. She wore a black PVC corset with metal clasps securing the front down to her panty line, where she was attired in black latex panties. Suspenders hooked long thigh-length black boots onto the corset.

Lady Raven was sitting cross-legged on a crimson crushed velvet lounge chair with gold tassels around the edges. She wore a black lace eye mask studded with tiny diamonds above the eyes. She was staring out at us, her thick, sensuous lips adorned with what looked like deep red lip gloss, exposing a slightly angular chin—it was a mean-looking chin—and a cruel smile. Her hands were black-gloved up to her elbows and were crossed in front of her. In one she held a tasseled flogger, its sharp metal ties glinting silver at the ends.

After three seconds, the hologram began to rotate, zooming around, her face turning slightly, following us from within the screen before returning full frontal for another three seconds.

"Are those augmented breasts?" asked Pieter breathlessly. "I wasn't sure last night." I glanced at him in slight surprise and then back at the hologram. Surely no response was required. I understood his curiosity, but, like me, he should learn to keep such thoughts to himself, especially at work. At the foot of the image a waveguide caption slowly scrolled across, in black ink that dripped holographically toward the foot of the image: *Lady Raven: Your mistress, your high-tech goddess.* And then her E-box address faded in.

"That's enough for you two," Lotte said as she deactivated screen mirroring. The image of Lady Raven vanished.

"So, if Gasper was gay, I assume he wasn't a client." Pieter shook his head. "Then what was he doing with Lady Raven?" I asked. Lotte had moved back around my console, facing me again.

"That's where my digging comes in," Lotte said, looking at me mysteriously. "My cryptography AI team has uncovered quite a significant thing." I glanced at her across the console. "The Catch and Kill audio. The second voice … once we enhanced the quality, we managed to recover a fragment. And this other voice does actually say, 'catch and kill,' which is what the female voice then repeats. Given we've placed our mysterious Gasper at Lady Raven's address, it got me wondering. Anyway, last night I had my team run an acoustic analysis on his voice print."

"It's Gasper, right?"

Lotte squinted at me. "We think so. We couldn't lift a voice print from the Catch and Kill audio. You only get that from live speech, you know—metadata from the acoustic signal using an LS scanning orb. So we had to do some reverse engineering. Forensic voice analysis," Lotte said proudly. "But we found a way, using recorded audio files of Mr. Gasper's voice recovered from his virtual locker. Then we matched a sample with the enhanced male voice in the Catch and Kill clip. I had a technician compare acoustic features of the two voice samples."

"And?" I asked impatiently.

"It wasn't conclusive. It couldn't be. But ..." Lotte began. I drummed my fingers on the console impatiently as she showed off. "Speech features are identified by using power spectral density estimation." I made a face. I could see from his expression that Pieter was nonplussed as well. "Basically, the power associated with a particular feature of speech, measured as a function of unit of frequency," Lotte announced. "Expressed typically in watts per hertz. And using statistical modeling, we were able to construct a digital map of Mr. Gasper's spectral density. We matched the relevant speech features with the utterance 'catch and kill.'"

"So what did you find? In plain English, please."

"A partial match—around sixty-five percent. Given the poor quality of the audio, it's a relatively high match. Normally you'd want over ninety percent to be convinced."

"But it's him," I said quietly, staring thoughtfully into Lotte's eyes. *So what was this Dhruv Gasper up to?* I wondered, genuinely perplexed. *What is 'catch and kill'? How is Lady Raven involved?* "Pieter, tell me about Drones Kineto. What does the company do?"

"It started small—an R&D venture developing AI solutions, primarily software packages used to run UAVs. It now employs around one thousand human assets and uses a walloping amount of AI, including physical synthetic units, androids, and gynoids. It also operates a mid-size manufacturing plant offering integrated drone solutions, both software and hardware. It's also branched out into mobile robotic surgical units. Last year it had a turnover approaching a billion e-Continentals."

"Anything else?"

"There is one more thing," Pieter said. "Mr. Gasper's partner, Dwayne Kline? He's asked to meet with you."

"With me?" I asked, completely taken aback.

"Yes! He asked for you *specifically*. By name."

"I'll be happy to facecall him."

Pieter shook his head. "He wants to meet you *in person*. He asked that you go to him. As soon as possible. He was very explicit. He claims to have important information—says he's been told to only talk to you."

"By whom?" I asked.

"He was very mysterious. Called yesterday evening, when you were still tied up at the Imperium. I explained you were busy with the outage. I said I'd let you know first thing today."

I studied Pieter's face as he finished talking, and I stood up. I moved around my console and began pacing, gazing idly out the window at the woods opposite, thinking. Then I turned around.

"And you said Drones Kineto is based in the Inland Empire?" I asked Pieter.

"Southern California. They have a twenty-hectare facility on the edge of the Colorado Desert."

"Hmmm ..." I muttered. Both Pieter and Lotte were

watching me. "Erebus McDenizen ..." Pieter's eyes narrowed. "Datashizzle, the Babelist I interrogated yesterday. He provided interesting intel that I have a feeling also points in the direction of our dead Dhruv Gasper. He intercepted an audio file from Appleton. I started telling Lotte yesterday ..."

"What did it say?" asked Pieter.

"Something along the lines of Operation False Flag being engaged. That the Inland Empire third party has deployed the drone. And that the fall guy would take the blame for the outage as planned."

"The Inland Empire?" Lotte asked.

"A third party. Could that be Mr. Gasper?" Pieter asked with renewed excitement.

"My thoughts exactly," I muttered. "Looks like I'll be heading to the Republic of California."

CHAPTER 20

I blink activated the Europol travel planner app before searching options. The Republic of California was nine hours behind Union Central Time. The Inland Empire was 8,951 kilometers away. An Interceptor-class scramjet was the only realistic option, given time constraints. Traveling in the hypersonic range, the journey would take just one hour. Formalities would also need to be observed, liaising with local law enforcement so as not to ruffle cross-jurisdiction feathers and to arrange a meet and greet. Executive-level authorization was required to book a scramjet. *Crap!* The director would never approve any of it. Not now he'd received a direct instruction from the High Representative that I was to stand down my investigation. His hands were tied. Which was precisely why I would call Lina instead.

There was something about Lina de Bolle. I had always felt it. And now my instinct told me I could rely on her to get me the authorization I needed. Especially as it wasn't yet official that I was off the case—and given what was at stake. I dismissed Lotte and Pieter. Then I called Lina's office. She agreed at once, told me to give her an hour to make it happen. It would be the small hours in the Republic. But Dwayne Kline's answering service responded immediately, agreeing to meet at his office. *It must be really important*, I thought.

It was almost noon by the time I had all the authorizations I required. An hour later I was airborne. As the scramjet began its climb away from the vertipad on top of the Europol communications tower, I squinted through the cabin window. I watched Scheveningen slowly dwindle into a miniature landscape beneath me as the aircraft ascended the long VTOL corridor reserved for Europol traffic. From there, the hypersonic jet would take me to a top-stacked skyway for intercity travel. At the apex of the VTOL corridor, I felt vibrations and heard a grinding sound. The aircraft undercarriage was auto-stowing. And within a minute I was already out, over the North Sea, heading up toward unrestricted airspace. Once the speed of sound was exceeded, the air-breathing engine kicked in. From that point, the scramjet reached its cruising speed of 7.25 mach in just a few minutes.

* * *

As the scramjet approached Californian airspace, it dropped back into subsonic mode. It was dark outside. The VTOL piloting system took over and the aircraft began descending the Drones Kineto VTOL corridor before coming to its parking position on the designated vertipad. While I waited for the safety lights to deploy and the door latch to unlock, I heard a ping in my ear implant. I had received priority mail. I gave my wrist chip a single press to activate my holotab—Pieter had sent through details of my itinerary. I would be escorted on site by a police captain, Atticus Snyder, from the Inland Empire Police Department, representing the three cities of Palm Springs, Riverside, and San Bernardino. I blinked through until I had his stillgram. The wide, puffy face of a European Californian floated across the screen. I would also be escorted by an Appleton security contractor, a Mr. Tylan Elrod. His was a lean face, an African Californian.

The hydraulic system of the butterfly-wing doorway hatch made a whooshing sound as it opened upward and out on the side of the scramjet.

"Commander, you may exit the aircraft," the piloting VirDa informed me in the standard metallic drawl of Europol communication devices. "I hope you had a pleasant flight," the drawl persisted in meaningless valedictory pleasantry. A metal stairway had auto-deployed and was already attached to the side of the scramjet.

The first thing that struck me was the dryness of the air. I stood at the top of the steps, trying to make out shapes in the blackness outside. And then the temperature hit me. It was cold, just above freezing. That was how things rolled, I guessed, in the middle of a desert in southern California at this time of year.

As I descended the small stairway, transit lighting booted on, illuminating the floor of the vertipad and the disembarkation zone. I had arrived at a large transit lot. In front of me, in the near distance, were the dark silhouettes of buildings—two tall towers on either side of a large dome. Behind, enclosing the large lot, was a high perimeter fence feathered by security lighting. Beyond was the dark landscape of California's Colorado Desert. To one side of the landing zone was a small glass shuttle. As my eyes adjusted to the uneven illumination of the light-infused blackness, I saw that two men were waiting adjacent to it.

I approached the pale arc of the shuttle headlights. The shorter, bulky shape moved forward, stifling a slack-jawed yawn.

"Commander Morgan," the man announced, using General American accent differentiators. He held out a white, pasty hand. I peered down at him. He was middle-aged, with a waistline that provided ample evidence that this was someone who didn't do denial. "I'm Atticus Snyder." I shook his hand. "Welcome to the Republic."

I glanced at the large coil pistol dangling from his beaten-up leather hip holster. Snyder was wearing the scruffiest suit I had ever seen, but he came across as an amiable enough type. He stretched out his arm, ushering me in the direction of the small shuttle and the second shape.

Snyder hissed a voice command and the interior lighting of the shuttle booted on. The second man, Tylan Elrod, was standing motionless next to the vehicle. He was athletic looking, wearing a sharp, dark suit. The guy clearly worked out. He was tall, although not quite my height, clean-shaven, and around forty years of age, I guessed. There had been nothing beyond name, job title, employer, and stillgram image in the file I'd received, which was surprising. Apparently, Europol had very little on him. He nodded at me. *Clearly the taciturn type.*

"This is Tylan Elrod, security specialist," Snyder said, speaking on the guy's behalf.

I was ushered on board. The two men followed and sat opposite me. As Elrod sat, I fleetingly saw the outline of his concealed weapon underneath his jacket. We were both packing heat.

The shuttle trundled past workshops, hangars, and a manufacturing plant, all illuminated by the pale flickers of ambient security lights and the beam of the shuttle's headlamps.

"Is that where they assemble the drones?" I asked, glancing at Elrod. He scowled at me in hostility without responding.

After a moment Snyder shook his head and patted Elrod lightly on one leg.

"Oh, don't let Tylan here get you riled up. He don't mean nothing by it," began Snyder. "The way Appleton sees it, and the way I see it, none of this is Europol's concern. Not your jurisdiction, you might say." I had mistaken Snyder's laconic hangdog face for amiableness. *Mental note to self: he just hides the hostility better.* Then Snyder looked away, while Tylan Elrod maintained his surveillance of me, now also giving me the fisheye.

After a few minutes, we pulled up at the entrance to one of the towers. The dark suit of Elrod led as we disembarked. The security console at the entrance scanned our LS rebounds as we approached, while Elrod spoke a voice command. The door slid open. Inside, floor lighting began booting up, tiles that came on one by one until a large lobby was revealed, marked out from the blackness of the cold desert air permeating the lobby atrium. And perhaps fittingly, in the center of the lobby was a large palm tree in a wide soil basin.

We moved in single file toward the elevator shaft. Snyder brought up the rear. The elevator VirDa addressed Elrod by name. He spoke to confirm the identity of his two *corporate guests* on a preassigned itinerary. It was now also confirmed, to me at least, who was really in charge. And that was Appleton, not the local police department. As we emerged from the elevator, a security light flickered on. At regular intervals, holographic LED wall signage activated as we reached corridor junctions, all addressing Elrod. We were being directed to the Executive Offices Suite. But Elrod clearly knew his way anyway. Finally, we passed through a set of large, automated glass doors. They parted silently as we approached, leading to a darkened antechamber. A gynoid stood motionless behind a console. A hibernation light flicked pale red behind one of her ears every few seconds.

I followed Elrod toward a second set of glass doors. This time we entered into light. A large office. At one end was a floor-to-ceiling window facing out onto blackness. I fleetingly wondered what kind of view it afforded during daylight. Perhaps the complex of industrial units I had just been transported past. And maybe beyond, toward the distant vista of the arid valley landscape.

A man in his mid-thirties was pacing up and down along the window wall behind a long work console. He was clearly ill at ease. I recognized him from his stillgram: Dwayne Kline. As he heard us enter, he spun around on his heels, stopping dead as he came to face us. His eyes appeared to bulge as he saw Elrod leading me in.

There were several chairs in front of the console. Without saying a word, Elrod walked to one and slowly eased himself down. He placed his hands firmly on the armrests and sat straight-backed, watching Kline, now frozen as if with fear, still standing on the other side of the console. I was now in the middle of the room, stationary, Snyder behind me. I tracked him in my peripheral vision as he positioned himself against a wall, arms crossed, watching.

Dwayne Kline was a good-looking man with a dark goatee and a quiff hairstyle. He was stylishly dressed in skinny white trousers, a sky-blue shirt, and a casual green knit blazer. It was unmistakably Canatalti, one of my favorite Italian luxury brands—no internal lining to better hug the body shape. The guy had taste. But he was also on edge. As I stepped forward, his hand visibly trembled as he reached across the console to shake mine. And all the while, he had one eye on Elrod's motionless form, seated in front of him.

Kline attempted a smile as he addressed me. "I'm Dwayne Kline. Welcome, Commander Morgan. I hope you had a swell trip." He spoke in the oddly clipped tones of Mid-Atlantic accent differentiators. Kline was clearly a high-end Appleton subscriber. His accent was effete, at least to my ears, and I found his old-fashioned lexicon amusing. It was a throwback to the twentieth-century East Coast elite, which blended prestigious New England accent patterns with elements of English received pronunciation: a cultivated, distinctively North American poshness that now only existed on Appleton's servers in space.

"Thank you," I responded. He gave the slightest of nods before sitting down in a chair on the other side of the work console, facing me. I helped myself to a chair opposite.

"You asked to see me ...?" Kline stammered at me. I felt my eyes widen in surprise.

"I understood it was *you* who asked to see *me*," I replied. "And that it had to be in person."

Kline glanced down at his hands before staring back at me. I glimpsed a brief flicker of translucence projecting from his wrist. *Has he activated his holotab?* I wondered. He looked down again, blinking quickly several times. *Yes, he has.* His eyes moved back up to me again before gulping. "Um ... there may have been a misunderstanding. I told your deputy, Mr. de Bruijn, everything I could think of. It's a huge shock for all of us."

"Look," I began, feeling myself becoming angry at having wasted my time. Just at that point there was a ping in my ear implant—a high-priority alert. I instinctively activated my holotab. It was a memoclip on my personal messaging service. It read: "Not safe to talk here. Say you need to call base. Step outside. Dwayne Kline." I was taken aback. I glanced back up and Kline was staring at me intently. As my eyes met his, he gave me the slightest of nods again. I coughed slightly.

"Mr. Kline, I've just been asked to facecall HQ. It may be urgent. Is there somewhere I can go, just for a few minutes, to place the call?"

"Of course. No problem at all," he responded instantly. "If you step outside, my assistant will escort you to a quiet room. Take your time."

I nodded, rose, and left the office. The opaque glass doors slid open and closed behind me, leaving the three men inside. Outside, the gynoid was no longer in hibernation mode. She was now standing alert, apparently expecting me.

"This way, Commander," the gynoid said quietly, leading me back out of the antechamber into the corridor but this time away from the elevator shaft. She led me to a single opaque door and presented her retinal fold to the sec-cam for ID confirmation by her Einstein chip. The door slid open and the ceiling lighting auto-booted to reveal a windowless room—a storage unit. There were shelves on three walls containing assorted boxes with serial numbers printed on them.

"Mr. Kline will be with you presently," the gynoid said mysteriously, and departed.

CHAPTER 21

Around thirty seconds later, the door opened again. This time it was Dwayne Kline, now even twitchier than before.

He glanced at me apologetically. "Sorry for the smoke and mirrors. We only have a few minutes before they suspect something. We can't both be absent too long." I wondered where this was going. "Dhruv had an *insurance policy*. At least that's what he called it. Should anything happen to him. I thought it was a joke …" Kline muttered the last phrase quietly, almost to himself.

"Mr. Gasper?" I asked. Kline nodded. A tear welled up in his eye and slowly trickled down his face. I suddenly felt sorry for him.

"It's been hell, the last few days," he confided, glancing up at me. "Marc Barron is bankrolling us. So we've had Appleton security crawling all over us since the accident. I'm being monitored twenty-four seven …" His words trailed off.

"I'm very sorry for your loss, Mr. Kline."

"Can I trust you, Emyr Morgan?" Kline asked.

I looked him square in the eyes. "You can trust me with the truth."

"I was told I could trust you and that I should only talk to you."

"Oh?" I asked, slightly startled.

"A woman—I'll explain. But first Dhruv. I received a notification three days ago to my E-box account, right after the outage. It was an access code for a numbered virtual locker in SwissSecure. There were two files: a video memoclip for me, and a facecall recording. Between Dhruv and Barron. He told me … Dhruv told me in the memoclip … that if I received this, he was already dead. That he loved me." Tears were now rolling down Kline's face in a stream. I looked away, slightly embarrassed, while he took out a handkerchief. I glanced back after a moment, once I'd sensed he had managed to pull himself together. "He told me he had messed up. That he was sorry."

"Messed up?" I asked.

"Barron had leverage on Dhruv. They go back some. But you have to understand, Dhruv is … *was* a good man. He never intended to hurt anyone."

"What happened?" I asked quietly.

"He was only twenty-five. He knew he shouldn't have. Dhruv just made a mistake, which he's been paying for ever since."

"What did he do?" I pressed.

"Took out a car in manual mode. With a friend. They were both high. They hit the VTOL beacon marker—a million-to-one freak accident. Dhruv didn't have a scratch on him, but his friend suffered a bad head injury. The doctors induced a coma. Irreversible brainstem damage. It would've been a shitshow. But Barron made it all go away—bought off the cops and compensated the guy's family. He still needs twenty-four seven intensive care, and for the rest of his life. Dhruv never forgave himself."

"And Marc Barron used his leverage?" I asked.

THE BABEL APOCALYPSE   203

Kline nodded. "Always. This time Dhruv had to deploy one of our high-spec military drones in foreign airspace on November 5th. He was provided with a software package which included place coordinates. Using weird codenames—typical Marc Barron. Operation False Flag, Operation Dark Court. That was always his thing. Melodramatic, if you ask me."

"Operation Dark Court. What's that?" I asked sharply. Kline shrugged and shook his head. "Which foreign territory?" I asked instead.

"The Russian Federation." My eyes widened as I finally had my growing suspicion confirmed. Kline saw my expression. "I know," he acknowledged. "It's a breach of international treaties, flying a drone in Russian airspace without a license. It could put us out of business."

I instinctively shook my head. He'd misunderstood. This provided confirmation that Appleton was likely involved in the plan to frame the Russians for the language outage. And more. I could barely wrap my head around it. After all, I knew that the origination point of the cyberattacks came from Lake Baikal in Siberia. But apparently not a boat, a drone!

Yet, the prospect of Appleton being responsible, now that I was uncovering actual evidence, still seemed as absurd as it had the day before during the Erebus McDenizen interrogation. And during the interview with Ebba Black. *Could Appleton really be responsible for the language outage?* But Marc Barron's apparent scheming to take over the commercial interests of the providers whose operations had been damaged certainly provided compelling circumstantial evidence. I sensed Kline staring at me, knowing he'd momentarily lost me.

"Did Dhruv give the coordinates for the drone's destination?" I asked almost breathlessly.

"He said he wanted to protect me. The less I knew, the better. But in the facecall, Marc Barron mentions Siberia." I felt myself tensing. *Siberia! There it was. The confirmation.* "I'll send you the file."

I watched as he issued blink commands on his holotab before hibernating it. Almost immediately, I felt a slight vibration in my ear implant—a high-priority incoming mail. There, I had it: the facecall file. I blinked to activate. Just twenty-seven seconds long. The feed had been recorded in stealth mode by Dhruv Gasper.

There was Marc Barron's familiar face from the news bulletins; but without the dermal filler and wrinkle slider of contemporary MyPlace broadcast trickery, this was a face full of the lines and creases of age. As he spoke, Barron's heavy jowls were the same, swaying with the strange orange hue that always clung to him; his famous boast about his perma-tan using Appleton's patented biomimetic technology had once made him a laughingstock in some circles. But what did he care? He was the world's richest man. The eyes were the same, though—dead, expressionless in a way that didn't seem normal, somehow absent yet possessed. It was difficult to explain. As Barron spoke, the corners of his mouth moved larger than life on the screen in a cruel, affected way. His customary manner. And the upward flick of his right hand, jabbing with the forefinger as if to emphasize a particular point as he spoke.

Marc Barron was issuing instructions. Dhruv would receive a software card for Operation False Flag from Darya Zao, with place coordinates for the drone. She would deliver in person. He then spoke about *the package*; I assumed that was the drone. It was to be dispatched on November 5th. Operation False Flag would initiate the first phase of Operation Dark Court. *Operation*

False Flag, that's now clear, I thought. *But what the hell is Operation Dark Court? Does that relate to the strange story of a Doomsday cult that Karen Hoekstra first came to me with five years ago?* For now, I put the speculation aside.

As the file finished playing, I looked back at Kline. "Can you tell me why Dhruv was in the Union on the 5th?"

"Business in Paris," Kline replied.

"Please think carefully. Anywhere else?"

Kline appeared mildly surprised by the question. "No, just Paris."

"Who told you to contact me, Mr. Kline?"

His eyes narrowed. "It was the weirdest thing. This woman, she appeared in my office yesterday morning out of nowhere ..." Kline smiled weakly.

"A woman? Someone known to you?"

Kline shook his head. "I'd never seen her before. But I knew I could trust her. When she touched me ... it's hard to explain ... she felt familiar, as if she knew me—really knew me. As if I knew her. But I felt calm—this sense of serenity. Makes no sense, right?" Kline asked, glancing at me. I didn't judge. Never did. I was just glad he had come to me with this, whatever the reason. "Anyway, she told me I had to come to you with this. That I could trust you. To trust only you. I know this all sounds crazy. But I'm telling you the truth."

I thought for a moment. "Did she give a name, this woman?"

Kline spoke slowly, deliberately. "Lilith King."

It was as if a bolt of electricity seared through me. "From Interpol?" I asked in bewildered amazement.

"From the future. At least, that's what she claimed," Kline muttered. "She even had me check my bioclock to give you the time coordinates. 9.16 a.m. Californian Standard Time. Said that was important, that I best not forget. Then when I looked up, she had vanished into thin air. Just like that." I felt my eyes bulging. "Look, I'm not inventing this," Kline said defensively.

I could tell from his eyes he was telling the truth. "Can you describe her to me?"

"I sure can. Not one to be readily forgot. Bright red-orange hair, real pretty, and her eyes ..."

"Bright green?" I asked. Kline's mouth opened slightly in surprise. He didn't need to reply. "I believe you, Mr. Kline. Lilith King works for Interpol—director of the International Cybercrime Directorate, based in Singapore."

"You know her, then?" Kline asked. "Darn, that would explain it." With that, he appeared to calm down. But I knew this explained nothing. I'd never met Lilith King. She was a big fish. "I need to go back in. Give me two minutes and then return, okay?" Kline asked, glancing at his bioclock. I heard his half-gasp as he realized we'd been away too long already. But I still needed more from him.

As he began to turn, I asked my final question. "Just one more thing. Did Dhruv ever mention anything about a Lady Raven to you? In Brussels?"

"In the Union? No, I don't think so ..." Kline paused. But then he stiffened. "But there was something odd ... now that I think over it."

"What's that?"

"A payment from Drones Kineto's private checking account a few days ago to a Brussels business account. The payment reference was Glanc MD. Probably a medical contractor. I would have gone ahead and asked Dhruv about it—usually we use a different account to pay MDs. I wouldn't have noticed otherwise. But ..."

"Might I ask a favor? Could I have details of the transaction and the account number of the payee?"

"I'll have my assistant see to it," he said.

"Thank you." Kline brushed a hand across his cheek and breathed out, taking a few seconds to compose himself.

I returned to Kline's office suite a few minutes later. By then, he was back behind his console. I was greeted by silence. Tylan Elrod stared at me coldly.

"I think I have things straightened out," I announced. "There seems to have been a misunderstanding at our end. I apologize for the inconvenience."

"Don't mention it. It's too bad I couldn't be of more help." Kline said apologetically. Then, glancing nervously toward Elrod and Snyder, he announced: "Guys, please show him to his ride."

CHAPTER 22

Within thirty minutes of departing the Inland Empire I was already back in daylight. And by the time the scramjet approached Union airspace, having re-crossed multiple time zones, I found myself in fading afternoon embers as the late fall sun began setting on the horizon.

My mind was still reeling from my new discoveries. Appleton was implicated dead center in the language outage. I was already on my second whiskey, procured from the onboard entertainment service unit, when I received an incoming facecall alert. I gave a half-tap behind my ear to shut off the vibration before activating my holotab. It was Lina. I quickly pushed the glass out of visual range before accepting the call.

Lina's stern face bobbed in front of me. "Emyr, you're to go straight to Gothenburg. The director's orders. I'm sending a revised itinerary authorization through to your autopilot VirDa." Lina never ceased to surprise me. I was prepared for pretty much anything, but this new instruction took even me aback.

"What's up?" I asked in startled surprise.

"An intruder alert has been activated at the Ebba Black mansion. Perimeter sensors to the estate have been triggered," she replied. *Doesn't local law enforcement pick that up?* I thought.

Why would Europol get involved? Still, I felt a prick of excitement that I might get to see Ebba Black again, and sooner than I'd thought.

"I expected to be off the case. After the meeting yesterday at the Imperium."

Lina stared at me with renewed curiosity. "How well do you know this Ebba Black?" *Strange question,* I thought. "I met her for the first time yesterday. Why?" I asked.

"The Gothenburg police chief contacted us five minutes ago." *Why would Gothenburg police contact Europol about this?* Now I was genuinely dumbfounded. "He had instructions to request we send you."

"Instructions? Who gives the police chief instructions?"

"Ebba Black, apparently," Lina replied. "The director wants you there as soon as possible. Your autopilot indicates you can be there in seven minutes."

"What's really going on?" I asked.

Lina sighed. "Between you and me, we think CyberForce is being even dumber than usual. The director suspects von Böhm has convinced the High Representative to authorize a black ops action targeting Ebba Black. A team sent in to sanction her."

"What! But what about jurisdiction? Are the Nordic authorities aware?"

"What do you think?" Lina replied. "That's kind of the point of black ops."

I sighed in exasperation. "What are my orders?"

"Prevent any assassination attempt. And provide safe passage for Ebba Black. We want her escorted to Europol HQ for protection. Authorized by the director himself—an informal arrangement with the Gothenburg police for now, based on safety protocols. We're liaising with the Nordic national authorities. As you and I both know, CyberForce and von Böhm have an unusual modus operandi."

"Shoot first, ask questions later?" I asked.

"We prefer to do it the other way around. And to avoid an international incident."

"Understood," I replied.

"How did it go in California?" Lina asked finally.

"You won't believe it. I'll brief you in the morning."

Lina looked at me strangely. "You'd be surprised what I would believe," she said tersely, before calling off. As her face disappeared, the autopiloting VirDa screen blinked in front of me and the VirDa began to talk in its metallic drawl from the cabin speaker overhead. The flight itinerary had been modified.

* * *

The scramjet touched down gently on Ebba Black's private vertipad in front of the dark silhouette of her mansion. I squinted out. There was no lighting from within as far as I could tell. The scramjet's sensors had detected no sign of another vehicle, no evidence of anything untoward. *Perhaps I've managed to get here before CyberForce. Perhaps the sensors were tripped by a wild animal.*

"VirDa, I need LiDAR night-vision goggles," I said as I picked up my jacket from the seat next to me. A metal cover in front of me opened and a drawer auto-deployed. Inside was a tray with various apparatus, including a small coil pistol, a mobile sec-cam, a mobile LS orb scanner, a first aid utility belt, and a pair of high-tech night goggles.

"The goggles have been programmed to work with your voice print, Commander," said the VirDa. I took the goggles and the first aid belt. The butterfly-wing door hissed open, and

I clambered out and jumped down onto the vertipad. I pulled on my suit jacket over the kydex shoulder holster and coil gun, put the goggles in my pocket, and wrapped the belt around my waist. I then proceeded quickly across the circular lawn in front of the house to avoid noise from the gravel driveway. I moved stealthily up one of the marble staircases that led to the front entrance. The windows were dark. I didn't know whether that was because no lights were on, or window shields had been activated. But I also knew from the day before that everything in the house was switched on manually. There were no VirDas to operate niceties such as lighting. Outside, a frosty moon appeared from behind a cloud, casting its pale light on the darkened building.

At the top of the staircase, I made out the paneled front doors in the moonlight. One door was ajar. *That's ominous*, I thought. I pushed it slightly and peeped in. Inside was a dark swirl of undifferentiated shapes. I paused and put on the goggles. They were a small compact unit, featuring a laser emitter and a forward-facing camera feeding a signal to a pair of eye viewers. The unit auto-adjusted around my head.

"Goggles, activate LiDAR," I said. I heard a soft click from the unit's integrated VirDa. And with that, the dark shapes I could barely discern a moment before popped into perfect acuity in three-dimensional splendor.

I walked through the entrance vestibule into the large hallway. I recognized the chandelier from the day before hanging above me. I paused and listened. Only silence. I scanned the scene. The large staircase opened out ahead of me before separating out from the half-landing on either side. As I was about to move on, I heard a slight groan coming from the mezzanine landing above, overlooking the hallway below. As

I focused my gaze, I saw a shape on the floor, partially hidden behind the row of marble balusters.

"Gun, activate," I said. I quickly pulled my jacket lapel back across my chest to prevent the glow of the gun's green capacitor giving away my presence.

I skipped swiftly and silently up the main staircase, before taking the right-hand stairs. As I reached the landing, I saw a figure lying on its back at the apex of the staircase. From the body armor, I knew this was a special forces commando, an elite human operator. *Lina was right. It is CyberForce!*

I kneeled next to the stricken commando, pulling back the visor and helmet. The face was female. I knew I shouldn't be surprised, but somehow I was. Her skin was pallid; she was drawing slow, rasping breaths. The commando was wearing special forces insignia—a sergeant in the CounterRevolutionary Warfare command. I checked the small VirDa screen inside her visor. Her health parameters were a mess. Her blood pressure was dangerously low. She wouldn't last thirty minutes without a medivac.

A standard-issue modular coil assault rifle lay at her side. The status lights on its side showed that it had recently been fired. Her coil pistol was still sheathed in her belt holster, unused. I touched her gently.

"Sergeant?" I whispered. She murmured. And then I saw it— the wound to her stomach. She was wearing tactical armored torso, arm, and leg casings, not a full suit. Light, flexible, and normally highly effective. But her torso casing had been dislodged, probably deliberately. And now the sergeant was bleeding out.

"Sergeant?" I said again. Her eyes flickered open. "I'm Commander Morgan, Europol. Please identify."

She drew in a breath. "CyberForce Alpha team. Three hostiles. Captain Törni has lead." Of course, it had to be *him*. "Hostiles?" I asked. "Please clarify."

"Executive Kill Order," she muttered.

"On whose authority, Sergeant?" I said in sudden alarm. The woman's eyes popped open, looking at me with fleeting surprise. I only realized I had raised my voice when the echo bounced back at me from the large hallway below. Her eyes peeled away from me, her eyelids flickering shut. Her blood pressure was dropping.

"Stay with me, Sergeant," I hissed, quickly searching through various pouches in the first aid belt. I used a vial of ammonia inhalants to bring her to. Her eyes, now slit-like, reopened. I fished out a hemostatic gauze to stop the blood flow and placed it firmly over the gunshot wound in her stomach. A weapon had been discharged at point blank range into her midriff. From the wound ballistics, I could already tell this was not the neat incision of modern coil weaponry. I activated my holotab, blinking on the magnifying weapons identifier app: a 9mm-caliber bullet that had distorted on impact. A Glock 19 fired 9mm rounds. *Ebba's bodyguard, Ursula!* I thought.

"Sergeant, has a medivac been dispatched?"

"BabelNet," the sergeant whispered.

"What?" I asked. "Is your Bravo team on its way?"

"We can't get through. All comms are jammed," she whispered before falling silent. I tried turning her gently to see whether there was an exit wound that also needed stanching. She groaned softly. Her tactical body armor was still in place at her back; there was no sign of blood underneath. Her intestines had been badly damaged. Her visor diagnostics also showed some kidney damage—I couldn't decipher the readings well enough to know how bad.

"So no one knows your status?" I asked. Her eyes glazed over. The sergeant twitched and coughed up blood. She suddenly opened her eyes wide. "I was jumped," she whispered hoarsely. "I tagged her ..." Her words trailed off as her eyes flickered shut. She had lost consciousness.

I stood and scanned my environs. A long, wide corridor led out from the large landing. There were closed doors on either side—but twenty meters along, dead ahead, one door had been left wide open. I jogged quietly toward the threshold. My LiDAR-powered night goggles revealed a medium-sized bedroom. At the far end was a double bed on a raised dais, with two steps up. And lying on the bed was the motionless figure of Horchata Chiu. I knew she was dead from the unnatural lack of motion.

As I moved into the room, I saw she was lying under a bloodied silver silk sheet that had been sprayed with a round of high-caliber bullets from a coil rifle. Very messy. Uncharacteristic for a Union special forces commando. Then I saw a body slumped over the bed, face down, also a member of the special forces A-Team. A male this time. His head was exposed; his helmet had fallen onto the floor next to him. He had a single bullet wound to the back of his head at the base of his skull. Again, a 9mm pistol wound. I turned him over. His eyes stared up at me, so I brushed my hands across his face to close them. From his position, I guessed he had been ambushed from behind as he stood at the foot of the bed, readying himself to execute Horchata Chiu. That would also explain the messy gunfire scatter.

I moved toward Horchata Chiu. Her pale albino face appeared serene, her eyes closed. She had been sleeping alone, judging by the bedding arrangement. I pulled up the sheet to cover her head.

Just at that point, I heard a groan. I turned around and saw a figure to my right, half sitting, half lying, propped up with their back against the legs of a lounge chair. It was the bodyguard. I moved toward her. She was badly injured. Part of her left shoulder had been destroyed by coil rifle rounds, probably from the sergeant back out on the landing. I winced involuntarily. Blood was oozing out of the wound, her left arm useless next to her. She had seen my shape moving in the darkness and fumbled for something. I saw the Glock handgun next to her on the carpet. Given that her injury was so severe, I was impressed she had managed to hold on. She was one tough woman. She placed her right hand on the gun.

"Ursula," I said quietly. "I'm Emyr Morgan, Europol. We met yesterday, remember?" I crouched beside her. She was breathing heavily. "I'm here to protect Ebba," I confirmed. Ursula relaxed her hand and moved it away from the pistol. She beckoned me toward her before dropping her good hand back down by her side.

"Help Ebba," she whispered into my ear. "Go, quickly ..."

"Where?" I asked with urgency. I could see she didn't have long.

"Downstairs—the basement. BabelNet Command and Control." Then she grabbed my hand and looked into my eyes. "Keep ... Ebba ... safe." And with that final exertion, her hand fell limply to the carpeted floor. She was gone.

CHAPTER 23

I sprang up and began jogging back the way I had come, passing the unconscious sergeant at the top of the landing. I went back down the stairs into the hallway below. I then turned 180 degrees, loping along a wide corridor into the unknown of the building's interior. The corridor was lined with oak paneling, and a few meters along I spotted a jib door that had been left ajar. It was well camouflaged. I never would have noticed it had it remained flush with the wall. Someone had clearly been in a hurry. I pulled it wide open, spying a secret flight of stairs bending down into darkness.

I entered and descended the narrow stone steps. At the bottom was a wide tunnel that ran in both directions, stretching away under the entire mansion. Lights booted on. *So, Ebba Black does have some uses for smart technology after all.*

I took off my night-vision googles and clipped them onto my belt. The tunnel's floor, walls, and ceiling were made from reinforced concrete. Thick cables ran along the ceiling, secured in plastic support ducts. I paused, listening, trying to detect any sound, seeking a clue as to which way to proceed. Nothing. Just then, up ahead to my left, where the tunnel bent away from view, I spotted something lying motionless on the tunnel floor. A body.

As I approached, I recognized the familiar attire of another CyberForce commando; from the physique, it was male. I caught myself hoping it was Törni and felt a twinge of regret when I saw that it wasn't. The head was twisted to one side, eyes still open, frozen in surprise. I wondered what it was that he had seen. This one wasn't wearing a helmet, although from his insignia it looked like he was a first lieutenant. A typical CyberForce A-Team had four operators. This was the third one, which meant there was only Törni left.

The dead lieutenant had a tiny ballistic wound in the center of his forehead, between his eyes. That ruled out Ursula and her Glock 19. This had to be the work of a second shooter—a first-rate marksman by the looks of it, as their aim would have had to be accurate to be lethal. The dead commando was well-armed. His assault rifle lay still sheathed in its magnetic cradle on his torso armor, while his coil pistol was still in his outstretched hand. I kneeled and quickly examined its ballistic status lights. The weapon hadn't been fired: he hadn't been quite quick enough on the draw.

Just ahead, the tunnel veered again, this time to the right. Around the bend there was a vault-like circular steel door, partially open, leading into another room. There was a numeric combination keypad on the wall adjacent to the vault's entrance. Numbered buttons to be physically pressed. Low tech, but nevertheless, extremely effective. As I approached, I realized that the door was thick, about a meter through, with deep deadbolts. Whatever was inside would be exceptionally well protected.

The circular entrance was large enough for a normal-sized person to step through, but not for me. As I was about to lower my head to pass through, I heard a male voice in the room on the other side. I froze. *Törni.* I immediately reached for my gun, drawing it out of its holster.

"Not running your mouth now, are you? Not like yesterday with that shit about your Chicken game." There was real hate in the Finn's voice.

I craned my neck, creeping a few centimeters farther forward to get a better view of the room beyond the door. Törni was standing with his back toward me around ten meters away. He was dressed in special forces fatigues. He had placed his coil pistol and assault rifle nearby, on a console surface a couple of meters from him. I saw, beyond him, the partially occluded figure of a seated and restrained Ebba. Glimpses of her body moved in and out of view around the edges of Törni's burly physique.

"Where is Freetown? Tell me and your death will be painless," Törni announced. Then I heard Ebba laugh—a hard, callous laugh. It was definitely her. I watched Törni stiffen; this wasn't the response he'd been expecting.

"I'm going to tell you your future, Captain dearest," Ebba began. It was the same husky voice, but now with malice in it. "You're going to die. You might respond with, 'But of course I am; we all are, one day.' But I am here to tell you your death is nigh—it will be swift and delivered by a single bullet. Do you know what a Baby Browning is?" I listened and couldn't help smirking. This woman was something. She was tied up yet issuing death threats. "Of course you don't," she continued snarkily, without awaiting a response. "Because you're an ignorant brute who lacks finesse as well as manners. It's a blowback-operated semiautomatic pistol. A design classic." At that, the Finn moved toward the seated Ebba. He struck her hard across the face before moving back, blocking her again from my line of sight.

"You're in no position to—" Törni began, before her laugh cut him off again.

"I have you exactly where I want you," Ebba spat at him. "And it will be between your eyes. Yes, I think that would be perfect for you. My single bullet."

As I listened, I quickly scanned the rest of the room. It was a cavernous underground chamber also made of reinforced concrete. Across one entire wall to my right, there was a bank of dozens and dozens of display screens, all with muted audio feeds. I squinted in amazement as I realized this place was running live streams of secure sec-cams from all the security agencies and governmental ministries of note in the automated world. The digital identifiers scrolling at the bottom of each screen revealed video capture from Union assets in the Proelium, the Imperium, and even Europol HQ. There was live streaming from inside Unilanguage HQ in California and a direct feed to the president's office in the United Federation of America's Capitol. Ebba Black had apparently achieved the impossible, hacking into the world's most secure venues. *This explains how she knows so much.*

Along the opposite wall stood racks of servers, emitting a pale blue light. The servers were encased in a sealed glass tunnel that extended in either direction out of the cavernous chamber through enclosed portals. Inside the server tunnel were cooling units and temperature thermostats, with ceiling grilles for ventilation. Server storage this big meant Ebba Black's operation didn't rely on the servers in space run by big tech.

At the far end of the chamber, beyond the looming figure of Törni, was a large cone-like device with an antenna on top. It was connected by myriad wires to an adjacent console the size and height of an Explorer-class droid unit, with blinking lights, buttons, and scrolling streams of text across digital displays. A small red light on the top flashed periodically. There was also a communication console, including a mobile telepresence unit for virtual communication.

Törni was now moving toward his weapons. He'd clearly had enough. I knew I needed to act. I aimed my gun and stepped through the open vault entrance. But the LiDAR goggles dangling from my utility belt scraped the metal frame. I paused. The noise wasn't loud, but it was enough to take away my element of surprise. Törni spun around.

His half-twisted frame revealed more of Ebba Black beyond him. He had secured her using liquid restraint webbing. She was tied with her wrists to her ankles, secured behind the front legs of the chair so that her torso was pulled forward. Ebba was attired as the day before. But now her blouse and pencil skirt were compressed by the restraint webbing. And the way her legs and arms were angled, her skirt was partially pulled up, revealing more of her stockings, while her hands had been thrust against her black patent leather stilettos. She looked uncomfortable. But for his trouble, Törni had received a series of deep scratches—four lines down his cheek, blood weeping, as if scratched by the talons of a bird of prey.

"You?" Törni said, part question, part snarled exclamation, as he gathered himself. Ebba's face glared, her dark, alert eyes watching me intently.

"I have orders to escort Dr. Black to Europol HQ," I said calmly.

Törni smiled at me wryly. "And I have *my* orders," he replied with a glint in his eye, now standing near the console where he had laid his coil pistol.

I frowned. "I'm asking you to stand down. Release Dr. Black into my custody."

"Or what, pretty boy?" Törni asked. "You'll fall over like last time in Cantina? I barely even touched you. This time it'll actually hurt." He took a step forward menacingly. *Keep cool, Emyr*, I thought, as I felt my blood beginning to boil. "I'm just glad you're stringing words into sentences now," I replied tersely. "Gun activate, stun rounds," I instructed quietly, staring at Törni with ferocity. His gray eyes remained devoid of emotion, his square face impassive, staring back at me. We both knew I had the drop on him. He would be incapacitated before he could reach his own weapon. He smirked as he appeared to reach down around his back.

"Look out," I heard Ebba call. I flinched and adjusted my body, turning to one side as a throwing knife sailed past my nose. I felt an unexpected displacement of air rush against my face and heard a gasp from Ebba.

Too late, I looked up. Törni had covered the few meters between us and was in my face. Before I had time to adjust, he caught me flush with an uppercut. *He had taken me by surprise again!*

I was sent spinning against the console on which he had placed his weapons, banging my face against the surface. My pistol spilled from my hand. I glimpsed it completing a series of 360-degree spins across the smooth concrete floor.

I heaved myself upright and brushed my face where I had hit the console. As I glanced at my hand, I saw a smear of red. It was blood from my nose. Now I was raging mad. As I straightened up, Törni's face leered at me from just a few paces away. It was the same expression as that time in the bar when his sucker punch had gone unanswered. "Not this time," I whispered, as I switched to combat stance.

"There's no military police to save your sorry ass this time," Törni hissed.

I saw red. I launched myself forward like a mountain lion. But Törni had good reflexes for such a big guy. He stepped adroitly to one side, and I clean missed him, grabbing air. He tutted, giving a slight shake of the head.

Now he moved forward again as I put up a tight guard with my fists. Törni feinted before throwing a stiff jab. He was a front foot super heavyweight, yet moved like a middleweight. His hand speed and punch angle beat me. It felt as if an electric bolt had coursed through my skull as my head snapped back. I stuttered back several steps in involuntary retreat before dropping to the floor. That one hurt.

"Get up, you pussy," Törni said, baiting me. On the floor next to me, I saw the glint of carbon steel. It was the knife he had launched at me. I picked it up, curling my fingers around the paracord-wrapped handle. I knew I needed to slow the guy down.

I moved forward, holding the knife out, circling as Törni's eyes narrowed, watching me intently. I lunged, making a slashing gesture. Again Törni slipped me with a sidestep. But this time, as I lurched forward past his flank, I drove the knife down, deep into the top of his left shoulder, pressing until I felt bone. Törni winced in pain, falling to one knee. I could tell he was hurt. I moved quickly toward my gun. But before I could reach it, I heard Ebba's warning cry again.

"Emyr!" I turned to see Törni, still on one knee, reaching across his body and pulling the knife out of his shoulder with his right hand. Blood began spurting from the wound. But the man seemed oblivious to the pain. He was shaping to throw again.

I glimpsed Ebba in my peripheral vision, still struggling with the webbing holding her fast in the chair. Yet she had somehow managed to free one hand and unhook one of her shoes. And just before Törni threw his knife, she launched her shoe at him. It knocked against his arm as he released. There wasn't much force behind it, but it was enough. The knife flew harmlessly past me, clattering across the concrete floor. Törni was quickly up and moving forward, cutting me off from my gun. But he was panting and losing blood. He positioned his body in an orthodox boxing stance, and I saw he was setting up a power punch. I narrowed my eyes while I did a quick mental reckoning. A spinning elbow strike it would be—my own personal tsunami of devastation.

As Törni leaned in, to jab, to set up his cross, I delayed for a split second before swiveling. And as his jab rushed past the side of my head, connecting only with air, I delivered my spinning elbow strike.

But Törni surprised me. Despite being committed, he somehow managed to pull away. Just a slight adjustment of his body, but it was enough. I caught him, but only a glancing blow. He staggered backward, a look of surprise spreading across his broad, dumb face.

I blew him a kiss. "Hurt, did it?" I watched as his face became strained with rage. Now I had gotten under his skin. Finally. He straightened up and moved toward me once more, relentless. I could tell he was again shaping to try and overpower me with a haymaker. He was leading with a jab; an uppercut would follow. This time there was no disguise. He was telegraphing it.

I readied myself to deliver my own coup de grâce: a roundhouse kick. I waited for just the right distance, pausing, holding for him to advance just a fraction more. I watched as Törni moved in, feeling the weight of my striking leg as I tensed, waiting for the precise moment. And as it arrived, I lifted and bent my right knee while simultaneously turning my left leg. I whipped my body around in a rapid semicircular motion, striking Törni with my shin and instep. I connected over his leading guard, directly on his cheek and the side of his eye. The man was a giant, but he toppled backward as if hit by a ton of bricks. As he staggered back under the force of the strike, he crashed into another desk console. The side of his head glanced in sickening fashion against the sharp edge of the unit. He crumpled to the floor, finally still. I lowered my leg deliberately, sucking in my cheeks.

"I love the sound you make when you shut up," I hissed at Törni's limp form on the concrete floor.

I heard a noise from across the chamber that drew my attention away from the fallen man. It was Ebba. She had almost managed to completely free herself. I watched in amazement as she used the stiletto heel of her one remaining shoe as a tool to cut through the webbing. The inside edge was razor-sharp. Custom made, I assumed, and potentially lethal. *The woman is literally walking on blades!* I mused wryly as I caught my breath. As she detached the last of the webbing from her lap and chest, she arched underneath, shimmying out of the seat she had been bound to.

Then, to my shock, I heard Törni's voice behind me. "Gun activate. Live rounds." I spun around. Somehow the man was both conscious *and* standing. And he had retrieved his fallen pistol. The gun was primed and ready to fire, but this Törni before me was not the same. This Törni had a deep, ugly-looking laceration across his one remaining good cheek where he had collided with the console edge. His lip was split and swelling before my eyes, while his nose was badly broken, twisted to the right in an unnatural-looking shape, a fragment of bone partially piercing his skin. And his left eye socket and eye were forming into a large purple bubble. I guessed his eye socket was broken. But the man wasn't.

Törni watched me through his good eye, squinting. I could see his hatred. I could almost feel it. I glanced across the chamber at my fallen gun.

He followed my gaze. "You'll be dead before you reach it," he lisped through his swollen lips, before spitting out a drizzle of blood. I knew he was right as I watched him beginning to squeeze the trigger.

I nodded, even then unable to help myself. "You know, I never quite realized it until now ..." I paused for effect, "... but ugly goes clean to the bone."

As dark anger rippled across his face, I heard another noise. It was a rustling from Ebba's direction. Törni had heard it too. I glanced to my left. Ebba had stooped and pulled her pencil skirt up to just below her panty line, revealing her stocking tops. Around her right thigh was a small lace gun holster. I sucked in my breath. She presented quite the sight.

Ebba pulled a tiny gun from her thigh holster. A *really* tiny gun. She hadn't been kidding about her Baby Browning, I thought in amazement. As she moved her small hand away from her leg, holding the antique pistol, I saw that this one had been customized. I took in the pearl handle, the hot blue metal of the body.

Still with her skirt around her upper thighs, Ebba stepped forward, one small, elegant step, pistol held aloft. She aimed at the one-eyed giant standing in front of her. This was no coil gun. This was a small work of art, one that fired six rounds without the need for a firing pin. Like everything about Ebba Black, it was petite, classy, and something to be underestimated at your peril.

Törni had turned, too. He jerked his arm, directing his coil pistol toward Ebba. At nearly two meters tall, Törni's firing angle was slightly downward. As he steadied his aim, he smirked at her. I watched as Ebba eyed him intently—his eyes, his hands, his movements. *She's watching for a tell*, I thought, *the slightest twitch that will give him away.*

"You won't hurt me with that," Törni sneered through his split lip. As he spoke, he revealed a newly broken front tooth, snapped at the gum. "It's just a toy."

Ebba's eyes narrowed as she aimed at his head, still watching him like a hawk. *Now we have a game of Chicken*, I thought. Who would blink first? The standoff only lasted a second or two, yet it felt like an eternity.

Törni's trigger finger made the slightest movement. At that precise moment, Ebba dropped to one knee, still holding her gun extended out in front of her. Törni fired. There was silence. The discharge from a coil gun produces no sound, no smoke, and no recoil. It is one-hundred-percent accurate. Yet Törni had missed.

With a slight tweak, Ebba adjusted her aim, changing her shooting angle upward from her lower position, now having a larger target to aim at. One eye narrowed further. Her full lips were still adorned with the same blood-red lipstick as the day before, puckered ever so slightly. She fired.

There was a bang, smoke, and a slight recoil. Ebba held her hands steady. Törni's one good eye looked startled. There was now a small mark on his forehead. The bullet had struck dead center, right between his eyes. Törni's gun clattered to the ground, the green capacitor glow fading, as the big man crashed back onto the cold concrete floor. Dead. I felt my mouth open slightly. I had never witnessed anything like it. Technique, precision, and a nerveless execution.

Ebba stood. "Welcome to your future," she spat at Törni's body. She holstered her pistol and pulled her skirt down; then she walked toward her shoes, picking up each one before sliding them onto her feet. She brushed down her stockings below the knees and walked back to the body, briefly staring down at Törni. She appeared to nod to herself before muttering, "Aapo Törni. Check." She turned back toward me. "What took you so long?"

"I'm sorry?" I asked, confused.

"I sent a request for you to come. You're here now, at least."

I nodded, speechless.

With that, Ebba marched toward the console beneath the large bank of screens. She pulled something out from underneath the console top—a long, flat object with buttons of some kind on it. She placed it on top of the console and began pressing. They made an unfamiliar clicking sound. To my surprise, the bank of screens responded. One by one, the screens were being shut down. Ebba glanced back at me and grinned as she saw my expression.

"It's a computer keyboard," she said as I looked on, nonplussed.

"I need to contact HQ," I said, glancing at Törni. "This will take some explaining."

"You can't contact anyone from here." Ebba glanced back at me as she worked. "See that over there?" She gestured to the large cone-like device I had seen earlier. "That's a satellite uplink jammer. It emits multiple barrage signals per second. The same frequencies as your satellite system."

"Could you turn it off?"

"I could ..." she replied, lapsing into silence while continuing to tap on her retro keyboard, now with an air of almost manic intent. I could tell from her demeanor that she wouldn't. "The

LS rebounds from your chip will give us away anyway, soon enough, outside," she muttered without taking her eyes off the keyboard. *I'll contact HQ once we're both in the scramjet*, I thought.

"What are you doing?" I asked finally, curiosity getting the better of me. She glanced back over her shoulder at me.

"Uploading the BabelNet database to the Freetown servers. Almost done. Then I'll disable the system here." I frowned.

"Uploading malware now. We won't be coming back," she explained, straightening up and turning toward the circular doorway. Her heels clicked as she moved across the concrete floor. I was still rooted to the spot, mesmerized. She glanced back. "Come on, Emyr. We don't have much time."

I felt I needed to do something for Törni. But I wasn't sure what. I followed meekly. Outside the chamber, Ebba stopped.

"Close that," she instructed, pointing to the circular metal door of the vault. I stared at her. "Quickly—just do it." To my surprise, I obeyed again and pushed the door slowly until it swung closed, tight as a clamshell. Ebba turned a circular mechanism on the door until it would turn no more.

"But Törni's still in there," I said.

"Lucky guy. A personal burial chamber," Ebba replied darkly.

CHAPTER 24

I followed Ebba up the narrow stone steps. She certainly moved quickly for someone in high heels. Back up in the main house, she flicked a switch on the wall. And then there was light. I marveled at the strangeness of the thing: an old-fashioned switch. She continued walking with clear intent into the magnificent entrance hallway. The chandelier illuminated the large vestibule in soft-glowing brilliance.

"Wait here," Ebba commanded. I watched as she moved all the way up the stairs to the apex of the landing, where I had left the wounded commando. Ebba bent over her. I heard the sergeant groan. Ebba straightened up and carried on walking. I lost sight of her as she disappeared down the corridor leading toward the open bedroom; I knew she would find nothing good there.

After a couple minutes of waiting, I was starting to become impatient. Just then, Ebba reappeared. She walked again toward the stricken sergeant, before stopping and leaning over her. Through the balustrade, I watched Ebba pull up her skirt and remove her pistol once more.

"Ebba, no!" I shouted. Too late. I watched in disbelief as she aimed deliberately at the fallen commando and fired a single shot. There was a small bang and some smoke. Little of consequence to signal that a life had been ended. Ebba re-holstered her weapon and returned down the stairs.

I gaped. "Why? She was injured," I mouthed at her, my words hoarse with shock, at the cold, calculated sang-froid. Ebba flicked her head, looking straight past me.

"I keep a list," Ebba replied. "She wanted to be on it."

"A list?" I had no idea what she was talking about. Ebba brushed past me and turned back down the paneled corridor, walking past the jib door that led down to the basement. She was moving away from the hallway and the front entrance.

"My vehicle is that way," I said, gesturing behind us toward the front of the house. But my words were only directed at Ebba's back. I could tell I was wasting my time. "I have orders to take you to Europol HQ," I called after her more insistently. Ebba stopped dead. She spun around, her small face upturned, gazing back at me as I caught up with her. Even then, with death all around us, I couldn't help but admire her beauty.

"We're not taking your vehicle," she countered. "We're taking mine." I frowned as she spoke. She sighed as she watched me. "My life is in danger. You have orders to protect me, right?" I nodded. "Then follow me."

"I can't let you leave." I placed my hand inside my jacket on my pistol handle.

"Then you'll have to kill me," Ebba said, flashing me the same waspish, evil-joker grin she had treated Törni to the day before in her library. She turned and again walked away. *Ughh! This woman is impossible.* I was gripping my pistol handle so tightly, I could feel my knuckles beginning to hurt. I briefly considered immobilizing her with a stun round. But then again, I would see how this played out. Maybe she would lead me to Freetown. I took a deep breath before releasing my gun and hurrying after her.

I caught up as she was about to exit the rear of the manor through a spacious conservatory. I glanced around in wonder. There was a large glass dome above us.

Ebba led us out into a garden, cloaked in darkness. She pressed another button on a support pillar, as she crossed the threshold to leave the conservatory. The lights in the house were instantly extinguished.

Directly outside, there was a small metal plate in the ground. Ebba crouched as she tapped a code into a keypad on its front. Then she pulled the metal plate up. I peered down over her shoulder, trying to get a better view of what she was doing. Underneath, there was plastic housing containing a sealed unit with a timer mechanism inside. Ebba punched numbers into another keypad. There was a click. Red digits on a revolving screen began to move. *Has she activated a countdown?* I wondered.

Ebba stood, straightened her skirt, and began walking quickly again without a backward glance. I followed along a small path. The pale moon cast an eerie penumbra around us. We were walking through a garden, its shrubs and flowerbeds now barren until spring. Ebba was leading us toward a large brick-built structure up ahead, partially hidden in a small copse at the rear of the house.

As we reached the entrance, Ebba turned abruptly. I stopped dead as she suddenly faced me. But she wasn't looking at me. Her gaze went straight past, over my shoulder: she was looking back at her family home. She stared for a few seconds. I wondered what she was thinking as I scrutinized the silhouette of her upturned face for clues. She gave nothing away, despite the brief flutter of her eyelashes, caught by the pale luster of the moon. And then her reverie was done, and she turned back toward the brick building.

The entrance consisted of a large door. On a wall to one side there was another combination keypad. Ebba stood in the darkness and pressed with her small fingers. There was a click. She twisted a handle and the metal up-and-over garage door rose slowly.

Light cast by the moon dropped into the building, illuminating the lines of a vehicle. To my surprise, I realized this was a two-seater sportscar. And it was jet black. Through the windshield I glimpsed an old-fashioned steering wheel, yet there was a canopy structure on the roof—that meant an autogyro VTOL system.

"It's a hybrid," I exclaimed in surprise. Ebba stared at me through the dark. I turned my head to glance down at her as she stood next to me on the driver's side. I could see from the curve of her top lip that she was smiling.

"Yes, it is. Get in," she said brusquely. *How?* I thought, at a loss as I looked around for a VirDa voice command mic port. Ebba was watching me. "You have to use the handle," she whispered. I could hear the amusement in her voice.

"I open it myself?" I asked. Then she laughed. The same tinkling sound I had heard the day before now punctured the eerie semidarkness. I stared in wonder, both at the vehicle and at her.

"Yes. Yourself!" With that, she pulled on a handle. Her door swung open, and she gestured to the other side before she climbed in. I walked around and pulled it open. *I've opened a door myself,* I thought in quiet wonder.

Once inside, Ebba pressed something; the engine started with a gentle roar. She glanced at my face. "An internal combustion engine," she said. "Except this one runs on biodiesel. It's carbon neutral."

"I've never heard anything like it," I murmured.

"That's because there aren't engines like this anymore."

Headlights flickered on. Ebba pushed something else, and I heard the familiar sound of an autogyro system deploying in the roof sheath. She pressed pedals with her feet, embedded somewhere in the vehicle floor under the steering wheel, and the vehicle moved slowly out of the large garage-like building. There were lights on the driving console, but still no sign of a VirDa or an autopiloting system.

"What kind of car is it?" I asked.

"The *Ebba Black*."

"I meant the make and model." And then there it was again—her laugh.

"No make or model—the only one of its kind. Custom built to my specifications. Old tech with twenty-second-century smarts." The *Ebba Black*, I thought, smiling to myself. Naming a car after herself! That told me everything I needed to know about the woman.

Ebba revved the engine before driving out. I heard its throb under the hood as we circled the copse. After that, she drove along a small dirt track away from her family home toward the moonlit cliff edge and the Kattegat. Except that Ebba showed no inclination of slowing down, of stopping, as we approached the edge. The car journey had quickly turned into a white-knuckle ride.

"Ebba!" I yelled.

She glanced at me. "It's only a cliff." She tutted. But that had been my point. *We're literally driving off a cliff!*

As we plunged off the high cliff, I glanced out the passenger window at the foaming sea beneath us, bathed in ghostly pale moonlight. *If this is the end, then I can confirm there is a white light!*

I thought. Ebba put both of her hands on top of the steering wheel. In that moment, despite my trepidation, I found myself admiring how beautifully manicured they were.

And with that, Ebba pulled the wheel toward her with an abrupt jerk. It moved forward and down, rotating in front of her. A new navigation system flipped into position, revealing an autogyro steering handle where the steering wheel had been just a moment before. Ebba pulled on the throttle stick as the vehicle's VTOL system began lifting us up into the sky.

Death seemingly averted, I attempted to relax. I glanced at the woman next to me. She was dressed as if about to go to the office, in pencil skirt, blouse, and ridiculous high-heeled shoes. I saw that she was staring at me too.

"We need to get you off the grid," she announced.

"Me?" I asked, smirking. "We need to get *you* to safety."

"*You* are the liability. This is a stealth vehicle. It can't be tracked. And neither can I. But you! You're a walking, talking homing beacon. Your language chip, your LS rebounds. They are giving our location away right now."

"We need to get you in for protection by my people," I replied.

"And those weren't your people?" Ebba asked, raising a sarcastic eyebrow.

I sighed. Törni's team, CyberForce—they weren't my people. But I also understood that the Union's internal politics and diverging agendas didn't inspire much confidence. Especially when two of her staff had just been assassinated and she had only just escaped with her life.

"I have a safehouse with a portable satellite jammer. We'll spend the night there. Then we can decide what to do next. Okay?" she asked.

"Do I have a choice?" She turned to me and smiled again, shaking her head, while the vehicle performed a 180-degree turn. We were no longer over water but traveling back toward her estate.

As we passed high over her mansion, it was the sound that hit me first. A low rumbling. As it grew in intensity, I looked down. I watched in morbid fascination as the mansion slowly collapsed, imploding as we flew overhead. The gorgeous roof dropped, falling as though sucked in. Then the walls were dragged after, toppling and crashing asunder, roof tiles blinking in the pale moonlight. Rubble rained down, creating a din that reached us even through the windows of the craft, a hundred meters up. And as we flew across the explosive destruction below, I glanced at Ebba, searching for something—a hint of emotion, maybe.

She was holding the autogyro steering handle hard. Her knuckles appeared white through her pale skin. It was almost as if she was attempting to deflect the sound by sheer force of will, despite the puny strength of her small hands and arms. But she didn't flinch. She did not look down; she did not look back. *Either she's completely mad or in total control of her emotions. Time will tell,* I thought. Her family home had been rigged to explode. There could be no going back now, no homecoming.

We traveled for a minute or two in silence.

"We're heading north," Ebba announced, finally breaking the quietude that had fallen between us. "In case you're curious."

"Where?"

"Frösön," she replied.

"Still old Swedish territory? I don't know the geography."

I knew, of course, that the Nordic Republic of Scandinavia encompassed the former kingdoms of Denmark, Norway, and

Sweden. And that her family was of old, northern Swedish stock.

Ebba ignored my question. "Frösön is an island. The largest in Lake Storsjön, over five hundred and fifty kilometers north of Stockholm. I have a place there. We'll be safe, at least for tonight."

"Frösön," I muttered quietly.

"It means Island of Freyr. The Norse god of sun and good harvest."

"Will there be snow?" I asked.

Ebba began chuckling. "I mention sun and you ask about snow."

"It is November," I responded huffily.

"Not yet—at least, not on Frösön. For that we'd need to go farther north. To Lappi territory."

CHAPTER 25

We were traveling fast through the sky. Ebba pointed out landmarks on the ground below. As we approached the island, we passed over the city of Östersund, the last dwelling before the lake. I gazed down at the dappled streetlights glinting up at us through the northern darkness. The city was nestled along the curve of the shoreline. Beyond, at the water's edge, the lights ceased abruptly. Ebba pointed to the dark contour of the island, way out in the middle of the lake's inky expanse.

We soon began our descent toward Frösön, dropping down onto a strip of sand on the far side of the island, adjacent to the shore. The distant lights of Östersund disappeared as we sank below the dense branches of the birch, aspen, and alder forest that Ebba had informed me dominated the island. The vehicle came to a brief standstill. Ebba again clicked and rotated the steering mechanism, returning the vehicle to conventional car mode. Then I heard the gentle thrum of the engine as we moved slowly along a dirt track, past tall trees on either side. The shadowy arc of the headlamps revealed a clearing ahead with a small house in the center, cloaked by the surrounding dark trees. As Ebba turned the vehicle before parking, the headlights shone directly on the house, lighting it up.

It had the air of a fortress rather than the cabin in the woods I had expected; a two-story structure, part brick and part reinforced log construction. There were galvanized steel shutters locked across the windows, and an iron-barred security gate protected the solid-wood front door. Wooden steps led up to a brick veranda that encircled the house. The roof was constructed from thick corrugated steel sheeting. It extended over the veranda, providing shelter from inclement weather, with a flat apex and a glass dome at the center. The dome gave the appearance of being an observation point.

Ebba pulled up in front of the building. Before she turned off the headlamps, I saw, to my surprise, that the steel shutters on all the windows actually contained sight holes of different sizes and shapes. They were clearly expressly designed with different caliber weapons in mind. *This is some stronghold.*

Ebba switched off the engine and climbed out, letting in the cold draft of the night. As I followed, she pressed on a small device in her hand. The doors clicked behind me, and the car's headlights blinked. *The vehicle's locking and security system?* I wondered.

On the veranda, there was a metal cover in the floor near the front door. Ebba tapped a code on top of the panel to gain access. Inside, there was a sealed plastic unit. She began tapping, pressing buttons. I heard a click inside the locking mechanism of the security gate. Ebba pulled it open before using a metal key she produced from a pocket to unlock the wooden door.

Still outside on the dark veranda, I listened to the stillness of the forest. Inside, I heard clicks. Ebba was pressing things— switches. Lights came on, filtering out through the doorway in a small arc and through the metal holes in the shutters in slivers. Behind me I heard a whirr and then perimeter lights booted up around the edge of the clearing. Something moved in the sky—a bat, fleeting; as the light struck it, it moved back into darkness. I heard a faint hum from somewhere on the other side of the house. A generator powering on, maybe. I caught sight of a small black surveillance drone. And then another, and two more, slowly crisscrossing the clearing. Then another two, making six in total. Ebba had her own security detail.

As I entered, Ebba was examining a small LED control panel mounted on a wall near the door. Next to it was a closed-circuit display divided into sectors, showing images projected from the six drones.

"I've activated the orbital jamming system," she said, glancing up at me. "You are now officially incognito. But don't worry, just an uplink jammer. You can still receive incoming signals, you won't be feral."

"And you have one super secure safehouse," I retorted, glancing around. The ground floor consisted of a large space divided into an open-plan kitchen and dining and lounge areas. In the very center was a wooden staircase leading up and down, encased by wooden panels at the sides and back. The lounge ran around and behind the staircase and was partially obscured from where I was standing at the entrance. As I glanced down at the wooden floorboards, I smiled to myself. They were partially covered with what I now took to be Ebba's trademark antique-style red rugs. To my right, in the kitchen area, were wooden cupboards, and to my left a large trestle table. Ebba brushed past me and pulled the metal security gate closed before shutting the wooden interior door.

"Now we're secure." I shot her a quizzical look. "It's quiet, isn't it?"

"Sure, I guess," I replied.

"See those?" Ebba pointed to speakers at each corner of the ceiling. "If perimeter sensors are tripped or if the drones detect an intruder, then the alarm is triggered. I'll show you around."

Ebba's high heels clicked as she walked across the wooden floor. I followed down the stairs to the basement. We reached a metal door. There was again a keypad on the wall.

"You like combinations, don't you?"

Ebba shot me a stern look. "What I like is ultimate security. Which means, in today's world, a system that can't be cracked by a digital algorithm. The irony is that in the era of digital security, low tech makes me more secure than any so-called digital fail-safe."

"But you have to remember combinations," I retorted.

Ebba stared straight back at me. "I have a good memory. And I use mnemonics." She began entering her code, using her hand to shield the combination. "If you saw the code, then I'd have to kill you," she said, winking as she turned, catching me watching her. I didn't reply. I actually believed her.

She turned the handle and the massive steel door glided open inward. She pulled on a lighting cord inside the room. Neon ceiling lights flickered on. We were in a large basement, the entire area of the house. Immediately in front of us was a large darkened-glass cabinet extending from floor to ceiling. Ebba moved toward it and pressed a switch; a light flickered on inside the display. To my astonishment, it contained an arsenal of firearms.

I stood and marveled at the array of conventional weaponry— there were no coil weapons here, just good old-fashioned live-action firearms. I was an aficionado and recognized design classics when I saw them. Ebba had a fine collection of some of the most lethal conventional weapons ever made. I spotted four shotguns. Ebba followed my gaze.

"That's a Benelli Super Black Eagle II. Then there's a Remington 870, a workhorse of a shotgun, and my personal favorite, the Ithaca Model 37. But the pièce de résistance is this one," she said, opening the glass casing and pulling a weapon out of the rack.

"A Connecticut A-10 American," I muttered. Ebba handed it to me. The shotgun featured a full side lock as well as over and under action. The shoulder stock was made of walnut with the finest hand-cut checkering detail. This specimen was a work of art. I gave it back to Ebba as I ran my gaze along the rack.

I saw carbines, submachines, and different types of both assault and sniper rifles. The distinctive bolt action of the sniper rifles was on display, designed for lethal force at a distance, while the assault rifles were all intermediate caliber and automatic. These were weapons that were no longer manufactured, let alone still in use.

On a second wall there was a tall chest of drawers. Ebba motioned for me to take a look. She saw my confusion and chuckled at my stupidity.

"You just pull, remember—no VirDas," she said, gesturing at a drawer. Within lay an exquisite range of old-fashioned high-caliber handguns. There was a Browning Hi-Power pistol, a Sig P226, a Walther P99 AS, a collection of different Beretta 92 models, a Heckler and Koch VP9, and even a Ruger SR9.

I pulled out another drawer, full of revolvers. And in another drawer there was a proprietary casing in which two machine pistols were stowed. The first was a CZ Scorpion EVO 3 S1. This one I knew and loved. It was one I had often practiced with in my Cymru police academy days, in my live-action shooting club. Ebba smiled as I handled it.

"You like that one?" she asked.

I nodded. "A large-format machine pistol with a folding brace. Effective as a larger rifle but ideal for enclosed spaces; easy to maneuver with limited recoil."

"You know your weapons," she muttered as I glanced at the second machine pistol. I recognized it as the Romanian-designed Draco. I nodded toward it. "A twenty-first-century design classic."

"Yes, it is. Inspired by the much older AK-47 Kalashnikov Soviet-era assault rifle. The stopping power of the AK-47, but in a more compact format."

Ebba then showed me another drawer stocked with knives and a cabinet stacked with ammunition, categorized and labeled with small, printed cards. There was also a cabinet containing grenades of different types—stun, sting, gas, and exploding. And in the center of the basement strong room was a low cushioned square green bench, which I guessed was the go-to place to suit up with all the weaponry going, ready for Armageddon.

I turned, gazing around the room, trying to absorb it all while whistling in wonder.

"What is this, a museum?" I asked.

Ebba laughed. "Does it look like a museum? I take home defense seriously."

"Home defense?" I scoffed. "You could start a war with this lot." Ebba shook her head, still laughing. "And you know how to use all this?"

"What do you think?" Ebba asked rhetorically. This woman was starting to intimidate the hell out of me. She might even be a better marksman than me—and that would be something, given I was the best I had ever met. "I have a practice range outside," she added. *I bet she does.*

Ebba moved toward the exit, and I followed her out. She locked the strong room behind her. She then used a small microfiber cloth to wipe the combination keypad, which she placed back into the recess she had taken it from.

"Removing fingerprints?" I asked.

"The only way to crack this combination is by using residue tells from my fingers." *She's thought of everything.* "I'll show you where you'll sleep," she said, gesturing up. I followed her back to the ground floor and then around and up the next set of steps.

The upper level was smaller than the ground floor, located under the pitch of the roof. At the top of the stairs was a wide landing. In its center was a small dais, allowing someone to stand and view outside via the glass dome in the roof.

Ebba pointed. "Go ahead."

I stepped onto the dais. The glass dome was high enough that even someone of my stature could stand comfortably, surveilling out around the clearing. It afforded a 360-degree bird's-eye view all around the house. Ebba pressed a switch and powerful search lamps, fixed on the sides of the house, illuminated the clearing. I could see the glint of water from the lake through a gap in the tall birch.

"The dome can be opened. You press there." Ebba pointed to a lever on the ceiling, adjacent to and below the dome. I nodded and knocked on the inside of the glass with my knuckles. "It's transparent armor. It can withstand high-caliber projectiles of most kinds."

"So you *are* expecting a war?" I asked.

Ebba studied me thoughtfully before replying. "CyberForce will certainly know by now that its Alpha team has been neutralized. This safehouse is invisible to the Union satellite tracking systems, as are you. But your language chip rebounds weren't cloaked on the journey here. It won't take them long to figure out that you're not among the dead. To determine this location. They *will* send someone."

"I need to contact my boss, Lina de Bolle, to get this all straightened out. To have CyberForce stand down."

Ebba shook her head firmly. "CyberForce won't stand down." She said it with such certainty that it took me aback. *What does she know that I don't?* "Let me finish showing you around."

There were three doors leading off the landing. Ebba pointed to the bathroom dead ahead at the end and gestured to her room, the door on the right at the top of the stairs. "And through here," she gestured, opening the third door on our left, "is where you sleep."

The room contained a king-size bed, another shuttered window, a small desk and chair, and a large wardrobe. Ebba walked into the room and opened the wardrobe. There was an array of men's clothes—shirts, jackets, pants, even shoes.

"These are for you," she announced, turning and looking at me coyly. I gaped over her shoulder into the cupboard. The clothes were all brand new, Italian designer items, exactly my style, taste, and colors. I moved forward to examine the label on one salmon-colored blended-silk shirt.

"It's my size!" I exclaimed. I glanced through the selection of items. They all were. A perfect fit. I was completely stunned. I turned back to Ebba, startled, not knowing what to say. "How exactly do you know so much about me?" I asked. Ebba remained silent, watching me with a furtive expression.

She pointed to some towels on the bed. "Those are also for you," she said, changing the subject. "The water pressure in the shower is surprisingly good for a cabin in the woods. I'll prepare something to eat and we can talk." With that, she turned and left. I heard the click of her heels as she descended the stairs, leaving me alone with my unspoken questions and thoughts.

CHAPTER 26

By the time I went back downstairs, Ebba had prepared a platter of sandwiches and was already sitting at the long wooden table. I was now wearing a salmon-colored shirt, new slacks, and Italian patent leather loafers. I felt better, clean. As I walked toward her, she looked me up and down, studying me.

"You were right about the water pressure," I said. She had set a place for me opposite her with utensils and an empty glass tumbler.

"Something to drink? A Rusty Nail, perhaps?" I glanced at Ebba sharply. *My tipple of choice. She knows that too.*

Ebba pointed to two covered containers on the table. "The ice is in there, and this one has the sugared orange slices." She reached down to pick something up, producing an unopened bottle of Irish whiskey. She placed it in front of me. "No service droids here. But luckily you have hands," she said with a wink.

I poured a good glass of whiskey. "Will you join me?"

She shook her head. "I never drink alcohol."

"Never?"

"I don't like the taste. I'm fine with water." I arched a brow. This was the most unusual woman I had ever met. She maintained a military arsenal in her basement yet didn't consume alcohol on account of the taste. *Not even the excuse of health or religion*, I mused. As I took a sip, I studied her with narrowed eyes. Now that I thought of it, she did give me a control-freak vibe. I wondered whether that explained her abstinence: not wanting to lose control. She smiled at me as she offered the platter of sandwiches.

"What are we doing here?" I asked.

"You mean what are *you* doing here? When you have orders to bring me in, right?" I smiled wryly. *She's good. Cuts right to the chase.*

"You brought me here for a reason. I'm kinda getting the feeling I've been *selected* ... for something."

Ebba sighed. "What I have to do, I can't do alone. And your own destiny is tied up in all this, whether you believe in such things or not."

"I get that. But look, I'm no idealist. I can't help you with undoing lang-laws, changing the world."

Ebba watched me thoughtfully for a moment. "This may sound strange, but I'm not really an idealist either. My parents and my poor Elias," she added in a whisper, glancing down. Then her black eyes looked up again, staring at me for a moment as if weighing her words. "You're compromised now. After tonight with CyberForce. And with that UG tech in your head, they'll always know where you are. You'll never be free."

Whatever it was that Ebba was up to, it was becoming less clear to me the more I got to know her. One thing I did know: I had to at least try to bring her in.

"Tonight, CyberForce acted illegally on foreign soil. You were entitled to defend yourself. What they did, killing your staff ..." I shook my head. "There will be consequences. We can explain what happened. Come in with me. Please." I took another sip of the whiskey. I savored its warmth in the roof of my mouth before allowing the liquid to trickle down my throat. "And I have to try and stop a war."

"You know who's really behind the language outage, don't you?"

"Not the Russian Federation," I said quietly.

"They're being set up by Appleton—by Marc Barron. You know that by now."

I smirked. "Operation False Flag," I said. "A drone was deployed by Drones Kineto, a tech company with connections to Appleton."

"The cyberattack was initiated deep inside Russian airspace."
So she knows too, I thought.

"What still puzzles me is why BeeDirect was spared. If Marc Barron's plan is market domination, why leave intact the main language streaming provider of the world's most populous Tier Two state?"

"Simple," Ebba said. "It makes Russia look guilty. And if there's war, the Union will aim to dismantle BeeDirect anyway. The Federation won't be allowed to retain its own infrastructure."

And there it was—my own personal epiphany. Ebba was right. Appleton was a carpetbagger; it would get a foothold in the Russian language streaming market anyway. Especially as Marc Barron now had leverage with the Union, which needed support for all the out-soc Tele3 subscribers. And Appleton would take over in the Russian Federation too.

"So basically, all this suffering, maybe even war, it's just about the bottom line?" I asked in amazement. It beggared belief that the people of the automated world were nothing more than pawns in a global marketing strategy dreamed up by Appleton executives, so that the company might become the dominant global force in commercial language streaming. "Is that why you've been targeting Appleton? You knew this was coming?"

Ebba shook her head solemnly. She paused, glancing down at my hands wrapped around the whiskey glass. "The outage. I only found out about that a month ago." I frowned. *So Ebba did have advance knowledge of what was to come.* "But the organization, I set it up years ago for my own ends ..." She lapsed into silence.

"Go on ..." I whispered.

"My parents, they didn't die in an accident ..." Ebba was silent again. I waited, giving her space to explain in her own time. "They were murdered," she said finally. "On Marc Barron's orders."

I recoiled. "You know that for sure?" Ebba stared back at me, her gaze unflinching, her eyes meeting mine. She leaned forward slightly. Her hands were gripping the edge of the table.

"My parents were allowed to challenge the legality of lang-law in the courts," she began.

"Everyone knows that. So ...?"

"If Californian lang-law had been ruled unconstitutional, that would have been a game-changer, not just in the Republic of California but everywhere." Ebba frowned before continuing. "Then came the dirty tricks. Not just the lawyers. Appleton even hired private investigators, trying to dig up whatever they could. They succeeded. The year my mother studied at Berkeley on a scholarship in her student days. Dad always said she was a free spirit. She definitely was back then, by all accounts. It was all horrific."

I watched Ebba intently. I wondered what kind of childhood she must have had with parents like hers. An itinerant lifestyle, growing up in the shadow of some mythical great cause, the fabled LangFree movement. Led by two oddball activist parents who toured the Tier One globe giving lectures, leading rallies, mounting lawsuits, becoming cult superstars, while in the mainstream popular consciousness they were viewed as anachronistic weirdos. I felt fleetingly sorry for her. With her background it was probably no surprise she was so screwed up. After all, what normal person had a basement full of guns and rigged their ancestral home to blow up? *What normal person even has an ancestral home?*

Ebba glanced across at me with an expression that spoke of keening sadness.

"It was ruled an accident. The hover car crash," she whispered. "The last one with fatalities in the entire Tier One world." Now she shook her head. "They had to be special, even with that."

"The day after the Supreme Court ruling. I know."

"They were traveling from Sacramento. The funny thing was that Elias had flown into San Francisco to meet them, with Karen—she was always playing mother to him in those days. It was supposed to be a celebration. I never really had their—" her words suddenly seem to catch in her throat, "—passion. For the cause." Ebba looked away before glancing back at me, smiling weakly. "Their hover car developed a fault midair. The autogyro system just failed. No one could explain it."

"But you suspected foul play?"

"What do you think? Coincidence?" Ebba said, crossing her arms. "The hire company had no explanation. The vehicle had only just been serviced. Less than a year old. Elias and Karen were too distraught to carry on with their legal challenge. They found comfort in each other, I suppose. And by the time Elias was ready, a bit older, well … the world had moved on. The momentum for the movement had evaporated. And a legal fight—that takes will, resolve, nerves of steel, and lots of money. It drags on for years. It was my father's hobby horse. Elias didn't have the stomach for it."

"I'm sorry for your loss."

Ebba smiled at me faintly, seemingly drifting away for a moment. Then she turned back to me. "But you know, that was my own personal inflection point. I decided I would use my tech and coding skills to become the world's most formidable hacker. Nothing would be hidden from me."

"And you found out something, right? That's what this is all really about, isn't it?"

Ebba stared at me intently before answering. "It took me ten years, but I got to the bottom of it—the conspiracy, the elaborate cover-up. Their vehicle had been tampered with. They fell to their deaths, a deep canyon. It took two days to recover their bodies. And I finally uncovered the identity of the engineer who sabotaged their car. He went straight on my list!"

"You mean a hit list, right?" I asked grimly. I had already seen Ebba execute a CyberForce commando in cold blood. "What happened to him?"

"Poetic justice happened. His bones lie in the same canyon," Ebba whispered. "He was bribed by Darya Zao. He confessed everything. It wasn't pretty ... they always beg in the end," she muttered.

My eyes widened. "The Appleton executive?" We had a file on Zao, a naturalized Californian with the sobriquet of 'the Rottweiler' for her less than subtle approach to protecting Appleton's business interests. I took another sip of whiskey as I mulled over what I had just heard.

"You didn't go after her?" I asked finally.

Ebba smirked. "Of course I did. She and Marc Barron are on my list. But he's protected. And he protects her."

"I'll bet. Probably the best money can buy," I mused.

Ebba shook her head. "No, that's not what I meant. This is something else. I even had the drop on him, but ..." She lapsed into silence again. Now she was being enigmatic.

Then it struck me as I did some mental calculations. If it had taken Ebba ten years to uncover the truth about her parents, that would have been around a decade ago; which was when she had announced the arrival of her organization with her manifesto.

"So the publication of the Babel Apocalypse, what was that? Cover for revenge? Nothing to do with repealing lang-laws?"

Ebba looked me dead in the eye. "It wasn't just about revenge. At least, not in the beginning. I wanted to do something. For Elias. He was hurting so badly after I discovered our parents' death wasn't an accident. I hadn't taken it seriously enough, while they were alive. None of it, the whole LangFree movement. And with the discovery that they had been murdered, it brought back all Elias's old pain too. He had never really recovered from losing them."

"So why did he go work for Appleton?" I asked. Ebba looked at me sharply.

"I blame myself for that, and for what happened. I told him too much. About how they died, our parents. I shouldn't have."

"What did happen to Elias?" I asked softly.

"We both wanted revenge, I guess. We had different strategies. His was to infiltrate Appleton. He wanted to get proof, to go to the authorities. It was naïve, but that was Elias all over. He never understood that others don't play fair."

"I heard he even got himself chipped."

Ebba nodded sadly. "Just over five years ago. He thought getting chipped was the only way. You can trick systems with wearables that simulate LS rebounds. But he wasn't like me. He was like my parents, especially my father. Gentle. He was vulnerable, really." She sighed. "And Appleton HR would never have hired the son of William Riggs and Alvinia Black, Marc Barron's tormentors-in-chief." Ebba sipped from her glass of water. "He communicated regularly at first. You have no idea what Marc Barron is into," she said, her eyes blazing.

"But Elias discovered something, didn't he?" I asked, intrigued.

"Marc Barron is part of a secret cult. The Brethren of the Sacred Vessels of the Grigori." As Ebba uttered the name, a bolt of recollection seared through me. This was the same name Karen Hoekstra had mentioned when she'd first made contact.

I stared at her. "We have the name logged. Never could establish what it was or whether it actually existed," I muttered. Talk of a secret cult, especially after a drink, always sounded like the beginning of a joke. Except that Ebba didn't look as if she was joking.

"It's an eschatology society," Ebba said, a smirk spreading across her features as she watched me. My expression of bafflement must have been priceless. I had to look it up.

"Eschatology ..." I repeated, giving a double tap behind my ear to get the full definition streamed from my lexical package. The metallic drawl of the Union-DEF lexical database began intoning inside my ear implant. *The science of last things. The part of theology concerned with death, judgment, and the final destiny of the soul and humankind.*

"From what we figured out, this Grigori cult has existed in one form or another throughout the entire history of the Catholic Church," Ebba said. "It even has its HQ in the Vatican

City, under papal seal. And its own sacred text that diverges from the canonical gospels." I watched her face as she spoke. *Is this all for real?* I wondered. "We didn't manage to uncover a thing at Europol," I muttered. *Despite our vast resources.*

"The Swiss Guard has surprisingly sophisticated security protocols," Ebba said.

"So, what is this cult supposed to do?"

"It predicts the end of days. The arrival of the Grigori. That the Grigori will be hosted by the chosen ones; the rest of humanity will perish. They brand it the *destiny of the lost.*"

"Grigori?" I asked, shrugging. My English database didn't register anything, but instead started auto-parsing Greek. I nodded to myself as I got it. "Watchers. In English."

"Right. The Grigori are supposed to be fallen angels who will bring eternal life on the day of judgment. This is where it gets good. Marc Barron believes that these Watchers will possess the chosen few. Human vessels. And these vessels will destroy the false messiah, referred to as the Sage. And this Sage will be replaced by the judge of all things, the Mashiach." Ebba looked at me and grinned.

"So, some kind of Doomsday cult," I muttered. Which was what Karen Hoekstra had also claimed when she'd first come to me. "And your brother linked this to Marc Barron?"

"That's where it gets weird. We could never identify the cult leader, but it must be someone close to Marc Barron. My brother died trying to get this information," Ebba snapped. "Someone thought it important enough to kill." Her hands were now scrunched into fists, pushing down onto the table. Her whole body was rigid and her eyes ablaze. She certainly believed what she was telling me.

I frowned. "Why don't you tell me about your brother?

What do you think happened to him?" I said, trying to placate her. "We have it down as suicide."

Ebba looked straight at me, nodding. "My legal team had to apply some pressure. But we managed to have his body returned for burial on our estate. I had my own autopsy performed ... his head was blown apart. From the inside. His language chip exploded. Three months after getting chipped in the first place and after moving to California—infiltrating Appleton."

I gawped at her without blinking. "He didn't shoot himself?"

"Does that sound like suicide to you?" Ebba asked, staring straight back at me. Now my heart was beating fast. *Exactly the same cause of death as Dhruv Gasper*, I thought.

"I'm sorry, Ebba," I mumbled absently. It was all I could manage.

"Death would have been instantaneous," Ebba explained. She was speaking softly now. "You know, I'm at least grateful for that. No suffering. His body was so small on the slab. The mortician ... worked on him. But I still ... I didn't recognize him. It wasn't the injury so much. Well, obviously ... the injury. But also, you know, the stillness. Weird. It just felt so ... I don't know ... *unnatural* somehow. Now there's just me. I'm the last one." I knew how she felt.

I paused, trying to contain my mounting excitement. "You're not going to believe this. We have a case with the exact same cause of death. Although our autopsy showed a second implant inserted under the surface of the skull."

Ebba's eyes narrowed. "That'll be a neural transmitter. Elias had one too. I only discovered it had been fitted when I received the autopsy report. He would never have agreed to it voluntarily. The last few weeks before he died, I had lost contact with him. He was being held against his will, I'm sure of it. They did that to him. But … they'll pay …"

"A neural transmitter?" I asked. "You know what it does?"

"It took several months' research to figure it out."

"And?" My heart was pounding again as I waited.

"Synced to Elias's sec-code. Remotely activated to deliver malware on a proximity share." I watched Ebba, nonplussed. "In a nutshell, the implant turned Elias's language chip into a bomb. Inside his head."

"You know this for sure?" I asked.

Ebba glanced at me grimly. "Confirmed by the best forensic cyberanalysis money can buy."

"And I'm guessing you think this was also Marc Barron's doing? He discovered who Elias actually was, is that it?" She didn't reply; she didn't need to. "But do you have actionable evidence?"

"I don't need evidence, actionable or otherwise. I know it was him." Ebba gave a hollow laugh before continuing. "This might be about my revenge. But it's also about averting war, helping billions of people who are being used as pawns in a commercial aggrandizement scheme that benefits no one other than Appleton. It's about bringing down Marc Barron, serving justice, and stopping whatever other evil he has going on with his cult. Those are things that you believe in, right, Emyr?"

"But why me?" I asked. "With your connections, you'd be able to find a gun for hire better suited to this."

Ebba watched me thoughtfully before replying. "Someone told me it had to be you."

"Someone?" I asked, intrigued.

Ebba threw me a strange smile. "You're not going to believe me."

Now I really wanted to know. "Just tell me already," I said with frustration.

"Lilith King." Ebba paused, watching for my reaction.

I nodded. "That figures." As I spoke, Ebba's mouth opened wide in surprise. I laughed, seeing Ebba Black rendered speechless. I hadn't thought it possible.

"What figures?" she demanded.

"Yesterday I was in California, at Drones Kineto. At the request of Dwayne Kline. He happens to be the partner of the guy whose head was blown up. Just like your brother. He left Kline evidence that Marc Barron was behind Operation False Flag. But here's the thing: it was Lilith King that told him to get the intel to me."

"Do you know her, then?" Ebba asked.

"That's just it. I've never even met her. I had no idea she'd ever heard of me. Something odd, though. Dwayne Kline said she claimed to be from the future. He had to note the time she appeared—yesterday at 9.16 a.m. Californian Standard Time in his office."

Ebba frowned. "There's more to this Lilith King than meets the eye ... she claims she has other names." I clearly had a confused expression, as Ebba carried on. "Abaddon, Apollyon, Exterminans."

I shrugged as my language chip began auto-parsing. "The first two mean 'destroyer' in Hebrew and Greek. The third name ..." I paused as I received an unknown signal in my ear implant. "The language doesn't exist."

Ebba smiled at me. "The language used to exist all right. Just not on your server, apparently. Exterminans is Latin. The names all mean the same thing in all three languages. A reference to the Book of Revelation."

"As in—what? The Bible?" I asked, perplexed.

"Abaddon is the Angel of the Abyss who appears on Judgment Day. The Alpha and the Omega, the First and the Last, the Beginning and the End." Ebba shook her head before throwing me a questioning look. "Lilith said you would help me. Will you?"

"With what?" I asked, taken aback. Ebba glanced away. Then the penny dropped. "Surely not your revenge mission?"

She turned back to me with a look of determination. "Didn't you hear anything I just said? Marc Barron has to be stopped. Millions are already suffering."

"All the more reason for you to turn yourself in," I countered.

Ebba shook her head fiercely. "Don't you see? Barron has unlimited technical and financial resources at his disposal. You can't do anything on the inside—not now, not anymore. CyberForce will be coming for me and for you. Come with me to Freetown. There you can undergo untethering; you can be set free. And then do some good. Stop all this madness."

I closed my eyes, thinking, before looking back at her. "Where is Freetown?"

Ebba threw me a wry grin. "Lappi. We'll head out tomorrow."

"Lappi!" I exclaimed. "Look, I can't follow you to the frozen north. I can't undergo untethering. Honestly, the best thing for us both is if I take you in to Europol."

"My path was determined for me a long time ago. And now an attempt on my life. This is your time to choose." I shook my head again. "Just think about it overnight. Please?"

"I can't just give up on everything—my job, my career, my status. And even my freedom to do as I please. And for what? A life on the run?" *I can't give them up, all the things I love, the things I have worked so hard to achieve—my apartment, my beautiful car, my comfort*, I thought.

"Freedom?" Ebba laughed. "You're a prisoner of the system, of your language chip, of your UG tech, and all the dirty politics that it has inflicted upon the world. Your freedom is an illusion. I am offering you real freedom. To truly fulfil your potential and make a real difference."

As she gazed at me with her wide black eyes, I didn't have the heart to say no. Although I knew I would have to, eventually. But *no* could wait until the morning.

I sighed. "Fine. I'll sleep on it."

"Sleeping on it is fine," Ebba replied insouciantly. "Now, we really should get some rest. And I also need a shower."

* * *

After Ebba had disappeared upstairs, I dawdled for a minute, finishing my whiskey. Then I too went upstairs and into my assigned room. I closed the door and sat on the bed, lost in thought. I could hear Ebba in the shower.

A few minutes later I heard floorboards creak. I stood up, startled. I opened my door and surreptitiously surveyed the landing. The light was off. Ebba's door was slightly ajar, with a light on inside.

"Ebba?" I whispered. There was no reply. I assumed it had been her. I was about to turn and return to my room when I glimpsed her inside her bedroom through the gap of the open door. I stood momentarily transfixed by what I saw. She had her back to me and was drying herself in front of a mirror. Her pale, slender body was naked. Her hair fell over her shoulders and down her back. As I made to turn back to my room before she realized I had seen her, she moved, turning toward me. The light from my own room partially illuminated me, and as

Ebba turned, her eyes looked straight into mine through the gap. She didn't flinch, she didn't move, she just stared at me, unashamed, her breasts daring me to avert my gaze. Then she stepped toward the door and pulled it wider open.

"Come in," she whispered.

CHAPTER 27

For the first few seconds after I woke, I didn't know where I was. Although I knew when: it was day four of the language outage. But the residual disorientation of sleep inertia meant I couldn't place the strange, darkened room and even stranger bed I found myself in. Early morning light darted like laser beams through tiny sight-holes in the window shutters. I tried to remember, but confusion reigned.

Then I felt a form next to me. A woman's naked form. It was Ebba! Everything flooded back all at once as I remembered the night before.

Ebba's body was nestled into mine, still asleep. I felt her warmth and the gentle pressure of her skin against mine. She was on her side, curled into my chest and stomach as I also lay on my side, with her back to me. One of my legs was pushed between hers, clamping her to me. My left arm was under her neck, stretched out. Her hand was holding mine. My other hand was wrapped over her side, cupping her left breast. I breathed deeply and moved my hand. I gently stroked her soft skin, enjoying the moment.

I heard a ping in my ear implant. I knew it would be Lina de Bolle even before I activated my holotab. I slowly moved my arm from underneath Ebba, turning, not wanting to wake her.

Lina had just left a facecall mail on my Europol service. I saw I had also missed the memoclip she had sent the night before, requesting an update on my status.

"Activate E-box playback, Lina de Bolle," I said softly into my mail app. "Audible to ear implant only." Ebba was still breathing slowly and softly next to me. Lina's stern face appeared on the screen as playback commenced, but now her face also showed signs of visible concern.

"Catastrophe at the Ebba Black mansion last night. Typical CyberForce—complete screw-up. An entire Alpha team taken out. Something is going on. Von Böhm is refusing calls from the director. Patchy signal from you, but we know you got out. Emyr, let me know your status, please …"

Just then there was another ping in my ear. An alert banner scrolled across my holotab, above me as I lay on my back. This one was a memoclip from Dwayne Kline. I blinked through to the message. He was as good as his word and had sent details of the payment made by Dhruv Gasper, with the payee reference: *Glanc MD*. It was a large payment, denominated in e-Continentals on November 5th. But what took me aback wasn't the amount but the payee address, listed as Rue d'Aerschot, Schaerbeek, Brussels. I stiffened. This was the same address as Lady Raven from the Catch and Kill audio file.

The slight movement of my body was enough to disturb Ebba's sleeping form. She stirred and turned toward me. As her eyes fluttered open, she smiled before leaning forward and kissing me.

"Hello."

"Hello," I whispered back. We stared at each other, for that instant cocooned in the surreal strangeness of our new-found intimacy.

"What is it?" Ebba asked, looking up at the holotab still projecting from my wrist.

"Something strange I need to check out. An address in Brussels—a high-class escort. Linked somehow to the language outage. From an anonymous lead, an audio file."

Ebba smiled. "Catch and Kill, by any chance?"

I froze. "You know?" I asked as she smirked back at me, raising one lacy eyebrow. And then the penny dropped. "You sent it!" I mouthed at her. Ebba watched me, still on her side, her black eyes sparkling. I smirked back at her. "So, as you know so much, what's the significance of Lady Raven, then? It'll save me a trip."

Ebba frowned as she propped her head up on one hand. Her long black hair fell around her shoulders. "Who?"

"The escort. She's apparently a dominatrix. The one mentioned in the audio clip." Ebba began chuckling. "What's so funny?" I asked, becoming slightly irritated.

"You," she began. "For such a smart guy, you're really not that smart."

Now I was becoming frustrated. "So tell me who she is, then," I demanded.

Ebba shook her head. "That's not it. If she's a dominatrix, she's not an escort. A pro-domme doesn't have sexual intercourse with her clients; she won't get naked in front of them. They won't even be allowed to touch her."

"You're well informed," I muttered. "But what about Lady Raven?" I insisted.

Ebba shook her head again. "My software runs voice and visual detection algorithms. We're following Appleton's activities. That's our main focus. That audio file was flagged because a keyword was detected, relating to ghost chips. We don't know what Appleton is up to. But we're working on it. And the dominatrix, Lady Raven, we don't yet know anything about her—how she's involved in any of this."

"But you do think she's involved in some way?" I asked.

"The woman speaking in the Catch and Kill file is Darya Zao," Ebba said, staring at me intently.

"Ahh," I replied. Ebba nodded in response. I knew what this meant. Dhruv Gasper had been on a call with Marc Barron's fixer. And they'd been discussing Lady Raven. And given Gasper was now dead, whatever it was that Darya Zao had orchestrated, then Lady Raven really was involved in all this in some way. Still, I felt some measure of satisfaction that while Ebba was well informed, she didn't have a complete monopoly on all intel. She apparently didn't know anything about Lady Raven.

"So why did you send us the Catch and Kill file?" I asked.

"I warned you when we met that you wouldn't have believed me if I'd told you who was behind the language outage. You needed to find your own way to that conclusion. Once you'd identified the female voice as Darya Zao, you'd then see that Marc Barron was up to something. You did ID her too, right?"

I ignored Ebba's question. I wasn't going to admit that we'd only identified the male voice, Dhruv Gasper. While I was pondering what Ebba had told me, a loudspeaker in the corner of the ceiling began emitting a low-decibel electronic sound.

"What's that?" I asked, tensing. "The intruder alert?"

Ebba glanced at me, slightly perplexed, giving a small shake of her head. "That's the generator warning signal. An outage. Never happened before."

"A warning of what?"

"That signal means a complete failure. The backup generator

should have kicked in," she muttered grimly as she sprang out of bed. "I need to see what's going on."

I watched as she moved across the room toward a chest of drawers, her tousled obsidian-black hair streaming down her naked back. She pulled out underwear and began to dress before turning back to me. "The security systems will be down. And your language chip signature visible." She faced me now in black lace underwear. "Both generators at once ..." She shook her head slowly.

"Where are the generators?"

"Outside, round the back. They work on solar power."

"Could it be a loose connection? A fault of some kind?"

Ebba looked at me grimly. "I don't believe in strange coincidences. Do you? Someone is here," she said quietly. "But we'll be armed."

I got up to dress too. The air on the landing was cold as I crossed back to the other room for fresh clothes. By the time I was done, Ebba was standing, watching me through the open door of my room. She was wearing her trademark blouse with a black jacket. But in place of her skirt, she was sporting black palazzo power pants and sequined black designer sneakers.

"No heels today?"

She gave me a stern look. "We have company, darling," she replied sardonically. "Come down to the basement with me."

"I thought you'd never ask," I replied, and she threw me another dark look.

* * *

The cold in the basement was bitter. There was no heating down here. I watched as Ebba furrowed her brow, scanning her arsenal. She selected her Connecticut shotgun, the A-10 American.

"Power dressing?" I asked as she held the double-barreled shotgun aloft.

"This is what I call accessorizing." With that, Ebba pulled a cartridge belt out of a cupboard and quickly filled it. Then she chose a handgun—an original Beretta 92 model. Italian design, with curved lines and a round smooth top. Ebba's Beretta was both beauty and beast, with deadly stopping power. She selected a black leather hip holster and holstered her weapon. Finally, she opened a drawer containing combat knives and daggers. She chose a long, thin fixed blade with a full tang. It was a commando fighting knife. As she held it in her small hand, it glinted under the ceiling light.

"Böhler steel," she said quietly as she saw my gaze. It had a red textured rubber grip. She placed the combat knife in its matching red leather sheath, which she strapped around her waist on the opposite hip to her holster. *She has definitely accessorized*, I thought. "Now you choose something. I may need you to provide covering fire."

"I have my coil pistol." I pointed to my kydex shoulder holster.

Ebba shook her head firmly. "That's traceable every time you activate it. Especially now that the jammer is down. That stays here, away from temptation," she commanded. I frowned while she continued opening the gun rack and drawers to entice me. Then I saw the Scorpion EVO machine pistol and my face lit up. I smiled and pointed. Ebba laughed. "That was easy." The short-barreled weapon was the ideal choice. It also worked as an automatic rifle, especially with the stock extended. "Magazines are over there," Ebba added.

I removed my holster and picked up my new weapon. I clicked on the laser sight. The Scorpion EVO was chambered with 9mm Luger. It offered low recoil and provided accurate shooting, with plenty of firepower, in semiautomatic or fully automatic bursts. I helped myself to a bag of magazines, which I attached to my belt.

Finally, Ebba took a pair of what I now knew to be walkie-talkies from a shelf. She switched on both devices.

"You press here to speak," she said. She spoke again, this time into one of the devices. Her voice came through on the other, loud and clear. She handed one to me. It was housed in a fabric case with a belt clip.

Back upstairs, Ebba examined the monitor screen adjacent to the front door. The signals from the drone video feeds were dead. She began unlocking the door.

"I'm coming with you," I said insistently.

Ebba glanced back at me and smiled. "As soon as we have power again, your LS rebounds will be invisible. But only if you stay in here. The uplink jammer doesn't have a wide range. And I need you to keep lookout. You can spot me from up there." I followed Ebba's gesture. She was pointing back up the stairs to the landing and the dome in the roof. Then she clicked on a small lever on the monitor screen. It unclipped from the wall bracket. She pulled it out and extended a carry handle from the top of the unit. "Take this with you. Once power is back on, the signal from the drones will reboot. So, if CyberForce has sent a team here, we'll know about it. There's a spot to hang the screen on up there."

Ebba opened the door and paused while I jogged up the stairs, taking up my position. I pressed on the lever to release the glass dome. It slid up and over on one side, allowing a completely uninterrupted view all around the clearing. I climbed onto the dais. There was a clip attached to the ceiling of the landing, allowing me to hang up the monitor. Now I could watch both the screen and events unfolding outside.

"I'm all set," I called down. From my position on the landing it was no longer possible to see the front door. But I heard her voice crackle over the walkie-talkie attached to my belt.

"Heading out now." I unclipped the device.

"Be careful," I replied, remembering to hold down the button as I spoke. I placed my Scorpion on the edge of the roof and unclipped my bag of detachable box magazines. I laid five aside. Each magazine contained thirty rounds. The Scorpion used a blowback action, with a muzzle velocity of 370 meters per second. I set the weapon to automatic fire, just as a precaution.

From downstairs I heard the scrape of the protective iron gate as Ebba opened it. And the same locking sound as she secured it behind her. Now I was alone in the house.

CHAPTER 28

I looked out over the roof, scanning the clearing around the house; all was still. The morning light was bright. The air was cold and fragrant with pine sap. I heard a bird screeching from beyond the trees, somewhere over the lake.

Ebba's petite shape moved fast from the front of the house around the side. Amid the stillness, it was difficult to imagine that anyone else was really here, hidden among the trees on this distant northern island. But I knew that appearances of calm could be deceiving.

I tracked Ebba's progress around to the rear of the building toward the generator. It was a large unit, fixed firmly in a concrete base and encased in a caged structure with a solid protective roof and a gated entrance door. Ebba paused as she reached it, pressing on something. One of her combination keypads, I guessed. Then she disappeared from view inside the cage. My walkie-talkie crackled again. It was Ebba.

"Do you want the bad news?"

I pressed down to talk. "That sounds ominous."

"We definitely have company. A robotic drone the size of a small rodent. That's how it evaded detection ..." Then a brief pause. "Looks as if it carried an EMP package. The main generator is knocked out, frazzled by the electrical pulse. But

269

the backup ... I wonder ..." Her voice trailed off in a crackle. Just then, my monitor feed began flickering. "I've reset the backup generator," she announced, with more than a hint of triumph.

"My video feed is coming back online," I replied.

"We'll have backup power for around two hours. As soon as the drones are airborne, you'll have the surveillance zone restored. See if you can spot the CyberForce commandos for me. The drones have heat-detection capabilities."

"Copy," I replied.

I heard the buzz of the drones before I saw them, as they rose from where they had dropped at various points in the clearing. The live feed from each flickered back on across the six divisions of the screen. Ebba remained inside the generator cage, awaiting my intel.

As I scanned the six sectors of the screen, each corresponding to a live drone feed, I couldn't help but draw in a sharp breath.

"Ebba?"

"What is it?" she replied, detecting the alarm in my voice.

"I have heat signatures for five hostiles hidden in the woods surrounding the house."

"Can you pick them out for me?" she asked.

I paused, just for a second. The house was facing toward the lake at twelve o'clock. Ebba was directly behind the house inside the generator cage at six o'clock.

"One in tree cover directly behind you, ground level. Another dead in front of the house at twelve o'clock, and two more at three and nine o'clock. All ground level."

"And the fifth?"

"High tree level at ten o'clock," I replied.

"Tree level?" Ebba asked.

"Probably on an omni-move robotic lift platform. That's definitely military grade. Ten o'clock will be the sniper in the crow's nest." I knew that normally a Union Alpha team had four commandos. But because we were special, this time we also got a sniper. I also knew this would be a well-drilled commando unit.

"How do I neutralize them? Do they have body armor?" Ebba asked. "Like before?"

I examined the screen. The heat signatures were strongest at the neck and groin. From those distinctive tells, I knew they would have leg, arm, and torso casings. And probably also lightweight helmets with protective visors. But they would be exposed in at least two places.

"They're vulnerable to fire at the neck and groin," I replied.

"With the signal jammer back on, outgoing comms won't be possible. They won't be able to communicate with each other. That gives us the advantage. I'll take care of the ones on the ground. You take the sniper—over?" Ebba said.

"Roger that and out."

I watched as her face peered out of the generator cage. Her blood-red lips stood out against her pale complexion. She dropped to one knee, staring intently around and past the side of the cage, searching the base of the tree line behind the house at six o'clock for the first target. Suddenly she sprang up and ran around one side of the structure, partially obstructed from my view, hugging the base of the generator cage as a protective shield. She sped toward the edge of the clearing, covering the distance in a couple of seconds. *Wow, she's fast.*

As she neared the tree line, she opened up the side of her body and fired her shotgun, shooting from the hip. I knew she was using a tight choke in her weapon for maximum effect.

She fired both barrels in quick succession into the foliage base directly at six o'clock. As I watched the drone feed, I made out the heat signature of a kneeling figure at ground level, just inside the tree line. The shape twitched before slumping to the ground. She had gotten her target.

As Ebba was about to disappear into the foliage, I noticed that the sniper's heat display, at ten o'clock, had changed shape. The sniper had assumed a new firing angle, now aiming at Ebba. Coil weapons don't produce recoil or noise, so you couldn't spot a shooter based on a weapon being discharged. But I saw enough from the drone feed to be certain that Ebba was in danger.

I snatched up the Scorpion, pulling it into position, and fired an entire magazine at the sniper's heat signature high up in the tree. I couldn't tell whether I'd hit the target; I had no direct visual and the sniper was camouflaged. But the thermal signature shape shifted. My fire had caused a distraction, allowing Ebba to make it to safety. She disappeared inside the tree cover.

I heard the crackle of her walkie-talkie. She was back on comms.

"Six o'clock dispatched," she confirmed.

"Nice shooting," I replied, smiling before remembering that she couldn't see me. *You dumbass*, I thought to myself.

"I'm heading round to three o'clock. The foliage is dense."

I no longer had a direct visual for Ebba, so I switched to the screen. I could make out her heat signature from one of the drone feeds. It was distinct from the others; she didn't have body armor. Now she was on the other side of the house, diagonally opposite the sniper at ten o'clock, which meant she was safe from sniper fire, protected by thick tree cover.

I ducked down slightly below the roof line to avoid having my own head blown off by sniper fire. But just then, I heard a slight noise. I craned up my head, scanning back up over the roof. It was the commando who had been positioned at nine o'clock. The tip of a special forces helmet was now visible over the top of the flat apex of the roof. The commando continued to rise above roof level, no doubt also using an omni-move lift platform. As the figure stepped onto the roof, I saw from its physique that this one was clearly male. He aimed his assault rifle across the roof at me. I swiveled around to direct my Scorpion, switching to the semiautomatic fire setting while adjusting the laser sighting system. I discharged a burst of fire directly into his neck. This time I didn't miss. I even glimpsed the look of surprise through his visor before he toppled back off the roof, landing in the clearing below, out of sight. I heard the heavy thud as he hit the ground decked with frosted pine needles.

A new crackle of static drew my attention back to the walkie-talkie. "Are you okay, Emyr?" I smiled as I detected a hint of concern in Ebba's voice.

"All fine. Thanks for asking. Nine o'clock has been taken care of." Just then there was a muffled sound and I heard static followed by two rounds of gunfire. It was Ebba's Beretta. My walkie-talkie crackled again.

"Neck and groin," Ebba explained. "Three o'clock eliminated."

Now there were just two commandos remaining. I knew the sniper would be the more difficult to dispatch, with the advantage of height. I saw from the drone feed that Ebba was making her way around to the commando at twelve o'clock, immediately in front of the house. That was where the narrow track led through the break in the trees toward the lake.

I followed Ebba's progress via the drone feed; her distinctive heat signature emerged onto the track we had driven along the night before. To my shock, I glimpsed another partial heat signature. It was the fourth commando, hidden by a tree, which she had her back to.

"Ebba, behind you!" I half shouted hoarsely into the walkie-talkie. On the video feed, I watched in grim horror as the red and orange of Ebba's infrared signature spun around, her hand holding the Beretta poised midair, while the distinctive partial shape of the commando stepped out from behind the tree.

Just then I lost the visual, as the feed from drone two was blocked by the dense foliage. But it was replaced by live feed from drone five on the bottom left sector of the screen, which had just moved into direct visual range. This gave me a close-up bird's-eye view through a gap in the trees directly above Ebba and the commando; I was now watching the action unfold directly underneath, without the guesswork of interpreting heat signatures.

But what I saw was not good. Not for Ebba. The commando was aiming an assault rifle at her less than three meters away. This one was also male, and he had the drop on her. Ebba appeared to see the danger mid-turn. She curled her body down and around into a forward roll, spinning forward beneath his shooting line, striking his legs with her feet as she reached him. Her Beretta fell out of her hand from the impact, while the commando was knocked backward, dropping his weapon.

He was a tall guy but was up quickly. As he stood, he moved forward, grabbing Ebba's prone form from behind, one arm around her neck in a stranglehold, lifting her off the ground. I looked on, helpless, as she writhed and twisted her small body, attempting to gain traction, to wriggle free in midair. I could see her eyes beginning to pop as she was being strangled. But somehow, powered by desperation and sheer force of will, she managed to unclip the knife sheathed on her hip. She pulled it out but flailed in midair as the commando held her aloft, his arm compressing her windpipe.

I could only watch on the screen, unable to intervene, lacking a direct visual through the trees from my perch and without anything close to a clear shot. Yet Ebba was relentless, ferocious, and utterly fearless. Even as the very life was being crushed from her, she refused to succumb. I marveled as she kicked with venomous intensity, swinging her body to gain momentum. She succeeded in driving one heel hard into the commando's midriff with enough force to cause him to loosen his grip around her neck. She dropped a little, almost touching the ground, and with that impetus she managed a half twist, enough to get a striking angle, despite still being held in a choke hold. As she drove her knife hand forward, the commando, seeing the danger, parried, deflecting her strike. Her knife fell harmlessly to the ground.

But Ebba was undeterred. With her free hand, she continued stretching forward, fingertips reaching underneath the commando's torso armor. I watched the video feed, transfixed, as she reached for the one vulnerable area on his body that she had access to: above the thigh casings, below the torso plate. She buried her hand in his crotch area. I saw the whites of her knuckles as she clenched through the fabric of the commando's camouflage pants, squeezing, twisting his genitals with all her might. He instantly dropped her, howling as he staggered back in clear agony, dropping to one knee.

Ebba fell to the floor, but quick as a flash, she was up. She scooped up the knife from the ground. And with that, I knew he was done for. Before he had time to block, to defend himself, Ebba darted behind him. She placed her left arm across his visored forehead, holding his head firmly. And with her right hand, she drew her blade across his neck with a swift gesture.

As her small hand moved across the commando's neck, I thought I was still seeing the colored handle of the knife. But from the eruption of red, I realized this was blood, and the jet of bright color could mean just one thing. Ebba had completely severed his carotid artery with a deep stroke of her blade. The man slumped forward, dead in the dirt. *Ebba Black is not to be messed with. One hell of a badass!* I made a mental note for future reference.

Something new distracted me on the feed from a different drone—sector one, top left on the screen. The sniper was descending from tree-level position. The hydraulics of the omni-move lift platform glinted in the morning sunlight through the foliage. And as the commando emerged at the tree base, I saw from the physique that this one was female. It stood to reason the sniper would be. Women were statistically better sharpshooters than men. In my police cadet days, one psychologist had informed us that the reason was that women were better at concentrating and focusing rage. My own experiences led me to suspect a more prosaic explanation: women were just better students—no egos getting in the way. But then again, that was before I'd met Ebba Black.

The sniper was now wending her way through the trees, heading for Ebba, for a decisive kill. I no longer had a direct visual, just fragments of thermal signature from the drone feed as the sniper appeared fleetingly between the trees before disappearing again. Meanwhile, on the other drone feed, I saw Ebba searching the ground for her fallen pistol. From what I could see, she no longer had her shotgun either. I needed to warn her. I pressed on the walkie-talkie and spoke, but she wasn't receiving. *What the hell?*

I grabbed my firearm, jumped from the dais, and ran down the stairs. All I could think was that I needed to warn Ebba of the danger approaching. I pulled open the wooden door. But the outer gate was secured fast. Only Ebba knew the combination, which meant I was locked in. Through the iron bars, I scanned the tree line for any sign of Ebba or the sniper. And at exactly that point, I flinched. I felt a sharp burning sensation in my left triceps. I had been hit. I ducked back inside and slammed the wooden door shut.

I examined my arm. I'd been caught by a high-caliber sniper's bullet, from a coil rifle. Fortunately, it was just a flesh wound; the bullet had passed clean through. I rummaged through some drawers in the kitchen, finally finding a kitchen towel. I spent a couple of minutes binding the wound, winding the cloth tightly around to stanch the blood.

I only remembered I had left the roof hatch open when I heard the sound of a soft thud from upstairs, on the landing. The sniper had found her way inside the house! I moved across the room, positioning myself behind the long trestle table, crouching low for tactical advantage. From the sniper's position at the top of the stairs, she wouldn't be able to see me; but once she descended a couple of steps, I would have her in my sights.

I heard the sniper clear the bathroom and bedrooms, checking for occupants—for me. I saw her armored boots first as she stepped onto the top step of the stairs.

The sniper began advancing down the stairs. I now had her shin casings in my line of sight. I needed her to advance slightly farther for me to have a clear shot of the lower point on her body, her groin area. She paused, waited, listened.

Come on! I thought, willing her on. She just needed to descend slightly farther—two more steps. What was she waiting for? But the sniper began carefully retreating, moving backward up the stairs before holding her position just at the top. *Dammit.*

As I watched and waited, I heard a sound behind, to my right. It was the front door opening. I glanced over my right shoulder to see Ebba on the threshold. If I called out to warn her, the sniper would be alerted to my position. But if I said nothing, she would walk in and be vulnerable to coil weapon fire. My heart was beating so fast, it felt as if it would burst through my chest.

I heard the sniper beginning to move down the stairs again to check out the noise. Ebba spotted me crouching. I placed my finger over my lips before gesturing to the staircase.

Ebba looked at me and smiled. It was her warm, radiant smile. In that moment, I knew that this woman whom I had studied, every comma of whose file I knew by heart, more than fascinated me. I had felt her mouth against mine, her breath on me. I knew this was something I hadn't felt before, something inexplicable. And for the first time in my adult life, I felt afraid.

I gave Ebba another gesture to retreat. She shook her head. *Arghh!* I pointed up the stairs and raised my shoulders to signal *why the hell not?* But Ebba just carried on smiling at me. The sniper was beginning to creep down again. I calculated that she would need to be around four steps down to have a firing angle on Ebba—three, if Ebba took one step across the threshold. And I needed the sniper to be on step three for my kill.

Ebba glanced at me, threw me a strange, macabre look, and to my horror she took one step in while lowering her Beretta—

she *had* retrieved it. The gun slid out of her hand and dropped onto the floor with a clatter. She now had the sniper's full attention. The sniper skipped down the three steps. I could see from her legs that she was making to shoot from the hip—a high-caliber coil assault rifle aimed directly at Ebba's chest. But now I had her entire lower half in my sights. I fired thirty rounds directly into the unprotected area underneath her torso armor. There was an explosive crack as my weapon discharged. Before the sniper was able to get off a single round, she fell forward down the stairs, landing with a sickening thud on her head at the base of the stairs before rolling onto her back. I stood up. By the time I took the few paces toward her, a large pool of blood was surrounding the body.

I turned to Ebba, anger flushing my face. "You risked your life!" I hadn't realized I was shouting until I heard my own words reverberate around the large room. "Why?"

Ebba studied me in silence.

I suddenly felt giddy, weak. I half fell, half sat on the stairs, looking at her across the dead sniper who lay between us. Fear and panic hit me. And rage that she had deliberately put herself in harm's way. She picked up her pistol.

"A duty to rescue," Ebba said finally, enigmatically, moving across to me and bending down to examine my arm.

"What?" I asked, bewildered, pushing her slightly so that her eyes met mine.

"A duty to rescue," she repeated.

"You risked your life so that I had a duty to save you?" I asked, completely perplexed. *What kind of high-stakes game is this woman playing?* I wondered. I still felt overcome with a kaleidoscope of emotions at having nearly lost her, having only just found her.

Ebba smiled and shook her head at me. "No. I have a duty to rescue you ... and now you have to come with me to Freetown. To be freed." I stared at her in amazement, unable to fully comprehend the stunt she had just pulled. She was clearly plain mad. I had never in my whole life met anyone quite like her.

CHAPTER 29

After Ebba had cleaned and bandaged my wound, we sat across from each other in her house in the pine clearing on Frösön. I watched her hands resting on the trestle table like small, splayed icicles. I idly reconstructed the way they had felt on my skin, tending to my injured arm. Soft, chilling to the touch. Yet soothing.

Ebba's communication device was in front of her. She'd called it a Freeband radio. I had never heard of such a thing. She was to speak to someone at Freetown—arrangements had to be made. I felt strangely light-headed.

In rational terms, I knew there was now no going back. They would say I had been aiding and abetting a known cyberterrorist, the sinister Ebba Black. After all, I had killed two CyberForce commandos, two *friendlies*, to save her. Even Lina de Bolle wouldn't approve of that. Lina would have wanted me to come in, to bring Ebba in. And to cap it all off, my language streaming rebounds would soon light up. We were on backup power, which was running out. I was running out of time to think, to delay, to postpone a decision.

I felt an emotional crisis looming, storm clouds in my mind. I was backed into a metaphorical corner. The decision wasn't even mine to take. Loss of control. Stripped of agency by events; somehow by her.

Ebba had asked me to pack *my* things. I had grinned inwardly —a resigned grin. They were *her* things! Intended for me, sure, but things *she* had picked out for me. The clothes, the shoes, the shirts, even a beautiful long leather coat. But they were also the things I would have picked for myself anyway. Exactly those.

She also asked me to choose weapons. I walked around as if in a trance. Yet I chose; I was still capable of that. I selected a Glock 19 pistol and a matching leather shoulder holster. The Scorpion, of course, and an assault rifle, the SA80 A3. It was a beast of weapon that could be fitted with an underslung 40mm grenade launcher, a far-sight aiming module, as well as night-vision scopes. It was light and packed a serious punch. I helped myself to plenty of ammunition. I would be leaving behind my old faithful coil pistol.

Ebba loaded the car. Soon, everything was packed. The decision had already been made—I just couldn't bring myself to accept it. Thus we sat looking at one another in a delicate, tacit standoff at her table, with a dead commando on the floor near us.

"If I do this, I'll become an outlaw," I said.

"You will."

"I won't be able to go back to my apartment." I felt giddy as I spoke.

"No."

"I'll lose my job," I complained.

"Probably."

"And my car." I sighed wistfully. I loved that car.

"You'll lose it all, Emyr. You'll be an outlaw." Ebba spoke bluntly. *Nothing like sugar-coating it to make me feel better*, I thought to myself. *Just tough love.*

"I'll be out-soc," I said plaintively. I somehow felt an

otherworldly numbness creeping over me. It was the strangest feeling; somehow, I no longer felt myself. I knew, logically, that it was just shock at the situation I found myself in—at what this all meant. *Would I really give up my life? Everything I had worked for? Could I?*

"No, not out-soc, not even feral. Just an outlaw," Ebba replied.

"But how will I support myself?" I asked.

"I've made all the necessary arrangements," she replied.

"Arrangements?"

Ebba nodded. "A new alias. You will have a new voice print linked to a sec-code, a constructed employment history. You will have a bank account, money. It's all taken care of." She was trying to be reassuring. But why, then, did I not feel reassured?

I knew there were two types of decisions: the reversible, and the irreversible. Mine was of the second variety. There could be no going back. Yet I couldn't identify the point where I had decided, definitively, that I would follow Ebba, that I would travel to Freetown, that I would agree to change my state from that of a tethered mute to that of an untethered free man, whatever that even meant.

The Cymru police cadet training manual advocated seven steps in decision-making. First, identify that there *was* a decision to be made. Next, gather and organize relevant information, leading to the third step: identification of the options. The fourth step required the weighing of evidence. What would each alternative feel like? What would the consequences be, the pros and cons? And which alternatives best matched the values of the decision-maker? Then came the step of selection— choose from one of the options. Step six entailed taking action to realize the chosen path.

I had done none of this. There had been no weighing of evidence. No careful reflection. No assessment of who the impacted parties would be, how my life would change. Nor was there a eureka moment—a before, when the decision remained unmade, delineated by a clear after. It had just happened. Engineered by Ebba, maybe. She had seduced me. But I had wanted it. And the gunfight. I had wanted to protect her, especially when she'd offered herself as a target. That had been part of her cunning. I saw it, belatedly. She had forced me to choose. And she had done so by giving me no choice at all. Of course I was going to save her.

"Liminality," Ebba said.

I started in surprise. "What?" I asked. Not because I didn't know what the word meant. That was the beauty of on-demand streaming. I knew that *liminality* concerned ambiguity and disorientation associated with a transition from one state to another, that it referenced a rite of passage meant to bring about some change, physical or metaphysical. What startled me was the realization, as Ebba highlighted the liminal, that this was exactly it. It explained the numbness, the shock. I was on a threshold, and I was unsettled. This was to be an untethering. I really was going to give it all up. And that meant giving up my language chip, being permanently severed from the entire language streaming ecosystem. From my life.

Step seven, the final step in the cadet manual, was acceptance. Be at peace with the decision. No ifs, no buts. Today, I didn't feel at peace.

* * *

The Freeband radio on the table was taller than it was wide, with a handle on top for ease of transportation. On one tall, narrow side there was a detachable handheld mic, attached by a clip. A black spiral cable connected the mic and the base station. The base station itself was silver, with a speaker grille on its front. Toward the top of the front was a long, thin LED display screen. And along the top were buttons, including those marked *on/off*, *speak*, and *signal booster*. There were also several knobs and dials on the front, running in a horizontal column down the right-hand side opposite the mic clip.

Ebba explained she'd had it custom designed, allowing two-way communication with Freetown.

"It's old tech but very effective."

"But is that secure?" I was skeptical.

Ebba smiled across at me while I fidgeted. "You're thinking, this is analog. Not digital. The signal isn't encrypted. Anyone could listen in. Right?" I shrugged. That was exactly what I was thinking. Ebba laughed her tinkling laugh before continuing. "The real beauty of this kind of old tech is that no one uses it. No one has the technology anymore, not even in museums. And if no one has it, no one uses it, and so no one listens in. And if they can't listen in, it really *is* totally secure."

I watched Ebba as she spoke. With her reveal, something else finally dawned on me. "So, if you can communicate quite literally under the radar, why were we able to track down Erebus McDenizen? Why wasn't he using this old tech?" Ebba fixed me with a dark stare. *How come my team was able to intercept an exchange between Datashizzle and The Tower?*

"You intercepted a digital signal," Ebba replied quietly.

"But why would you use digital transmission when you have old tech that wouldn't be tracked? Unless …" I stopped. "Unless you did want us to intercept it. You wanted me to know about

False Flag," I stammered as dawning lucidity hit me.

Ebba gave me a faint smile. "Look, CyberForce is run by trigger-happy fools. They're itching to get back at the Federation. This is their perfect opportunity. I knew that once you realized it was a setup, you'd be able to do something."

"So you sacrificed your guy?" I asked, more in rhetorical incredulity than anything else.

"He's courageous. He volunteered. We anticipated his location might be compromised—at worst, that he might be detained." Ebba's face became dark. "However, neither he nor I expected you to put him on your NocioPerception rack."

I studied Ebba for a moment. "As you know so much about me, you must have known exactly what I was capable of."

Ebba's eyes narrowed as she watched me.

As I finished speaking, quite suddenly, everything fell into place. Ebba had Erebus McDenizen contact Karen Hoekstra. Ebba knew she was my informant. Of course she did. And once McDenizen had fed Hoekstra some juicy details, talked about Freetown, then Ebba Black would definitely have had all my attention.

Ebba was watching me with hooded eyes.

"You wanted me to treat Babel—you—as the prime suspect, rather than the Russian Federation," I whispered.

"That would be logical," Ebba replied. "If the Russians weren't behind the outage, you'd figure it was the organization; you'd suspect me."

"But why? When you had nothing to do with it? Why have me suspect you?" I asked. Ebba smiled, watching as my mind whirred. "Precisely because you had nothing to do with it!" I whispered, answering my own question as it hit me.

"I told you, you're very astute." That was all she said. I gazed at her.

"You've gamed all this. You dropped breadcrumbs for me that led all the way to you. But why? That's what I really want to know. What do you want with me?"

Ebba gave me an otherworldly look, then sighed. "I have it on good authority that you'll save my life." My mouth opened in surprise. That was not the response I'd been expecting. Ebba nodded at me, at my expression of disbelief. "But I believed her," she whispered.

"Lilith King?" I asked. Ebba continued to stare at me. She didn't need to reply. Now I sighed with resignation.

"Make the call. Let's get this over with."

Ebba flashed me a broad smile as she pulled out a long antenna from the top of the device; she pressed the button that read *signal booster*. I heard a crackle over the transmitter. Then she pushed the button marked *speak*.

"Freetown, come in. This is The Tower, over."

There was a slight pause before a female voice responded.

"Great to hear you. This is Freetown, over."

"I'm coming in with the patient. Alert Doc and the team, over."

"Will do. We've been expecting you," the operator said. I made a slight sound of surprise, causing Ebba to glance across at me. "What's your ETA? Over," the female voice queried.

"Around fifteen minutes."

"And the patient's LS signature is still hot?"

"It is," Ebba replied.

"We have our new venue prepped, over."

"See you soon, Freetown. Over and out." Ebba switched off. She began packing up her radio system.

"They've been expecting me?" I asked. Ebba stood, ignoring my question, and walked to the door. She looked back at me and gestured with her head for me to follow.

I nodded and rose. By the time I reached her outside on the veranda, she had again opened the metal compartment encased in the wooden floor. She was tapping numbers into a timer device similar to the one at her mansion the night before. She finished and closed the metal plate.

"We won't be coming back," she whispered.

"Do you make a habit of blowing up all your houses?" I asked. She smiled at me ruefully.

We got into the car and Ebba started it up, setting the vehicle in VTOL manual flight mode. As we lifted up, out of the clearing, I heard the rumble of the explosives bringing down the small house. This time I didn't look back either.

CHAPTER 30

As we flew north, we began to move across terrain with a fine dusting of white on the ground. The snow gradually became thicker. Then we passed through a squall. Gusting eddies of whiteness danced all around us, buffeting the sides of the vehicle.

Ebba told me that Freetown was located on the edge of Lake Torneträsk, north of the Arctic Circle. It was near Abisko, a small village in the old Swedish Lappi wilderness, nestled at the foot of a mountain range that sheltered reindeer and lemmings. She said the mountains were a great place to view the northern lights, especially at this time of year.

We emerged through the whiteout over the mountain peak into clear air, revealing a crystal lake laid out below in white, icy stillness. I half tapped on my wrist to activate my bioclock. It wasn't even 2 p.m., yet the light was already fading. The sun would be setting soon. November days were short this far north. Below, some streetlights were booting up as we passed over the tiny Arctic community at the edge of the remote Abisko National Park.

I glanced across at Ebba as she began dropping us down onto a transit corridor. "How do you keep Freetown hidden from prying eyes?" I asked. "Especially if it's near a community."

"You'll see," she replied mysteriously. As we landed, she switched to manual drive. "We're now on the E10."

I glanced out into the white gloom of dusk. The transit corridor was constructed from standard prefabricated plastic sunk into the Arctic soil. But this far north, the modular structure contained embedded heating coils. They were clearly doing their job, as the driving surface was covered in a film of slush from the melted snow.

"The heated transit lanes were installed when I was a girl," Ebba said. "Before that, there were still snowplows."

I watched the dark Arctic lake to our right as we traveled along the transit corridor. From the land, the water underneath the ice crystals looked somber, forbidding.

After a few minutes, as we moved over a rise, a large compound came into view on our left. I guessed it was a couple of hectares square. Much of it was obscured from view by fencing, save for the distinct contour of a huge transport craft. The vehicle's darkening silhouette rose high above the perimeter markers. The compound was enclosed by tall automated prefabricated fencing units with perimeter sensors. A dim waveguide holographic display ran across the outer fencing. It read: *Arctic Geological Survey*. Ebba pulled off the road toward it.

As we approached the entrance, I saw that it was guarded. *Human guards!* There was a small portacabin at the entrance with two silhouettes inside. Ebba wound down the driver's side window, and one guard walked out. He was dressed in a thick brown Arctic coat with a fur-lined hood. His livery and insignia designated the Arctic Geological Survey. He was a big man with a rugged face and a scar down one cheek—he didn't look like a geologist. He peered in and smiled in acknowledgment at Ebba. I saw that one of his front teeth was broken.

"Welcome back, Ebba." He spoke with General American accent differentiators. "Doc is all set in the medical unit. Penny has the evacuation underway. The *Black Albatross* has also been readied for you."

"Thanks, Sam," Ebba replied. The guard stared directly at me. I sensed his curiosity. He was clearly in good shape; I could tell he could handle himself. As I met his gaze, he nodded at me in acknowledgment. I nodded back. He straightened up as Ebba wound up her window. To my surprise, I saw that Sam was wearing a coil pistol in his hip holster. *Hmm, I thought Ebba was all about old tech.*

Sam waved us through. As we drove into the compound, I turned to Ebba.

"That was a real guard. He had a coil gun!"

"Flesh and blood," she said, clearly enjoying my confusion. "Former Delta Force commando. Now an employee of the Arctic Geological Survey."

"So where's Freetown?" I asked.

"Hiding in plain sight." Ebba smirked at me.

And what a sight. Now inside the perimeter fencing, I took in around twenty large, prefabricated container-like units in front of me, with doors and windows. They were clearly habitable. The units were arranged in two rows of five, stacked two up and with a few meters between each container. Enclosed, collapsible air bridges connected each unit, both horizontally and vertically, with more collapsible air staircases at each end connecting the lower and upper stories.

Beyond and along one side of the small city of containers, there were a number of transport hover vehicles. I spotted one large aircraft, a human transporter, with windows revealing cabins and sleeping berths.

But most striking of all was the shape I had seen protruding high above the perimeter fencing as we approached. Even as the light faded, I could see this was a jumbo hover transport, a cavernous beast of a vehicle and perhaps the largest civilian transport I had ever seen. It had multiple—ten, maybe a dozen—VTOL autogyro units fitted along its massive roof.

At its rear, there was a large ramp, which had been dropped to the snowy ground. Robotic hyper-lift loading units were moving up and down the ramp, loading other container units into its interior. I realized that the entire operation—this place, Freetown—was being packed away, stowed into the large transport. *Freetown is a portable city!*

I also realized that Freetown must consist of far more than the twenty or so habitable containers that still remained in situ in the middle of the vast compound. I could see the silhouettes of people moving through air bridges between containers as lights went out inside individual units. A line of people, each carrying bags, emerged at one end as we faced the assembly of containers. They were filing toward the smaller passenger cruiser. As we drew closer, I saw that the much larger craft, the jumbo transporter, was already nearly two-thirds full. I could tell that when in its normal state, Freetown would be a mini city of interconnected work- and home-space containers—a hive of activity, full of life. A community of kindred spirits.

"Welcome to Freetown," Ebba said, laughing at my amazement.

"How many people do you have here?"

"Around four hundred."

"And all untethered?"

"Every single one. All committed to the cause. All true believers," she replied. "And we carry on recruiting."

"Do you really *do* work for the Arctic Geological Survey?" I asked, still amazed. It was a well-established NGO.

"We *are* the Arctic Geological Survey," Ebba replied.

Now I was flabbergasted. The Survey's executive director was a well-known figure; she sat on the Union's New Green Deal advisory committee. Lina had even name-dropped her—Penelope Maes—and knew her socially.

"That can't be right," I exclaimed. "My boss is friends with the Survey director."

"Oh, you mean Penny," Ebba replied, smirking. "Yes, I hired her. In fact, I'm one of the founders of the Survey and chair of the Board of Directors. I spoke to Penny earlier; you heard me."

"On your radio? That was Penelope Maes?" I asked in bemusement.

"Penny's coordinating the evacuation now. And the Survey does do important work—work we all believe in. Everyone here wears two hats. You might think of them as white hats and black hats." Ebba winked at me.

"But we don't have a record of you having any links to the Survey," I stammered. I was still perplexed. The make-up of the Arctic Geological Survey, its board of trustees, directors, was all public knowledge. How was any of this possible? It felt far-fetched that the whole thing was a front for Babel. I could hear Ebba chuckling as she saw my expression.

"I have multiple roles, and more than one hat, too," she began. "As Ebba Black, I'm of course a university professor who intellectualizes the decommissioning of language chips and develops a language retraining program. I'm also an heiress, the beneficiary of funds from the Johansson-Black Trust, courtesy of my maternal grandparents. And as Ebba Black, I am also labeled a Babelist by our friends at CyberForce. Also sometimes by Europol. But you could say that my involvement in the Arctic Geological Survey is more that of the white hat."

"White hat?"

"The beauty of being a *ghost*, as you mutes love referring to me, is that assuming aliases is as easy as putting on a wearable and syncing it to a VirDa. The joy of our digital landscape is that I can become anything and anyone."

Ebba glanced across at me as we drove through the eerie spectacle. A community of researchers, scientists, and idealists, all wearing two hats, with the assistance of state-of-the-art robotic units, packing up their site, loading their supersized transports, and moving on.

She pulled up the car. "We're heading in there," she said, pointing to an entrance in one of the few containers that still had lights on. "We don't have much time. We need to get you prepped, untethered, and out of here. All of us, in fact. CyberForce will be here soon."

CHAPTER 31

I squinted as my eyes adjusted to the brightly lit interior of the medical unit I now found myself in. I absorbed its gleaming surfaces, brilliant white, and a window onto the fading gray landscape outside. Through the window, I glimpsed distorted flickers of security lights, oranges and reds from the robotic loading units as they stowed dark shapes.

I followed Ebba as she opened another door. I was still amazed to see door handles. This new door let out the distinctive odor of antiseptic from the room within. Ebba paused, half turning toward me. She smiled gently as she watched me follow her across the threshold. I felt tentative but committed now, finally.

Inside was the medical chamber. I took in an involuntary breath. They would be messing with my head; quite literally opening me up. I suddenly felt trepidation. And nausea. The funny thing was, I hated needles. No one ever got that as they looked at me. I got it, and their judgment. *What does a big guy like him have to be afraid of? He looks like he could stop a rhino.* It wasn't rational. Phobias never were.

The medical chamber was partitioned into two areas: a preclinical antechamber, and the operating theater itself. The operating theater was separated from us by a hermetically sealed glass partition fitted above a low microfiber wall. The whiteness of the place gave me the creeps.

A medic was seated at one end of the preclinical area. He had his back to us. His distinctive head gestures showed he was engrossed in issuing blink commands at the large translucent screen in front of him, projecting from the fusion bar inlaid in a large console surface.

"Thom," Ebba said. The medic turned and then stood, beaming as he saw her. He moved forward instinctively and gave her a hug.

"So good to see y'all," he replied, using General American accent differentiators, as he stepped back, holding Ebba by the shoulders, glancing at me before staring back at her.

I cursorily eyed him up and down. He was in his mid-thirties, I guessed, and wore thick-rimmed black glasses. He was a good head shorter than me. Despite having a thin, almost gaunt upper torso, his waistline pulled at the buttoned lower front of his white medical tunic.

"Emyr, meet Doc," Ebba gestured. Doc turned toward me and offered his hand, his eyes twinkling through his glasses as he studied me.

"We've been expecting you," he said.

"So it seems." I glanced quickly at Ebba.

"I'm Thomas Breckenheid," he stated.

"Doc is a leading light in New York," Ebba announced with pride.

"Was," he corrected her.

"Professor of Neurology at Columbia University," Ebba revealed, undeterred. "Fellow of the American Association of Neurologists and brain surgeon at Columbia's Neurological Institute."

"She likes embarrassing me." Doc squinted, now slightly red-faced. I already liked him.

"And he gave it all up to become the Chief Medical Officer for a lowly NGO in the frozen north."

Doc laughed at her, shaking his head. "Ebba made me an offer I couldn't refuse," he explained, glancing at me. "How many neuromedics get the opportunity, the resources, to achieve what we've done here?"

"We should probably get on," Ebba said quietly to Doc. He turned back to the console, gesturing for me to take the seat next to him. I wasn't sure whether I wanted us to *get on*.

As I moved forward, I glanced nervously through the glass partition on my left again. On the other side was a large surgical chair. And over it stood a robotic surgeon, with arms, levers, lights, and protruding needles poised in seeming menace. Adjacent was a health monitoring daemon. Behind were further temperature-controlled sealed glass units.

As I sat at the console next to him, Doc glanced at me, following my gaze through the glass.

"See the sealed unit in the middle with the circular aperture?" I nodded. "Your memory chip is in a cradle. We're going to connect to it, using my console here, and program it according to your preferences. When you're all set up, the robotic surgeon will implant the chip. We'll have you off the grid in no time."

"How do we do the language selection?" I asked.

"Here." He pointed at the screen. To my surprise, I saw that we were in a menu featuring Appleton proprietary logos. We were actually inside the Appleton database, in the state official language menu. Doc had the menu open, set at the letter A, with five state official varieties listed for Arabic—Arabic (New Modern Standard), Arabic (Egyptian), Arabic (Maghrebi),

Arabic (Gulf), and Arabic (Levantine)—each with nested menus of multiple accent differentiators. "Choose wisely," Doc advised. "Once the language selection is made, it's fixed for life. There's no going back."

I coughed. "English," I replied.

"Of course." Doc issued a blink command. The menu refreshed. There were five state official varieties available— English (African Standard), English (North American Standard), English (Oceanic Standard), English (Singlish), and English (Indian Standard), while King's English (Old Standard) was grayed out.

"That's now on the proscribed list—no longer available for streaming, as you're probably aware," Doc explained. "We can't steal King's English for you anymore."

There were also dozens of non-standard varieties available, associated with premium lexical upgrade packages, none of which had state official status, but which could be streamed for a price. I skipped through the large array of blinkables. The high-end non-standards for English ranged from Anglo-Cornish to Gullah to New Blinglish to Uglish.

But what I wanted was a state official variety. That was what all public VirDas used. That was what made most sense. And the majority of VirDas in the English-speaking world operated on North American Standard. I pointed.

Doc gave me a slight nod. "That takes care of the grammar and vocabulary. But what about an accent?" I knew he was right. After all, I didn't want the undifferentiated drawl of no accent differentiators. You could spot the Unskills a mile off precisely because of that—a lack of accent. The Union provided a monolexemic streaming package free of charge—or at least it *did* before Tele3 went up in smoke. But accents came at a premium, and the public aid program only paid for the basic subscription. Here and now, I could choose whatever accent differentiator package I wanted. Doc had them listed on his VirDa screen, quite literally only a blink away. As I sat next to him, I found it ironic that after a career spent guarding against cybercrime, I was about to steal an advanced language and accent package from Appleton.

Finally, I pointed at the screen, at an accent.

"Cardiff English it is," Doc said quietly.

"Good choice," murmured Ebba from behind us. I glanced over my shoulder. "Similar to the old Severnside accents of the Old Kingdom, but yours differs in being non-rhotic." Both Doc and I must have looked confused, because she sniggered. "That means you won't have an 'r' sound after a vowel."

Ebba then proceeded to pronounce *farmer* with and without the two "r" sounds to show me what she meant. I nodded as I got it, sitting back, somehow feeling now at peace with my decision to untether as I looked back at my selection on the screen.

This was to be the reliquary to contain my disdain for my father. He'd always been a boastful man. I remembered, once he was chipped, he'd always claimed he would get a multilexical package. He wanted Cardiff English. But he couldn't afford anything beyond the basic state package. Thus he had only ever streamed one language: the state official. Cymraeg it was, right until his untimely end. I curled my top lip as I sneered. In life, beyond death, I would have the last laugh. *At least that,* I thought.

After issuing some voice commands, Doc turned back to me. He gestured behind us to a hygiene unit. "You'll need to put on a gown in that cubicle. For the procedure." There was now urgency in his voice. I glanced down, activating my bioclock in my wrist chip. He watched me. "That won't work anymore either, afterward," he said, gesturing to my wrist. I nodded.

I stood and walked to the cubicle. The sliding door opened and then closed behind me. It was a large unit with an undressing area. The VirDa instructed me to remove my clothes, which were stowed in a sealed compartment while I was prepped for the cleansing procedure. It was a three-minute process. Light-green LED ceiling tiles glowed softly above me once the unit autoactivated. I was sprayed with a liquid jet of two percent chlorhexidine gluconate solution while massaging units cleaned me. I was then rinsed and finally blow-dried.

When I emerged in my slippers and surgical gown, Doc and Ebba turned. I felt strangely calm for what was next. The twinkle in Doc's eyes had been replaced by clear focus.

"The surgeon will shave a small area of your crown," he explained hurriedly. "The skin sterilized and a local anesthetic. Topical and by needle. Then a sonic shock to your ear implant. That will feel a little strange. Feral for a few minutes."

"But on the upside, the implant will have been permanently disabled," Ebba interjected.

I knew what that meant. No more language streaming rebounds. Although CyberForce would already have a fix on me—and, as a consequence, on Freetown's location here. They would be on their way.

"The memory implant will be inserted just below your skull," Doc explained. "Input cords sewn into the input jack in the language chip. When the incision has been closed, I get the green light from here," he said, pointing to his console. "I then activate the memory chip. Once it's switched on, it's yours for life. And that's it. We have a closed loop. You'll be done in twenty minutes. Then change back into your civvies and be on your way."

"Deep breaths," Ebba said. She was trying to be reassuring.

"Any questions?" Doc asked. I shook my head. A glass aperture opened, allowing me to pass through into the operating chamber.

Once closed in on the other side of the glass, it was the silence that struck me. A soundproofed stillness muffled my ears. And the room gleamed, a white sterility. I glanced back and saw Ebba watching me through the glass.

The robotic surgeon began speaking in banal welcome, oddly intersex, no gendered inflections. Once I was seated, the lower part of the seat, below my knees, folded up so that my legs were supported, stretched out in front of me. Chest and arm straps deployed from the frame, securing me to the brilliant whiteness of the seat's medical padding. A head brace deployed slightly unexpectedly from somewhere behind the seat's back. Now I was at the mercy of the robotic surgeon, locked in a forward-facing, vise-like grip.

The surgeon deployed over my head, its rotating arms positioning themselves around me. I heard a sound above and something brushing against my scalp. Then I felt the tiniest of pricks, a pop, and then … nothing. I stared at Ebba through the glass, enveloped in the surreal stillness of the absence of sound. Was the unit working above me, inside my head? This new silence was of a different quality to the muffled soundproofed silence.

I wondered whether, when this was done, I would experience an epiphany, whether I would feel different. Would I think in a new way with a new set of words, and a new accent that would now be my one single default, that I would have for life?

As my thoughts banged violently around my silent mind, it was done. I heard the robotic surgeon speak: "You might experience a slight headache, and possibly nausea. Such side effects can last for up to twenty-four hours." The clamps were released.

Once I was dressed, Ebba asked me how I felt. I didn't answer immediately. I felt strangely nervous—still myself, yet different. I would even sound different. I wasn't quite ready to speak. I shook Doc's hand.

"Tonight we celebrate," Ebba whispered to me as I followed her out.

Outside, it was now dark. The compound was almost completely packed away. The medical container where I had been treated was all that remained of the assembly of containers. The security booth had disappeared. Even the fencing panels were sliding back, auto-closing into upright poles, which a robotic loader was collecting.

There was a large shape in front of us, the shape of a passenger vehicle. The craft was a large luxury cruiser the size of several large trucks but with the curvature of an oversized bird. It didn't have wings; it didn't need them. I could see that much. It had a powerful VTOL autogyro system. I could tell that this beast would be able to approach the transonic speed range.

"My home away from home," Ebba said, "The *Black Albatross*." As the lighting flickered behind us from the medical container before shutting down, I saw the livery briefly. As the name suggested, all black. Of course.

The vehicle had a large windowless storage compartment at the rear, a piloting cabin, and a living area in the central portion, arranged as a duplex apartment. I thought I even glimpsed stairs, glinting for an instant in the reflected light from outside, as I regarded the small windows.

"The *Black Albatross*," I repeated, tasting the words, before I even realized I had spoken. *I have a new accent*, I thought. Ebba smiled at me. She seemed to like it. I liked it. "It's quite a beast," I murmured, impressed. "And your car, the *Ebba Black*?"

"Stowed in there," she said, pointing to the rear of the Albatross. "That's the garage." As we approached, Ebba beckoned toward the piloting cabin, with driver and passenger doors on either side of the front. She pressed on a small handheld device and steps deployed. She gestured and I climbed up the five steps. I now knew to use door handles, so I pulled my door open and climbed in.

"Where are we heading?" I asked.

"Tomorrow we will go see Lady Raven. But tonight, it's dinner at my place, in the Albatross, under the northern lights."

* * *

We landed on the lakeside summit of the mountain, overlooking the now-empty site that had hosted the Arctic Geological Survey just a short time before. I watched the stream of wing-mounted piloting lights through the domed windshield as the convoy of hover vehicles slowly lifted, departing into the dark evening sky.

Ebba was still sitting at her piloting console as she activated the craft's cloaking system. She then turned toward me and explained that this peak was known as the Aurora Sky station.

"The Scandinavian mountain range begins or *ends* at Abisko," she said, laughing. *I guess whether it's a beginning or an ending depends on your perspective*, I thought.

Once the *Black Albatross* VTOL system had powered down, Ebba stood. The piloting cabin contained two rows of three seats, with an aisle on one side. Ebba walked toward the rear of the cabin, beneath the lighting console that bent round the concave sides away from the windshield. I followed her toward a doorway, which led us into the spacious living quarters that opened up in the belly of the craft. There was a large open-plan lounge area, a raised dining deck with long windows at one end, and stairs up to a mezzanine-level sleeping deck.

"I need a drink," I muttered.

"That's on the menu," Ebba chuckled, pointing, as I followed her up the four steps to the dimly lit dining deck. She was in a good mood.

As I reached the top, I whistled in amazement. The deck featured the most exquisite black marble dining table I had ever seen. It was inlaid with colored motifs, swirling flowers of turquoise, yellow, and deep reds. Ebba glanced at me and then at the table.

"Handcrafted by artisans in Italy to my own specifications."

But that wasn't all. Outside, through the viewing pane, flickering lights were rippling across the dark sky. Ebba watched me.

"The Aurora Borealis," she muttered.

Glowing swirls of green and yellow all along the sky, as if painted by a master impressionist, reached down from the heavens, rippling through sensuous oil paint. And the darkening sky was the canvas.

"It's beautiful," I whispered, still testing my new accent, as I leaned on one of the black lacquered chairs surrounding the table.

"So are you," Ebba muttered. I started in surprise as I felt an unexpected constriction in my throat. "I have something for you, Emyr." As she used my name, I became aware of a pounding in my chest. *That's new, an elevated heart rate*, I thought.

As the northern lights illuminated her silhouette, I realized that Ebba was holding something. She raised her hand, offering what I saw was a long, black, cloth-bound box. Now it was her turn to seem oddly nervous. She turned slightly, staring up into my eyes as she handed it to me. I looked at the box blankly as it lay in my hands, and then down at her.

"Open it," she said gently.

Inside, I found an exquisite gentleman's Bulgori wristwatch. Old-fashioned, analog, expensive, and also extremely rare. These things weren't even manufactured anymore; they were collectors' items. The watch had a rose gold strap and small diamond studs around the gold rim of the face, and the face itself was a deep green. It was the most beautiful thing I'd ever seen. I held it up in my hands.

"I don't know what to say … it's stunning," I stuttered.

"I know you like Italian design," Ebba whispered. "Look on the other side."

I turned the watch over. There were words engraved on the back: *So that I'm always with you … Ebba.*

After a moment, Ebba took the watch from me and gently strapped it onto my right wrist. "Just in case you still need that for a while longer," she muttered, glancing in the direction of the chip embedded in my left wrist. I didn't reply. I was speechless.

CHAPTER 32

It was day five of the outage. That morning, as I awoke, I knew exactly where I was. I was lying in Ebba's bed on the *Black Albatross*. I rolled over, searching tentatively with my leading hand. But Ebba was already up. I could hear her somewhere downstairs, on the lower level.

Snatched remembrances of the evening before drifted briefly before my mind's eye, wispy tendrils of recollection. We had talked for hours. She had explained how language used to be learned; how individual languages evolved naturally, over time, before Unilanguage, before the extinction of over six thousand natural languages; and what's at stake when a language dies. Like loss of life, language death was an undoing, Ebba said. A reversal that we should mourn, that should shame us. It sounded powerful, bewitching, mysterious. Like her. I had studied the shifting shape of her mouth, in transfixed fascination as she spoke. Her charm, passion, and the strength of her views were intoxicating.

As I sat up in Ebba's bed, streams of white light floated through the small oval windows in the sides of the mezzanine. Opposite, at the edge as the mezzanine overlooked the lower level, there was a long glass panel, waist high, with a brushed steel rail at the top. And at the far end was the spiral staircase down.

I put on the dressing gown Ebba had left for me and walked to the mezzanine edge. I leaned against the rail, looking down. Ebba was below. I absorbed her in silence without saying anything. I studied her face, full of dark focus and concentration. She was seated adjacent to the lounge area, working at a desk with a bulky contraption in front of her. It was some kind of antique computer, I guessed, with a beveled screen attached to what I now knew to be a keyboard. Ebba pushed against the top of the screen. I watched it move back slightly. On the desk, there were various other items of equipment—digital and analog comms devices and something that I was relieved to finally be familiar with, a 3D printer.

I watched for a moment as Ebba worked. She had told me she could create wearables that simulated voice command implants, such as wrist chips. The woman was savvy. As I looked on, my knee knocked quietly against the glass panel, giving me away. Ebba glanced up and smiled at me.

"Good morning, sleepyhead. I was about to wake you. She's agreed to meet."

"Lady Raven? You managed to reach her?" I asked. *That's fast.* But then again, I knew by now that Ebba didn't mess around.

"We're meeting her at noon. Somewhere off-grid in Brussels—a bar near Rue Brabant. She says she's in trouble. I told her you're with Europol, that we could help."

"What kind of trouble?" I asked.

Ebba shrugged. "She was keen to get off facecall. She claims she's being watched."

* * *

Ebba was navigating us south in the *Black Albatross*, in manual mode, several hundred meters above the Scandinavian mountain range.

"I wonder what makes a woman like that tick? Doing *that* for a living. She could make money other ways," I mused.

"It's not about money," Ebba announced decisively. I glanced across at her, surprised. "It's a lifestyle decision."

"But how can it be about lifestyle?" I scoffed. "That woman could have anyone ..."

"Poor Emyr. You're a big boy, but you still don't know much about women, do you?" She glanced across at me in amusement. "Oh, stop pouting. You're still gorgeous," she teased.

"So what don't I understand?" I asked huffily.

"For someone like Lady Raven, it's not about money. Or at least, not just about money. She's a dominatrix. She needs control. She relishes exercising it over rich and powerful men. And she's selling a service."

"And what's that?" I asked.

"Release. That's what they're paying her for. These are men who are masters of all they survey. Strong men, in control of themselves, their families, their careers, at the top of their game—control freaks, even."

"But it's humiliating, what they do, allowing her to dominate ... them."

Ebba shook her head. "You need to understand their psychological profiles and hers. Lady Raven's clients are willing to pay a lot of money to escape their zones of control, just briefly, with the guarantee of absolute discretion. That's what she is selling. She's a sadist, both professionally and personally. She craves obedience and submissiveness. Without obedience, there can be no domination. I doubt she can live without it."

"But she's still selling her body," I retorted.

Again, Ebba shook her head. "I told you before, that's just it—she isn't. She's a dominatrix. They don't get to have sex with her. She's the one in control. If anything, it is her performing on them, not the other way around." I fell into thoughtful silence for a moment.

"How do you know so much about all this?" I asked. And there it was again, Ebba's distinctive laugh before she lapsed into silence of her own. I could see I wasn't going to get an answer.

As we approached the Brussels airways perimeter marker, a warning beacon began transmitting over the cabin comms. We were in an oversized vehicle, not permitted in restricted city airspace. We were required to land in a designated lot outside the city's R zone and travel in from there.

Ebba glanced at me. "We'll take the *Ebba Black* in," she muttered as she began dropping down the Park and Drive VTOL corridor at the edge of the restricted sky lanes zone.

Once the *Black Albatross* was secured in an oversized terrestrial parking berth, I followed Ebba through to the tail of the craft. There, locked in strong magnetic wheel clamps, was the *Ebba Black*. Ebba pressed a button on a control panel on one side of the *Black Albatross*, and the rear door slowly opened and dropped to the ground outside, creating an exit ramp. We climbed in. Ebba started the engine and we slowly reversed out. I watched the *Albatross*'s rear ramp close as we left. Soon we were airborne again, but this time in Ebba's hybrid sports car.

We parked in an underground parking zone near Laboratoire Rouge, the bar where we were scheduled to meet Lady Raven. Ebba sat for a moment while I watched. She put on a wearable wrist chip she had created that morning while I slept. It was attached to a thin elasticated transparent band. She wore it on her slender left wrist, just under the sleeve of her scarlet blouse.

"It's synced to an e-Continental account. In the name of an alias," Ebba said. I idly wondered how many aliases she had.

The bar was located on a small side street, a haunt for high-class escorts and their clients. We crossed the pedestrian lane and descended a few steps. The bar name, Laboratoire Rouge, and the tagline, *discret et ouvert 24/7*, scrolled across the doorway's holographic display. To one side was the entrance VirDa screen.

I was curious how Ebba was going to pull this one off, getting us inside using just a wearable. After all, she was unchipped. Multiple times per second, the unique radio frequency of an individual's language chip was transmitted to external receivers via the paired ear implant. These were the language streaming rebounds that identified each and every individual in the Tier One and Tier Two world. There was no way any normal person would be able to bypass voice command tech and fool the VirDa. But as I'd come to see for myself, Ebba Black was no ordinary lady.

"Bienvenue à Laboratoire Rouge," a standard waveform said, flickering across the VirDa screen before a female holographic facegram appeared. I grimaced. With my untethering, I had lost my ability to comprehend any language other than English. I had no idea what the words meant, which was pretty frustrating.

Ebba spoke into the VirDa's beveled mic in what I assumed to be fluent French. I knew from her file it was a language she spoke. *"J'ai déjà un compte."*

"J'ai bien peur que je n'arrive pas à détecter une empreinte vocale," the VirDa replied.

"Passez à mon compte de puce de poignet," Ebba responded.

"Avec plaisir. Veuillez placer votre puce de poignet contre l'écran," I heard.

Ebba placed her wrist chip against the VirDa screen. *What's going on?* I thought.

"Entrez, s'il vous plaît. Passez un bon moment au Lab Rouge," the VirDa said.

And with that, the door slid open. Ebba gestured with her head for me to follow. The door slid closed behind us.

"What the hell?" I asked, frustrated at my lack of comprehension but impressed anyway.

"The VirDa couldn't detect a voice print for me," Ebba said.

"Because you don't have one," I muttered.

"So I asked it to switch to wrist chip mode. For entry. As I already have an account with them—I created one earlier." Ebba winked at me before turning on her heel and leading us in. *This woman is certainly something,* I caught myself thinking for the umpteenth time.

CHAPTER 33

I glanced around the joint, a large low-lit cocktail parlor full of sumptuous ethnic, Congolese-themed booths, tables, and private recesses. There weren't many people in yet—just a few couples dotted around. Lady Raven hadn't arrived. Ebba walked toward a red velvet semicircular sofa in a secluded corner. As I followed, I eyed the high walls with their enclosed balcony boxes, glimpses of chairs and tables visible through the curtain partings. Narrow individual staircases serviced each box.

I lowered myself onto the sumptuous velvet cushions next to Ebba. From our booth, I could see the bar at the far end. Low-lit reds and deep yellows ebbed across its holographic frontage. Along the bar were automated drink-making machines and a rotating holographic menu pop-up, projecting at regular intervals along the counter surface from diffusion bars. Garish advertising displayed almost every variety of cocktail imaginable.

Ebba crossed her stockinged legs. The table surface booted up, its smart LEDs rippling with an intimate soft pink waveguide display. A translucent VirDa screen appeared before us, projected from the fusion sensor bar. Ebba held her wrist chip against the screen's ID sensor.

"*Comment puis-je vous aider, madame?*" the VirDa asked.

"*Un cocktail Rusty Nail et un soda,*" Ebba replied.

A short while later the drinks arrived, delivered by a serving unit. And after a couple more minutes, Lady Raven appeared, sashaying through the curtained entrance hall. It was the purple hair I recognized first. And as the curtains parted, I spotted the red latex boots below a long fur coat. But this Lady Raven was glancing nervously around. She had the same angular chin but looked like a fraught version of the hologram I had seen. As she moved forward, scanning the people, dark circles under her eyes were highlighted by the violet lighting.

I tapped Ebba, gesturing. Ebba stood and stared at Lady Raven. She paused before nodding and moving toward us.

"How do you do? You're Ebba Black, correct?" Lady Raven asked once she was standing across the table from us. She spoke with upper-class King's English accent differentiators. Expensive, modeled on how monarchs used to speak. The posh accent was now all that remained of the once default Old Standard English. Her grammar and vocabulary, like mine, was North American Standard. "And you're from Europol?" She was now staring at me.

"I'm Emyr Morgan. Division head for Cybercrime. Thanks for agreeing to meet." I stood and offered my hand.

Lady Raven shook it quickly while glancing around, touching her hair twitchily, before dropping into the seat opposite. She shimmied out of her coat as she sat. She was wearing a figure-hugging red dress, revealing plenty of cleavage. But her hands were shaking.

"Ebba said you would help me," Lady Raven said. I wasn't quite sure if this was a statement or a question. "I've been thrown to the wolves." She was clearly spooked.

"I *might* be able to help," I replied, trying to manage expectations despite being curious what kind of trouble Lady Raven found herself in.

Lady Raven gave her wrist chip a tap. She'd activated her holotab, but as she was directly facing us, the screen wasn't visible. Then she spoke a voice command quietly into the on-screen app. "Low repeating dosage."

"Activated. Thanks for using nicosafe," the app replied before she deactivated the screen. Lady Raven looked back up at us. She breathed in deeply, now appearing visibly calmer. Even in the dim light, the shimmering sapphire of her eyes was just as arrestingly purple as in her advertising image. *Iris replacement surgery, probably.* I studied her face. I could also see that she was wearing permanent make-up. Her lip coloring, eyeshadow, even her rouge had been carefully and expensively tattooed onto her face.

"Would you like something to drink?" Ebba offered.

Lady Raven shook her head, while absently tapping her knuckles on the table surface.

"Why don't you tell us what's going on?" I suggested.

Lady Raven glanced across at me sharply. She exhaled before starting speaking. "It started with a woman contacting me out of the blue. Darya, she called herself." I felt Ebba tense next to me. "She said she represented someone important. She wouldn't say who. Confidentiality. I understood. That's my world too ..."

"Darya Zao?" Ebba asked.

Lady Raven shrugged. "I only got Darya." Then she glanced at me. "Do you think Europol can help me? I need protection. I think someone is tailing me."

"Why don't you carry on? We can discuss the possibility of

protection once I understand the particulars of your situation."
I had wanted to ask about the Catch and Kill audio and what
her connection with Dhruv Gasper was. But somehow, I had a
feeling that would emerge anyway.

Lady Raven watched me for a moment before continuing.
"All right. This Darya, she had a business proposition. Said it
would be lucrative. She wanted to meet in person. She came
across from California with her protection—a tall guy, sharp
suit, athletic looking, not the talkative type."

"Did he give a name?" I asked. I wondered whether this
might be Tylan Elrod, the Appleton security guy I'd met at
Drones Kineto.

Lady Raven shook her head. She leaned forward. "But this
Darya, hell, was she one creepy lady."

"Creepy in what way?"

"Let's just say she didn't give me a good vibe. And I'm a good
judge of people. I could tell straight away."

"And what was her business proposition?" I asked.

Lady Raven gave a short, hard laugh. "The bitch just wanted
to blackmail me ..." Lady Raven stopped. She glanced around
again. "There was a carrot, too—money—not all stick. But I
had no choice."

"Blackmail?" I asked. She seemed to brush a tear away,
before composing herself and continuing.

"She had a complete list of my clients. Names, dates of
contact, payment details, even client preferences. My virtual
locker was supposed to be unhackable." She gulped. "If any of
that got out ... well ... these are seriously powerful men."

"Let me guess—your provider is Appleton?" Ebba asked.
Lady Raven threw her a look of surprise. "That accent ..." Ebba
explained. Lady Raven nodded.

"So what did this Darya want?" I asked.

"Her employer had a special interest in one of my clients. She claimed her employer had the ability to make it possible to give him, my client, what he was craving. His ultimate fantasy."

"And who was Darya interested in?" Ebba asked. I glanced sideways at her and smiled wryly. That was Ebba, no beating about the bush, direct as always.

Lady Raven shook her head. "My most powerful client. I can't tell you. Not yet, I'm afraid. Or I'm dead. That's why I'm being followed. I need to know you can protect me." We waited for a moment while she fixed herself a higher nicotine dosage on her app before continuing. "Sorry ..." Lady Raven murmured finally, when she was ready.

"But can you at least tell us anything about this ultimate fantasy of your client that Darya was interested in?" I asked.

Lady Raven glanced at Ebba, then back at me. "My client, he's a switch."

"A switch?" I asked, now thoroughly confused. But to my surprise, it was Ebba who answered.

"A dominant in their everyday life who relinquishes control in the bedroom." I glanced at Ebba, again wondering how she knew so much about all this.

Lady Raven nodded before continuing. "One of my specialisms is slave training and submissive conditioning. I don't mean to boast, but I'm very experienced. My client, he comes to escape his daily life of control, to unburden himself by exploring his submissive side."

"And his ultimate fantasy?" I asked.

"To relinquish control in places where he's normally dominant." She took a gulp. "Like his family home. Impossible, under normal circumstances. But Darya said her employer was a close friend of his. It was to be a special gift to make the fantasy a reality."

I furrowed my brow. "I don't follow. How would that be possible outside your dungeon? Your LS rebounds would show up, wouldn't they?"

Lady Raven nodded. "Correct. And he lives in a very exclusive part of Brussels—a luxury gated community. And married, two grown-up children and a granddaughter. But that's where the medical procedure came in."

"Medical procedure?" And then I gasped as it hit me. "Darya offered you a neural transmitter, a ghost chip, didn't she?"

Lady Raven looked at me in slight surprise. "A neural thing, right. The other chip you mention, I don't know ... sorry, I'm not good with technical terms." Her voice trailed off.

I shook my head. "The name doesn't matter. Did Darya explain what it was for, the implant?"

"That it would cloak my sec-code. A simple procedure, she said. Not even available in the UFA yet. But it would be soon. She said my client already knew about it, these new implants. Approval in the Union was still some way off."

"And you agreed?" I asked.

Lady Raven stared at me thoughtfully. "Like I had a choice! Let's just say this Darya wasn't the subtle type. If my client list came out, well ... I'd be ruined, reputation shredded, career over. Not to mention lawsuits. All my clients have mutually-binding, non-disclosure agreements." She paused. "And Darya seemed to know a hell of a lot about him—the client. I knew he would go for it. She did too. She knew his profile as well as me." Then she sighed. "And they were going to pay me ... a lot. Enough to retire. If I ever wanted to."

"So what happened?" I asked.

Lady Raven placed her head in her hands before looking back up at us.

"Shit happened. That's what." She shook her head. "I had mentioned to him that I had, you know, an opportunity for this procedure. I wanted to sound him out. Given it's not legal yet here and everything, and who he is. But when he found out, well, he was super excited. He just wanted to know when. A week later, another guy came with a mobile surgical robot. It was the afternoon just before the outage. My client insisted we meet as soon as it was done. I met him straight after, at his home. His family was away. His security guys collected me, scanned me for LS rebounds and the rest. And that was it. Until the next day."

"The next day?" I asked.

"The day after the outage. Given who he is, I thought he would have been too busy ... for me. But he facecalled, all panicked. And scared me—I'd never seen him like that, the threats."

"Why was he panicking? Why the threats?"

"He accused me of recording our session. Claimed he'd received an anonymous drop to his SwissSecure account. He wanted to know who had put me up to that."

"Recording? As in, what, audio recording?" I asked.

Lady Raven shook her head. "He claimed there was a complete audio and video file. Recorded from my POV. Accused me of wearing a body camera, of wanting to blackmail him. He was frog tied, full bondage." Lady Raven was now panting as she ran her hands through her hair. "Fuck-a-doodle-do. What a shitshow!" she muttered, finally.

"And you didn't record anything?" I queried.

"Of course not," Lady Raven exclaimed vehemently. "I was fully vetted. Checked by his security. It was impossible." She looked broken as she continued. "Now my lawyer ... disappeared. His office was ransacked."

"And the other guy you mentioned, who fitted the implant. Did he give a name?"

"He said his name was Dhruv. An Indian name, he told me. He was from the Republic, though, he said. He looked scared. He was gentle. He told me he hoped I'd be okay." As I listened, I knew this confirmed Pieter's mind-mapping intel on Dhruv Gasper. He *had* been in Brussels.

"Was there also a medic with him—someone called Glanc MD, maybe?" I asked.

Lady Raven looked at me, slightly surprised, before shaking her head. "Glanc market domination. That's what Darya called the procedure, when she spoke with her security guy. No idea what Glanc is. But only one guy came to fit it—Dhruv."

"Any ideas?" I asked, turning to Ebba.

"Glanc could be an acronym? Ghost language chip, maybe."

I looked at Ebba thoughtfully before turning back to Lady Raven. "And your lawyer—have you filed a missing person report?"

"Tried to get through to city police, but ... with the outage ..." I nodded. When there were millions now feral, many hundreds of thousands missing and unidentified, who cared about one lawyer?

"Ideally, we would want some evidence of the blackmail attempt by Darya. And if you really didn't record the session, well ..." I began before Lady Raven's expression changed. I paused as a faint smile appeared on her face.

"But there *is* evidence. The dungeon is off limits. But I have a small meeting room adjacent. And there, I have a hidden sec-cam. I know, strictly speaking that's a violation of Union's privacy laws unless I get consent from the other party. But it was my lawyer's advice. All business meetings recorded. Tax purposes."

"The meeting with Darya?" I asked excitedly.

"I have a video record. The entire meeting with her. Obviously, you know, I didn't let her know I was recording. I didn't trust her."

"Can we have the footage?"

Lady Raven studied me for a moment. "First you guarantee my safety."

"I'll need to talk to my boss," I replied. "Do you have somewhere safe to go?"

"My dungeon. No one gets in there. Totally secure. There's a secret tunnel entrance from another block. There's even a panic room—I'm staying there for now."

"We'll be in touch later today. Can we escort you back, just in case you're being followed?"

"I think I lost them. I'm careful." She glanced around her. Then she stood, picked up her coat, looked down at us, and without saying another word, abruptly walked away.

"What do you make of that?" I asked, turning to Ebba. "If she didn't film the session, who did?"

"Glanc MD. I think she's been fitted with a ghost chip. And whatever its real purpose, I suspect Appleton is up to something big—probably more than just cloaking LS rebounds," Ebba announced finally.

"Like a language outage? That's pretty big," I said.

"Maybe this is something even bigger." Ebba studied me thoughtfully.

"Well, I think we should follow her," I said as I gulped down the remainder of my drink.

Ebba smiled. "My thoughts exactly."

CHAPTER 34

The November midday air was chilly despite the pale sun. We emerged up the steps onto the side street and turned back onto Rue Brabant. I gestured down the street toward the slim fur-clad figure with the striking red boots. Ebba and I began walking after Lady Raven, languidly so as not to draw attention to ourselves.

As we followed the pedestrian lane, I noticed a thin-looking man ahead, loitering in a way that was less casual and more deliberate. He walked quickly before slowing to avoid catching up with Lady Raven. And each time Lady Raven shot a fearful glance over her shoulder, he paused, feigning absentminded nonchalance. Ebba glanced at me knowingly as we followed at a distance.

The street was busy with taxiing hover cars, e-scooters, and pedestrians, each in their own lanes. Up ahead, Lady Raven disappeared into some kind of doorway on the right. The man turned in behind her, disappearing from view too.

We quickened our pace to catch up. As we neared the spot where we had lost sight of them, I saw that in fact they had disappeared through the open entrance to an alleyway.

We squinted in, scanning the semidarkness. The alleyway was a narrow tunnel, brick walls with a curved brick ceiling.

Around ten meters ahead, there was a metal grille that prevented further access. Ebba made a face. I knew what she was thinking. Dark and claustrophobic.

I began moving into the alleyway, Ebba following behind me, and immediately saw the gate in the grille was slightly ajar. Then I heard sounds of a scuffle beyond it, farther in. As my eyes adjusted to the dim light, I saw that the thin man had caught up with Lady Raven; she had slipped to the ground as he pursued her. And now he had his back to us. But to my horror, I realized he had both hands clasped around her neck as she kneeled on the brick ground. He was asphyxiating her. Lady Raven's eyes were bulging, her hands pressing on his arms to no avail as he throttled the life out of her.

I was vaguely aware of Ebba brushing against me, close behind in the narrow alley, as she tried to draw her weapon. She had her Beretta in a shoulder holster under her jacket. But she didn't have a clean shot; the metal gate intervened between us and the assassin. And Lady Raven was becoming limp, beginning to slump to the cold ground.

I threw the metal gate open and stepped immediately behind the standing man, who was focused on his target. It wasn't until he heard the metal gate clatter against the brick that he was alerted to my presence—but by then it was too late. I knew what I would do. I always did when violence drew me in. No mercy. I raised my right fist and delivered a firm blow to the base of his skull.

The rabbit punch was illegal in the combat sport I was trained in, Muay Thai, and for good reason. It delivered a devastating blow to the cervical vertebrae. With enough force and precision, it could detach the brain from its stem, leading to instant death. The assailant was dead before his head hit the ground.

I quickly bent down, shaking Lady Raven. *Is she still breathing? Do I need to administer CPR?* Her throat bore red weals from strangulation. I felt for a pulse. It was weak but there. And then her breathing resumed. After a moment, her eyes flickered open as I helped her up.

"Give her a moment," Ebba instructed, moving forward. I carefully detached my arms from around Lady Raven's waist, allowing her diaphragm to expand as she took in gulps of air.

"Is this the tunnel?" I asked. "To your place?" Lady Raven was clearly badly shaken. She stared at me for a moment, eyes wide with shock that delayed her reaction, before nodding.

Ebba began leading her farther down the alley while I attended to the dead man. I grabbed him by his arms and pulled him toward the alleyway entrance, out of Lady Raven's metal gate. This wasn't an Appleton security type, that was clear. Probably a local hitman. Hired by Lady Raven's client, maybe. And it confirmed that whatever her client believed she had on him, he really was willing to kill for it.

I staged the corpse so that he was sitting with his back against the wall just inside the mouth of the alleyway. His head lolled; his eyes were closed. To passers-by, he would resemble another midday drunk. This was certainly the seedy neighborhood for it.

As I returned, walking back inside the metal gate, Lady Raven issued her voice command into a small wall-mounted VirDa I hadn't noticed previously. The gate locked behind us. Lights in the brick ceiling of the tunnel booted up ahead. Just a few meters farther on, we reached a solid steel door with an embedded VirDa screen at eye level. Lady Raven issued a further voice command and the door slid open.

We entered a plush vestibule with velvet seats. I recognized them from her advertising image. There was a small cloakroom to one side, a restroom, and even a shower room. Farther along, to the left, there were other doors; perhaps one led to the meeting room she had spoken of. And on the right, a larger door bore a striking holographic display that read *Lady Raven's Dungeon*. As we approached, the dungeon door slid open. We followed Lady Raven inside and dim lights booted up. She dropped onto a red leather tuxedo-style sofa on one side of the room.

I glanced around with prurient curiosity. It was a large chamber, the floor tiled in black. The ceiling was also black, fitted with parallel rows of metal struts, which supported numerous hooks for different kinds of suspension equipment. There were meat hooks as well as different types of shackles, metal looped D-gates with spring-loaded gates, and other sorts of carabiners. The walls were fitted with smart LED panels, which emitted a deep rippling red glow. There was a glass cabinet on one wall containing latex gimp masks and costumes. A rack of whips, and floggers was in another, including electric shock rods. I also spotted a shelf containing strap-on apparatus including, to my horror, extra-large dildos. It was all on display. Ebba sniggered quietly as she saw the color drain from my face.

There were various items of grotesque-looking furniture dotted around the room. I was drawn with grim fascination to a long red leather bench with restraint slots, in the center of the dungeon. It included straps for hands, neck, arms, and torso. Against one wall was a large red throne-like chair with further restraints and holes at the neck and back, and in the seat. In one corner there was a glass cube with a small sliding entry panel and breathing holes. And in another, there was what I assumed to be a sealed torture unit—I had heard of them—a high-tech simulator that aroused the pain and pleasure centers of the brain, using electric impulses in a non-invasive way.

There was a console adjacent to the leather sofa with a large 3D printer, presumably to create items for special requests. And in another display case I spotted an assortment of surgical scalpels and other bladed devices.

"Quite the place," I whispered nervously to no one in particular. Meanwhile, Ebba had joined Lady Raven, sitting next to her on the leather sofa.

"Do you have anyone who can come and stay with you?" Ebba asked.

"You have to help me," Lady Raven exclaimed, turning her face pleadingly toward Ebba.

"We will," Ebba said reassuringly. "But you have to give us more information. To be able to protect you, we need to know who your client is."

"That was probably his hitman," I added quietly.

"You have to believe me, I didn't film him. I would never do that. This is all a misunderstanding. Utter madness." She began hyperventilating.

"We believe you," Ebba whispered. Lady Raven gradually calmed down, nodding before seemingly bracing herself to utter the name she barely dared speak. She stared up at me as I stood before her and Ebba.

"Josep Lopez," she whispered finally.

"High Representative Lopez?" I asked, almost choking. Lady Raven looked at me without blinking.

"Third most powerful man in the Union," she sighed pitifully, tears beginning to trickle down her face. "Maybe even Europol can't help."

I watched Lady Raven, now incredulous. I knew that, according to gossips like Marchaud, Lopez was in fact the single most powerful man in the Union. And based on current evidence,

Marchaud might be right. After all, Lopez could seemingly even bend the joint presidents in the Magisterium to his will.

Ebba glanced at me with a knowing look. It wasn't only Lady Raven who had been blackmailed, but the High Representative too. It all fell into place. Catch and Kill was a plot to entrap Lopez and then coerce him. *But for what purpose?* Darya Zao worked for Marc Barron. This was an Appleton plot, like the language outage. And if we were right, and Glanc MD referred to the new secret ghost chip that Appleton had developed, it had been used to entrap Lopez.

Lady Raven was racked with sobs. Ebba produced a handkerchief from her coat before standing and whispering in my ear, "I wonder, was the High Representative coerced into blaming the Russian Federation for the outage?"

"If so, that means Lopez in fact knows that Russia isn't involved. And he also knows the evidence CyberForce has is a fake."

"Marc Barron, Appleton. This has all the hallmarks of his modus operandi," Ebba continued quietly, so that I alone could hear. I looked down into her eyes. I knew she was right.

"Lady Raven, it would really help if we could also have the file of your meeting with Darya," I said, addressing the seated woman gently.

Lady Raven shook her head firmly. "Go talk to your boss," she replied. "Please! If Europol guarantees my security, you can have it when you come back."

I sighed. But I also knew that the sec-cam file was the only leverage Lady Raven had. And as her life might depend on it, I hardly blamed her.

CHAPTER 35

After we left Lady Raven, Ebba and I headed back to the *Black Albatross*. Once on board, Ebba booted up her strange physical computer with the lid that folded up from an old-fashioned keyboard.

"So, what's the plan?" she asked.

I studied her thoughtfully. "We need to get to The Hague, to Europol HQ. I have to tell Lina de Bolle what we've uncovered. She'll help," I replied.

"Your Lina, she may not believe you. You know that, right? She'll probably need some convincing."

"Lady Raven has the evidence. If we can get her into Europol's witness protection program, then we'll get the sec-cam footage of Darya Zao. That'll establish a link with Appleton. I have faith in Lina."

As my thoughts were racing, Ebba let out an exclamation.

"Oh, that's not good," she said, suddenly alarmed. She was staring into her folding computer. I ogled over her shoulder as she sat at her desk—I was taken aback as I realized where she was. She had hacked into the Union's defense satellite system, which had one of the world's most difficult firewalls to breach.

"What isn't?" I asked as I focused on the screen. It was a little grainy.

"Emyr," Ebba said, slightly distressed, "an arrest warrant has been issued … for you. Executive level—the High Representative himself." I felt my face draining of color. Ebba was pointing to the screen. I realized that she was inside the secure Europol E-warrant portal. The warrant was addressed to Director Dominguez of Europol.

I frowned. "We're going to have to adjust our plan," I said. "We won't be able to just walk into Europol HQ now and ask to see Lina."

"What, then?" Ebba asked.

"We'll visit her later, back at her apartment after work."

"What about her family?"

"She lives alone. Just her and a cat."

***

Ebba and I arrived in The Hague's chic Belgisch Park district shortly after dark. Ebba monitored Lina's location via her uplink hack to the Union-DEF system. We waited until Lina's LS rebounds showed that she had returned home for the evening. We left the *Black Albatross* outside The Hague and traveled on a downtown airway in the *Ebba Black*, parking in an underground zone a few blocks from where Lina lived. From there we proceeded on foot.

Lina's apartment was on the top floor of a very exclusive building. We were opposite Lina's apartment building in a small park when Ebba revealed she had VTOL hoverboards that would get us to the roof terrace. *Of course she does!* I smirked to myself.

Each board was fitted with two diminutive turbine engines and a small tank of liquid CO_2. Ebba showed me how they worked. Burning fuel was driven through rotating blades, creating thrust. The rider was locked onto the board by magnetic foot clamps. Lift and descent were controlled by pressing on foot levers and direction by body shape, which the onboard VirDa detected from highly sensitive pressure pads on the hoverboard's base.

"I've disabled the apartment's VirDa security," Ebba said as she took her board out of its bag and stepped onto it. "Ready?"

Before I could reply, Ebba was off, ascending gracefully into the night sky. She flew noiselessly up, over the transit corridor and above the building opposite. I followed through the chilly air. As I caught up, Ebba was already dropping down onto the wide terrace outside Lina's apartment.

We stowed our hoverboards in their covers, out of sight in a dark corner of the terrace. I peered through the sliding glass doors. Inside was a dimly lit lounge. The backup security lights were on. There was no sign of Lina. As the security system had been disabled, I wedged my fingers between the opening of the two doors and gained sufficient purchase to prize them open. Ebba moved quickly through the narrow aperture first.

Inside, I listened intently in the dim evening stillness. Faint music from somewhere. A party in another apartment, perhaps. Ebba and I glanced at one other. Beyond the large lounge was a hallway. Footsteps were approaching; it was Lina. She stood on the threshold and froze when she saw our dark silhouettes. I heard her fumbling—for her weapon, maybe.

"Lina, it's Emyr." I spoke quietly. The rumble of my deep voice reverberated in the stillness of the apartment. I heard a gasp, which attached itself to Lina as her face bore toward me.

"Emyr. You're okay!" she exclaimed with a mixture of surprise and relief. "My home VirDa system has just blacked out. Now I know why."

"I just need a few minutes." I saw Lina looking at Ebba suspiciously. "This is Ebba Black."

"I know who she is," Lina replied with her customary sternness. She watched us both with narrowed eyes through her horn-rimmed glasses. "You'd better sit down." We sat on a sofa opposite her in semidarkness. "How did you manage to get in?" Before I could reply, she swept her hand to one side as if brushing the question away. "Better if I don't know."

"Lina, I ... we need your help."

"I'm listening."

"My trip to California," I began. I wondered whether Lina would believe what I was about to tell her. "The language outage. I've uncovered a plot by Appleton—by Marc Barron. He used a drone to launch the DDoS strikes on November 5th, targeting competitor satellite systems. But he had a drone initiate the attack from Russian airspace."

"Over Lake Baikal, Siberia?" Lina asked rhetorically. I was slightly startled. *She knew that?*

"Right. We originally thought the attack might have been launched from a boat. Marc Barron wanted to frame the Federation."

"And you have evidence for that, right?" Lina asked.

"A facecall between Barron and a dead CEO, Dhruv Gasper— the hover car crash I told you about in London." Lina nodded at me. "Anyway, in the facecall, Barron issues instructions to send a drone into Russian airspace on November 5th. Specifically, Siberia. Gasper's dead, so we can't verify what was intended. Barron's legal team could probably argue it's circumstantial ... but it at least gives us probable cause ..." I held out my hands.

"And BeeDirect?" Lina asked.

"A cyberattack launched from Russian airspace affecting all other commercial providers ..."

"That would make the Federation the likely suspect," Lina said quietly.

"While Appleton cleans up, becoming the world's near-exclusive provider of language streaming services," I added.

Lina gazed at us in silence for a moment before speaking. "There's been a total collapse in streaming services in the Chinese states. Zhengfei's infrastructure is inoperable. Appleton has just been appointed as the replacement state provider. The authorities are desperate. We heard from the Imperium earlier that Appleton's also reportedly taking over in Japan. And in the Indian Republic, and the Confederation of South American Republics. An update from the High Representative's office."

I didn't know whether to be more surprised that Lina seemed to believe me or that she appeared so well informed. But in any case, I wasn't done. I still needed to get her buy-in with Lady Raven.

"There's one more thing. Marc Barron has dirt on one of the Union's most senior leaders. I suspect Barron is using blackmail to have the Union wage war against the Russian Federation."

Lina's eyes narrowed. "Who's being blackmailed?"

"You may not believe me," I whispered.

"Try me," Lina said insistently.

"High Representative Lopez," I replied.

"That actually figures," Lina muttered. "But why set up the Russians?" she asked, looking directly at Ebba. "Babel would have been a more obvious target, especially as it's been hacking the Appleton servers."

"An obvious target, maybe, but hard to kill. CyberForce has already tried and failed," Ebba said archly.

Lina chuckled quietly.

"The Russians would never cede control of their internet-of-things ecosystem to a foreign provider," I said. "Unless the Federation were to come under Union control and its language streaming was outsourced to a third-party provider."

"So you're saying that Marc Barron is engineering war, using blackmail, to take over there too?" Lina asked. I nodded. She was watching me thoughtfully. "So how is Lopez being blackmailed?"

This was my cue. "We believe a video file exists of Lopez engaging in S&M bondage in his home with a high-end escort."

"Dominatrix," Ebba corrected.

"A dominatrix from Brussels," I added. "Interviewed her earlier today. We need to get her into Europol's protection program."

I could immediately tell from Lina's reaction that something was off. She began shaking her head. I was about to protest that Lina needed to agree when she held up her hand.

"Lady Raven, right?" she asked. I was taken aback again. *How did Lina know her name?* "You say you saw her today?"

"Around noon," I replied.

"She was found dead this afternoon around three p.m. Her silent alarm had been activated in her dungeon. Otherwise, it might have been weeks till the local cops found her." I could feel Ebba start next to me. "We were called in due to the unusual cause of death ..." Lina paused. "The same as your hover car crash case, according to Pieter."

"Dhruv Gasper?" I whispered in quiet amazement.

Lina activated her holotab. In the dark, the thin translucent screen glimmered silver. She blinked through the menu screen before reading out loud: "CoD likely due to massive internal brain trauma due to explosion of language chip. Possible failure of microbattery." She paused. "That's the medical examiner's preliminary assessment. Still waiting on the autopsy for a definitive report."

I narrowed my eyes while my mind reeled. Then I looked back across at Lina. "Lady Raven claimed she had a new neural implant recently fitted. We suspect it's what's being called a ghost chip. It cloaks LS rebounds. Was there any sign of that in the report?" I asked.

Lina looked back down at the open report, reading aloud from the screen: "Small microprocessor attached to brain surface, not subcortical. Scar tissue shows recent surgery. Evidence of sensor probes connected to optical and auditory nerves. Function of microprocessor undeterminable due to damage to brain vasculature. Placement and remnants appear analogous to autopsy ID 2125/NOV./13741 Dhruv Gasper."

"That's it!" I exclaimed, gasping. I felt two sets of eyes on me as both Lina and Ebba gave me their full attention. "The implant doesn't just cloak LS rebounds. It provides back-door access to sense perception input from the visual and auditory brain regions. That's how Appleton was able to harvest video footage and blackmail Lopez."

"By capturing and recording what Lady Raven was actually hearing and seeing," exclaimed Ebba.

"And somehow turning the language chip into a bomb," I added.

"Like Elias," Ebba whispered quietly as the pieces fell into place for her too. I felt her gaze on me. I glanced at her before turning back to Lina.

"Lady Raven said she had footage of her meeting with Darya Zao on a hidden sec-cam. Could you get Pieter to have a look?"

Lina shook her head solemnly. "He's spent most of the afternoon on site. The place has been cleaned out. All data in the virtual locker of the deceased wiped, all VirDa and sec-cam data gone."

I smiled to myself wryly. We were back to square one. The evidence that Lopez was being blackmailed by Appleton had been destroyed. Lina might believe it, but without evidence, no one else would.

Lina was observing me, my deflated expression. "Emyr," she whispered, "it gets worse. The Union is set to launch a surprise attack on the Russian Federation tomorrow at eleven p.m. A massive cyberattack once tactical biomechanical battalions are in strike positions along the eastern borders. A massive droid army. A full-scale invasion. Alojzija Žagar has operational command." *Ha, Alojzija Žagar again*, I thought.

"How do we stop it?" I muttered. Lina stared back at me, her brow furrowed as she thought. Then an idea struck me. "We show the evidence is fake. Does Europol have the facecall file yet—the one where CyberForce claims Bulchovi takes responsibility for the language outage?" I asked excitedly.

Lina shook her head. "Rodrigo has asked von Böhm for a copy. But so far he's been stonewalled."

I turned to Ebba. I could see her smiling at me even in the dim light. "I can get you what you need," she said before I could ask. Apparently, she was now also able to read my mind.

"Then we prove it's fake. After all, it's a hoax, right? The Russians are being set up."

"But how?" asked Lina.

"For that I'll need Lotte, to do an analysis. She'll get us the evidence."

"Emyr, an arrest warrant has been issued … for you," Lina said.

"So I hear," I replied grimly.

"The director's not happy about it either, but our hands are tied. I've been ordered to shut down your Union-DEF account."

I sighed. That wasn't good news. I would still need access to my Europol account to stop the madness of war.

"I haven't actioned it yet," Lina said. "I can give you another twenty-four hours or so, until, say, eleven p.m. tomorrow… It's not yet been marked a high-priority action on my daily schedule. Get the evidence. Let's try and stop this."

Before I could thank her, I heard a slight hissing sound. It came from a small dark shape on the floor—the distinctive outline of a cat next to Lina. I glimpsed fierce eyes glinting at me with unfriendly menace.

"Oh, Jerry," Lina muttered. I knew from previous interactions at Lina's annual social event for her management team that her cat was wary of strangers, and had taken a particular dislike to me. But to my irritation, the wretched cat moved toward Ebba, arching its back in feline greeting.

"Hello, cutie," Ebba said softly as the cat brushed against her stockinged legs. She bent forward to stoke it. The cat promptly jumped onto her lap, beginning to purr furiously as it burrowed its head into her pencil skirt. "Wow, what a beauty—a Ragdoll," Ebba whispered.

"You know your cats," Lina announced, clearly impressed. "I've never seen Jerry do that before …" I glanced across at Lina sharply. "To take to a stranger. Animals can sense a person …"

"We should probably go," I said, standing. *Animals can sense a person. Really! Whatever that means*, I thought indignantly.

"Now I get my home VirDa back, right?" Lina asked, glancing up at me. "I was about to have something fixed for dinner."

"You bet," I replied, as Ebba gently placed the cat back down before turning to follow me outside onto the roof terrace.

CHAPTER 36

By the time we arrived back at the *Black Albatross*, it was late. But Ebba was immediately at work. She soon had the file of the Russian Federation president's facecall, Viktor Bulchovi, from the CyberForce server. He spoke slowly, ponderously, taking himself way too seriously. *Politicians!* I despised them all.

"How's your Russian?" I asked. Mine was now nonexistent. Ebba ignored me. She was in full concentration mode, listening, frowning, her red lips puckered, her small forefinger pressing her nose up. She began running an acoustic analysis. Waveforms rippled across her computer screen, highlighted in red at certain points, as she re-ran the facecall file.

"He's claiming responsibility for the outage all right, but something is off," she said, pointing to the red peaks on the display. "There's evidence of a McGurk effect."

"A *what* effect?" I asked.

"His mouth shape doesn't match some of the words uttered—the vowels," Ebba replied. "It's clearly a fake, but—" she shrugged, "—I don't have the tools to prove it."

"Lotte will get what we need," I said definitively. I would send her the file. "I'll set up a meeting with her for tomorrow." Ebba glanced at me strangely, it was a haunted look; a shadow had come over her face. I frowned. *What's up now?* Ebba shook her head, changing the subject.

"What then?" she asked, watching me intently.

"Then we confront the High Representative. Show him we know it's a fake. Have him call off the war, or we'll expose it ourselves. Easier if he agrees to stand down the military strike. Can you send me the file?" I asked as I pressed my wrist chip to activate my holotab.

Ebba studied me thoughtfully. "Have you considered that the High Representative likely won't cooperate? Especially as he's being blackmailed. He's under extreme duress—perhaps an existential threat, for his career and family life. That's kind of the point of blackmail."

I glanced at her, a knowing look on her face, before frowning in irritation at my holographic screen.

"Strange ..." I muttered. My holotab was projecting from my wrist chip, but the *connection* icon was still spinning on the screen. "It can't sync to my sec-code. Can't access my account ..." I scratched my forehead, perplexed. "It's never done that before," I grumbled.

I was startled by Ebba's tinkling laugh in response.

"D'oh. Your language chip is now on a closed loop. Remember?"

I smiled sheepishly, feeling foolish. *Of course. I no longer have access to the Union-DEF servers.* I wasn't language streaming anymore. Ebba began tapping on her computer keyboard. I watched as the console lights on her 3D printer began glowing. The machine whirred. Ebba opened the lid and picked out what seemed to be a translucent earpiece, then handed it to me.

"Synced to your sec-code. It's a wearable ear implant, programmed to recognize your DNA. Now you can connect to your Union-DEF account whenever you want—or at least until it gets deactivated," she announced with a flourish.

"Like this?" I asked as I inserted the small blob of plastic into my ear, pondering how Ebba had obtained a sample of my DNA. Just then, the *connection* icon stopped spinning. My Europol secure portal menu popped up. I jumped as I felt a notification alert vibrate in my ear. Ebba laughed again.

"It works just like your old ear implant," she explained, smiling. I saw from my holotab that I had a proximity share. Ebba had sent me the file. I paused, just for a second, as I wondered how to begin my message to Lotte. *Hi, Lotte. Dear Lotte.* Or was it now just *Lotte*? I shook my head. *Damn it! That's way too abrupt.* I began with a simple *Hi!*

Only once I was done and had sent the file off to Lotte did I become aware that Ebba had been busy too. She held up a second translucent earpiece, newly minted from her 3D printer, and a wearable wrist chip just like the one I had seen her use earlier.

"While you're now officially an outlaw, that doesn't mean you have to be out-soc. Both the organization and I personally have a responsibility to provide you with an alias," Ebba said, mock bowing in her chair.

"You're too kind," I replied, laughing, as I took the second earpiece and wearable wrist chip that she held out.

"So, along with a name, you have a whole new identity. A unique sec-code from an unassigned language chip, courtesy of the Appleton database, of course. And that now belongs to you—or rather, Melker Nagrom."

I made a face. Ebba sniggered as she watched my expression.

"Melker Nagrom," I repeated quietly. *A bit weird*, I thought. I looked at Ebba. "You know, my given name is exactly that—

given, by my father. And my family name was his too, not mine ..." My voice lapsed into silence. My name had always been a reminder of choices I hadn't made. "But I guess where we start is not where we have to end up," I said finally, glancing back at Ebba.

"Wow, that's deep," she replied with mock solemnity, before laughing again. "And there I was just talking about a simple alias."

I shook my head and glanced away, avoiding eye contact. I didn't want her to see that I had become suddenly affected, emotional. I must have been taken by surprise by the unexpected offering of a new name.

Now Ebba had stopped laughing. She was serious too. "The names we carry have significance, a heritage," she said gently. "This name is no different."

I stared at her as I recovered my composure. I took in her deep black hair, her coal-black eyes. But most of all, it was her attitude.

"But Melker Nagrom. What sort of name is that?"

"Melker was my maternal grandfather's name. In old Swedish it refers to a *king*," Ebba replied. I felt surprise well up in me anew.

"That's what Emyr means, too. In Cymraeg." As I spoke, I saw from Ebba's expression that she already knew that. *But of course she does.*

"That's the first reason. The meaning remains in your new given name."

"And there's a second reason?" I asked.

"He was someone I loved ... still love," Ebba whispered. I glanced away quickly, embarrassed. I didn't know how to respond to that.

"And Nagrom? What sort of family name is that?"

"That's all you. The same pieces rearranged," Ebba replied. I frowned, not understanding. "Nagrom is a semordnilap."

I smiled. I knew what *semordnilap* meant. That was the beauty of having Appleton's entire lexical database for English stored on a memory implant inside my head. I could now instantly access definitions for over a million words.

"A word that spells a different word in reverse," I announced proudly. My new family name was in fact my old family name. *Morgan* backwards.

Ebba began explaining how my exotic-sounding alias worked. Once my Europol account was deactivated, the ear wearable that she had just given me would no longer function. My former self, Emyr Morgan, no longer emitted LS rebounds anyway, as my language chip no longer streamed. But reborn as Melker Nagrom, I would not only have a unique sec-code, but would also be able to fool any language scanning orb with simulated LS rebounds, generated from my wearable translucent earpiece, synced with my alias, stored on the Freetown servers.

And with my new wrist chip, also synced to my new alias, I would be able to communicate with any public VirDa. I simply requested wrist chip identification to avoid having to issue voice commands. After all, I could no longer produce a voice print, as my language chip now operated on a closed loop. And Emyr Morgan's sec-code, and hence Emyr Morgan as an in-soc persona, would be deactivated at 11 p.m. tomorrow.

Then Ebba handed me a small clamshell device. I flipped it open, revealing an LED screen that booted on. Ebba called it a touchtab. It was also synced to my alias on the Freetown servers, and it enabled a real-time translation into English to my wearable earpiece of any public VirDa anywhere in the Tier One and Two world, no matter the state official language. *That'll definitely come in handy. Not too shabby living without language streaming after all*, I thought. I was now most definitely back in-soc.

"This touchtab is programmed to respond only to your fingerprints," Ebba revealed. "That panel there." She was pointing to a small square sensor on the bottom of the screen. "If you press any finger or thumb here, it will activate. Then you can select from the range of apps."

"How did you get my fingerprints?" I asked. Ebba ignored the question.

"Your alias has an associated bank account. You are now quite well off. And use the touchtab to set up a retail account in advance—the Freetown server will connect you to nearly any retail outlet in the Union. We have encrypted uplink patches to all the main commercial providers."

"But my alias ... this isn't something you've just created, is it?" I asked, beginning to wonder how long she'd been planning all this.

"Of course not. Melker Nagrom has a back history, a full employment record, an education with some fancy college degrees, even a small criminal record." I raised an eyebrow at that while Ebba sniggered. "Yes, sorry about that. But I wanted you to be authentic. And Melker Nagrom does seem the type," she added. *I'll have to learn a new back story, a new biography.*

I looked at Ebba, now deadly serious. "How long have you been planning this?"

"Don't you want to know how rich you are?" Ebba asked, brushing away my question. I was perplexed, but I could also tell, for the time being at least, that I would get nothing further from her. I took the wrist chip and placed the band around my hand. I held the touchtab and examined it.

"So now I belong to your organization?" I asked.

Ebba looked at me coyly. "Now you belong to me." She laughed as she saw the ashen look come over my face. "It's okay, I'm joking." I nodded slowly. It wasn't clear to me that she was. "But seriously," she continued, "we are now bound together. If you ever feel that you've been abandoned, I will always come for you. I will always find you. If you ever feel you've been given up on, handed over, imprisoned, I will find you. I will bring you back to me."

"Thanks. I think," I replied lamely. "It sounds like you know something I don't."

"It's just that after you've averted this war, I need you to help me with something else even bigger."

"Your revenge mission?" I asked with a hint of bitterness that surprised even me. Ebba fell silent, studying me thoughtfully.

CHAPTER 37

It was day six of the language outage. I had spent my second night sleeping next to Ebba on board the *Black Albatross*. When I checked my Europol account, Lotte had already responded. She was waiting on the results of the tech analysis of the Bulchovi file; she would have them by late morning. We agreed to meet at noon. Lotte proposed somewhere safe, off the beaten track. In Scheveningen, at Café de Renbaan; our old haunt. It would be safe, but still my heart sank. Old ghosts. I glanced at Ebba. She would be coming too—she insisted. I could already tell this was going to be awkward.

Ebba asked if I wanted to drive us in, to drive the *Ebba Black*! I gladly agreed, of course. I felt like a little kid. Before we set off, she gave me a full tour of the car. She handed me the remote control to operate the security settings. I pressed to unlock it. We opened the rear storage compartment in the trunk, which contained the two VTOL hoverboards. There was a metal case with ammo for our pistols, as well as another strange-looking box.

"What's that?" I asked.

"A breaking-and-entering kit," Ebba replied mysteriously.

"As in …?"

"A kit to break and enter … buildings … highly secure buildings." Ebba laughed as she saw my expression. Apparently,

I was surprised a lot around her. She opened the box and picked up a thin piece of folded webbing. She unfolded it, revealing a wide webbed mat with a flat metallic coil embedded in its surface. "You operate it from this tab on your touchtab," Ebba said, pointing.

"Is that what I think it is?" I asked.

"A heating coil to weaken armored glass. Heated to over a hundred and twenty-five degrees Celsius, the glass gets cloudy, less resistant to bullets. When the coil glows green, that's when you shoot. That's when it'll shatter." My mouth opened slightly as Ebba spoke. *Why on earth would she ever need such a thing?*

"Forward planning?" Ebba shrugged in response. "And what's this?" I asked, picking up a flimsy poncho. Except, as I examined it, I saw it was covered with tiny sequin-like cameras.

"An invisibility cloak," Ebba replied. Now I was seriously impressed. I'd heard of them. The science behind the technology had existed for decades, but the suits were still very expensive to manufacture. Only a few specialist units in the Union's special forces directorate had invisibility suits. I knew from a briefing memo that the tiny cameras reflected visible light, causing it to shift slightly, bending around the wearer, so that the wearer was, quite literally, hidden in plain sight.

I nodded in admiration as Ebba closed the trunk. She led me round to the driver's side and gestured for me to sit behind the steering wheel.

"You push there." I pressed and the gentle thrum of the engine sprang into life. Ebba showed me how to drive the car in manual mode, as a conventional car. It took me a few tries to get the hang of the gear shift system and pressing the pedals underneath the steering wheel proved confusing. Ebba grimaced as I changed gear without depressing the clutch.

The car made an awful whining sound and lurched to a stop. "You've stalled it!" she said.

"I've what?" I exclaimed, shrugging. "Old tech isn't all it was cracked up to be."

"Let's use VTOL mode," Ebba proposed. I agreed. I began navigating us across the airways of The Hague to Scheveningen.

* * *

We arrived at Café de Renbaan a few minutes after noon. I suddenly felt oddly nervous in a way I hadn't expected or anticipated. I glimpsed Ties Saaps, the bartender, through the window, leaning against the bar. The place felt unfamiliar, as if part of another life; that of a different person. Lunchtime trysts with Lotte—all that now belonged to a different age.

As we entered, Ties glanced across and smiled at me. Lotte was already there. She hadn't seen us yet. I paused, watching her as she gazed into her glass absently, a few, stray wisps of hair lingering over one shoulder. Lotte was seated at *our* table. *She couldn't have picked another one, could she?* I groaned inwardly.

As we neared, I paused, a sense of foreboding coming over me, just as Lotte looked up—spotting us. And with that, Ebba turned toward me and, without warning, pulled my head down toward hers and kissed me full on the mouth. She released me, smirking as she saw the expression on my face. She shrugged.

"I just felt like it," she muttered, handing me a small handkerchief. I glanced at it, puzzled. "For your mouth." I rubbed my lips, glancing at the smeared lipstick. As I looked back up, I glimpsed Lotte frowning before looking resolutely back down at her glass.

Ebba marched toward the table and seated herself on the opposite side to Lotte, glancing up at me expectantly. I sighed quietly and sat next to her. Lotte looked across at me and tried to smile before shooting a suspicious glance at Ebba.

"Hi," I said.

"Hi. I was only expecting *you*," Lotte murmured. I could feel the tension.

"This is Ebba Black," I stammered. Lotte gave a curt nod.

"I think she knows who I am," Ebba said, radiating a broad smile as if nothing were amiss. Lotte looked away. She was her made-up best, with her trademark psybient-style rings around her eyes. I gazed at her. I had once found her so appealing, provocative, sensual. But at the same table as Ebba, she now appeared almost plain—insignificant, somehow.

"So you're on the run?" Lotte asked in a hoarse whisper. She took a sip of her drink.

"There's an arrest warrant out."

"I think you're being very courageous," Lotte said trying to sound firm, although her voice quavered. "You always were." She smiled at me faintly. Then she noticed my new wristwatch. "Wow. That's beautiful. Never seen one before." I unclasped it and handed it to her without thinking. She gazed at the watch face, the rose gold, the diamonds. "And it tells the time too?" She turned it over. I realized too late—she saw the inscription. She quickly turned the watch back over, pretending to carry on admiring it before handing it back. I put it back on.

Lotte said nothing and kept her eyes down, as if studying a spot on the table.

"The Bulchovi file?" I prompted.

"You were right," Lotte replied, looking up now, but still not quite at me. She stared past my shoulder as if studying something on the wall behind me. Her eyes were sad. "It's definitely a fake …" She paused and sighed before continuing. "Each sound, in any language, is produced with a distinctive mouth shape …"

At that point Ebba jumped in. "Caused by speech articulators: the lips, tongue, throat, and different parts of the oral cavity—the hard palate, alveolar ridge, esophagus, and so on. To create each speech sound, each of these points combine in unique language-specific ways. A sound can be matched to a distinctive mouth shape. A visual cue."

Lotte glanced at her in surprise.

"That's what you get for hanging out with a professor of linguistics," I muttered.

"Right," Lotte said, still looking at Ebba but now frowning. "And in this case, our analysis has identified over one hundred discrepancies."

"So it's not Bulchovi speaking?" I asked.

"The speech sounds are those of Bulchovi. They're all him. He just didn't say them in this video. A different audio track has been created, harvesting his speech signature and superimposing that onto the visuals."

"Creating a mashup," Ebba said.

Lotte pursed her lips. "It's done a bit better than that," she replied with a hint of sarcasm. "The funny thing is, after all the effort to make it convincing, there's a basic error."

"What's that?" I asked softly. Lotte threw me a faint smile.

"During the merging process of the Bulchovi visual with the audio. Our forensic analysis shows that the digital properties of the lab that did this have been left in the metadata. It was probably done quickly."

I chuckled. "They weren't deleted. And you know who did it?"

"An acoustic lab in Brussels. But there's more," Lotte said with seeming triumph. I raised my eyebrows. "This is the most ludicrous of all. We actually have the original facecall on file."

"I don't follow," I said.

"Bulchovi's original facecall. CyberForce intercepted it several months ago. They shared that one with us—we have it in the Europol database. Except that in the original, the president is talking about a rescue operation for Federation sailors trapped on a submarine in the Black Sea."

"What?" I asked incredulous. "You have the original facecall?"

"With the original audio," Lotte confirmed.

"If this was done in Brussels, then maybe it's not actually Appleton's work," Ebba suggested, glancing at me.

"CyberForce?"

"Or maybe the High Representative, the Imperium," Ebba whispered ominously, giving me her knowing look.

"In any case, to force the hand of the Magisterium. The order for war ..." I said. Ebba and I stared at each other for a moment before I turned back to Lotte. "I'll need the evidence it's a fake."

Lotte stared straight back at me. "I knew you would. I've prepared a brief report, including the acoustic analysis, the metadata showing the source lab in Brussels, and a comparison with the original facecall. I've already sent it to your Europol account."

"Thanks," I replied as Lotte stood to leave. I could tell she was uncomfortable.

"What will you do?" Lotte asked.

"I'm not sure yet. But one way or another, I will stop this."

As Lotte put on her coat, she glanced down at me. "Emyr, one more thing." I jumped slightly as I heard her say my name.

"I put in my transfer request, in the end—you know, after what happened. My husband said he didn't want to wait ..." Lotte clearly felt awkward about sharing something of a more personal nature in front of a stranger. In front of Ebba.

"I understand," I replied softly.

"Lina cleared it this morning."

"I see," I replied.

"That's it then, I suppose," Lotte whispered.

"I suppose," I muttered, not knowing what else to say now that we really were at the end of things. Lotte watched my face for a moment. But now I was the one who could no longer look her in the eye.

"Good luck, Emyr," she said. "I hope you find what you're looking for." Lotte turned and began walking hurriedly away. It was only then that I looked up, watching her back as she left the café.

"That was tense," Ebba said. "Between the two of you." I stared at Ebba thoughtfully. I disliked her, momentarily. She was a piece of work. I felt bad about Lotte. "At least she and Jaap will be happier away from here," Ebba concluded.

"Jaap?" I asked, taken aback.

"Lotte's husband," Ebba replied. I turned in my seat to face her side on. She smirked sheepishly. "Lotte didn't mention his name, did she?" I shook my head.

"How do you know his name?"

Ebba shrugged. "Relax. It's no big deal. I'm sure they'll both be happier somewhere else, away from your shadow."

"My shadow? What do you know about me and Lotte?" I involuntarily clenched my jaws, and felt my face becoming flushed and hot. The din in the café quietened as people at nearby tables looked across.

"Calm down, Emyr, you're attracting attention," Ebba said quietly.

"I want to know," I said, still speaking loudly.

"You two … were lovers," she said. "Please keep your voice down. You're on the run, remember."

"How do you know that?" I hissed. "Female intuition?" I asked sarcastically. "Or because you were spying on me through sec-cam footage?" I looked into her black eyes, which stared back at me defiantly, unblinking. She wasn't going to deny it. That wasn't her style. "How long have you been watching me, Ebba?" I knew we had been careful. There was only one place we had ever been intimate—and then it struck me. Ebba couldn't have, surely. That would be perverted, sick.

"What is it, Emyr?" Ebba asked, becoming alarmed, probably at the way I was looking at her.

"You hacked into my isolation room," I announced hoarsely, breathing hard, staring at her. "Didn't you? You watched me, us …" I saw Ebba gulp. "You better start talking," I said menacingly. I could see, for the first and perhaps only time, a flicker of trepidation on Ebba's face, a hint of something—if not fear, then at the very least momentary uncertainty.

"It's not what you think," Ebba stammered.

"Then what is it? How do I fit into all this?" I asked. "Lilith King put you on to me, is that it? But you had no right to spy on me."

"It's true I started watching you."

"You mean studying, doing your psychological profiling," I said.

Ebba sighed. "You were perfect. A loner, a leader, strong, and a mental toughness that I hadn't seen before …"

"Perfect for what, exactly? I was happy. I had a job, a career.

I had Lotte. But you did something to take it away from me. That's why you know about Jaap. What did you do, Ebba?"

"Please keep your voice down, Emyr," Ebba whispered again. "If I tell you, I want you to stay calm. Don't do anything rash. Promise?" I nodded. "Promise me," she insisted. I shook my head. "If you don't promise, I can't tell you."

"I promise," I said through gritted teeth.

Ebba nodded. "Okay. The only thing that really tied you here, to your old life, was Lotte."

"And you couldn't have that," I retorted snidely. Ebba ignored me.

"I sent Jaap a message, anonymously, that he should look at his wife's video journal. That's all."

"Come on, Ebba, you did more than that. You set everything up. What else did you do?" Ebba took my hand in hers. I let her. I wanted her to comply, to tell me the truth. She clasped my hand tightly. I didn't withdraw it, not yet.

"I deactivated her video journal lock. I sent Jaap a message saying his wife was having an affair and activated an alarm in the apartment to create a window of opportunity."

And just like that, I knew it was over. Ebba had played me. She had entrapped me in her dark web of deceit for her own ends. She had made a fool of me. She had hurt Lotte. But what did Ebba care about Lotte? Lotte meant nothing to Ebba, with her full red lips, which now seemed crueler than ever. Lotte was collateral damage. And what of me? I was the court jester who had fallen for a twisted monster, as I now saw her—a woman who manipulated people, their lives, for her own ends, for her own purpose, to suit her own needs and desires. *Always the same; in the end, everyone I let get close to me betrays me.* That was why I had refused to love. Until now. *It serves me right.*

At that moment, in that café, I hated Ebba more than I had ever hated anyone or anything—or almost anyone. The Bastard still held that dubious honor. But most of all, I wanted to be away from her, from her clutches.

"You promised, Emyr. Nothing rash," Ebba implored as she watched my expression, the rage etched across my face. I stood up and moved away from the table.

"You're a monster. I never want to see you again!" As I spat my final words at her, I dashed out of the café. And before she could catch up, I walked away fast. I turned the corner of the block and glanced back. There was no sign of Ebba. I kept walking, loathing and hate swelling within me. I felt wretched.

Before I knew it, I had arrived at the parking zone where we had parked the *Ebba Black*. I still had the security remote control. Did I dare? Could I? She still had the *Black Albatross*, after all. And in my emotional flux, lying somewhere between rage and heartache, I reasoned that she owed me. I clicked on the remote, opened the car, and climbed in.

I taxied the vehicle out of the underground parking lot. There was still no sign of Ebba. I approached a nearby vertipad and set the vehicle to VTOL manual mode. And as I rose up into the sky, high above Scheveningen, I glanced down at the familiar surroundings that now appeared strange and otherworldly.

I turned onto an airway. At first, I didn't know where I was going. For the first time in my adult life, I suddenly had no plan. Just then, as the rage began to subside, the grief hit me. It was an uncontrollable, overpowering grief, a loss born of betrayal. The image of my mother suddenly popped into my head as I steered the vehicle. She had betrayed me too, as a child. I had suffered at the hands of the Bastard while she looked the other way.

"I'll cut you off without a penny," he had said after beating me. The cruelty of the words, uttered to a child, came back to me—a trail of pain across the years. The echoes from a distant past whispered to me, as I flew along the airway, calling up emotional scars that had never healed.

I had promised myself that never again would I allow myself to be hurt. Yet I had made myself vulnerable. I had trusted her; I had allowed myself to fall in love with Ebba. And now I was lost once more. Tears rolled down my cheeks for the first time in years. As I sobbed, I piloted the car away from The Hague. And just like that, a plan slowly formed in my mind, out of my blackness: how to stop the war.

CHAPTER 38

My crazy plan might as well have been a suicide mission, but I no longer cared about myself. That in itself was empowering. It rendered me both reckless and very dangerous. For an interloper who had no detectable language streaming signature and the means to become invisible, there might be a chance to gain a few minutes alone with the High Representative in his chamber. And one way or another, I would compel him to stop the looming war.

But I knew I didn't have long. I glanced at my wristwatch. It was 2 p.m. Cyberstrikes against the Federation were scheduled to begin in just nine hours, followed by a ground invasion. And by that point, I would no longer have access to my Europol account and Lotte's evidence that the basis for war was a hoax. *High stakes, no margin for error—just the way I like it*, I thought wryly.

I parked the *Ebba Black* in an underground parking zone a few blocks away from the Imperium building. I was wearing my Glock 19 in the leather holster under my jacket, and the touchtab Ebba had given me was clipped to my belt. I opened the trunk of the car and placed extra ammo clips in a belt holder. I removed the translucent earpiece that connected to my Europol account and left that in the trunk. No LS rebounds. Now I couldn't be detected as I broke into one of the most fortified buildings in the world. I selected the armored glass heating mat and the invisibility cloak, and placed them inside a small shoulder bag. Finally, I took one of the VTOL hoverboards in its carrier. I closed the trunk and clicked on the car's remote, setting the vehicle to secure mode.

I walked toward the elevator and ascended to street level. It was only a few minutes to the Imperium on foot. I took a narrow side street that provided service access to retail outlets in an adjacent street. Walking along the pedestrian corridor, I glanced around to ensure I was alone; then I took out the VTOL hoverboard, along with the invisibility cloak. I stepped onto the hoverboard, clamped my feet in position, and put on the cloak.

The cloak consisted of a hood attached to an enveloping garment that fell below my feet. The hood and cloak were secured on the inside by self-adhesive fabric tape. When it was pressed together, I was completely enclosed. The fabric was thin enough that I could still see out with near-perfect acuity, but with the hundreds of reflector cameras, it was surprisingly heavy. I took out the touchtab from my belt and activated the cloak. I felt a slight rigidity as the cameras went live. The app showed that I was now invisible to sec-cams and the naked eye alike. I activated the hoverboard with the foot pedal and flew up the narrow side street, rising above the tall buildings that loomed over me.

Once above the buildings, I directed my hoverboard toward the gleaming Imperium building. The triangular postmodern structure was an unmistakable edifice on the Brussels skyline. I moved over the Imperium and touched down on the roof. I remained hidden from the multiple roof-mounted sec-cams due to the cloak, as well as the fleet of surveillance drones that I knew patrolled the building's perimeter airspace.

Picking up the hoverboard, I held it underneath the cloak and jogged toward the enclosed light shaft. It was protected at roof level by a glass dome. I gaped through the glass into the wide artery that ran hundreds of meters down inside the center of the building.

I knew from security briefings that the dome was impossible to penetrate with conventional weaponry. It was constructed from multiple layers of armor-plated glass sandwiched with bullet-resistant acrylic. If a bullet were to be fired at the glass, the compressed layers would absorb its forward momentum, causing it to bounce harmlessly away. Moreover, the dome was nigh on impossible to melt, at least with standard portable equipment.

However, I had learned from Ebba that there was a hack to overcome the armor's resistance. And I had a heating mat for just that purpose.

I took the folded mat from my shoulder bag. Reaching out, I quickly placed it over the dome. Then, under cover of my cloak, I selected the app on my touchtab and activated the heating coil.

I knew I wouldn't have long once I managed to shatter the armored dome. Sensors in the glass would alert building security of a perimeter breach. I removed my invisibility cloak and placed it in my shoulder bag. I needed room to fire accurately, and couldn't do so while wearing the heavy garment. My presence would be given away soon enough anyway.

I readied myself, locking my feet back into the magnetic clamps on my hoverboard. I pulled out my pistol, waiting for any sign that the integrity of the dome was compromised. As the glass began to turn cloudy, I positioned myself at an angle four meters away to avoid ricochets, and began firing. The noise from the Glock was deafening. Vibration sensors would already be transmitting my location to the droid security detail.

Each magazine of my Glock 19 contained fifteen rounds. I aimed at a single spot near the dome's center, discharging two magazines before the dome shattered. As I watched the splinters of glass fall in a cascade of sound, in my peripheral vision I caught sight of a large surveillance drone with a fixed-wing weapon station. It rose quietly above the edge of the building. I had been spotted!

I activated my hoverboard and swooped down through the shaft, descending quickly. I could hear the falling glass crashing against the interior walls of the building as it tumbled down ahead of me. I dropped several stories until I recognized the looming sight of the High Representative's stained-glass windows; then I tilted my body back, causing the hoverboard to stop, hovering in midair a few meters from the windows as I fired my weapon at them. These panes were made of regular glass. They shattered in a crescendo of sound, and with a quick gesture of my body, I made my hoverboard move through into the High Representative's cabinet chamber. I recognized the table and long room from my previous visit.

The falling stained glass made a crashing din. As I flew in, a door in one wall of the cabinet chamber flung open and the High Representative raced out of an adjacent office. I glanced through the doorway from which he had emerged. It was a small private work area with a console and some shelving. I also saw that I was in luck. He was alone.

Lopez froze as he saw me, his eyes suddenly wide, his mouth agog. For a split second, I almost wanted to laugh out loud at the look of shock on his bearded face. But this man was scum. He didn't deserve my mirth. I stepped off my hoverboard onto the floor of the cabinet chamber. Still holding my pistol, I aimed it squarely at him.

"Josep Lopez, sit there," I commanded, pointing to a chair at the cabinet table.

The man's face transformed into a mask of contempt. "Are you crazy?" Lopez asked, recovering his composure as he recognized me. "How dare you! Do you have any idea what I can do to you?"

"Sit," I repeated.

Lopez's eyes narrowed slightly. "You're the Europol Commander whose arrest I ordered."

I laughed defiantly, striking him on the side of his temple. He stumbled back, falling into the seat I had indicated.

"I don't like repeating myself," I said with menace. A trickle of blood began oozing from a small gash on the side of Lopez's head.

"What do you want?" he asked quietly.

"I want you to call off the war."

With that, it was Lopez's turn to laugh. "You really are crazy, then," he said finally. "I couldn't do that even if I wanted to. It's all been approved in the Magisterium, by the joint presidents, signed off by the Council of Leaders."

"On your say-so," I retorted.

He shook his head. "They've seen the evidence. There's no other way. We have no choice."

I laughed again, this time sardonically. "So that's what you're going with." Lopez frowned, watching me, slightly perplexed. He reached up to his temple, touching his wound before looking at the blood on his fingers. "We both know that your so-called evidence has been fabricated. The Federation has been set up. The work of a lab here in Brussels."

"Who told you that?" Lopez shot back, a mixture of alarm and genuine surprise tugging at his mouth, twisting his black beard as he spoke.

"I have the evidence here." I tapped my wrist chip menacingly without activating it. "Europol even has Bulchovi's original facecall. You're setting the Federation up as the fall guy for the outage."

Lopez began shaking his head. "You don't understand. How could you? You don't see everything. The big picture. I am the High Representative."

"What don't I understand? Please do enlighten me."

"The end always justifies the means," Lopez muttered, as if to himself. And then, more loudly, "Let's say for argument's sake that you're right. The evidence used to justify war isn't all it seems. That doesn't mean the conclusion isn't correct. And if the conclusion is correct, then the decision is justified."

"You don't mean to say that you actually believe the Federation did it?" I asked. "The outage?"

"It doesn't matter whether they did or not. The Russians have done other things. And will do more damage in the future as their state fails, as the Bulchovi family takes it down. It's in the Russian DNA. Harming everything around them for over a thousand years. It has to end. War—" the High Representative stretched out his hands as if appealing to me, "—is inevitable. A necessary evil. For the greater good."

I felt my blood beginning to boil. "You can't take us to war just like that, risking the lives of millions of people. You know there will be retaliation. You may have convinced yourself that the Federation will be decimated—that they'll roll over—but war is unpredictable. It's easier to start one than end it. You're playing with global peace. You are playing god!" The man stared back at me, defiant, unspeaking, a faint hint of a smile on his face, a look of slight pity puckering his bearded mouth.

"Playing god?" Lopez smirked. "That's a good one. But you see, I am always right, so maybe you're on to something after all." And it was only then that it hit me. The man really did have a god complex. He really did believe he was right—that the end justified the means, that nothing could harm him, that he was too big to fail. I tried a different tack.

"You've been coerced by Marc Barron, by Appleton, haven't you? Don't you think that Appleton is a more likely suspect?"

Lopez suddenly shot me a dark, fearful look. "What are you saying?" he asked hoarsely, tension now etched across his face.

"Lady Raven," I said. I watched as his micro-expression gave him away, as he flinched.

"The name means nothing to me."

"There's video footage. Of you and her. Damaging footage for a man like you, I imagine."

Lopez eyed me carefully. "That woman is dead. There's no evidence. Nothing." I was about to retort that if he really didn't know who Lady Raven was, then he wouldn't know she was dead. But my riposte was interrupted by the sound of droids from outside the chamber. Security would be here at any moment. Lopez looked at me defiantly. "You can't stop this. It's beautiful. The logic of war, the purity of it ..." A twisted smile came over his face as he spoke, manic, convinced of his own infallibility.

At that precise moment, two Warrior-class Einstein-chipped droids burst into the room. The one in the lead was holding a coil pistol aloft; the second was holding a long coil assault carbine. I had no time to lose. I holstered my own pistol and ducked down behind the high table, running back toward my hoverboard and escape at the end of the chamber near the smashed windows. I was saved from coil fire by the tall back of the High Representative's chair, which now featured charred holes. I clamped my feet onto the hoverboard. With a deft twist of my body, I was airborne. I flew out of the chamber the way I had come, moving rapidly back up the air shaft.

I heard Lopez shouting instructions at the droids from inside the chamber below. And before either could fire up at me, I was already at the top of the air shaft.

But now I faced another problem. The dark shape of a large surveillance drone was stationed above the building, facing down into the shaft. It was too large to enter, but it had its weapons trained on me. And a remote drone operator would no doubt have me in their sights, about to fire, waiting until I was out of the shaft to avoid damage to Union property or personnel.

I rose fast, soon reaching the opening where the shaft gave out onto the roof. That was where I would be vulnerable to the hardpoint weaponry. As I emerged above the brow of the roof, I fired my own semiautomatic weapon, aiming my Glock directly at the underside of the large drone, discharging an entire magazine. It was enough to momentarily nudge the drone slightly sideways just as it fired its fixed-wing automatic coil guns, which missed.

I ducked low on the hoverboard, using my feet to steer away from the drone across the roof and down the side of the building. I dropped quickly, disappearing between two nearby buildings into a side street. When I landed at ground level, I quickly unclamped my feet and retrieved the invisibility cloak. I threw it over my head as the drone appeared ominously in the sky above, searching. I made out its silhouette clearly through the cloak, flying high above, its sec-cams and LS scanners trained downward in vain.

I paused for a moment as I caught my breath, as a maelstrom of emotions raged within me. I knew now what I had to do. The High Representative had to die.

CHAPTER 39

I made my way back to where I had parked the *Ebba Black*. I stowed the hoverboard and other equipment in the trunk, and reinserted the earpiece Ebba had given me to access my Europol account. At my rank, I had access to relevant details of senior Union officials for protection duties, including home addresses. With a few blinks on my holotab, I had Lopez's exact address. I started the car. I would wait for him at his home and ambush him there.

I descended the vertipad that serviced Avenue Molière. It was an exclusive street that housed foreign consulates, luxurious residences, and the high-security gated community where the High Representative's villa was located. I parked the car in a nearby underground parking zone. Before securing the car, I left the earpiece behind again to avoid LS rebounds being detected, while I helped myself to more ammo magazines along with the invisibility cloak. This time I also took a noise suppressor for my pistol, which I placed in my jacket pocket. I went up to street level to wait for Lopez's arrival.

I sat on a bench beside a fountain in a small park opposite the entrance to the gated community. Darkness slowly descended. Streetlights began to boot up as vehicles taxied past.

Around 6 p.m., a large sports utility hover vehicle descended onto the adjacent vertipad. The vehicle had blacked-out armored windows and the distinctive Union livery that designated a high-ranking official. It had to be Lopez. I threw on my invisibility cloak before emerging into the pedestrian zone of the transit corridor, then watched as the vehicle taxied down the ramp from the vertipad. To my surprise, a second vehicle descended just behind the first, with the same markings. I smiled wryly to myself. This amounted to a doubling of the security detail for Lopez. He'd clearly had a scare earlier: an interloper—me—breaking into his office and still at large. Both vehicles continued along the transit corridor toward the high wrought-iron gates at the perimeter of the walled compound.

The vehicles turned onto the short driveway in front of the gates, slowing to a near standstill as they approached. The gates began to open slowly inward. The vehicles moved off, entering the gated perimeter. Before the gates closed, I slipped through on foot, unseen in my cloak. I jogged after the vehicles, following their lights. The compound contained around half a dozen villas situated on ample plots of land. Despite it being dark, I could tell from the perimeter lighting that these were magnificent residences.

I followed the vehicles toward a Palladian-style luxury villa. There was a rolling grassy mound in front of it, with a driveway disappearing around it toward a basement garage. A wide double garage door slid upward as the vehicles approached. Rows of lights illuminated the descending driveway at each edge as I followed. There were sec-cams mounted along the driveway, and as I approached the bottom, I spotted a large rotating security LS orb above the garage door. Just before the door could fully close, I ducked under it, undetected.

Ahead of me, the vehicles had already been parked. Four security guards—human assets—had gotten out and were talking with the High Representative ahead of them at the far end. Two other vehicles were already parked in the large basement garage.

Two of the security guards walked toward an elevator beyond the parked vehicles. They were wearing dark suits. They got in, leaving Lopez with the two remaining guards. He began chatting with them. I heard one laugh at something he said. But I was too far away, crouched down behind one of the bulletproof vehicles, to hear what they were saying. After a few minutes, one of the first two guards returned in the elevator and approached Lopez before speaking. I moved slightly closer so that I could hear.

"Interior sweep completed. All secure. Interior sensors and alarms deactivated," the security guard said quietly. Lopez nodded in acknowledgment and followed the guard back into the elevator, disappearing from view as the door closed.

The remaining two guards moved to one corner of the large garage. There was a spiral staircase I hadn't spotted. They walked heavily up it, their shoes clanging on the metal.

I took off my cloak and carefully placed it in my bag, which I secured over my shoulder. I waited a few minutes until the voices of the men had faded, then jogged to the spiral staircase and slowly, quietly, moved up it. At the top was another door, slightly ajar. I could hear the sound of voices from within—the High Representative, a woman, and a second woman. There was also the sound of a child—the voice of a small girl. Then I heard the sound of a service unit, dinner plates, and the smell of food being served from somewhere within the house. I crept back down into the garage, sitting perfectly still at the bottom of the steps. After a few minutes, the garage lights faded out. I would now wait, biding my time.

*   *   *

I glanced at the wristwatch Ebba had given me. The photoluminescent pigment on the hands and numerals glowed at me through the dark. It was approaching 8 p.m., nearly two hours since Lopez had entered the house. I stood, ready to go back up the stairs. The garage lights booted up. I froze, barely daring to breathe. The lighting was clearly motion-activated, and I wasn't wearing the invisibility cloak. I waited to see whether any security had been triggered.

After thirty seconds of nothing, I concluded all was safe. The alarms had clearly been deactivated, as I'd overheard. I could move around freely. But I knew I would need to remain vigilant, especially for the security guards.

I reached into my jacket pocket and took out the noise suppressor for my pistol. I attached it to my Glock. Then I moved up the metal spiral staircase. As I reached the top, I pushed the door, which was slightly ajar. I stood on the threshold and listened. Silence. I moved through the doorway and found myself in a hall. At one end, there was a soft light from another room. I crept toward it.

The light was emanating from a large lounge with big, sumptuous sofas and dim lighting from LED smart walls. I stopped dead. The High Representative was seated in the center on a high-backed sofa. It seemed serendipitous. He was completely alone in the room, his head lolling back, resting against the sofa, with his back to me. There was no one else around. I had the perfect opportunity, without security guards, witnesses, or even the concern that I would be detected.

I walked stealthily into the room, holding my pistol complete with suppressor. Lopez was about fifteen meters from me. From the silence and his heavy breathing, I suspected he was asleep. I walked across the room and aimed my pistol squarely at the back of his head. I was standing over the seated figure, my weapon angled down. One shot and he would meet his maker.

As I was about to fire, I heard a slight sound—a whimper. I crept half a meter farther forward and looked over Lopez's head. To my shock, I saw there was a small child, a girl, lying with her head on his lap, apparently dozing. She was dressed in pajamas ready for bed. Lopez was still holding a children's storybook in one hand, which had dropped against the sofa seat.

As I processed the scene, I sucked in my breath. The child's eyes flickered open. She looked up at me, dark brown eyes staring directly into mine. As she saw me, fear stole over her face. It was an expression that I recognized, recalled from my own childhood trauma. And in that split second, I knew I could no longer take the shot. Not now.

I cursed inwardly and lowered my gun. And then the girl screamed. At that, Lopez started, sitting up smartly in alarm, the girl pointing at me over his shoulder. I grabbed my cloak from out of my bag and threw it over myself. I activated it from my touchtab and watched the child's amazed face as I vanished from view. She was pointing at thin air by the time Lopez managed to turn to see what she was gesturing at.

I carefully retreated to one corner of the room, as there was a further commotion. Two security guards rushed in, followed by a middle-aged woman and a younger woman. The younger woman scooped up the child, who was sobbing. Lopez and the security guards began talking to her, clearly panicked, attempting to figure out what she had seen.

I saw my chance to slip away. Quickly retracing my steps, I moved backward out of the large lounge. Still under cover of the cloak, I unscrewed the suppressor and put the gun away in my shoulder holster. Once back out in the hall, the agitated voices from the lounge were less distinct. I ducked through the doorway leading to the spiral staircase and the garage.

Once down in the garage, I could hear more noise, chatter. It was the other two security guards. As luck would have it, they were leaving, probably going off duty for the evening. They were climbing into one of the armored hover vehicles.

The garage door opened while the hover car turned around 180 degrees, ready to move out. But just at that moment, a shrill alarm began sounding from somewhere, and a red warning light on the garage door began flashing. The door began to auto-close, while the security guards in the vehicle shut down the engine and clambered out quickly, drawing their coil weapons.

I watched my window of opportunity for escape shrinking, quite literally, as the garage door re-closed, drawing down to seal shut against the ground. I threw myself forward and slid underneath, brushing against the base of the door as I made it out in the nick of time.

Outside, I rolled to my feet and began sprinting back along the driveway as it curved up, toward the grass mound and the gates at the perimeter of the compound. Just then, I heard the hum of surveillance drones and saw the small machines buzzing ahead as the perimeter security lights booted on. I still had my cloak, so for now I was safe from visual detection. But I was also hampered, as the cloak reduced my ability to move as freely as I would have wished.

I reached the perimeter and had to make a decision. The walls were too high; without equipment, I couldn't scale them. The angry buzz of the smaller drones was starting to irritate the hell out of me as they darted back and forth across the gated compound, clearly searching for me. Behind me, I heard shouts in the distance. And then I spotted the silhouette of one of the security guards emerging over the grassy mound. I needed to do something—and fast. The only way out was over the gate. And I couldn't do that draped in the cloak, loaded with cameras.

The gate was at least three meters high, with spikes at the top. I would need to take a running jump and try to grab onto the top without impaling a hand. I sucked in my breath and quickly ripped at the cloak's fastening, pulling it off. I let it fall to the ground. Now I was visible, I would need to work fast.

I set off, sprinting hard toward the gate, judging when I would need to leap. As I approached, I jumped off my right leg, throwing my left foot against the gate around a third of the way up. Using the purchase that gave me, I threw myself farther up, grabbing the top rail. My right hand scraped painfully between two spikes, grazing either side, but I managed to hold fast. I secured a grip with my left hand and pulled myself up until my chin was level with the top.

Just at that moment, I heard hoarse grunts behind me, and a spotlight shone full on me from one of the drones. A security guard was about ten meters away, looking up at me from the driveway.

I pulled myself up until I was crouching precariously on the top of the gate, attempting to avoid being caught by the spikes. The security guard was drawing a coil pistol, readying a shot. I glimpsed the status lights flickering on the barrel of the pistol just as he discharged the weapon. And with that, I launched myself off the top of the gate onto the polycarbonate walkway on the other side. As the surface rose up beneath me, I scrunched myself into a ball and rolled forward to avoid the worst of the impact, coming to a sitting position. For a moment the breath was knocked out of me. Then I was up and sprinting away before they could get the gates open behind me.

Once back in the park opposite, I hid in the bushes, listening to the sounds of shouts from the security guards and the buzz of drones searching for me. As the noises faded, I moved quickly, remaining in the shadows, running the few blocks to where I had left the *Ebba Black*. Now I knew what I still had to do. *Why didn't I think of this before?* I wondered. *My emotional state, maybe.*

I reached the vehicle and opened it. I put in my earpiece to connect with my Europol account and sat, breathing heavily, in the driver's seat. I gave myself thirty seconds to catch my breath, to compose myself, then I pressed on my wrist chip, activating my holotab. I glanced down at the analog watch on my other wrist. *Yes! I still have time.*

I blinked through the holotab menu to the secure personal messaging service. The mail app activated. Then I spoke my in-app voice command. "Send priority mail to the Union Commission president, the president of the Council of Leaders, and the director of Europol."

"Yes, Commander," the app responded. Their details populated the addressee list in the messaging service. *Thank god for the LS rebounds from the earpiece Ebba gave me.*

"Message reads as follows," I began, dictating. "The Russian Federation has no responsibility for the language outage. The video evidence of President Bulchovi claiming responsibility is a hoax. It is a doctored facecall. The original undoctored facecall file is attached. Also attached is a report from Europol with detailed evidence of the hoax. The order for war must be canceled and all forces stood down." With that, I blinked on the files to be attached. "Send."

"Message sent, Commander."

"Notify me when it's been read," I instructed. I waited.

"Message read by the president of the Council of Leaders," the app informed me after a few seconds. And within two minutes it had been read by all three addressees.

I blinked to close the app and set the holotab to hibernate. The translucent screen vanished back into my wrist chip. Soon it would be useless anyway. I took out the earpiece that connected me to my holotab and rolled it over in my hand. I wound down the car window and threw it out. I heard it skittering across the floor. My Europol account was about to become permanently deactivated anyway. I had made my final play. And I didn't want to be tracked by the LS rebounds from the earpiece.

As I started up the car, I felt suddenly hollow. I had no job, nowhere to be, and no one to be with. I was on my own, just like I'd always been. I hadn't realized how fully alone I was until that precise moment—and I was sitting in a vehicle that wasn't even mine. So, I decided to go to the one place where I had once, for a time at least, felt at home.

CHAPTER 40

I maneuvered out of the parking zone back up to street level. Driving the car toward the nearest vertipad, I switched to VTOL mode. The VTOL corridor's red safety lights blinked at me as I ascended. I piloted the car onto a city airway before turning off and ascending further to reach an intercity skyway. I was heading across the sea, over the Old Kingdom Channel, back to Bridgend, in Cymru.

Bridgend was thirty kilometers west of the city of Cardiff and thirty-two kilometers east of Swansea. It was located at the head of the River Ogmore. Before I had moved to Scheveningen, my home, life, and career had been centered around Bridgend, where the south Cymru territorial Heddlu force was headquartered and where the Celtic Partnership civil CyberForce command was based. Bridgend was the closest I had to a home, and I was going back.

After around fifteen minutes, I approached Cymru's airspace, dropping down across the southern coastline. As I neared, I saw the lights of Bridgend below. I moved down into lower stacked airways before finally dropping through a VTOL corridor in the city center. I taxied down the familiar vertipad and parked the vehicle in the municipal parking zone beneath the central retail park.

Once stationary, I sat in the parked car and took out the touchtab Ebba had given me. I clicked on an app and set myself up with an account at the local Maple convenience store. I took an elevator up to the retail level and walked in. Selecting a large bottle of Irish whiskey, I paid at the automated teller using the wrist chip Ebba had printed for me.

I returned to the *Ebba Black* in the underground parking zone and opened the trunk. I took out my long leather overcoat. That I would take. I took off my shoulder holster and pistol, and placed them inside the trunk. I didn't want or need them anymore. I took out my touchtab and slid off the wrist chip. I left those in there, too. I unclasped the wristwatch and held it in my hand. That was also from Ebba. I turned it over, glancing at the inscription: *So that I'm always with you … Ebba.* Yet, somehow, I couldn't bring myself to part with it. That was too much of a wrench. I sighed. *You fool, Emyr!* I thought. That I would keep. It wasn't how rare or expensive it was, but rather the care and thought that had gone into the gift, the inscription. I clasped it back on, despite a nagging sense that I would live to regret it.

But the rest, it didn't belong to me. I locked the vehicle using the remote control for the final time. I dropped the remote to the floor and stamped on it hard with my heel, crushing it. I kicked the broken device underneath the vehicle, out of sight. No one could get into the vehicle now. And I had no doubt that Ebba would be able to track her beloved custom-made sports car and retrieve it. I had divested myself of it and of her. I picked up my bottle of whiskey and put on my leather coat.

I headed toward the elevator. Out on the street it was cold and dark. Streetlights booted up as I walked, and I pulled my coat collar up around my neck to guard against the wind. I had no plan and nowhere to be, except to be still and calm and to drink.

I walked through Oldcastle, the quarter on the right bank of the river. I made my way toward the Old Bridge, *Yr Hen Bont* in Cymraeg. I crossed the old stone bridge into Newcastle on the other side of the river and carried on walking toward Newcastle Hill. Lights booted up around me. My feeling of hollowness had given way to a fatalistic dolor. I glanced up at the night sky. It was cold and clear; glinting stars peppered the darkness above me. I reached Newcastle Hill and climbed over a fence, entering the grounds of the ancient Norman castle that overlooked Bridgend. I carried on walking inside the thousand-year-old castle ruins. In the middle, I sat on an ancient rock. I looked down at the town below, listening to the distant sounds of people, the rush of water.

I opened my bottle and took a sip. The fiery taste of the whiskey felt good in my throat. I closed my eyes and breathed in. The wind tickled against my hair. I no longer had any ties to anyone or anything. I had nothing more to do. I sat in momentary tranquility, with only the night-time breeze for company.

As I sat, I saw a distant glow. I watched as it grew brighter, slowly moving up the hill, approaching through the dark and the wind. As it neared, it attached itself to dark figures—a group of people. The silhouettes were holding LED torch sticks, which were lighting their way on the path through the castle walls. As the group drew close, a few meters from me, I saw the unmistakable silhouette of Director Dominguez of Europol, my director! And finally, he stood in front of me. Behind him, with coil pistols in hip holsters, was an armed detachment of uniformed Europol officers.

Dominguez contemplated me through the dark, holding up his LED glow stick, searching my face with his gaze.

"Hello, Emyr," he said softly. I didn't reply. "You didn't expect to see me." I shook my head. The uniformed officers stood about seven or eight meters farther back. "Do you mind if I sit?" he asked.

"Director, I—"

He raised his hand.

"Rodrigo. Call me Rodrigo. Can I join you?" I glanced at him; he was looking at the whiskey. I handed him my bottle. "Thanks," he replied. He sat next to me on the ancient rock and unscrewed the cap. Then he took a gulp and handed the bottle back to me. I took a gulp too. "That's very welcome," he said.

"It's fortifying," I said. "Against the cold."

"The attack against the Russians," the director began. "All forces have been ordered to stand down. Twenty minutes ago. I had a call from the Commission president: the Council of Leaders has unanimously agreed."

I nodded. "That's good," I said blankly. I no longer felt much.

"You did well," he acknowledged. "Thank you." He glanced at me. I took another sip of whiskey.

"You're here to arrest me?" I asked.

"It was either us or CyberForce," he said. "And you know …"

I laughed bitterly. "They shoot first and ask questions later… what will happen to me?"

"I will ask for clemency, but you'll be sent off-world. The High Representative's orders."

"The High Representative!" I repeated, curling my lips in a sneer. "Has Lina briefed you?"

The director nodded. "She's told me everything you told her. For now, there's not much I can do. Not without evidence. He claims you attempted to assassinate him. He has witnesses. But at least you've spared us war."

"How did you find me?" I asked.

The director creased his brow. "An anonymous tip. I was sent a link to an app that is tracking you."

I glanced at him, suddenly perplexed.

"Tracking me?" I asked, taking another sip from the bottle.

"Apparently linked to that," he said, pointing to my wristwatch. I glanced down at the watch on my right wrist. "Who gave you that?" he asked with genuine curiosity. My face froze. I didn't reply. And then I started laughing, a crazy laugh. The director stared at me through the darkness as I cackled. And as my body convulsed with crazy, hysterical laughter, tears began to roll down my face. I'd been betrayed again. I brushed my sleeve across my eyes and cheeks. I felt the sting of my salty tears as the cold breeze paddled my face.

"No one important. Not anymore," I whispered. I unclasped the watch and took it off, dropping it onto the damp grass. It fell with a soft thud in the darkness. Now I was finally free. Now Ebba no longer possessed me. I gazed out into the dark sky peppered with the feathery light of distant stars. One seemed to twinkle.

"One more drink, then I'll be ready." The director nodded. He understood.

EPILOGUE

The Exoplanet was a purpose-built penitentiary in space. I arrived on day seven of the outage. I had traveled with eleven other inmates from the Union's spaceport near the equator in French Guiana. During the one-hour trip on the prison transport shuttle, we were required to watch the onboarding video. I had been fitted with a compliance wrist chip, linked to my health and attention biomedical parameters. It began delivering small electric shocks if my gaze wandered from the presentation or if I attempted to sleep.

I learned that the Exoplanet was some feat of engineering. Powered by a nuclear fusion core, which operated an ion drive and a gravitation engine, its geostationary orbit was fixed 35,786 kilometers above the Earth. It hurtled through space at around 11,000 kilometers an hour and consisted of scores of levels organized around parabolic courtyards in glass chambers, radiating out from the core like spokes in a wheel.

Upon arrival on the Exoplanet, all inmates were processed before being escorted to individual detention units. My cell was small, with LED wall panels that were nearly always white. There was a humming air grille in the ceiling, providing a steady supply of oxygen, and a sec-cam in one corner that blinked at me in watchful silence. At one end was the window, a reinforced glass pane that overlooked the Zone Max courtyard below. It became transparent twice a day for one hour. During these periods, I sat in aimless silence and gazed out at nothing: no one passed, no one came. I studied the curved windows of the opposite wing, stretching up and up, resembling long, drawn faces.

The cell had a semi-enclosed hygiene unit in the corner near the sealed entrance. On the adjacent wall there was a small square delivery chute. Food was auto-dispensed three times per day and clean Zone Max overalls once per day. And on the far side of the room, underneath the window, was the bed: a small single bunk with an auto-cleaning foam mattress.

For the first three weeks, the routine was the same. The white LED smart walls booted on at 6 a.m. and breakfast was dispensed—a tasteless protein bar and a large cup of syrupy juice. At 7 a.m., the hygiene unit activated for the daily three-minute clean cycle. A new set of overalls was then dispensed. At 9.30 a.m., the cell's window became transparent for one hour. At 12.30 lunch was dispensed. The second transparent window slot activated at 1.30 p.m. And at 4 p.m., my cell door unlocked and I took an elevator down to the long parabolic courtyard, a restricted yard away from the general population, for my one hour of daily exercise.

Rows of cells ran up on either side of my courtyard like giant honeycombs made of a light-gray thermoformed polycarbonate substance. High overhead were walkways with armed droid sentry units. The units rotated, following my movements, as I paced from one distant end to the other, where the glass dome gave out to the blackness of space.

After returning to my cell, an evening protein bar, a piece of fruit, and a hot drink were dispensed at 6.30 p.m. And at 8.30

p.m., the bright white light faded, leaving me in total darkness until the next day of enervating boredom.

In the cell, I exercised, making good use of my calisthenics routine. I distracted myself by setting physical targets and challenges. My routine included jumping jacks, trunk twists, push-ups, sit-ups, planks, lunges, and burpees. By the end of my third week, I had set a new personal best and could rip out 1,727 push-ups in just one hour and thirty-five one-finger push-ups in thirty seconds. I varied my physical targets for duration and speed, focusing on the number of reps as well as stamina. The exercise kept me sane, helping deflect me from dark thoughts centering around Ebba. I was serving time at her pleasure. Some days I felt sick with anger at her betrayal, and others sick with despair.

Once a week was NocioPerception rack day. On those days, at 11 a.m., I was escorted from my cell by two correctional droids, heavily armed. I was taken to the NocioPerception preparation suite and prepped for the procedure. I watched in fascination as the human medical technician supervised the droid that inserted electrodes into my body. As this was done, I prepared myself mentally, separating my mind from my body and the pain that my body would experience. Each interrogation lasted around an hour. Afterward, I underwent a physical and psych exam by a droid medical unit before being escorted back to my cell. On those days, I was too sick for lunch. I would lie on my bunk until late afternoon, when it was time to exercise in the parabolic courtyard.

The NocioPerception sessions were pointless—and they knew it. Which was kind of the point. I knew neither Freetown's new location nor where Ebba was. She had vanished into thin air and her organization with her. They had my baseline measures;

they knew I was telling the truth. It surprised me that they didn't seem aware that her organization was hiding in plain sight, masquerading as the Arctic Geological Survey. And despite having been betrayed by Ebba, as they never asked, I didn't volunteer it—I wouldn't give them the pleasure of free intel; they had to earn it through my pain. At least that secret of Ebba's remained safe.

All the while, my interrogators remained unseen, faceless voices. I was required to admit high treason against the state I had traduced. *Traduced?* I laughed bitterly to myself. I was the one who had been traduced.

As I entered my fourth week, I knew something had changed. My cell VirDa announced that the prison governor would address me personally. Albrecht Schmidt's long face appeared on the LED smart wall, holographically projected from his office in the Exoplanet administrative zone. He had thin purple lips, splashes of faint red veins across his cheeks, a bulbous nose, and thin-rimmed glasses.

"Ah, Emyr," he said as if picking up the thread of some earlier conversation. His narrow face made it appear as if he was crying as he pronounced each word. Yet Schmidt spoke in the expressionless monotone of an administrator who couldn't care less. "I'm glad to be able to finally welcome you face-to-face to Exoplanet. This is a courtesy call to inform you of a development in your custodial schedule." I stared back at the governor defiantly. Schmidt paused for a moment. But I didn't say anything, not yet. "You're to be confined to a PseudoComa Stasis Pod," he informed me, smiling as if this was the most normal thing anyone could say to someone else. "Effective tomorrow. This evening will be your last meal. Any special requests?" he asked, nodding sympathetically as he saw my dumbfounded expression. "I know this must be a shock, which is why I prefer to deliver the news personally." I stared at him. *A shock? What the hell!* I was screaming in my head.

"On what grounds?" I managed. No charges had been brought against me. I had been convicted of no crime; there had been no due process. I had been denied access to a lawyer. Yet here I was.

"Under the State of Emergency, the executive order cannot be appealed. And this comes direct from the High Representative himself."

I stared at Albrecht Schmidt in disbelief. All I could think of was how ridiculous his large nose seemed as he gazed out at me. I was still attempting to process the news. The death penalty was illegal under Union law. So, the powers-that-be had come up with the PseudoComa Stasis Pod instead. In some ways, it was a fate far worse than death. I should know—I'd spent my entire career in law enforcement.

"The procedure ..." I began.

"A brainstem infarction. It's actually quite quick. It takes less than fifteen minutes, performed under local anesthetic," Schmidt explained, as if this fact were somehow a selling point. "The lower pons is damaged, causing permanent paralysis."

I nodded. "Thereafter, neither movement nor speech is possible. Even breathing is impossible without ventilatory support. The only physical movement still possible is eye movement, controlled by a different brain pathway, the dorsal area of the pons. But the upper part of the brain—the cortex, the thought center, the seat of consciousness—that remains intact."

Schmidt nodded at me and smiled. "You know your stuff."

I grimaced. The consequence of this particularly cruel type of brain damage was locked-in syndrome: a fully functioning human mind trapped in a non-responsive body. Some likened it to being buried alive. And once the body had been permanently disabled, they inserted you into a PseudoComa Stasis Pod, which provided life support for the remainder of your natural life.

A PCS Pod consisted of a white casing around three meters in height and two meters across, with a square bottom merging into an oval-shaped top. There were cables and tubes extending out the back of each pod, which fed into ducts in the floor behind. The pods were positioned in a row on a specially designated corridor at the top of the Exoplanet, so that they were facing out, looking through the armored glass into the depths of space, with a large glass viewing screen at head height on each pod. Prisoners, trapped inside, would spend the remainder of their lives staring out into black nothingness, a room without a view.

Inside the pod, each inmate was set up with an IV drip and suspended in a fluid preparation, with auto-massagers to stimulate muscle mass retention. They were fitted with a mouthpiece breathing apparatus and special protective eyewear. I knew from the protocols that I'd be removed once per year for a full manual physical exam and so that the pod could be serviced. And by law, the High Representative had to review the sentence every five years. There would be no chance of a reprieve; it was all about paper-pushing and ticking boxes.

"The Union has only sentenced twenty-two inmates to the PCS Pod since the program was inaugurated over twenty years ago," Schmidt added.

"It's reserved for those convicted of the most heinous crimes," I muttered. "And for me." I knew the stats. Survival rate was around ten years on average. Death was usually due to atrophying muscle mass. Although two inmates—two of the earliest, Prisoners B and D—had reached the twenty-year mark.

"You'll be our twenty-third PCS Pod inmate: Prisoner W," Schmidt announced. "The Stasis Pod provides muscle stimulation. But ultimately, it's down to the conditioning and mental fortitude of the individual. Some inmates on the PCS Pod corridor simply give up. I have the feeling that won't be your case." My voice cracked as I laughed.

ABOUT THE AUTHOR

Vyvyan Evans is a native of the ancient Roman cathedral city of Chester, England. He holds a PhD in linguistics from Georgetown University, Washington, D.C., and has lived and worked extensively in Asia, Europe, and North America as a professor of linguistics. He has published numerous acclaimed popular science and technical books on language and linguistics. His popular science essays and articles have been featured in numerous publications ranging from *The Guardian* to *Psychology Today*, from the *New York Post* to *New Scientist*, from *Newsweek* to *The New Republic*. His award-winning writing focuses, in one way or another, on the nature of language and mind, the impact of technology on language, and the future of communication. His science fiction work explores the status of language and digital communication technology as potential weapons of mass destruction. For further biographical details, visit his official website: **www.vyvevans.net**. For details of his science fiction writing, visit the Songs of the Sage book series website: **www.songs-of-the-sage.com**.

CPSIA information can be obtained
at www.ICGtesting.com
Printed in the USA
JSHW050013110423
39961JS00020B/377